D0834053

GREAT FAIRY STORIES

THE EMPEROR WALKED ALONG UNDER THE GORGEOUS CANOPY.

[*page* 100]

GREAT FAIRY STORIES

FROM ANDERSEN, GRIMM, AND THE ARABIAN NIGHTS

Illustrated by

T. H. ROBINSON, W. H. ROBINSON,
R. ANNING BELL, ETC.

DAILY SKETCH PUBLICATIONS
LONDON

MADE AND PRINTED IN GREAT BRITAIN BY
HAZELL, WATSON AND VINEY, LTD.
LONDON AND AYLESBURY

ILLUSTRATIONS

GREAT FAIRY STORIES FROM ANDERSEN

THE MERMAID

FAR out at sea the water is as blue as the bluest cornflower, and as clear as the clearest crystal; but it is very deep, too deep for any cable to fathom, and if many steeples were piled on the top of one another they would not reach from the bed of the sea to the surface of the water. It is down there that the Mermen live.

Now don't imagine that there are only bare white sands at the bottom; oh no! the most wonderful trees and plants grow there, with such flexible stalks and leaves, that at the slightest motion of the water they move just as if they were alive. All the fish, big and little, glide among the branches just as, up here, birds glide through the air. The palace of the Merman King lies in the very deepest part; its walls are of coral and the long pointed windows of the clearest amber, but the roof is made of mussel shells which open and shut with the lapping of the water. This has a lovely effect, for there are gleaming pearls in every shell, any one of which would be the pride of a queen's crown.

The Merman King had been for many years a widower, but his old mother kept house for him. She was a clever woman, but so proud of her noble birth that she wore twelve oysters on her tail, while the other grandees were only allowed six. Otherwise she was worthy of all praise, especially because she was so fond of the little mermaid princesses, her grandchildren. They were six beautiful children, but the youngest was the prettiest of all; her skin was as soft and delicate as a rose-leaf, her eyes as blue as the deepest sea, but like all the others she had no feet, and instead of legs she had a fish's tail.

All the livelong day they used to play in the palace in

THE MERMAID

FAR out at sea the water is as blue as the bluest cornflower, and as clear as the clearest crystal; but it is very deep, too deep for any cable to fathom, and if many steeples were piled on the top of one another they would not reach from the bed of the sea to the surface of the water. It is down there that the Mermen live.

Now don't imagine that there are only bare white sands at the bottom; oh no! the most wonderful trees and plants grow there, with such flexible stalks and leaves, that at the slighest motion of the water they move just as if they were alive. All the fish, big and little, glide among the branches just as, up here, birds glide through the air. The palace of the Merman King lies in the very deepest part; its walls are of coral and the long pointed windows of the clearest amber, but the roof is made of mussel shells which open and shut with the lapping of the water. This has a lovely effect, for there are gleaming pearls in every shell, any one of which would be the pride of a queen's crown.

The Merman King had been for many years a widower, but his old mother kept house for him; she was a clever woman, but so proud of her noble birth that she wore twelve oysters on her tail, while the other grandees were only allowed six. Otherwise she was worthy of all praise, especially because she was so fond of the little mermaid princesses, her grandchildren. They were six beautiful children, but the youngest was the prettiest of all, her skin was as soft and delicate as a roseleaf, her eyes as blue as the deepest sea, but like all the others she had no feet, and instead of legs she had a fish's tail.

All the livelong day they used to play in the palace in

the great halls, where living flowers grew out of the walls. When the great amber windows were thrown open the fish swam in, just as the swallows fly into our rooms when we open the windows, but the fish swam right up to the little princesses, ate out of their hands, and allowed themselves to be patted.

Outside the palace was a large garden, with fiery red and deep blue trees, the fruit of which shone like gold, while the flowers glowed like fire on their ceaselessly waving stalks. The ground was of the finest sand, but it was of a blue phosphorescent tint. Everything was bathed in a wondrous blue light down there; you might more readily have supposed yourself to be high up in the air, with only the sky above and below you, than that you were at the bottom of the ocean. In a dead calm you could just catch a glimpse of the sun like a purple flower with a stream of light radiating from its calyx.

Each little princess had her own little plot of garden, where she could dig and plant just as she liked. One made her flower-bed in the shape of a whale, another thought it nice to have hers like a little mermaid; but the youngest made hers quite round like the sun, and she would only have flowers of a rosy hue like its beams. She was a curious child, quiet and thoughtful, and while the other sisters decked out their gardens with all kinds of extraordinary objects which they got from wrecks, she would have nothing besides the rosy flowers like the sun up above, except a statue of a beautiful boy. It was hewn out of the purest white marble and had gone to the bottom from some wreck. By the statue she planted a rosy red weeping willow which grew splendidly, and the fresh delicate branches hung round and over it, till they almost touched the blue sand where the shadows showed violet, and were ever moving like the branches. It looked as if the leaves and the roots were playfully interchanging kisses.

Nothing gave her greater pleasure than to hear about the world of human beings up above; she made her old grandmother tell her all that she knew about ships and towns, people and animals. But above all it seemed strangely beautiful to her that up on the earth the flowers were scented, for they were not so at the bottom of the sea; also that the woods were green, and that the fish which were to be seen among the branches could sing so loudly and sweetly that it was a delight to listen to them. You see the grandmother called little birds fish, or the mermaids would not have understood her, as they had never seen a bird.

"When you are fifteen," said the grandmother, "you will be allowed to rise up from the sea and sit on the rocks in the moonlight, and look at the big ships sailing by, and you will also see woods and towns."

One of the sisters would be fifteen in the following year, but the others,—well, they were each one year younger than the other, so that the youngest had five whole years to wait before she would be allowed to come up from the bottom, to see what things were like on earth. But each one promised the others to give a full account of all that she had seen, and found most wonderful on the first day. Their grandmother could never tell them enough, for there were so many things about which they wanted information.

None of them was so full of longings as the youngest, the very one who had the longest time to wait, and who was so quiet and dreamy. Many a night she stood by the open windows and looked up through the dark blue water which the fish were lashing with their tails and fins. She could see the moon and the stars, it is true, their light was pale but they looked much bigger through the water than they do to our eyes. When she saw a dark shadow glide between her and them, she knew that it was either a whale swimming above her, or else a ship laden with human beings. I am certain they never dreamt that a lovely little mermaid was standing down below, stretching up her white hands towards the keel.

The eldest princess had now reached her fifteenth birthday, and was to venture above the water. When she came back she had hundreds of things to tell them, but the most delightful of all, she said, was to lie in the moonlight, on a sandbank in a calm sea, and to gaze at the large town close to the shore, where the lights twinkled like hundreds of stars; to listen to music and the noise and bustle of carriages and people, to see the many church towers and spires, and to hear the bells ringing; and just because she could not go on shore she longed for that most of all.

Oh! how eagerly the youngest sister listened, and when, later in the evening she stood at the open window and looked up through the dark blue water, she thought of the big town with all its noise and bustle, and fancied that she could even hear the church bells ringing.

The year after, the second sister was allowed to mount up through the water and swim about wherever she liked. The sun was just going down when she reached the surface, the most beautiful sight, she thought, that she had ever seen. The whole sky had looked like gold, she said, and as for the clouds! well, their beauty was beyond description, they floated in red and violet splendour over her head, and, far faster than they went, a flock of wild swans flew like a long white veil over the water towards the setting sun; she swam towards it, but it sank and all the rosy light on clouds and water faded away.

The year after that the third sister went up, and being much the most venturesome of them all, swam up a broad river which ran into the sea. She saw beautiful green, vine-clad hills; palaces and country seats peeping through splendid woods. She heard the birds singing, and the sun was so hot that she was often obliged to dive, to cool her burning face. In a tiny bay she found a troop of little children running about naked and paddling in the water; she wanted to play with them, but they were frightened and ran away. Then a little black animal came up, it was a dog, but she had never seen one before; it barked so furiously at her that she was frightened and made for the open sea. She could never forget the beautiful woods, the green hills and the lovely children who could swim in the water although they had no fishes' tails.

The fourth sister was not so brave, she stayed in the remotest part of the ocean, and, according to her account, that was the most beautiful spot. You could see for miles and miles around you, and the sky above was like a great glass dome. She had seen ships, but only far away, so that they looked like sea-gulls. There were grotesque dolphins turning somersaults, and gigantic whales squirting water through their nostrils like hundreds of fountains on every side.

Now the fifth sister's turn came. Her birthday fell in the winter, so that she saw sights that the others had not seen on their first trips. The sea looked quite green, and large icebergs were floating about, each one of which looked like a pearl, she said, but was much bigger than the church towers built by men. They took the most wonderful shapes, and sparkled like diamonds. She had seated herself on one of the largest, and all the passing ships sheered off in alarm when they saw her sitting there with her long hair streaming loose in the wind.

In the evening the sky became overcast with dark clouds; it thundered and lightened, and the huge icebergs glittering in the bright lightning, were lifted high into the air by the black waves. All the ships shortened sail, and there was fear and trembling on every side, but she sat quietly on her floating iceberg watching the blue lightning flash in zigzags down on to the shining sea.

The first time any of the sisters rose above the water she was delighted by the novelties and beauties she saw; but once grown up, and at liberty to go where she liked, she became indifferent and longed for her home; in the course of a month or so they all said that after all their own home in the deep was best, it was so cosy there.

Many an evening the five sisters interlacing their arms would rise above the water together. They had lovely voices, much clearer than any mortal, and when a storm was rising, and they expected ships to be wrecked, they would sing in the most seductive strains of the wonders of the deep, bidding the seafarers have no fear of them. But the sailors could not understand the words, they thought it was the voice of the storm; nor could it be theirs to see this Elysium of the deep, for when the ship sank they were drowned, and only reached the Merman's palace in death.

When the elder sisters rose up in this manner, arm-in-arm, in the evening, the youngest remained behind quite alone, looking after them as if she must weep, but mermaids have no tears and so they suffer all the more.

"Oh! if I were only fifteen!" she said, "I know how fond I shall be of the world above, and of the mortals who dwell there."

At last her fifteenth birthday came.

"Now we shall have you off our hands," said her grandmother, the old queen dowager. " Come now, let me adorn you like your other sisters! " and she put a wreath of white lilies round her hair, but every petal of the flowers was half a pearl; then the old queen had eight oysters fixed on to the princess's tail to show her high rank.

" But it hurts so! " said the little mermaid.

" You must endure the pain for the sake of the finery! " said her grandmother.

But oh! how gladly would she have shaken off all this splendour, and laid aside the heavy wreath. Her red flowers in her garden suited her much better, but she did not dare to make any alteration. " Good-bye," she said, and mounted as lightly and airily as a bubble through the water.

The sun had just set when her head rose above the water, but the clouds were still lighted up with a rosy and golden splendour, and the evening star sparkled in the soft pink sky, the air was mild and fresh, and the sea as calm as a millpond. A big three-masted ship lay close by with only a single sail set, for there was not a breath of wind, and the sailors were sitting about the rigging, on the cross-trees, and at the mast-heads. There was music and singing on board, and as the evening closed in, hundreds of gaily coloured lanterns were lighted—they looked like the flags of all nations waving in the air. The little mermaid swam right up to the cabin windows, and every time she was lifted by the swell she could see through the transparent panes crowds of gaily dressed people. The handsomest of them all was the young prince with large dark eyes; he could not be much more than sixteen, and all these festivities were in honour of his birthday. The sailors danced on deck, and when the prince appeared among them hundreds of rockets were let off making it as light as day, and frightening the little mermaid so much that she had to dive under the water. She soon ventured up again, and it was just as if all the stars of heaven were falling in showers round about her. She had never seen such magic fires. Great suns whirled round, gorgeous fire-fish hung in the blue air, and all was reflected in the calm and glassy sea. It was so light on board the ship that every little rope could be seen, and the people still better. Oh! how handsome the prince was, how he laughed and smiled as he greeted his guests, while the music rang out in the quiet night.

It got quite late, but the little mermaid could not take her eyes off the ship and the beautiful prince. The coloured lanterns were put out, no more rockets were sent up, and the cannon had ceased its thunder, but deep down in the sea there was a dull murmuring and moaning sound. Meanwhile she was rocked up and down on the waves, so that she could look into the cabin; but the ship got more and more way on, sail after sail was filled by the wind, the waves grew stronger, great clouds gathered, and it lightened in the distance. Oh, there was going to be a fearful storm! and soon the sailors had to shorten sail. The great ship rocked and rolled as she dashed over the angry sea, the black waves rose like mountains, high enough to overwhelm her, but she dived like a swan through them and rose again and again on their towering crests. The little mermaid thought it a most amusing race, but not so the sailors. The ship creaked and groaned, the mighty timbers bulged and bent under the heavy blows, the water broke over the decks, snapping the main mast like a reed, she heeled over on her side and the water rushed into the hold.

Now the little mermaid saw that they were in danger and she had for her own sake to beware of the floating beams and wreckage. One moment it was so pitch dark that she could not see at all, but when the lightning flashed it became so light that she could see all on board. Every man was looking out for his own safety as best he could, but she more particularly followed the young prince with her eyes, and when the ship went down she saw him sink in the deep sea. At first she was quite delighted, for now he was coming to be with her, but then she remembered that human beings could not live under water, and that only if he were dead could he go to her father's palace. No! he must not die; so she swam towards him all among the drifting beams and planks, quite forgetting that they might crush her. She dived deep down under the water, and came up again through the waves, and at last reached the young prince just as he was becoming unable to swim any further in the stormy sea. His limbs were numbed, his beautiful eyes were closing, and he must have died if the little mermaid had not come to the rescue. She held his head above the water and let the waves drive them whithersoever they would.

By daybreak all the storm was over, of the ship not a trace was to be seen; the sun rose from the water in radiant brilliance and his rosy beams seemed to cast a glow of life into the prince's cheeks, but his eyes remained closed. The mermaid kissed his fair and lofty brow, and stroked back the dripping hair; it seemed to her that he was like the marble statue in her little garden, she kissed him again and longed that he might live.

At last she saw dry land before her, high blue mountains on whose summits the white snow glistened as if a flock of swans had settled there; down by the shore were beautiful green woods, and in the foreground a church or temple, she did not quite know which, but it was a building of some sort. Lemon and orange trees grew in the garden and lofty palms stood by the gate. At this point the sea formed a little bay where the water was quite calm, but very deep, right up to the cliffs; at their foot was a strip of fine white sand to which she swam with the beautiful prince, and laid him down on it, taking great care that his head should rest high up in the warm sunshine.

The bells now began to ring in the great white building and a number of young maidens came into the garden. Then the little mermaid swam further off behind some high rocks and covered her hair and breast with foam, so that no one should see her little face, and then she watched to see who would discover the poor prince.

It was not long before one of the maidens came up to him, at first she seemed quite frightened, but only for a moment, and then she fetched several others, and the mermaid saw that the prince was coming to life, and that he smiled at all those around him, but he never smiled at her; you see he did not know that she had saved him; she felt so sad that when he was led away into the great building she dived sorrowfully into the water and made her way home to her father's palace.

Always silent and thoughtful, she became more so now than ever. Her sisters often asked her what she had seen on her first visit to the surface, but she never would tell them anything.

Many an evening and many a morning she would rise to the place where she had left the prince. She saw the fruit in the garden ripen, and then gathered, she saw the snow melt on the mountain-tops, but she never saw the prince, so she always went home still sadder than before. At home her only consolation was to sit in her little garden with her arms twined round the handsome marble statue which reminded her of the prince. It was all in gloomy shade now, as she had ceased to tend her flowers and the garden had become a neglected wilderness of long stalks and leaves entangled with the branches of the tree.

At last she could not bear it any longer, so she told one of her sisters, and from her it soon spread to the others, but to no one else except to one or two other mermaids who only told their dearest friends. One of these knew all about the prince, she had also seen the festivities on the ship; she knew where he came from and where his kingdom was situated.

"Come, little sister!" said the other princesses, and, throwing their arms round each other's shoulders, they rose from the water in a long line, just in front of the prince's palace.

It was built of light yellow glistening stone, with great marble staircases, one of which led into the garden. Magnificent gilded cupolas rose above the roof, and the spaces between the columns which encircled the building were filled with life-like marble statues. Through the clear glass of the lofty windows you could see gorgeous halls adorned with costly silken hangings, and the pictures on the walls were a sight worth seeing. In the midst of the central hall a large fountain played, throwing its jets of spray upwards to a glass dome in the roof, through which the sunbeams lighted up the water and the beautiful plants which grew in the great basin.

She knew now where he lived and often used to go there in the evenings and by night over the water; she swam much nearer the land than any of the others dared, she even ventured right up the narrow channel under the splendid marble terrace which threw a long shadow over the water. She used to sit here looking at the young prince who thought he was quite alone in the clear moonlight.

She saw him many an evening sailing about in his beautiful boat, with flags waving and music playing, she used to peep through the green rushes, and if the wind happened to catch her long silvery veil and anyone saw it, they only thought it was a swan flapping its wings.

Many a night she heard the fishermen, who were fishing by torchlight, talking over the good deeds of the young prince; and she was happy to think that she had saved his life when he was drifting about on the waves, half dead, and she could not forget how closely his head had pressed her breast, and how passionately she had kissed him; but he knew nothing of all this, and never saw her even in his dreams.

She became fonder and fonder of mankind, and longed more and more to be able to live among them; their world seemed so infinitely bigger than hers; with their ships they could scour the ocean, they could ascend the mountains high above the clouds, and their wooded, grass-grown lands extended further than her eye could reach. There was so much that she wanted to know, but her sisters could not give an answer to all her questions, so she asked her old grandmother who knew the upper world well, and rightly called it the country above the sea.

"If men are not drowned," asked the little mermaid, "Do they live for ever, do they not die as we do down here in the sea?"

"Yes," said the old lady, "they have to die too, and their life time is even shorter than ours. We may live here for three hundred years, but when we cease to exist, we become mere foam on the water and do not have so much as a grave among our dear ones. We have no immortal souls, we have no future life, we are just like the green sea-weed, which, once cut down can never revive again! Men, on the other hand, have a soul which lives for ever, lives after the body has become dust; it rises through the clear air, up to the shining stars! Just as we rise from the water to see the land of mortals, so they rise up to unknown beautiful regions which we shall never see."

"Why have we no immortal souls?" asked the little mermaid sadly. "I would give all my three hundred years to be a human being for one day, and afterwards to have a share in the heavenly kingdom."

"You must not be thinking about that," said the grandmother, "we are much better off and happier than human beings."

"Then I shall have to die and to float as foam on the water, and never hear the music of the waves or see the beautiful flowers or the red sun! Is there nothing I can do to gain an immortal soul?"

"No," said the grandmother, "only if a human being so loved you, that you were more to him than father or mother, if all his thoughts and all his love were so centred in you that he would let the priest join your hands and would vow to be faithful to you here, and to all eternity; then your body would become infused with his soul. Thus and only thus, could you gain a share in the felicity of mankind. He would give you a soul while yet keeping his own. But that can never happen! That which is your greatest beauty in the sea, your fish's tail, is thought hideous up on earth, so little do they understand about it; to be pretty there you must have two clumsy supports which they call legs!"

Then the little mermaid sighed and looked sadly at her fish's tail.

"Let us be happy," said the grandmother, "we will hop and skip during our three hunderd years of life, it is surely a long enough time, and after it is over, we shall rest all the better in our graves. There is to be a court ball to-night."

This was a much more splendid affair than we ever see on earth. The walls and the ceiling of the great ball room were of thick but transparent glass. Several hundreds of colossal mussel shells rose-red and grass-green, were ranged in order round the sides holding blue lights, which illuminated the whole room and shone through the walls, so that the sea outside was quite lit up. You could see countless fish, great and small, swimming towards the glass walls, some with shining scales of crimson hue, while others were golden and silvery. In the middle of the room was a broad stream of running water, and on this the mermaids and mermen danced to their own beautiful singing. No earthly beings have such lovely voices. The little mermaid sang more sweetly than any of them and they all applauded her. For a moment she felt glad at heart, for she knew that she had the finest voice either in the sea or on land. But she soon began to think again about the upper world, she could not forget the handsome prince, and her sorrow in not possessing, like him, an immortal soul. Therefore she stole out of her father's palace, and while all within was joy and merriment, she sat sadly in her little garden. Suddenly she heard the sound of a horn through the water, and she thought, " now he is out sailing up there; he whom I love more than father or mother, he to whom my thoughts cling and to whose hands I am ready to commit the happiness of my life. I will dare anything to win him and to gain an immortal soul! While my sisters are dancing in my father's palace, I will go to the sea witch of whom I have always been very much afraid, she will perhaps be able to advise and help me! "

Thereupon the little mermaid left the garden and went towards the roaring whirlpools at the back of which the witch lived. She had never been that way before; no flowers grew there, no seaweed, only the bare grey sands, stretched towards the whirlpools, which like rushing mill-wheels swirled round, dragging everything that came within reach down to the depths. She had to pass between these boiling eddies to reach the witch's domain, and for a long way the only path led over warm bubbling mud, which the witch called her " peat bog." Her house stood behind this in the midst of a weird forest. All the trees and bushes were polyps, half animals and half plant; they looked like hundred-headed snakes growing out of the sand, the branches were long slimy arms, with tentacles like wriggling worms, every joint of which from the root to the outermost tip was in constant motion. They wound themselves tightly round whatever they could lay hold of and never let it escape. The little mermaid standing outside was quite frightened, her heart beat fast with terror and she nearly turned back, but then she remembered the prince and the immortal soul of mankind and took courage. She bound her long flowing hair tightly round her head, so that the polyps should not seize her by it, folded her hands over her breast, and darted like a fish through the water, in between the hideous polyps which stretched out their sensitive arms and tentacles towards her. She could see that every one of them had something or other, which they had grasped with their hundred arms, and which they held as if in iron bands. The bleached bones of men who perished at sea and sunk below peeped forth from the arms of some, while others clutched rudders and sea chests, or the skeleton of some land animal; and most horrible of all, a little mermaid whom they had caught and suffocated. Then she came to a large opening in the wood where the ground was all slimy, and some huge fat water snakes were gambolling about. In the middle of this opening was a house built of bones of the wrecked; there sat the witch, letting a toad eat out of her mouth, just as mortals let a little canary eat sugar. She called the hideous water snakes her little chickens, and allowed them to crawl about on her unsightly bosom.

"I know very well what you have come here for," said the witch. "It is very foolish of you! all the same you shall have your way, because it will lead you into misfortune, my fine princess. You want to get rid of your fish's tail, and instead to have two stumps to walk about upon like human beings, so that the young prince may fall in love with you, and that you may win him and an immortal soul." Saying this, she gave such a loud hideous laugh that the toad and the snakes fell to the ground and wriggled about there.

"You are just in the nick of time," said the witch, "after sunrise to-morrow I should not be able to help you until another year had run its course. I will make you a potion, and before sunrise you must swim ashore with it, seat yourself on the beach and drink it; then your tail will divide and shrivel up to what men call beautiful legs, but it hurts, it is as if a sharp sword were running through you. All who see you will say that you are the most beautiful child of man they have ever seen. You will keep your gliding gait, no dancer will rival you, but every step you take will be as if you were treading upon sharp knives, so sharp as to draw blood. If you are willing to suffer all this I am ready to help you!"

"Yes!" said the little princess with a trembling voice, thinking of the prince and of winning an undying soul.

"But remember," said the witch, "when once you

have received a human form, you can never be a mermaid again, you will never again be able to dive down through the waters to your sisters and to your father's palace. And if you do not succeed in winning the prince's love, so that for your sake he will forget father and mother, cleave to you with his whole heart, let the priest join your hands and make you man and wife, you will gain no immortal soul! The first morning after his marriage with another your heart will break, and you will turn into foam of the sea."

"I will do it," said the little mermaid as pale as death.

"But you will have to pay me, too," said the witch, "and it is no trifle that I demand. You have the most beautiful voice of any at the bottom of the sea, and I daresay that you think you will fascinate him with it, but you must give me that voice, I will have the best you possess in return for my precious potion! I have to mingle my own blood with it so as to make it as sharp as a two-edged sword."

"But if you take my voice," said the little mermaid, "what have I left?"

"Your beautiful form," said the witch, "your gliding gait, and your speaking eyes, with these you ought surely to be able to bewitch a human heart. Well! have you lost courage? Put out your little tongue and I will cut it off in payment for the powerful draught."

"Let it be done," said the little mermaid, and the witch put on her cauldron to brew the magic potion. "There is nothing like cleanliness," said she, as she scoured the pot with a bundle of snakes; then she punctured her breast and let the black blood drop into the cauldron, and the steam took the most weird shapes, enough to frighten anyone. Every moment the witch threw new ingredients into the pot, and when it boiled the bubbling was like the sound of crocodiles weeping. At last the potion was ready and it looked like the clearest water.

"There it is," said the witch, and thereupon she cut off the tongue of the little mermaid, who was dumb now and could neither sing nor speak.

"If the polyps should seize you, when you go back through my wood," said the witch, "just drop a single drop of this liquid on them, and their arms and fingers will burst into a thousand pieces." But the little mermaid had no need to do this, for at the mere sight of the bright liquid which sparkled in her hand like a shining star, they drew back in terror. So she soon got past the wood, the bog, and the eddying whirlpools.

She saw her father's palace, the lights were all out in the great ballroom, and no doubt all the household was asleep, but she did not dare to go in now that she was dumb and about to leave her home for ever. She felt as if her heart would break with grief. She stole into the garden and plucked a flower from each of her sister's plots, wafted with her hand countless kisses towards the palace, and then rose up through the dark blue water.

The sun had not risen when she came in sight of the prince's palace and landed at the beautiful marble steps. The moon was shining bright and clear. The little mermaid drank the burning, stinging draught, and it was like a sharp two-edged sword running through her tender frame; she fainted away and lay as if she were dead. When the sun rose on the sea she woke up and became conscious of a sharp pang, but just in front of her stood the handsome young prince, fixing his coal black eyes on her; she cast hers down and saw that her fish's tail was gone, and that she had the prettiest little white legs any maiden could desire, but she was quite naked, so she wrapped her long thick hair around her. The prince asked who she was and how she came there, she looked at him tenderly and with a sad expression in her dark blue eyes, but could not speak. Then he took her by the hand and led her into the palace. Every step she took was, as the witch had warned her beforehand, as if she were treading on sharp knives and spikes but she bore it gladly; led by the prince she moved as lightly as a bubble, and he and every one else marvelled at her graceful gliding gait.

Clothed in the costliest silks and muslins she was the greatest beauty in the palace, but she was dumb and could neither sing nor speak. Beautiful slaves clad in silks and gold came forward and sang to the prince and his royal parents; one of them sang better than all the others, and the prince clapped his hands and smiled at her; that made the little mermaid very sad, for she knew that she used to sing far better herself. She thought, "Oh! if he only knew that for the sake of being with him I had given up my voice for ever! " Now the slaves began to dance, graceful undulating dances to enchanting music; thereupon the little mermaid lifting her beautiful white arms and raising herself on tiptoe glided on the floor with a grace which none of the other dancers had yet attained. With every motion her grace and beauty became more apparent, and her eyes appealed more deeply to the heart than the songs of the slaves. Everyone was delighted with it, especially the prince, who called her his little foundling, and she danced on and on, notwithstanding that every time her foot touched the ground it was like treading on sharp knives. The prince said that she should always be near him, and she was allowed to sleep outside his door on a velvet cushion.

He had a man's dress made for her, so that she could ride about with him. They used to ride through scented woods, where the green branches brushed her shoulders, and little birds sang among the fresh leaves. She climbed up the highest mountains with the prince, and although her delicate feet bled so that others saw it, she only laughed and followed him until they saw the clouds sailing below them like a flock of birds, taking flight to distant lands.

At home in the prince's palace, when at night the others were asleep, she used to go out on to the marble steps; it cooled her burning feet to stand in the cold sea water, and at such times she used to think of those she had left in the deep.

One night her sisters came arm in arm; they sang so sorrowfully as they swam on the water that she beckoned to them and they recognised her, and told her how she had grieved them all. After that they visited her every night, and one night she saw, a long way out, her old grandmother (who for many years had not been above the water), and the Merman King with his crown on his head; they stretched out their hands towards her, but did not venture so close to land as her sisters.

Day by day she became dearer to the prince, he loved her as one loves a good sweet child, but it never entered his head to make her his queen; yet unless she became his wife she would never win an everlasting soul, but on his wedding morning would turn to sea foam.

"Am I not dearer to you than any of them?" the little mermaid's eyes seemed to say when he took her in his arms and kissed her beautiful brow.

"Yes, you are the dearest one to me," said the prince, "for you have the best heart of them all, and you are fondest of me; you are also like a young girl I once saw, but whom I never expect to see again. I was on board a ship which was wrecked, I was driven on shore by the waves close to a holy Temple where several young girls were ministering at a service; the youngest of them found me on the beach and saved my life; I saw her but twice. She was the only person I could love in this world, but you are like her, you almost drive her image out of my heart. She belongs to the holy Temple, and therefore by good fortune you have been sent to me, we will never part!"

"Alas! he does not know that it was I who saved his life," thought the little mermaid. "I bore him over the sea to the wood, where the Temple stands. I sat behind the foam and watched to see if anyone would come. I saw the pretty girl he loves better than me." And the mermaid heaved a bitter sigh, for she could not weep.

"The girl belongs to the holy Temple, he has said, she will never return to the world, they will never meet again, I am here with him, I see him every day. Yes! I will tend him, love him and give up my life to him."

But now the rumour ran that the prince was to be married to the beautiful daughter of a neighbouring king, and for that reason was fitting out a splendid ship. It was given out that the prince was going on a voyage to see the adjoining countries, but it was without doubt to see the king's daughter; he was to have a great suite with him, but the little mermaid shook her head and laughed; she knew the prince's intentions much better than any of the others. "I must take this voyage," he had said to her; "I must go and see the beautiful princess; my parents demand that, but they will never force me to bring her home as my bride; I can never love her! She will not be like the lovely girl in the Temple whom you resemble. If ever I had to choose a bride it would sooner be you with your speaking eyes, my sweet, dumb foundling!" And he kissed her rosy mouth, played with her long hair, and laid his head upon her heart, which already dreamt of human joys and an immortal soul.

"You are not frightened of the sea, I suppose, my dumb child?" he said, as they stood on the proud ship which was to carry them to the country of the neighbouring king; and he told her about storms and calms, about curious fish in the deep, and the marvels seen by divers; and she smiled at his tales, for she knew all about the bottom of the sea much better than anyone else.

At night, in the moonlight, when all were asleep, except the steersman who stood at the helm, she sat at the side of the ship trying to pierce the clear water with her eyes, and fancied she saw her father's palace, and above it her old grandmother with her silver crown on her head, looking up through the cross currents towards the keel of the ship. Then her sisters rose above the water, they gazed sadly at her, wringing their white hands; she beckoned to them, smiled, and was about to tell them that all was going well and happily with her, when the cabin boy approached, and the sisters dived down, but he supposed that the white objects he had seen were nothing but flakes of foam.

The next morning the ship entered the harbour of the neighbouring king's magnificent city. The church bells rang and trumpets were sounded from every lofty tower, while the soldiers paraded with flags flying and glittering bayonets. There was a *fête* every day, there was a succession of balls, and receptions followed one after the other, but the princess was not yet present, she was being brought up a long way off, in a holy Temple they said, and was learning all the royal virtues. At last she came. The little mermaid stood eager to see her beauty, and she was obliged to confess that a lovelier creature she had never beheld. Her complexion was exquisitely pure and delicate, and her trustful eyes of the deepest blue shone through their dark lashes.

"It is you," said the prince, "you who saved me when I lay almost lifeless on the beach?" and he clasped his blushing bride to his heart. "Oh! I am too happy!" he exclaimed to the little mermaid.

"A greater joy than I had dared to hope for has come to pass. You will rejoice at my joy, for you love me better than any one." Then the little mermaid kissed his hand, and felt as if her heart were broken already.

His wedding morn would bring death to her and change her to foam.

All the church bells pealed and heralds rode through the town proclaiming the nuptials. Upon every altar throughout the land fragrant oil was burnt in costly silver lamps. Amidst the swinging of censers by the priests, the bride and bridegroom joined hands and received the bishop's blessing. The little mermaid dressed in silk and gold stood holding the bride's train, but her ears were deaf to the festal strains, her eyes saw nothing of the sacred ceremony, she was thinking of her coming death and of all that she had lost in this world.

That same evening the bride and bridegroom embarked, amidst the roar of cannon and the waving of banners. A royal tent of purple and gold softly cushioned was raised amidships where the bridal pair were to repose during the calm cool night.

The sails swelled in the wind and the ship skimmed lightly and almost without motion over the transparent sea.

At dusk lanterns of many colours were lighted and the sailors danced merrily on deck. The little mermaid could not help thinking of the first time she came up from the sea and saw the same splendour and gaiety; and she now threw herself among the dancers, whirling, as a swallow skims through the air when pursued. The onlookers cheered her in amazement, never had she danced so divinely; her delicate feet pained her as if they were cut with knives, but she did not feel it, for the pain at her heart was much sharper. She knew that it was the last night that she would breathe the same air as he, and would look upon the mighty deep, and the blue starry heavens; an endless night without thought and without dreams awaited her, who neither had a soul, nor could win one. The joy and revelry on board lasted till long past midnight, she went on laughing and dancing with the thought of death all the time in her heart. The prince caressed his lovely bride and she played with his raven locks, and with their arms entwined they retired to the gorgeous tent. All became hushed and still on board the ship, only the steersman stood at the helm, the little mermaid laid her white arms on the gunwhale and looked eastwards for the pink tinted dawn; the first sunbeam, she knew would be her death. Then she saw her sisters rise from the water, they were as pale as she was, their beautiful long hair no longer floated on the breeze, for it had been cut off.

"We have given it to the witch to obtain her help, so that you may not die to-night! she has given us a knife, here it is, look how sharp it is! Before the sun rises, you must plunge it into the prince's heart, and when his warm blood sprinkles your feet they will join together and grow into a tail, and you will once more be a mermaid; you will be able to come down into the water to us, and to live out your three hundred years before you are turned into dead, salt, sea-foam. Make haste! you or he must die before sunrise! Our old grandmother is so full of grief that her white hair has fallen off as ours fell under the witch's scissors. Slay the prince and come back to us! Quick! Quick! do you not see the rosy streak in the sky? In a few moments the sun will rise and then you must die!" saying this they heaved a wondrous deep sigh and sank among the waves.

The little mermaid drew aside the purple curtain from the tent and looked at the beautiful bride asleep with her head on the prince's breast; she bent over him and kissed his fair brow, looked at the sky where the dawn was spreading fast; looked at the sharp knife, and again fixed her eyes on the prince who, in his dream called his bride by name, yes! she alone was in his thoughts!—For a moment the knife quivered in her grasp, then she threw it far out among the waves now rosy in the morning light and where it fell the water bubbled up like drops of blood.

Once more she looked at the prince, with her eyes already dimmed by death, then dashed overboard and fell, her body dissolving into foam.

Now the sun rose from the sea and with its kindly beams warmed the deadly cold foam, so that the little mermaid did not feel the chill of death. She saw the bright sun and above her floated hundreds of beauteous ethereal beings through which she could see the white ship and the rosy heavens, their voices were melodious but so spirit-like that no human ear could hear them, any more than an earthly eye could see their forms. Light as bubbles they floated through the air without the aid of wings. The little mermaid perceived that she had a form like theirs, it gradually took shape out of the foam. "To whom am I coming?" said she, and her voice sounded like that of the other beings, so unearthly in its beauty that no music of ours could reproduce it.

"To the daughters of the air!" answered the others, "a mermaid has no undying soul, and can never gain one without winning the love of a human being. Her eternal life must depend upon an unknown power. Nor have the daughters of the air an everlasting soul, but by their own good deeds they may create one for themselves. We fly to the tropics where mankind is the victim of hot and pestilent winds, there we bring cooling breezes. We diffuse the scent of flowers all around, and bring refreshment and healing in our train. When, for three hundred years, we have laboured to do all the good in our power we gain an undying soul and take a part in the everlasting joys of mankind. You, poor little mermaid, have with your whole heart, struggled for the same thing as we have struggled for. You have suffered and endured, raised yourself to the spirit world of the air; and now, by your own good deeds you may, in the course of three hundred years, work out for yourself an undying soul."

Then the little mermaid lifted her transparent arms towards God's sun, and for the first time shed tears.

On board ship all was again life and bustle, she saw the prince with his lovely bride searching for her, they looked sadly at the bubbling foam, as if they knew that she had thrown herself into the waves. Unseen she kissed the bride on her brow, smiled at the prince and rose aloft with the other spirits of the air to the rosy clouds which sailed above.

"In three hundred years we shall thus float into Paradise."

"We might reach it sooner," whispered one. "Unseen we flit into those homes of men where there are children, and for every day that we find a good child who gives pleasure to its parents and deserves their love, God shortens our time of probation. The child does not know when we fly through the room, and when we smile with pleasure at it, one year of our three hundred is taken away. But if we see a naughty or badly disposed child, we cannot help shedding tears of sorrow, and every tear adds a day to the time of our probation."

HANS CLODHOPPER

THERE was once an old mansion in the country, in which an old squire lived with his two sons, and these two sons were too clever by half. They had made up their minds to propose to the king's daughter, and they ventured to do so, because she had made it known that she would take any man for a husband who had most to say for himself. These two took a week over their preparations; it was all the time they had for it, but it was quite enough with all their accomplishments, which were most useful. One of them knew the Latin Dictionary by heart, and the town newspapers for three years either forwards or backwards. The second one had made himself acquainted with all the statutes of the Corporations, and what every alderman had to know. So he thought he was competent to talk about affairs of state; and he also knew how to embroider harness, for he was clever with his fingers.

"I shall win the king's daughter," they both said, and their father gave each of them a beautiful horse. The one who could repeat the Dictionary and the newspapers had a coal-black one, while the one who was learned in Guilds and embroideries had a milk-white one. Then they smeared the corners of their mouths with oil to make them more flexible. All the servants were assembled in the court-yards to see them mount, but just then the third brother came up, for there were three, only nobody made any account of this one, Hans Clodhopper, as he had no accomplishments like his brothers.

"Where are you going with all your fine clothes on?" he asked.

"To court, to talk ourselves into favour with the princess. Haven't you heard the news which is being drummed all over the country?" And then they told him the news.

"Preserve us! then I must go too," said Hans Clodhopper. But his brothers laughed and rode away.

"Father, give me a horse. I want to get married too. If she takes me, she takes me, and if she doesn't take me, I shall take her all the same."

"Stuff and nonsense," said his father, "I will give no horse to you. Why you have got nothing to say for yourself, now your brothers are fine fellows."

"If I mayn't have a horse," said Hans Clodhopper, "I'll take the billy-goat, he is my own and he can carry me very well!" And he seated himself astride the billy-goat, dug his heels into its sides, and galloped off down the highroad. Whew! what a pace they went at.

"Here I come," shouted Hans Clodhopper, and he sang till the air rang with it.

The brothers rode on in silence, they did not say a word to each other, for they had to store up every good idea which they wanted to produce later on, and their speeches had to be very carefully thought out.

"Halloo!" shouted Hans Clodhopper, "here I come; see what I've found on the road," and he shewed them a dead crow.

"What on earth will you do with that, Clodhopper?" said they.

"I will give it to the king's daughter."

"Yes, I would do that," said they, and they rode on laughing.

"Halloo, here I come; see what I have found; one doesn't find such a thing as this every day on the road." The brothers turned round to see what it was.

"Clodhopper," said they, "it's nothing but an old wooden shoe with the upper part broken off. Is the princess to have that too?"

"Yes indeed she is," said Hans, and the brothers again rode on laughing.

"Halloo, halloo, here I am," shouted Hans Clodhopper. "Now this is famous."

"What have you found this time?" asked the brothers.

"Won't the princess be delighted!"

" Why," said the brothers, " it's only sand picked up out of the ditch! "

" Yes, that it is," said Hans Clodhopper, " and the finest kind of sand, too. You can hardly hold it." And he filled his pockets with it. The brothers rode on as fast as they could, and arrived at the town gates a whole hour before him. At the gate the suitors received tickets, in the order of their arrival, and they were arranged in rows, six in each file, and so close together that they could not move their arms which was a very good thing, or they would have torn each other's garments off, merely because one stood in front of the other. All the other inhabitants of the town stood round the castle, peeping in at the windows to see the king's daughter receive the suitors, and as each one came into the room he lost the power of speech.

" No good," said the princess, " away with him! "

Now came the brother who could repeat the Lexicon, but he had entirely forgotten it while standing in the ranks. The floor creaked and the ceiling was made of looking-glass, so that he saw himself standing on his head; and at every window sat three clerks and an alderman, who wrote down all that was said, so that it might be sent to the papers at once, and sold for a halfpenny at the street corners. It was terrible, and the stoves had been heated to such a degree that they got red-hot at the top.

" It is terribly hot in here," said the suitor.

" That is because my father is roasting cockerels to-day," said the princess.

Bah! There he stood like a fool; he had not expected a conversation of this kind, and he could not think of a word to say, just when he wanted to be specially witty.

" No good," said the king's daughter, " away with him," and he had to go.

Then came the second brother. " There's a fearful heat here," said he.

" Yes, we are roasting cockerels to-day," said the king's daughter.

" What did—what? " said he, and all the reporters duly wrote " What did—what? "

" No good," said the king's daughter, " away with him."

HE SEATED HIMSELF ASTRIDE THE BILLY-GOAT.

Then came Hans Clodhopper. He rode the billy-goat right into the room.

"What a burning heat you have here," said he.

"That is because I am roasting cockerels," said the king's daughter.

"That is very convenient," said Hans Clodhopper, "then I suppose I can get a crow roasted, too?"

"Yes, very well," said the king's daughter; "but have you anything to roast it in? For I have neither pot nor pan."

"But I have," said Hans Clodhopper. "Here is a cooking pot!" And he brought out the wooden shoe and put the crow into it.

"Why you have enough for a whole meal," said the king's daughter; "but where shall we get any dripping to baste it with?"

"Oh, I have some in my pocket," said Hans Clodhopper; "I have enough and to spare;" and he poured a little of the sand out of his pocket.

"Now I like that," said the princess; "you have an answer for everything, and you have something to say for yourself. I will have you for a husband. But do you know that every word we have said will be in the paper to-morrow; for at every window sit three clerks and an alderman, and the old man is the worst, for he doesn't understand." She said this to frighten him. All the clerks sniggered and made blots of ink on the floor.

"Oh, those are the gentry," said Hans Clodhopper, "then I must give the alderman the best thing I have;" and he turned out his pockets and threw the sand in his face.

"That was cleverly done," said the princess; "I couldn't have done it, but I will try to learn."

So Hans Clodhopper became king, gained a wife and a crown and sat upon the throne. We have this straight out of the alderman's newspaper, but it is not to be depended upon.

Then came Hans Clodhopper. He rode the billy-goat right into the room.

"What a burning heat you have here," said he.

"That is because I am roasting cockerels," said the king's daughter.

"That is very convenient," said Hans Clodhopper; "then I suppose I can get a crow roasted, too."

"Yes, very well," said the king's daughter; "but have you anything to roast it in? For I have neither pot nor pan."

"But I have," said Hans Clodhopper. "Here is a cooking pot." And he brought out the wooden shoe and put the crow into it.

"Why you have enough for a whole meal," said the king's daughter; "but where shall we get any dripping to baste it with?"

"Oh, I have some in my pocket," said Hans Clodhopper; "I have enough and to spare," and he poured a little of the sand out of his pocket.

"Now I like that," said the princess; "you have an answer for everything, and you have something to say for yourself. I will have you for a husband. But do you know that every word we have said will be in the paper to-morrow, for at every window sit three clerks and an alderman, and the alderman is the worst, for he doesn't understand." She said this to frighten him. All the clerks sniggered and made blots of ink on the floor.

"Oh, those are the gentry," said Hans Clodhopper; "then I must give the alderman the best thing I have," and he turned out his pockets and threw the sand in his face.

"That was cleverly done," said the princess, "I couldn't have done it, but I will try to learn."

So Hans Clodhopper became king, gained a wife and a crown and sat upon the throne. We have this straight out of the alderman's newspaper, but it is not to be depended upon.

THE FLYING TRUNK

THERE was once a merchant who was so rich that he might have paved the whole street, and a little alley besides, with silver money. But he didn't do it—he knew better how to use his money than that: if he laid out a penny, he got half a crown in return, such a clever man of business was he—and then he died.

His son got all the money, and he led a merry life; he used to go to masquerades every night, made kites of bank notes, and played ducks and drakes with gold coins instead of stones. In this way the money soon went. At last he had only a penny left, and no clothes except an old dressing-gown and a pair of slippers. His friends cared for him no longer, they couldn't walk about the streets with him; but one of them who was kind sent him an old trunk, and said, "Pack up." Now this was all very well, but he had nothing to pack, so he got into the trunk himself.

It was a most peculiar trunk. If you pressed the lock the trunk could fly; and this is what happened: with a whiz it flew up the chimney, high above the clouds, further and further away. The bottom of it cracked ominously, and he was dreadfully afraid it would go to pieces, and a nice fall he would have had! Heaven preserve us! At last he arrived in the country of the Turks. He hid the trunk in a wood under the dead leaves, and walked into the town; he could easily do that, as all the Turks wear dressing-gowns and slippers, you know, just like his. He met a nurse with a baby. "I say, you Turkish nurse," said he, "what is that big palace close to the town, where all the windows are so high up?"

"That's where the king's daughter lives," said she;

"it has been prophesied that she will be made very unhappy by a lover, so no one is allowed to visit her except when the king and queen go with them."

"Thank you," said the merchant's son, and then he went back to the wood and got into his trunk again, and flew on to the roof of the palace, from whence he crept in at the princess's window.

She was lying on a sofa, fast asleep. She was so very beautiful that the merchant's son was driven to kiss her. She woke up and was dreadfully frightened, but he said that he was the Prophet of the Turks and he had flown down through the air to see her, and this pleased her very much.

They sat side by side and he told her stories about her eyes; he said they were like the most beautiful deep, dark lakes, in which her thoughts floated like mermaids; and then he told her about her forehead, that it was like a snow mountain, adorned with a series of pictures. And he told her all about the storks, which bring beautiful little children up out of the rivers. No end of beautiful stories he told her, and then he asked her to marry him, and she at once said "Yes." "But you must come here on Saturday," she said, "when the king and the queen drink tea with me. They will be very proud when they hear I am to marry a prophet; but mind you have a splendid story to tell them, for my parents are very fond of stories: my mother likes them to be grand and very proper, but my father likes them to be merry, so that he can laugh at them."

"Well, a story will be my only wedding-gift!" he said, and then they separated: but the princess gave him a sword encrusted with gold. It was the kind of present he needed badly.

He flew away and bought himself a new dressing-gown, and sat down in the wood to make up a new story; it had to be ready by Saturday, and it is not always so easy to make up a story.

However he had it ready in time, and Saturday came.

The king, the queen and the whole court were waiting for him round the princess's tea-table. He had a charming reception.

"Now will you tell us a story," said the Queen, "one

which is both thoughtful and instructive."

"But one that we can laugh at too," said the King.

"All right!" said he, and then he began: we must listen to his story attentively.

"There was once a bundle of matches, and they were frightfully proud because of their high origin. Their family tree, that is to say the great pine tree of which they were each a little splinter, had been the giant of the forest. The matches now lay on a shelf between a tinder box and an old iron pot, and they told the whole story of their youth to these two. 'Ah, when we were a living tree,' said they, 'we were indeed a green branch! Every morning and every evening we had diamond-tea, that was the dew-drops. In the day we had the sunshine, and all the little birds to tell us stories. We could see, too, that we were very rich, for most of the other trees were only clad in summer, but our family could afford to have green clothes both summer and winter. But then the wood-cutters came, and there was a great revolution, and our family was sundered. The head of the tribe got a place as mainmast on a splendid ship, which could sail round the world if it chose; the other branches were scattered in different directions, and it is now our task to give light to the common herd, that is how such aristocratic people as ourselves have got into this kitchen.'

"'Now my lot has been different!' said the iron pot, beside which the matches lay. 'Ever since I came into the world I have passed the time in being scoured and boiled, over and over again! Everything solid comes to me, and in fact I am the most important person in the house. My pleasure is when the dinner is over, to lie clean and bright on the shelf, and to have a sensible chat with my companions; but with the exception of the water-bucket which sometimes goes down into the yard, we lead an indoor life. Our only newsmonger is the market-basket, and it talks very wildly about the Government and the People. Why the other day an old pot was so alarmed by the conversation, that it fell down and broke itself to pieces! It was a Liberal you see!'

"'You are talking too much,' said the tinderbox, and the steel struck sparks on the flint. 'Let us have a merry evening.'

" 'Yes, pray let us settle which is the most aristocratic among us,' said the matches.

" 'No, I don't like talking about myself,' said the earthen pipkin; 'let us have an evening entertainment! I will begin. I will tell you the kind of things we have all experienced; they are quite easy to understand, and that is what we all like: By the eastern sea and Danish beeches——'

" 'That's a nice beginning to make!' said all the plates; 'I am sure that will be a story I shall like!'

" 'Well, I passed my youth there, in a very quiet family; the furniture was bees-waxed, the floors washed, and clean curtains were put up once a fortnight!'

" 'What a good story-teller you are,' said the broom; 'one can tell directly that it's a woman telling a story, a vein of cleanliness runs through it!'

" 'Yes, one feels that,' said the water-pail, and for very joy it gave a little hop which clashed on the floor.

" The pipkin went on with its story, and the end was much the same as the beginning.

" All the plates clattered with joy, and the broom crowned the pipkin with a wreath of parsley, because it knew it would annoy the others; and it thought, 'If I crown her to-day, she will crown me to-morrow.'

" 'Now I will dance,' said the tongs, and began to dance; heaven help us, what a way into the air she could get her leg. The old chair-cover in the corner burst when she saw it! 'Mayn't I be crowned too,' said the tongs, so they crowned her.

" 'They're only a rabble after all,' said the matches.

" The tea-urn was called upon to sing now, but it had a cold, it said; it couldn't sing except when it was boiling; but that was all because it was stuck-up; it *wouldn't* sing except when it was on the drawing-room table.

" There was an old quill pen, along on the window-sill, which the servant used to write with; there was nothing extraordinary about it, except that it had been dipped too far into the inkpot, but it was rather proud of that. 'If the tea-urn won't sing, it can leave it alone,' it said. 'There is a nightingale hanging outside in a cage, it can sing; it certainly hasn't learnt anything special, but we needn't mind that to-night.'

" 'I think it is most unsuitable,' said the kettle, which was the kitchen songster, and half-sister of the urn, 'that a strange bird like that should be listened to! Is it patriotic? I will let the market-basket judge.'

" 'I am very much annoyed,' said the market-basket. 'I am more annoyed than any one can tell! Is this a suitable way to spend an evening? Wouldn't it be better to put the house to rights? Then everything would find its proper place, and I would manage the whole party. Then we should get on differently!' "

" 'Yes, let us make a row!' they all said together.

" At that moment the door opened, it was the servant, and they all stood still, nobody uttered a sound. But not a pot among them which didn't know its capabilities, or how distinguished it was, 'If *I* had chosen, we might have had a merry evening, and no mistake,' they all thought.

" The servant took the matches and struck a light; preserve us! how they spluttered and blazed up.

" 'Now everyone can see,' they thought, 'that we are the first. How brilliantly we shine! What a light we shed around!'—And then they were burnt out."

" That was a splendid story," said the Queen; " I quite felt that I was in the kitchen with the matches. Yes indeed you shall marry our daughter."

" Certainly!" said the King. " Thou shalt marry her on Monday!" They said " du " (thou) to him now, as they were to be related.

So the wedding was decided upon, and the evening before the town was illuminated. Buns and cakes were scattered broadcast; the street boys stood on tiptoe and shouted hurrah, and whistled through their fingers. Everything was most gorgeous.

" I suppose I shall have to do something too," said the merchant's son; so he bought a lot of rockets, squibs, and all sorts of fireworks, put them in his trunk, and flew up into the air with them.

All the Turks jumped at the sight, so that their slippers flew into the air, they had never seen a flight of meteors like that before. They saw now without doubt that it was the prophet himself, who was about to marry the princess.

As soon as the merchant's son got down again into the wood with his trunk, he thought, " I will just go into the town to hear what was thought of the display," and it was quite reasonable that he should do so.

Oh, how every one talked, every single man he spoke to had his own opinion about it, but that it had been splendid was the universal opinion.

"I saw the prophet myself," said one; "his eyes were like shining stars, and his beard like foaming water."

"He was wrapped in a mantle of fire," said another. "The most beautiful angels' heads peeped out among the folds." He heard nothing but pleasant things, and the next day was to be his wedding-day. He went back to the wood to get into his trunk—but where was it? The trunk was burnt up. A spark from the fireworks had set fire to it and the trunk was burnt to ashes. He could not fly any more, or reach his bride. She stood all day on the roof waiting for him; she is waiting for him still, but he wanders round the world telling stories, only they are no longer so merry as the one he told about the matches.

THE ROSE ELF

IN the middle of a garden grew a rose tree; it was full of roses, and in the loveliest of them all lived an elf. He was so tiny that no human eye could see him. He had a snug little room behind every petal of the rose. He was as well made and as perfect as any human child, and he had wings reaching from his shoulders to his feet. Oh, what a delicious scent there was in his room, and how lovely and transparent the walls were, for they were palest pink, rose petals. All day he revelled in the sunshine, flew from flower to flower, and danced on the wings of fluttering butterflies. Then he would measure how many steps he would have to take to run along all the high roads and paths on a linden leaf. These paths were what we call veins, but they were endless roads to him. Before he came to the end of them the sun went down, for he had begun rather late.

It became very cold, the dew fell and the wind blew; it was high time for him to get home. He hurried as much as ever he could, but the rose had shut itself up, and he could not get in,—not a single rose was open. The poor little rose elf was dreadfully frightened, he had never been out in the night before; he had always slept so safely behind his cosy rose leaves. Oh, it would surely be his death!

At the other end of the garden he knew there was an arbour covered with delicious honeysuckle, the flowers looked like beautiful painted horns. He would get into one of those and sleep till morning.

He flew along to it. Hush! There were already two people in the arbour, a young handsome man and a lovely maiden. They sat side by side and wished they might never more be parted, so tenderly did they love each other. They loved each other more dearly than the best child can even love its father and mother.

"Still, we must part," said the young man: "your brother is not friendly to us, therefore he sends me on such a distant errand, far away over mountains and oceans. Good-bye, my sweetest bride, for you are that to me, you know!"

Then they kissed each other, and the young girl wept, and gave him a rose, but before she gave it to him she pressed a kiss upon it, a kiss so tender and impassioned that the rose spread its petals. Then the little elf flew in and leant his head against the delicate fragrant walls, but he could hear them saying, "Farewell, farewell," and he felt that the rose was placed upon the young man's heart—Ah, how it beat! The little elf could not go to sleep because of its beating.

The rose did not remain long undisturbed on that beating heart; the young man took it out, as he walked alone through the dark wood, and kissed it passionately many, many times; the little elf thought he would be crushed to death. He could feel the young man's burning lips through the leaves, and the rose opened as it might have done under the midday sun.

Then another man came up behind, dark and angry; he was the pretty girl's wicked brother. He took out a long sharp knife, and while the other was kissing the rose the bad man stabbed him. He cut off his head and buried it with the body in the soft earth under the linden tree.

"Now he is dead and done with," thought the wicked brother. "He will never come back any more. He had a long journey to take over mountains and oceans where one's life may easily be lost, and he has lost his. He will never come back, and my sister will never dare to ask me about him."

Then he raked up the dead leaves with his foot, over the earth where it had been disturbed, and went home again in the darkness of the night. But he was not alone, as he thought; the little elf went with him. He was hidden in a withered linden leaf which had fallen from the tree on to the bad man's head while he was digging the grave.

It was covered by his hat now, and it was so dark inside, where the little elf sat trembling with fear and anger at the wicked deed. The mad man got home in the early morning; he took off his hat, and went into his sister's bedroom. There lay the pretty, blooming girl dreaming about her beloved, whom she thought was so far away, beyond mountains and woods. The wicked brother leant over her with an evil laugh, such as a fiend might laugh. The withered leaf fell out of his hair upon the counterpane; but he never noticed it, and went away to get a little sleep himself. But the elf crept out of the dead leaf, and into the ear of the sleeping girl, and told her, as in a dream the tale of the terrible murder. He described the place where her brother had committed the murder, and where he had laid the body; he told her about the flowering linden tree, and said, "So that you may not think all I have told you is a mere dream, you will find a withered leaf upon your bed."

This she found, as he had said, when she woke. Oh! what bitter, bitter tears she shed. To no one did she dare betray her grief. Her window stood open all day, and the little elf could easily have got into the garden to the roses and all the other flowers, but he could not bear to leave the sorrowing girl. A monthly rose-bush stood in the window, and he took up his place in one of the flowers, whence he could watch the poor girl. Her brother often came into the room, he was merry with an evil mirth, but she dared not say a word about the grief at her heart.

When night came she stole out of the house, and into the wood, to the place where the linden tree stood. She tore away the leaves from the ground and dug down into the earth, and at once found him who had been murdered. Oh how she wept and prayed to God, that she too might soon die. Gladly would she have taken the body home with her could she have done so. But she took the pale head with the closed eyes, kissed the cold lips and shook the earth out of his beautiful hair.

"This shall be mine!" she said, when she had covered up the body with earth and leaves. Then she took the head home with her and a little spray of the jasmine tree which flowered in the wood where he was killed.

As soon as she reached her room she fetched the biggest

flower pot she could find, and laid the head of the dead man in it, covered it with earth, and planted the sprig of jasmine in the pot.

"Farewell, farewell!" whispered the little elf. He could no longer bear to look at such grief, so he flew away into the garden to his rose, but it was withered, and only a few faded leaves hung round the green calyx. "Alas! how quickly the good and the beautiful pass away!" sighed the elf. At last he found another rose, and made it his home. He could dwell in safety behind its fragrant petals.

Every morning he flew to the poor girl's window, and she was always there, weeping by the flower pot. Her salt tears fell upon the jasmine, and for every day that she grew paler and paler the sprig gained in strength and vigour. One shoot appeared after another, and then little white flower buds showed themselves, and she kissed them; but her wicked brother scolded her, and asked if she was crazy. He did not like to see, and could not imagine why, she was always hanging weeping over the flower pot. He did not know what eyes lay hidden there, closed for ever, nor what red lips had returned to dust within its depths. She leant her head against the flower pot, and the little elf found her there, fallen into a gentle slumber. He crept into her ear, and whispered to her of that evening in the arbour, about the scented roses, and the love of the elves. She dreamt these sweet dreams, and while she dreamt her life passed away. She was dead—she had died a peaceful death, and had passed to heaven to her beloved! The jasmine opened its big white blossoms, and they gave out their sweetest scent. They had no other way of weeping over the dead.

The wicked brother saw the beautiful flowering plant, and he took it for himself as an inheritance. He put it into his own bedroom, close by his bedside, because it was so beautiful to look at, and smelt so sweet and fresh. The little rose elf accompanied it and flew from blossom to blossom; in each lived a little elf, and to each one he told the story of the murdered man, whose head now rested under the earth. He told them about the wicked brother and his poor sister.

"We know it," said each little creature. "We know it;

did we not spring from those murdered eyes and lips? We know it, we know it! " and then they nodded their heads so oddly.

The rose elf could not understand how they could be so quiet about it, and he flew to the bees who were gathering honey. He told them the story about the wicked brother, and the bees told it to their queen, who commanded them all to kill the murderer next morning.

But in the night, the first night after his sister's death, when the brother was asleep in his bed, close to the fragrant jasmine tree, every blossom opened wide its petals, and out of every flower stepped invisibly, but armed each with a tiny poisoned spear, the little spirits from the flower. First they took their places by his ear, and told him evil dreams; then they flew over his mouth and pierced his tongue with their poisoned darts.

" Now we have revenged the dead! " said they, and crept back again into the white bells of the jasmine.

When morning came, the window all at once flew open, and in flew the rose elf and all the swarm of bees with their queen to kill him.

But he was already dead; people stood round the bed and said, " The scent of the jasmine has killed him! "

Then the rose elf understood the vengeance of the flowers, and told it to the queen bee, and she with all her swarm buzzed round the flower pot; the bees would not be driven away. Then a man took up the flower pot, and one of the bees stung his hand, and he let the flower pot fall, and it was broken to bits.

Then they saw the whitened skull, and they knew that the dead man lying on the bed was a murderer. The queen bee hummed in the air, and sang about the vengeance of the flowers to the rose elf, and that behind each smallest leaf, lurks a being who can discover and revenge every evil deed.

THE ELF-HILL

SOME lizards were nimbly running in and out of the clefts in an old tree. They understood each other very well, for they all spoke lizard language.

"What a rumbling and grumbling is going on inside the old Elf-hill," said one of the lizards. "I have not closed my eyes for the last two nights for the noise. I might just as well be having toothache, for all the sleep I get!"

"There is something up inside," said the other lizard. "They propped up the top of the hill on four red posts till cockcrow this morning, to air it out thoroughly; and the elf maidens had been learning some new dancing steps, which they are always practising. There certainly must be something going on."

"Yes, I was talking to an earthworm of my acquaintance about it," said the third lizard. "He came straight up out of the hill, where he had been boring into the earth for days and nights. He had heard a good deal, for the miserable creature can't see, but it can feel its way, and plays the part of eavesdropper to perfection. They are expecting visitors in the Elf-hill, grand visitors; but who they are the earthworm refused to say or perhaps he did not know. All the will-o'-the-wisps are ordered for a procession of torches, as it is called; and the silver and gold plate, of which there is any amount in the hill, is all being polished up and put out in the moonlight."

"Whoever can the strangers be?" said all the lizards together.

"What on earth is happening? Hark! what a humming and buzzing?"

At this moment the Elf-hill opened, and an elderly elf-maiden tripped out. She was hollow behind,[1] but otherwise quite attractively dressed. She was the old elf-king's housekeeper, and a distant relative. She wore an amber heart upon her forehead. She moved her legs at a great pace, "trip, trip." Good heavens! how fast she tripped over the ground; she went right down to the night-jar in the swamp.

"You are invited to the Elf-hill for to-night," said she to him. "But will you be so kind as to charge yourself with the other invitations. You must make yourself useful in other ways, as you don't keep house yourself. We are going to have some very distinguished visitors, goblins, who always have something to say, and so the old elf-king means to show what he can do."

"Who is to be invited?" asked the night-jar.

"Well, everybody may come to the big ball, even human beings, if they can only talk in their sleep, or do something else after our fashion. But the choice is to be strictly limited for the grand feast. We will only have the most distinguished people. I have had a battle with the elf-king about it; because I hold that we mustn't even include ghosts. The merman and his daughters must be invited first. I don't suppose they care much about coming on dry land, but I shall see that they each have a wet stone to sit on, or something better; so I expect they won't decline this time. All the old demons of the first-class, with tails, the River-god, and the wood-sprites. And then I don't think we can pass over the Grave-pig,[2] the Hell-horse, and the Church-grim, although they belong to the clergy, who are not of our people; but that is merely on account of their office, and they are closely connected with us, and visit us very frequently."

"Croak," said the night-jar, and he flew to issue the invitations.

The elf-maidens had already begun to dance, and they danced a scarf dance, with scarves woven of mist and

[1] According to a superstition these elf-maidens are hollow, like the inside of a mask.

[2] According to Danish superstition, a living horse or pig has been buried under every church; their ghosts are said to walk at night.

moonshine; these have a lovely effect to those who care for that kind of thing. The great hall in the middle of the Elf-hill had been thoroughly polished up for the occasion. The floor was washed with moonshine, and the walls were rubbed over with witches' fat, and this made them shine with many colours, like a tulip petal. The kitchen was full of frogs on spits, stuffed snake skins, and salads of toad stool spawn, mouse snouts and hemlock. Then there was beer brewed by the marsh witch, and sparkling salt-petre wine from the vaults. Everything of the best, and rusty nails and church window panes among the kickshaws.

The old elf-king had his golden crown polished with pounded slate-pencil, ay, and it was a head-boy's slate-pencil too, and they are not so easy to get. They hung up fresh curtains in the bedroom, and fixed them with the slime of snails. Yes, indeed, there was a humming and a buzzing.

"Now we will fumigate with horse-hair and pig's bristles, and then I can do no more!" said the old elf-servant.

"Dear father!" said the youngest of the daughters, "are you not going to tell me who these grand strangers are?"

"Well, well," he said, "I suppose I must tell you now. Two of my daughters must prepare themselves to be married,—two will certainly make marriages. The old Trold chieftain from Norway, that lives on the Dovrefield, among his many rock castles and fastnesses and gold works, which are better than you would expect, is coming down here with his two sons. They are coming to look for wives. The old Trold is a regular honest Norwegian veteran, straightforward and merry. I used to know him in the olden days, when we drank to our good fellowship. He came here to fetch a wife, but she is dead now. She was a daughter of the king of the chalk cliffs at Möen. As the saying is, 'he took his wife on the chalk,' viz., bought her on tick. I am quite anxious to see the old fellow. The sons, they say, are a pair of overgrown, ill-mannered cubs; but perhaps they are not so bad; I daresay they will improve as they grow older. See if you can't lick them into shape a bit."

"And when do they come?" asked one of the daughters.

"That depends upon wind and weather," said the elf-king. "They travel economically, and they will take their chance of a ship. I wanted them to come round by Sweden, but the old fellow can't bring himself to that yet. He doesn't march with the times, but I don't hold with that!"

At this moment two will-o'-the-wisps came hopping along, one faster than the other, so of course one arrived before the other.

"They are coming, they are coming!" they cried.

"Give me my crown, and let me stand in the moonlight," said the elf-king.

The daughters raised their scarves and curtseyed to the ground.

There stood the Trold chieftain from the Dovrefield; he wore a crown of hardened icicles and polished fir cones, and besides this, he had on a bearskin coat and snow-shoes. His sons, on the other hand, had bare necks and wore no braces, because they were strong men.

"Is that a hill?" asked the youngest of the brothers, pointing to the Elf-hill. "We should call it a hole in Norway."

"Lads!" cried the old man, "holes go inwards, hills go upwards! Haven't you got eyes in your heads?"

The only thing that astonished them, they said, was that they understood the language without any trouble.

"Don't make fools of yourselves," said the old man; "one might think you were only half baked."

Then they went into the Elf-hill, where the company was of the grandest, although they had been got together in such a hurry; you might almost say they had been blown together. It was all charming, and arranged to suit every-one's taste. The merman and his daughters sat at table in great tubs of water, and said it was just like being at home. Everybody had excellent table manners, except the two young Norwegian Trolds; they put their feet up on the table, but then they thought anything they did was right.

"Take your feet out of the way of the dishes," said the old Trold, and they obeyed him, but not at once. They tickled the ladies they took into dinner with fir cones out of their pockets; then they pulled off their boots, so as to be quite comfortable, and handed the boots to the ladies to hold. Their father, the old Trold chieftain, was very different; he told no end of splendid stories about the proud Norwegian mountains, and the waterfalls dashing down in white foam with a roar like thunder. He told them about the salmon leaping up against the rushing water, when the nixies played their golden harps. Then he went on to tell them about the sparkling winter nights when the sledge bells rang and the lads flew over the ice with blazing lights, the ice which was so transparent that you could see the startled fish darting away under your feet. Yes, indeed, he could tell stories, you could see and hear the things he described; the saw mills going, the men and maids singing their songs and dancing the merry Halling dance. Huzza! All at once the old Trold gave the elf housekeeper a smacking kiss, such a kiss it was, and yet they were not a bit related. Then the elf-maidens had to dance, first plain dancing, and then step dancing, and it was most becoming to them. Then came a fancy dance.

Preserve us, how nimble they were on their legs, you couldn't tell where they began, or where they ended, you couldn't tell which were arms and which were legs, they were all mixed up together like shavings in a saw-pit. They twirled round and round so often that it made the hell-horse feel quite giddy and unwell and he had to leave the table.

"Prrrrr!" said the old Trold. "There is some life in those legs, but what else can they do besides dancing and pointing their toes and all those whirligigs?"

"We will soon shew you!" said the elf-king, and he called out his youngest daughter; she was thin and transparent as moonshine, and was the most ethereal of all the daughters. She put a little white stick in her mouth and vanished instantly; this was her accomplishment.

But the Trold said he did not like that accomplishment in a wife, nor did he think his boys would appreciate it. The second one could walk by her own side as if she had a shadow, and no elves have shadows.

The third was quite different; she had studied in the marsh witches' brewery, and understood larding alder stumps with glow-worms.

"She will be a good housewife," said the Trold, and then he saluted her with his eyes instead of drinking her health, for he did not want to drink too much.

Now came the turn of the fourth; she had a big golden harp to play, and when she touched the first string everybody lifted up their left legs (for all the elfin folk are left legged). But when she touched the second string everybody had to do what she wished.

" She is a dangerous woman! " said the Trold, but both his sons left the hill, for they were tired of it all.

" And what can the next daughter do? " asked the old Trold.

" I have learnt to like the Norwegians," she said, " and I shall never marry unless I can go to Norway! "

But the smallest of the sisters whispered to the Trold, " that is only because she once heard a song which said that when the world came to an end, the rocks of Norway would still stand, and that is why she wants to go there, she is so afraid of being exterminated."

" Ho, ho! " said the Trold, " so that slipped out. But what can the seventh do? "

" The sixth comes before the seventh," said the elf-king, for he could reckon, but she would not come forward.

" I can only tell people the truth," she said. " Nobody cares for me, and I have enough to do in making my winding sheet."

Now came the seventh and last, what could she do? Well she could tell stories as many as ever she liked.

" Here are my five fingers," said the old Trold, " tell me a story for each one."

" The elf-maiden took hold of his wrist, and he chuckled and laughed, till he nearly choked. When she came to the fourth finger, which had a gold ring on it, as if it knew there was to be a betrothal, the Trold said, " Hold fast what you have got, the hand is yours, I will have you for a wife, myself! " The elf-maiden said that the stories about Guldbrand, the fourth finger, and little Peter Playman, the fifth, had not yet been told.

" Never mind, keep those till winter. Then you shall tell us about the fir, and the birch, and the fairy gifts, and the tingling frost. You shall have every opportunity of telling us stories; nobody up there does it yet. We will sit in the Stone Hall, where the pine logs blaze, and drink mead out of the golden horns of the old Norwegian kings.

The river god gave me a couple. When we sit there the mountain sprite comes to pay us a visit, and he will sing you the songs of the Sæter girls. The salmon will leap in the waterfalls, and beat against the stone wall, but it won't get in. Ah, you may believe me when I say that we lead a merry life there in good old Norway. But where are the lads?"

Yes, where were the lads? They were running about the fields, blowing out the will-o'-the-wisps, who came so willingly for the torchlight procession.

"Why do you gad about out there?" said the Trold. "I have taken a mother for you, now you can come and take one of the aunts."

But the lads said they would rather make a speech, and drink toasts; they had no wish to marry. Then they made their speeches, and drank toasts and tipped their glasses up to shew that they had emptied them. After that they pulled off their coats and went to sleep on the table, to show that they were quite at home. But the old Trold danced round and round the room with his young bride, and exchanged boots with her, which was grander than exchanging rings.

"There is the cock crowing!" said the old housekeeper. "Now we must shut the shutters, so that the sun may not burn us up."

Then the hill closed up. But the lizards went on running up and down the clefts of the tree; and they said to each other. "Ah, how much I liked the old Trold."

"I liked the boys better," said the earthworm, but then it couldn't see, poor, miserable creature that it was.

THE REAL PRINCESS

THERE was once a prince, and he wanted a princess, but then she must be a *real* princess. He travelled right round the world to find one, but there was always something wrong. There were plenty of princesses, but whether they were real princesses he had great difficulty in discovering; there was always something which was not quite right about them. So at last he had to come home again, and he was very sad because he wanted a real princess so badly.

One evening there was a terrible storm; it thundered and lightened and the rain poured down in torrents; indeed it was a fearful night.

In the middle of the storm somebody knocked at the town gate, and the old king himself went to open it.

It was a princess who stood outside, but she was in a terrible state from the rain and the storm. The water streamed out of her hair and her clothes, it ran in at the top of her shoes and out at the heel, but she said that she was a real princess.

"Well we shall soon see if that is true," thought the old Queen, but she said nothing. She went into the bedroom, took all the bedclothes off and laid a pea on the bedstead: then she took twenty mattresses and piled them on the top of the pea, and then twenty feather beds on the top of the mattresses. This was where the princess was to sleep that night. In the morning they asked her how she had slept.

"Oh terribly badly!" said the Princess. "I have hardly closed my eyes the whole night! Heaven knows what was in the bed. I seemed to be lying upon some hard thing, and my whole body is black and blue this morning. It is terrible!"

They saw at once that she must be a real princess when she had felt the pea through twenty mattresses and twenty feather beds. Nobody but a real princess could have such a delicate skin.

So the prince took her to be his wife, for now he was sure that he had found a real princess, and the pea was put into the Museum, where it may still be seen if no one has stolen it.

Now this is a true story.

A PICTURE FROM THE RAMPARTS

IT is autumn, and we are standing on the ramparts round the citadel, looking at the ships sailing on the Sound, and at the opposite coast of Sweden which stands out clearly in the evening sun-light. Behind us the ramparts fall away steeply; around are stately trees from which the golden leaves are falling fast. Down below us we see some dark and gloomy buildings, surrounded with wooden palisades, and inside these, where the sentries are walking up and down, it is darker still, yet not so gloomy as it is behind yon iron grating; that is where the worst convicts are confined. A ray from the setting sun falls into the bare room. The sun shines upon good and bad alike! The gloomy savage prisoner looks bitterly at the chilly sunbeam. A little bird flutters against the grating. The bird sings to good and bad alike! It twitters softly for a little while, and remains perched, flutters its wings, picks a feather from its breast, and puffs its plumage up. The bad man in chains looks at it, a milder expression steals over his hideous face. A thought which is not quite clear to himself steals into his heart; it is related to the sunshine coming through the grating, related to the scent of violets, which in spring grow so thickly outside the window. Now is heard the music of a huntsman's horn clear and lively, the bird flies away from the grating, the sunbeam disappears, and all is dark again in the narrow cell, dark in the heart of the bad man. Yet the sun has shone into it, and the bird has sung its song.

Continue ye merry notes! The evening is mild, the sea is calm and bright as any mirror.

THE RED SHOES

THERE was once a little girl; she was a tiny, delicate little thing, but she always had to go about barefoot in summer, because she was very poor. In winter she only had a pair of heavy wooden shoes, and her ankles were terribly chafed.

An old mother shoemaker lived in the middle of the village, and she made a pair of little shoes out of some strips of red cloth. They were very clumsy, but they were made with the best intention, for the little girl was to have them. Her name was Karen.

These shoes were given to her, and she wore them for the first time on the day her mother was buried; they were certainly not mourning, but she had no others, and so she walked bare-legged in them behind the poor deal coffin.

Just then a big old carriage drove by, and a big old lady was seated in it; she looked at the little girl, and felt very, very sorry for her, and said to the Parson, "Give the little girl to me and I will look after her and be kind to her." Karen thought it was all because of the red shoes, but the old lady said they were hideous, and they were burnt. Karen was well and neatly dressed, and had to learn reading and sewing. People said she was pretty, but her mirror said, "you are more than pretty, you are lovely."

At this time the Queen was taking a journey through the country, and she had her little daughter the Princess with her. The people, and among them Karen, crowded round the palace where they were staying, to see them. The little Princess stood at a window to show herself. She wore neither a train nor a golden crown, but she was dressed all in white with a beautiful pair of red morocco shoes. They were indeed a contrast to those the poor old mother shoemaker had made for Karen. Nothing in the world could be compared to these red shoes.

The time came when Karen was old enough to be confirmed; she had new clothes, and she was also to have a pair of new shoes. The rich shoemaker in the town was to take the measure of her little foot; his shop was full of glass cases of the most charming shoes and shiny leather boots. They looked beautiful, but the old lady could not see very well, so it gave her no pleasure to look at them. Among all the other shoes there was one pair of red shoes like those worn by the Princess; oh, how pretty they were. The shoemaker told them that they had been made for an earl's daughter, but they had not fitted. "I suppose they are patent leather," said the old lady, "they are so shiny."

"Yes, they do shine," said Karen, who tried them on. They fitted and were bought; but the old lady had not the least idea that they were red, or she would never have allowed Karen to wear them for her Confirmation. This she did however.

Everybody looked at her feet, and when she walked up the church to the chancel, she thought that even the old pictures, those portraits of dead and gone priests and their wives, with stiff collars and long black clothes, fixed their eyes upon her shoes. She thought of nothing else when the priest laid his hand upon her head and spoke to her of holy baptism, the covenant with God, and that from henceforth she was to be a responsible Christian person. The solemn notes of the organ resounded, the children sang with their sweet voices, the old precentor sang, but Karen only thought about her red shoes.

By the afternoon the old lady had been told on all sides that the shoes were red, and she said it was very naughty and most improper. For the future, whenever Karen went to the church, she was to wear black shoes, even if they were old. Next Sunday there was Holy Communion, and Karen was to receive it for the first time. She looked at the black shoes and then at the red ones—then she looked again at the red, and at last put them on.

It was beautiful, sunny weather; Karen and the old lady went by the path through the cornfield, and it was rather dusty. By the church door stood an old soldier, with a crutch; he had a curious long beard, it was more red than white, in fact it was almost quite red. He bent down to the ground and asked the old lady if he might dust her shoes. Karen put out her little foot too. "See, what beautiful dancing shoes!" said the soldier. "Mind you stick fast when you dance," and as he spoke he struck the soles with his hand. The old lady gave the soldier a copper and went into the church with Karen. All the people in the church looked at Karen's red shoes, and all the portraits looked too. When Karen knelt at the altar-rails and the chalice was put to her lips, she only thought of the red shoes; she seemed to see them floating before her eyes. She forgot to join in the hymn of praise, and she forgot to say the Lord's Prayer.

Now everybody left the church, and the old lady got into her carriage. Karen lifted her foot to get in after her, but just then the old soldier, who was still standing there, said, "See what pretty dancing shoes!" Karen couldn't help it; she took a few dancing steps, and when she began her feet continued to dance; it was just as if the shoes had a power over them. She danced right round the church; she couldn't stop; the coachman had to run after her and take hold of her, and lift her into the carriage; but her feet continued to dance, so that she kicked the poor lady horribly. At last they got the shoes off, and her feet had a little rest.

When they got home the shoes were put away in a cupboard, but Karen could not help going to look at them.

The old lady became very ill; they said she could not live; she had to be carefully nursed and tended, and no one was nearer than Karen to do this. But there was to be a grand ball in the town, and Karen was invited. She looked at the old lady, who after all could not live; she looked at the red shoes; she thought there was no harm in doing so. She put on the red shoes, even that she might do; but then she went to the ball and began to dance! The shoes would not let her do what she liked: when she wanted to go to the right, they danced to the left; when she wanted to dance up the room, the shoes danced down the room, then down the stairs, through the streets and out of the town gate. Away she danced, and away she had to dance, right away into the dark forest. Something shone up above the trees, and she thought it was the moon, for it was a face, but it was the old soldier with the red beard, and he nodded and said, " See what pretty dancing shoes! "

This frightened her terribly and she wanted to throw off the red shoes, but they stuck fast. She tore off her stockings but the shoes had grown fast to her feet, and off she danced, and off she had to dance over fields and meadows, in rain and sunshine, by day and by night, but at night it was fearful.

She danced into the open churchyard but the dead did not join her dance, they had something much better to do. She wanted to sit down on a pauper's grave where the bitter wormwood grew, but there was no rest nor repose for her. When she danced towards the open church door, she saw an angel standing there in long white robes and wings which reached from his shoulders to the ground, his face was grave and stern, and in his hand he held a broad and shining sword.

" Dance you shall! " said he, " you shall dance in your red shoes till you are pale and cold. Till your skin shrivels up and you are a skeleton! You shall dance from door to door, and wherever you find proud vain children, you must knock at the door so that they may see you and fear you. Yea you shall dance——"

" Mercy! " shrieked Karen, but she did not hear the angel's answer, for the shoes bore her through the gate into the fields over roadways and paths, ever and ever she was forced to dance.

One morning she danced past a door she knew well; she heard the sound of a hymn from within, and a coffin covered with flowers was being carried out. Then she knew that the old lady was dead, and it seemed to her that she was forsaken by all the world, and cursed by the holy angels of God.

On and ever on she danced; dance she must even through the dark nights. The shoes bore her away over briars and stubble till her feet were torn and bleeding; she danced away over the heath till she came to a little lonely house. She knew the executioner lived here, and she tapped with her fingers on the window pane and said,

"Come out! come out! I can't come in for I am dancing!"

The executioner said, "You can't know who I am? I chop the bad people's heads off, and I see that my axe is quivering."

"Don't chop my head off," said Karen, "for then I can never repent of my sins, but pray, pray chop my feet off with the red shoes!"

Then she confessed all her sins, and the executioner chopped off her feet with the red shoes, but the shoes danced right away with the little feet into the depths of the forest.

Then he made her a pair of wooden legs and crutches, and he taught her a psalm, the one penitents always sing; and she kissed the hand which had wielded the axe, and went away over the heath.

"I have suffered enough for those red shoes!" said she. "I will go to church now, so that they may see me!" and she went as fast as she could to the church door. When she got there, the red shoes danced up in front of her, and she was frightened and went home again.

She was very sad all the week, and shed many bitter tears, but when Sunday came, she said "Now then, I have suffered and struggled long enough; I should think I am quite as good as many who sit holding their heads so high in church!" She went along quite boldly, but she did not get further than the gate before she saw the red shoes dancing in front of her; she was more frightened than ever, and turned back, this time with real repentance in her heart. Then she went to the parson's house, and begged to be taken into service, she would be very industrious and work as hard as she could, she didn't care what wages they gave her, if only she might have a roof over her head and live among kind people. The parson's wife was sorry for her, and took her into her service; she proved to be very industrious and thoughtful. She sat very still, and listened most attentively in the evening when the parson read the Bible. All the little ones were very fond of her, but when they chattered about finery and dress, and about being as beautiful as a queen, she would shake her head.

Next Sunday they all went to church, and they asked her if she would go with them; but she looked sadly, with tears in her eyes, at her crutches, and they went without her to hear the word of God, and she sat in her little room alone. It was only big enough for a bed and a chair; she sat there with her prayer book in her hand, and as she read it with a humble mind, she heard the notes of the organ, borne from the church by the wind; she raised her tear stained face and said, "Oh, God help me!"

Then the sun shone brightly round her, and the angel in the white robes whom she had seen on yonder night, at the church door, stood before her. He no longer held the sharp sword in his hand, but a beautiful green branch, covered with roses. He touched the ceiling with it and it rose to a great height, and wherever he touched it a golden star appeared. Then he touched the walls and they spread themselves out, and she saw and heard the organ. She saw the pictures of the old parsons and their wives; the congregation were all sitting in their seats singing aloud—for the church itself had come home to the poor girl, in her narrow little chamber, or else she had been taken to it. She found herself on the bench with the other people from the Parsonage. And when the hymn had come to an end they looked up and nodded to her and said, "it was a good thing you came after all, little Karen!"

"It was through God's mercy!" she said. The organ sounded, and the children's voices echoed so sweetly through the choir. The warm sunshine streamed brightly in through the window, right up to the bench where Karen sat; her heart was so over-filled with the sunshine, with peace, and with joy that it broke. Her soul flew with the sunshine to heaven, and no one there asked about the red shoes.

THUMBELISA

THERE was once a woman who had the greatest longing for a little tiny child, but she had no idea where to get one; so she went to an old witch and said to her, "I do so long to have a little child, will you tell me where I can get one?"

"Oh, we shall be able to manage that," said the witch. "Here is a barley corn for you; it is not at all the same kind as that which grows in the peasant's field, or with which chickens are fed; plant it in a flower pot and you will see what will appear."

"Thank you, oh, thank you!" said the woman, and she gave the witch twelve pennies, then went home and planted the barley corn, and a large, handsome flower sprang up at once; it looked exactly like a tulip, but the petals were tightly shut up, just as if they were still in bud. "That is a lovely flower," said the woman, and she kissed the pretty red and yellow petals; as she kissed it the flower burst open with a loud snap. It was a real tulip, you could see that; but right in the middle of the flower on the green stool sat a little tiny girl, most lovely and delicate; she was not more than an inch in height, so she was called Thumbelisa.

Her cradle was a smartly varnished walnut shell, with the blue petals of violets for a mattress and a rose-leaf to cover her; she slept in it at night, but during the day she played about on the table where the woman had placed a plate, surrounded by a wreath of flowers on the outer edge with their stalks in water. A large tulip petal floated on the water, and on this little Thumbelisa sat and sailed about from one side of the plate to the other; she had two white horse hairs for oars. It was a pretty sight. She could sing, too, with such delicacy and charm as was never heard before.

One night as she lay in her pretty bed, a great ugly toad hopped in at the window, for there was a broken pane. Ugh! how hideous that great wet toad was; it hopped right down on to the table where Thumbelisa lay fast asleep, under the red rose-leaf.

"Here is a lovely wife for my son," said the toad, and then she took up the walnut shell where Thumbelisa slept and hopped away with it through the window, down into the garden. A great broad stream ran through it, but just at the edge it was swampy and muddy, and it was here that the toad lived with her son. Ugh! how ugly and hideous he was too, exactly like his mother. "Koax, koax, brekke-ke-kex," that was all he had to say when he saw the lovely little girl in the walnut shell.

"Do not talk so loud or you will wake her," said the old toad; "she might escape us yet, for she is as light as thistledown! We will put her on one of the broad water lily leaves out in the stream; it will be just like an island to her, she is so small and light. She won't be able to run away from there while we get the state-room ready down under the mud, which you are to inhabit."

A great many water lilies grew in the stream, their broad green leaves looked as if they were floating on the surface of the water. The leaf which was furthest from the shore was also the biggest, and to this one the old toad swam out with the walnut shell in which little Thumbelisa lay.

The poor, tiny little creature woke up quite early in the morning, and when she saw where she was she began to cry most bitterly, for there was water on every side of the big green leaf, and she could not reach the land at any point.

The old toad sat in the mud decking out her abode with grasses and the buds of the yellow water lilies, so as to have it very nice for the new daughter-in-law, and then she swam out with her ugly son to the leaf where Thumbelisa stood; they wanted to fetch her pretty bed to place it in the bridal chamber before they took her there. The old toad made a deep curtsey in the water before her, and said, "Here is my son, who is to be your husband, and you are to live together most comfortably down in the mud."

"Koax, koax, brekke-ke-kex," that was all the son could say.

Then they took the pretty little bed and swam away with it, but Thumbelisa sat quite alone on the green leaf and cried because she did not want to live with the ugly toad, or have her horried son for a husband. The little fish which swam about in the water had no doubt seen the toad and heard what she said, so they stuck their heads up, wishing, I suppose, to see the little girl. As soon as they saw her, they were delighted with her, and were quite grieved to think that she was to go down to live with the ugly toad. No, that should never happen. They flocked together down in the water round about the green stem which held the leaf she stood upon, and gnawed at it with their teeth till it floated away down the stream carrying Thumbelisa away where the toad could not follow her.

Thumbelisa sailed past place after place, and the little birds in the bushes saw her and sang, "what a lovely little maid." The leaf with her on it floated further and further away and in this manner reached foreign lands.

A pretty little white butterfly fluttered round and round her for some time and at last settled on the leaf, for it had taken quite a fancy to Thumbelisa: she was so happy now, because the toad could not reach her and she was sailing through such lovely scenes; the sun shone on the water and it looked like liquid gold. Then she took her sash and tied one end round the butterfly, and the other she made fast to the leaf which went gliding on quicker and quicker, and she with it for she was standing on the leaf.

At this moment a big cockchafer came flying along, he caught sight of her and in an instant he fixed his claw round her slender waist and flew off with her, up into a tree, but the green leaf floated down the stream and the butterfly with it, for he was tied to it and could not get loose.

Heavens! how frightened poor little Thumbelisa was when the cockchafer carried her up into the tree, but she was most of all grieved about the pretty white butterfly which she had fastened to the leaf; if he could not succeed in getting loose he would be starved to death.

But the cockchafer cared nothing for that. He settled with her on the largest leaf on the tree, and fed her with honey from the flowers, and he said that she was lovely although she was not a bit like a chafer. Presently all the other chafers which lived in the tree came to visit them; they looked at Thumbelisa and the young lady chafers twitched their feelers and said, " she has also got two legs, what a good effect it has." " She has no feelers," said another. " She is so slender in the waist, fie, she looks like a human being." " How ugly she is," said all the mother chafers, and yet little Thumbelisa was so pretty. That was certainly also the opinion of the cockchafer who had captured her, but when all the others said she was ugly, he at last began to believe it too, and would not have anything more to do with her, she might go wherever she liked! They flew down from the tree with her and placed her on a daisy, where she cried because she was so ugly that the chafers would have nothing to do with her; and after all, she was more beautiful than anything you could imagine, as delicate and transparent as the finest rose-leaf.

Poor little Thumbelisa lived all the summer quite alone in the wood. She plaited a bed of grass for herself and hung it up under a big dock-leaf which sheltered her from the rain; she sucked the honey from the flowers for her food, and her drink was the dew which lay on the leaves in the morning. In this way the summer and autumn passed, but then came the winter. All the birds which used to sing so sweetly to her flew away, the great dock-leaf under which she had lived shrivelled up leaving nothing but a dead yellow stalk, and she shivered with the cold, for her clothes were worn out; she was such a tiny creature, poor little Thumbelisa, she certainly must be frozen to death. It began to snow and every snow-flake which fell upon her was like a whole shovelful upon one of us, for we are big and she was only one inch in height. Then she wrapped herself up in a withered leaf, but that did not warm her much, she trembled with the cold.

Close to the wood in which she had been living lay a large cornfield, but the corn had long ago been carried away and nothing remained but the bare, dry, stubble which stood up out of the frozen ground. The stubble was quite a forest for her to walk about in: oh, how she shook with the cold. Then she came to the door of a field-mouse's home. It was a little hole down under the stubble. The field-mouse lived so cosily and warm there, her whole room was full of corn, and she had a beautiful kitchen and larder besides. Poor Thumbelisa stood just inside the door like any other poor beggar child and begged for a little piece of barley corn, for she had had nothing to eat for two whole days.

"You poor little thing," said the field-mouse, for she was at bottom a good old field-mouse. "Come into my warm room and dine with me." Then, as she took a fancy to Thumbelisa, she said, "you may with pleasure stay with me for the winter, but you must keep my room clean and tidy and tell me stories, for I am very fond of them," and Thumbelisa did what the good old field-mouse desired and was on the whole very comfortable.

"Now we shall soon have a visitor," said the field-mouse; "my neighbour generally comes to see me every week-day. He is even better housed than I am; his rooms are very large and he wears a most beautiful black velvet coat; if only you could get him for a husband you would indeed be well settled, but he can't see. You must tell him all the most beautiful stories you know."

But Thumbelisa did not like this, and she would have nothing to say to the neighbour for he was a mole. He came and paid a visit in his black velvet coat. He was very rich and wise, said the field-mouse, and his home was twenty times as large as hers; and he had much learning but he did not like the sun or the beautiful flowers, in fact he spoke slightingly of them for he had never seen them. Thumbelisa had to sing to him and she sang both "Fly away cockchafer" and "A monk, he wandered through the meadow," then the mole fell in love with her because of her sweet voice, but he did not say anything for he was of a discreet turn of mind.

He had just made a long tunnel through the ground from his house to theirs, and he gave the field-mouse and Thumbelisa leave to walk in it whenever they liked. He told them not to be afraid of the dead bird which was lying in the passage. It was a whole bird with feathers and beak which had probably died quite recently at the beginning of the winter and was now entombed just where he had made his tunnel.

The mole took a piece of tinder-wood in his mouth, for that shines like fire in the dark, and walked in front of them to light them in the long dark passage; when they came to the place where the dead bird lay, the mole thrust his broad nose up to the roof and pushed the earth up so as to make a big hole through which the daylight shone. In the middle of the floor lay a dead swallow, with its pretty wings closely pressed to its sides, and the legs and head drawn in under the feathers; no doubt the poor bird had died of cold. Thumbelisa was so sorry for it; she loved all the little birds, for they had twittered and sung so sweetly to her during the whole summer; but the mole kicked it with his short legs and said, "Now it will pipe no more! it must be a miserable fate to be born a little bird! Thank heaven! no child of mine can be a bird; a bird like that has nothing but its twitter and dies of hunger in the winter."

"Yes, as a sensible man, you may well say that," said the field-mouse. "What *has* a bird for all its twittering when the cold weather comes? it has to hunger and freeze, but then it must cut a dash."

Thumbelisa did not say anything, but when the others turned their backs to the bird, she stooped down and stroked aside the feathers which lay over its head, and kissed its closed eyes. "Perhaps it was this very bird which sang so sweetly to me in the summer," she thought; "what pleasure it gave me, the dear pretty bird."

The mole now closed up the hole which let in the daylight and conducted the ladies to their home. Thumbelisa could not sleep at all in the night, so she got up out of her bed and plaited a large handsome mat of hay and then she carried it down and spread it all over the dead bird, and laid some soft cotton wool which she had found in the field-mouse's room close round its sides, so that it might have a warm bed on the cold ground.

"Good-bye, you sweet little bird," said she, "good-bye, and thank you for your sweet song through the summer when all the trees were green and the sun shone warmly upon us." Then she laid her head close up to the bird's breast, but was quite startled at a sound, as if something was thumping inside it. It was the bird's heart. It was not dead but lay in a swoon, and now that it had been warmed it began to revive.

In the autumn all the swallows fly away to warm countries, but if one happens to be belated, it feels the cold so much that it falls down like a dead thing, and remains lying where it falls till the snow covers it up. Thumbelisa quite shook with fright for the bird was very, very big beside her who was only one inch high, but she gathered up her courage, packed the wool closer round the poor bird, and fetched a leaf of mint which she had herself for a coverlet and laid it over the bird's head. The next night she stole down again to it and found it alive but so feeble that it could only just open its eyes for a moment to look at Thumbelisa who stood with a bit of tinder-wood in her hand, for she had no other lantern.

"Many, many thanks, you sweet child," said the sick swallow to her; "you have warmed me beautifully. I shall soon have strength to fly out into the warm sun again."

"Oh!" said she, "it is so cold outside, it snows and freezes, stay in your warm bed, I will tend you." Then she brought water to the swallow in a leaf, and when it had drunk some, it told her how it had torn its wing on a black thorn bush, and therefore could not fly as fast as the other swallows which were taking flight then for the distant warm lands. At last it fell down on the ground, but after that it remembered nothing, and did not in the least know how it had got into the tunnel.

It stayed there all the winter, and Thumbelisa was good to it and grew very fond of it. She did not tell either the mole or the field-mouse anything about it, for they did not like the poor unfortunate swallow.

As soon as the spring came and the warmth of the sun penetrated the ground, the swallow said good-bye to Thumbelisa, who opened the hole which the mole had made above. The sun streamed in deliciously upon them, and the swallow asked if she would not go with him, she could sit upon his back and they would fly far away into the green wood. But Thumbelisa knew that it would grieve the old field-mouse if she left her like that.

"No, I can't," said Thumbelisa.

"Good-bye, good-bye, then, you kind pretty girl," said the swallow, and flew out into the sunshine. Thumbelisa looked after him and her eyes filled with tears, for she was very fond of the poor swallow.

"Tweet, tweet," sang the bird, and flew into the green wood.

Thumbelisa was very sad. She was not allowed to go out into the warm sunshine at all; the corn which was sown in the field near the field-mouse's house grew quite long, it was a thick forest for the poor little girl who was only an inch high.

"You must work at your trousseau this summer," said the mouse to her, for their neighbour the tiresome mole in his black velvet coat had asked her to marry him. "You shall have both woollen and linen, you shall have wherewith to clothe and cover yourself when you become the mole's wife." Thumbelisa had to turn the distaff and the field-mouse hired four spiders to spin and weave day and night. The mole paid a visit every evening and he was always saying that when the summer came to an end, the sun would not shine nearly so warmly, now it burnt the ground as hard as a stone. Yes, when the summer was over he would celebrate his marriage; but Thumbelisa was not at all pleased, for she did not care a bit for the tiresome mole. Every morning at sunrise and every evening at sunset she used to steal out to the door, and when the wind blew aside the tops of the cornstalks so that she could see the blue sky, she thought how bright and lovely it was out there, and wished so much to see the dear swallow again; but it never came back; no doubt it was a long way off, flying about in the beautiful green woods.

When the autumn came all Thumbelisa's outfit was ready.

"In four weeks you must be married," said the field-mouse to her. But Thumbelisa cried and said that she would not have the tiresome mole for a husband.

"Fiddle-dee-dee," said the field-mouse; "don't be obstinate or I shall bite you with my white tooth. You are going to have a splendid husband; the queen herself hasn't the equal of his black velvet coat; both his kitchen and his cellar are full. You should thank heaven for such a husband!"

So they were to be married; the mole had come to fetch Thumbelisa; she was to live deep down under the ground with him, and never to go out into the warm sunshine, for he could not bear it. The poor child was very sad at the thought of bidding good-bye to the beautiful sun; while she had been with the field-mouse she had at least been allowed to look at it from the door.

" Good-bye, you bright sun," she said as she stretched out her arms towards it and went a little way outside the field-mouse's house, for now the harvest was over and only the stubble remained. " Good-bye, good-bye! " she said, and threw her tiny arms round a little red flower growing there. " Give my love to the dear swallow if you happen to see him."

" Tweet, tweet," she heard at this moment above her head. She looked up; it was the swallow just passing. As soon as it saw Thumbelisa it was delighted; she told it how unwilling she was to have the ugly mole for a husband, and that she was to live deep down underground where the sun never shone. She could not help crying about it.

" The cold winter is coming," said the swallow, " and I am going to fly away to warm countries. Will you go with me? You can sit upon my back! Tie yourself on with your sash, then we will fly away from the ugly mole and his dark cavern, far away over the mountains to those warm countries where the sun shines with greater splendour than here, where it is always summer and there are heaps of flowers. Do fly with me, you sweet little Thumbelisa, who saved my life when I lay frozen in the dark earthy passage."

" Yes, I will go with you," said Thumbelisa, seating herself on the bird's back with her feet on its out-spread wing. She tied her band tightly to one of the strongest feathers, and then the swallow flew away, high up in the air above forests and lakes, high up above the biggest mountains where the snow never melts; and Thumbelisa shivered in the cold air, but then she crept under the bird's warm feathers, and only stuck out her little head to look at the beautiful sights beneath her.

Then at last they reached the warm countries. The sun shone with a warmer glow than here; the sky was twice as high, and the most beautiful green and blue grapes grew in clusters on the banks and hedgerows. Oranges and lemons hung in the woods which were fragrant with myrtles and sweet herbs, and beautiful children ran about the roads playing with the large gorgeously-coloured butterflies. But the swallow flew on and on, and the country grew more and more beautiful. Under magnificent green trees on the shore of the blue sea stood a dazzling white marble palace of ancient date; vines wreathed themselves round the stately pillars. At the head of these there were countless nests, and the swallow who carried Thumbelisa lived in one of them.

" Here is my house," said the swallow; " but if you will choose one of the gorgeous flowers growing down there, I will place you in it, and you will live as happily as you can wish."

" That would be delightful," she said, and clapped her little hands.

A great white marble column had fallen to the ground and lay there broken in three pieces, but between these the most lovely white flowers grew. The swallow flew down with Thumbelisa and put her upon one of the broad leaves; what was her astonishment to find a little man in the middle of the flower, as bright and transparent as if he had been made of glass. He had a lovely golden crown upon his head and the most beautiful bright wings upon his shoulders; he was no bigger than Thumbelisa. He was the angel of the flowers. There was a similar little man or woman in every flower, but he was the king of them all.

" Heavens, how beautiful he is," whispered Thumbelisa to the swallow. The little prince was quite frightened by the swallow, for it was a perfect giant of a bird to him, he who was so small and delicate, but when he saw Thumbelisa he was delighted; she was the very prettiest girl he had ever seen. He therefore took the golden crown off his own head and placed it on hers, and asked her name, and if she would be his wife, and then she would be queen of the flowers! Yes, he was certainly a very different kind of husband from the toad's son, or the mole with his black velvet coat. So she accepted the beautiful prince, and out of every flower stepped a little lady or a gentleman so lovely that it was a pleasure to look at them. Each one brought a gift to Thumbelisa, but the best of all was a pair of pretty wings from a large white fly; they were fastened on to her back, and then she too could fly from flower to flower. All was then delight and happiness, but the swallow sat alone in his nest and sang to them as well as he could, for his heart was heavy, he was so fond of Thumbelisa himself, and would have wished never to part from her.

" You shall not be called Thumbelisa," said the angel of the flower to her; " that is such an ugly name, and you are so pretty. We will call you May."

" Good-bye, good-bye," said the swallow, and flew away again from the warm countries, far away back to Denmark; there he had a little nest above the window where the man lived who wrote this story, and he sang his " tweet, tweet " to the man, and so we have the whole story.

THE STEADFAST TIN SOLDIER

THERE were once five and twenty tin soldiers, all brothers, for they were the offspring of the same old tin spoon. Each man shouldered his gun, kept his eyes well to the front, and wore the smartest red and blue uniform imaginable. The first thing they heard in their new world, when the lid was taken off the box, was a little boy clapping his hands and crying, "Soldiers, soldiers!" It was his birthday and they had just been given to him; so he lost no time in setting them up on the table. All the soldiers were exactly alike with one exception, and he differed from the rest in having only one leg. For he was made last, and there was not quite enough tin left to finish him. However, he stood just as well on his one leg, as the others on two, in fact he is the very one who is to become famous. On the table where they were being set up, were many other toys; but the chief thing which caught the eye was a delightful paper castle. You could see through the tiny windows right into the rooms. Outside there were some little trees surrounding a small mirror, representing a lake, whose surface reflected the waxen swans which were swimming about on it. It was altogether charming, but the prettiest thing of all was a little maiden standing at the open door of the castle. She, too, was cut out of paper, but she wore a dress of the lightest gauze, with a dainty little blue ribbon over her shoulders, by way of a scarf, set off by a brilliant spangle, as big as her whole face. The little maid was stretching out both arms, for she was a dancer, and in the dance, one of her legs was raised so high into the air that the tin soldier could see absolutely nothing of it, and supposed that she, like himself, had but one leg.

"That would be the very wife for me!" he thought; "but she is much too grand; she lives in a palace, while I only have a box, and then there are five and twenty of us to share it. No, that would be no place for her! but I must try to make her acquaintance!" Then he lay down full length behind a snuff box, which stood on the table. From that point he could have a good look at the little lady, who continued to stand on one leg without losing her balance.

Late in the evening the other soldiers were put into their box, and the people of the house went to bed. Now was the time for the toys to play; they amused themselves with paying visits, fighting battles, and giving balls. The tin soldiers rustled about in their box, for they wanted to join the games, but they could not get the lid off. The nut-crackers turned somersaults, and the pencil scribbled non-sense on the slate. There was such a noise that the canary woke up and joined in, but his remarks were in verse. The only two who did not move were the tin soldier and the little dancer. She stood as stiff as ever on tip-toe, with her arms spread out: he was equally firm on his one leg, and he did not take his eyes off her for a moment.

Then the clock struck twelve, when pop! up flew the lid of the snuff box, but there was no snuff in it, no! There was a little black goblin, a sort of Jack-in-the-box.

"Tin soldier!" said the goblin, "have the goodness to keep your eyes to yourself."

But the tin soldier feigned not to hear.

"Ah! you just wait till to-morrow," said the goblin.

In the morning when the children got up they put the tin soldier on the window frame, and, whether it was caused by the goblin or by a puff of wind, I do not know, but all at once the window burst open, and the soldier fell head foremost from the third storey.

It was a terrific descent, and he landed at last, with his leg in the air, and rested on his cap, with his bayonet fixed between two paving stones. The maid-servant and the little boy ran down at once to look for him; but although they almost trod on him, they could not see him. Had the soldier only called out, "here I am," they would easily have found him, but he did not think it proper to shout when he was in uniform.

Presently it began to rain, and the drops fell faster and faster, till there was a regular torrent. When it was over two street boys came along.

"Look out!" said one; "there is a tin soldier! He shall go for a sail."

So they made a boat out of a newspaper and put the soldier into the middle of it, and he sailed away down the gutter; both boys ran alongside clapping their hands. Good heavens! what waves there were in the gutter, and what a current, but then it certainly had rained cats and dogs. The paper boat danced up and down, and now and then whirled round and round. A shudder ran through the tin soldier, but he remained undaunted, and did not move a muscle, only looked straight before him with his gun shouldered. All at once the boat drifted under a long wooden tunnel, and it became as dark as it was in his box.

"Where on earth am I going to now!" thought he. "Well, well, it is all the fault of that goblin! Oh, if only the little maiden were with me in the boat it might be twice as dark for all I should care!"

At this moment a big water rat, who lived in the tunnel, came up.

"Have you a pass?" asked the rat. "Hand up your pass!"

The tin soldier did not speak, but clung still tighter to his gun. The boat rushed on, the rat close behind. Phew, how he gnashed his teeth and shouted to the bits of stick and straw.

"Stop him, stop him, he hasn't paid his toll! he hasn't shewn his pass!"

But the current grew stronger and stronger, the tin soldier could already see daylight before him at the end of the tunnel; but he also heard a roaring sound, fit to strike terror to the bravest heart. Just imagine! Where the tunnel ended the stream rushed straight into the big canal. That would be just as dangerous for him as it would be for us to shoot a great rapid.

He was so near the end now that it was impossible to stop. The boat dashed out; the poor tin soldier held himself as stiff as he could; no one should say of him that he even winced.

The boat swirled round three or four times, and filled with water to the edge; it must sink. The tin soldier stood up to his neck in water, and the boat sank deeper and deeper. The paper became limper and limper, and at last the water went over his head—then he thought of the pretty little dancer, whom he was never to see again, and this refrain rang in his ears:

> "Onward! Onward! Soldier!
> For death thou canst not shun."

At last the paper gave way entirely and the soldier fell through—but at the same moment he was swallowed by a big fish.

Oh! how dark it was inside the fish, it was worse than being in the tunnel even; and then it was so narrow! But the tin soldier was as dauntless as ever, and lay full length, shouldering his gun.

The fish rushed about and made the most frantic movements. At last it became quite quiet, and after a time, a flash like lightning pierced it. The soldier was once more in the broad daylight, and some one called out loudly, "a tin soldier!" The fish had been caught, taken to market, sold, and brought into the kitchen, where the cook cut it open with a large knife. She took the soldier up by the waist, with two fingers, and carried him into the parlour, where everyone wanted to see the wonderful man, who had travelled about in the stomach of a fish; but the tin soldier was not at all proud. They set him up on the table, and, wonder of wonders! he found himself in the very same room that he had been in before. He saw the very same children, and the toys were still standing on the table, as well as the beautiful castle with the pretty little dancer.

She still stood on one leg, and held the other up in the air. You see she also was unbending. The soldier was so much moved that he was ready to shed tears of tin, but that would not have been fitting. He looked at her, and she looked at him, but they said never a word. At this moment one of the little boys took up the tin soldier, and without rhyme or reason, threw him into the fire. No doubt the little goblin in the snuff box was to blame for that. The tin soldier stood there, lighted up by the flame, and in the most horrible heat; but whether it was the heat of the real fire, or the warmth of his feelings, he did not know. He had lost all his gay colour; it might have been from his perilous journey, or it might have been from grief, who can tell?

He looked at the little maiden, and she looked at him; and he felt that he was melting away, but he still managed to keep himself erect, shouldering his gun bravely.

A door was suddenly opened, the draught caught the little dancer and she fluttered like a sylph, straight into the fire, to the soldier, blazed up and was gone!

By this time the soldier was reduced to a mere lump, and when the maid took away the ashes next morning she found him, in the shape of a small tin heart. All that was left of the dancer was her spangle, and that was burnt as black as a coal.

THE BUTTERFLY

THE butterfly was looking out for a bride, and naturally he wished to select a nice one among the flowers. He looked at them, sitting so quietly and discreetly upon their stems, as a damsel generally sits when she is not engaged; but there were so many to choose among, that it became quite a difficult matter. The Butterfly did not relish encountering difficulties, so in his perplexity he flew to the Daisy. She is called in France *Marguerite*. He knew that she could " spae," and that she did so often; for lovers plucked leaf after leaf from her, and with each a question was asked respecting the beloved:—" Is it true love? " " From the heart? " " Love that pines? " " Cold love? " " None at all "—or some such questions. Everyone asks in his own language. The Butterfly came too to put his questions; he did not, however, pluck off the leaves but kissed them all one by one, with the hope of getting a good answer.

" Sweet Marguerite Daisy," said he, " you are the wisest wife among all the flowers; you know how to predict events. Tell me, shall I get this one or that? or whom shall I get? When I know, I can fly straight to the fair one, and commence wooing her."

But Marguerite would scarcely answer him; she was vexed at his calling her " wife." He asked a second time, and he asked a third time, but he could not get a word out of her; so he would not take the trouble to ask any more, but flew away without further ado on his matrimonial errand.

It was in the early spring, and there were plenty of Snowdrops and Crocuses. " They are very nice-looking," said the Butterfly, " charming little things, but somewhat too juvenile." He, like most very young men, preferred elder girls. Thereupon he flew to the Anemones, but they were rather too bashful for him; the Violets were too enthusiastic; the Tulips were too fond of show; the Jonquils were too plebeian; the Linden-tree blossoms were too small, and they had too large a family connection; the Apple blossoms were certainly as lovely as Roses to look at, but they stood to-day and fell off to-morrow, as the wind blew. It would not be worth while to enter into wedlock for so short a time, he thought. The Sweet-pea was the one that pleased him most; she was pink and white, she was pure and delicate, and belonged to that class of notable girls who always look well, yet can make themselves useful in the kitchen. He was on the point of making an offer to her when at that moment he observed a pea-pod hanging close by, with a withered flower at the end of it. "Who is that?" he asked. "My sister," replied the Sweet-pea. "Indeed! then you will probably come to look like her, by-and-by," screamed the Butterfly as he flew on.

The Honeysuckles hung over the hedge; they were extremely ladylike, but they had long faces and yellow complexions. They were not to his taste. But who was to his taste? Ay! ask him that.

The spring had passed, the summer had passed, and autumn was passing too. The flowers were still clad in brilliant robes, but, alas! the fresh fragrance of youth was gone. Fragrance was a great attraction to him, though no longer young himself, and there was none to be found among the Dahlias and Hollyhocks.

So the Butterfly stooped down to the Wild Thyme.

"She has scarcely any blossom, but she is altogether a flower herself, and all fragrance—every leaflet is full of it. I will take her."

So he began to woo forthwith.

But the Wild Thyme stood stiff and still, and at length she said, "Friendship, but nothing more! I am old, and you are old. We may very well live for each other, but marry—no! Let us not make fools of ourselves in our old age!"

So the Butterfly got no one. He had been too long on the look-out, and that one should not be. The Butterfly became an old bachelor, as it is called.

It was late in the autumn, and there was nothing but drizzling rain and pouring rain; the wind blew coldly on the old willow trees till the leaves shivered and the branches cracked. It was not pleasant to fly about in summer clothing; this is the time, it is said, when domestic love is most needed. But the Butterfly flew about no more. He had accidentally gone within doors, where there was fire in the stove—yes, real summer heat. He could live, but "to live is not enough," said he; "sunshine, freedom, and a little flower, one must have."

And he flew against the window pane, was observed, admired, and stuck upon a needle in a case of curiosities. There they could not do for him.

"Now I am sitting on a stem, like the flowers," said the Butterfly; "very pleasant it is not, however. It is almost like being married, one is tied so fast. And he tried to comfort himself with this reflection.

"That is poor comfort!" exclaimed the plants in the flower pots in the room.

"But one can hardly believe a plant in a flower pot," thought the Butterfly; "they are too much among human beings."

THE STORKS

A STORK had built his nest on the roof of the last house in a little town. The mother stork was sitting on the nest with her little ones, who stuck out their little black beaks, which had not turned red yet. The father stork stood a little way off on the ridge of the roof, erect and stiff, with one leg drawn up under him, so as at least to be at some trouble while standing sentry. One might have thought he was carved out of wood, he stood so still!

"It will look so grand for my wife to have a sentry on guard by the nest!" he thought. "People won't know that I am her husband, I daresay they think I have orders to stand there—it looks smart!" and so he remained standing on one leg.

A party of children were playing in the street, and when they saw the stork, one of the boldest boys, followed by the others, sang the old song about the storks, but he sang it just as it came into his head,

"Oh! father stork, father stork, fly to your nest,
Three featherless fledglings await your return.
The first of your chicks shall be stuck through the breast
The second shall hang and the third shall burn."

"Hark! what are the boys singing?" said the little storks; "they say we are to be hanged and burnt!"

"Don't bother your heads about them!" said the mother stork; "don't listen to them and then it won't do you any harm."

But the boys went on singing and pointing their fingers at the storks; only one boy, whose name was Peter, said that it was a shame to make fun of the creatures and he would take no part in it.

The mother bird comforted her little ones saying, "Do not trouble yourselves about it, look at your father how quietly he stands, and on one leg too!"

"But we are so frightened," said the young ones, burying their heads in the nest.

The next day when the children came back to play and they saw the storks they began their old song,

"The first of your chicks shall be stuck through the breast,
The second shall hang and the third shall burn."

"Are we to be hanged and burnt?" asked the little storks.

"No, certainly not!" said the mother; "you are to learn to fly, see if I don't drill you, then we will go into the fields and visit the frogs; they curtsey in the water to us and sing 'Koax, Koax,' and then we gobble them up; that's a treat if you like!"

"And what next?" asked the young ones.

"Oh, then all the storks in the country assemble for the autumn manœuvres, and you will have to fly your best, for the one who cannot fly will be run through the body by the general's beak, so you must take good care to learn something when the drills begin."

"After all then we may be staked just as the boys said, and listen, they are singing it again now!"

"Listen to me and not to them," said the mother stork. "After the grand manœuvres we shall fly away to the warm countries, ever such a way off, over the woods and mountains. We go to Egypt where they have three-cornered houses the points of which reach above the clouds; they are called Pyramids, and they are older than any stork can imagine. Then there is a river which overflows its banks and all the land round turns to mud. You walk about in mud devouring frogs."

"Oh!" said all the young ones.

"Yes, it is splendid, you do nothing but eat all day; while we are so well off there, there is not a leaf on the trees in this country, and it is so cold that the clouds freeze all to pieces and fall down in little bits."

She meant snow, but did not know how to describe it any better.

"Do the naughty boys freeze to pieces?" asked the young storks.

"No, they don't freeze to pieces, but they come very near to it and have to ssit moping in dark rooms; you, on the other hand, fly about in strange countries, in the warm sunshine among flowers."

Some time passed and the little ones were big enough to stand up in the nest and look about them. The father stork flew backwards and forwards every day, with nice frogs and little snakes, and every kind of delicacy he could find. It was so funny to see the tricks he did to amuse them; he would turn his head right round on to his tail, and he would clatter with his beak, as if it was a rattle. And then he told them all the stories he heard in the swamps.

"Well, now you must learn to fly," said the mother stork one day; and all the young ones had to stand on the ridge of the roof. Oh, how they wobbled about trying to keep their balance with their wings, and how nearly they fell down.

"Now look at me," said the mother; "this is how you must hold your heads! And move your legs so! one, two, one, two, this will all help you to get on in the world."

Then she flew a little way, and the young ones made a clumsy little hop, and down they came with a bump, for their bodies were too heavy.

"I don't want to fly," said one of the young ones, creeping down into the nest again. "I don't care about going to the warm countries."

"Do you want to freeze to death here when the winter comes? Shall the boys come and hang or burn or stake you? I will soon call them!"

"No, no," said the young one, hopping up on to the roof again, just like the others.

By the third day they could all fly fairly well; then they thought they could hover in the air, too, and they tried it, but flop!—they soon found they had to move their wings again.

Then the boys began their song again:

"Oh! father stork, father stork, fly to your nest."

"Shall we fly down and pick their eyes out?" asked the young ones.

"No, leave them alone," said their mother; "only pay attention to me, that is much more important. One, two, three, now we fly to the right; one, two, three, now to the left, and round the chimney! that was good. That last stroke of the wings was so pretty and the flap so well done that I will allow you to go to the swamp with me to-morrow! Several nice storks go there with their children; now just let me see that mine are the nicest. Don't forget to carry your heads high; it looks well, and gives you an air of importance."

"But are we not to have our revenge on the naughty boys?" asked the young storks.

"Let them scream as much as they like; you will fly away with the clouds to the land of the pyramids, while they will perhaps be freezing. There won't be a green leaf or a sweet apple here then!"

"But we *will* have our revenge!" they whispered to each other, and then they began their drilling again.

Of all the boys in the street, not one was worse at making fun of the storks than he who first began the derisive song. He was a tiny little fellow, not more than six years old. It is true, the young storks thought he was at least a hundred, for he was so much bigger than their father and mother, and they had no idea how old children and grown-up people could be. They reserved all their vengeance for the boy who first began to teaze them, and who never would leave off. The young storks were frightfully irritated by the teazing, and the older they grew the less they would stand it. At last their mother was obliged to promise that they should have their revenge, but not till the last day before they left.

"We shall first have to see how you behave at the manœuvres! If you come to grief and the general has to run you through the breast with his beak, the boys will after all be right, at least in one way! Now let us see!"

"That you shall!" said the young ones; and didn't they take pains. They practised every day, till they could fly as lightly as any feather; it was quite a pleasure to watch them.

Then came the autumn; all the storks began to assemble, before they started on their flight to the warm countries, where they spend their winters.

Those were indeed manœuvres! They had to fly over woods and towns, to try their wings, because they had such a long journey before them. The young storks did everything so well, that they got no end of frogs and snakes as prizes. They had the best characters, and then they could eat the frogs and snakes afterwards, which you may be sure they did.

"Now we shall have our revenge!" they said.

"Yes, certainly," said the mother stork. "My plan is this, and I think it is the right one! I know the pond where all the little human babies lie, till the storks fetch them, and give them to their parents. The pretty little creatures lie there asleep, dreaming sweet dreams, sweeter than any they ever dream afterwards. Every parent wishes for such a little baby, and every child wants a baby brother or sister. Now we fly to the pond and fetch a little brother or sister for each of those children who did not join in singing that horrid song, or in making fun of the storks. But those who sang it shall not have one."

"But what about that bad wicked boy who first began the song!" shrieked the young storks; "what is to be done to him?"

"In the pond there is a little dead baby, it has dreamed itself to death, we will take it to him, and then he will cry, because we have brought him a little dead brother. But you have surely not forgotten the good boy, who said 'It is a shame to make fun of the creatures!' We will take both a brother and a sister to him, and because his name is Peter, you shall all be called Peter too."

It happened just as she said, and all the storks are called Peter to this day.

LITTLE TUK

NOW there was little Tuk; as a matter of fact his name was not Tuk at all, but before he could speak properly he called himself Tuk. He meant it for Carl, so it is just as well we should know that. He had to look after his sister Gustave, who was much smaller than he was, and then he had his lessons to do, but these two things were rather difficult to manage at the same time. The poor boy sat with his little sister on his lap and sang all the songs he knew, at the same time glancing at his geography book which was open in front of him. Before the next morning he had to know all the towns in the island of Zealand by heart, and everything there was to know about them.

At last his mother came home, for she had been out, and then she took little Gustave. Tuk ran to the window and read as hard as ever he could, for it was getting dark, and mother could not afford to buy candles.

" There's the old washerwoman from the lane," said his mother, as she looked out of the window. " She can hardly carry herself, and yet she has to carry the pail from the pump; run down little Tuk and be a dear boy. Help the old woman! "

Tuk jumped up at once and ran to help her, but when he got home again it was quite dark, and it was useless to talk about candles, he had to go to bed. He had an old turn-up bed, and he lay in it thinking about his geography lesson, the island of Zealand, and all that the teacher had told him. He ought to have been learning the lesson, but of course he could not do that now. He put the geography book under his pillow, because he had heard that this would help him considerably to remember his lesson, but that can't be depended upon.

He lay there thinking and thinking, and then all at once it seemed just as if some one kissed him on his eyes and his mouth, and he fell asleep, yet he was not quite asleep either. It seemed to him as if the old washer-woman was looking at him with her kind eyes and saying: "It would be a great shame if you were not to know your lesson. You helped me, and now I will help you, and our Lord will always help you." And all at once the book under his head went "cribble crabble."

"Cluck, cluck, cluck!" and there stood a hen from the town of Kiöge. "I am a Kiöge hen," and then it told him how many inhabitants there were, and about the battle which had taken place there, which after all was not a very important one.

"Cribble, crabble, bang!" something plumped down; it was a wooden bird which now made its appearance—the popinjay from the Shooting Association in Præstö. It told him that there were just as many inhabitants as it had nails in its body, and it was very proud of this. "Thorvaldsen used to live close by my corner; the situation is beautiful."

Now little Tuk no longer lay in bed, he was on horse-back. Gallop a gallop he went. He was sitting in front of a splendidly dressed knight with a shining helmet and a waving plume. They rode through the woods to the old town of Vordingborg,[1] and this was a big and populous town. The castle towered over the royal city, and the lights shone through the windows; there was dancing and singing within, and King Waldemar led out the stately young court ladies to the dance. Morning came, and as the sun rose the town sank away and the king's palace, one tower after the other; at last only one tower remained on the hill where the castle had stood, and the town had become tiny and very poor. The schoolboys came along with their books under their arms, and they said "two thousand inhabitants," but that was not true, there were not so many.

Little Tuk was still lying in his bed; first he thought he was dreaming, and then he thought he was not dreaming, but there was somebody close to him.

[1] Under King Waldemar a place of great importance, now insignificant, only one of the towers of its castle remaining.

A sailor, a tiny little fellow, who might have been a cadet, but he was not a cadet, was saying to him, " Little Tuk! Little Tuk! I am to greet you warmly from Korsöer," which is a rising town. It is a flourishing town, which has steamers and coaches. At one time it used to be called a tiresome town,[1] but that was an old-fashioned opinion. " I lie close to the sea," says Korsöer. " I have good high roads and pleasure gardens, I have given birth to a poet who was amusing, and that is more than they all are. I wanted to send a ship round the world, I did not do it, but I might have done it; then there is the most delicious scent about me, because there are beautiful rose gardens close by the gates! "

Little Tuk saw them, the green and red flowering branches passed before his eyes; and then they vanished and changed into wooded heights, sloping to the clear waters of the fiord. A stately old church towered over the fiord, with its twin spires. Springs of water flowed from the cliff and rushed down in rapid bubbling streams. Close by them sat an old king with a golden crown round his flowing locks; this was King Hroar of the Springs and Roeskilde,[2] (Hroars-springs) is now the name of the town. Down over the slopes and past the springs, walked hand in hand all Denmark's kings and queens wearing their crowns. On and on they went into the old church to the pealing music of the organ, and the rippling of the springs. " Don't forget the Estates of the Realm," said King Hroar. All at once everything vanished—where were they? Now an old peasant woman stood before Tuk; she was a weeding woman, and came from Sorö, where the grass grows on the market-place. She had put her grey linen apron over her head and shoulders, it was soaking wet, there must have been rain. " Yes, indeed, it has been raining," she said. She knew some of the comic parts of Holberg's plays, and she knew all about Waldemar and Absolom; just as she was going to tell him these stories she shrank up and wagged her head, it looked just as if she was about to take a leap. " Koax," she

[1] It was a dull town on the Great Belt before the establishment of steamboats. Birthplace of the poet Baggesen.

[2] The former capital of Denmark, and the burial-place of all the Danish kings and queens.

said, "it is wet, it is wet, it is dull as ditch water—in good old Sorö!" She had become a frog, "koax," and then once more she was the old woman. "One must dress according to the weather!" said she. "It is wet, it is wet, my town is like a bottle, you get in by the neck, and you have to come out the same way again! I used to have beautiful fish [1] there once, now I have rosy-cheeked boys down at the bottom of the bottle; they get a great deal of wisdom there; Greek! Greek![2] Hebrew! koax!" It was just like the croaking of frogs or the creaking of fishing boots when you walk in a swamp. It was always the same sound, so tiresome, so tiresome that little Tuk fell into a deep sleep, which was the best thing for him.

But even in this sound sleep he had a dream or something of the sort. His little sister, Gustave, with the blue eyes and golden, curly hair, had all at once become a lovely grown up girl, and without having wings she could fly. They flew together right across Zealand, over the green woods and deep blue waters.

"Do you hear the cock crowing, little Tuk? Cock-a-doodle-doo. The hens come flying up from Kiöge town. You shall have such a big, big chicken yard. You will be a rich and happy man! Your house shall hold up its head like King Waldemar's towers, and it shall be richly built up with marble statues, like those in Præstö. You understand me, I suppose. Your name will spread round the world with praise, like the ship which was to have sailed from Korsöer; and it will be known in Roeskilde town."

"Remember the Estates of the Realm," said King Hroar.

"You shall speak well and wisely in Parliament, little Tuk; and when you are in your grave you shall sleep as quietly as——"

"As if I were in Sorö!" said little Tuk, and then he woke up. It was bright daylight, and he remembered nothing about his dream; but that was as it should be, one must not look into the future.

[1] Maller, Siluris glanis, only found in Sorö Lake, and now extinct.

[2] Sorö is an old public school, founded by Holberg, the Danish Molière.

He sprang out of bed and read his book till he knew his lesson, which he did almost at once. The old washer-woman put her head in at the door, nodded to him, and said—

" Many thanks for your help yesterday, you dear child! May the Lord fulfil the dream of your heart! "

Little Tuk did not know a bit what he had dreamt, but One above knew all about it!

THE EMPEROR'S NEW CLOTHES

MANY years ago there was an Emperor who was so excessively fond of new clothes that he spent all his money on them. He cared nothing about his soldiers nor for the theatre, nor for driving in the woods except for the sake of showing off his new clothes. He had a costume for every hour in the day, and instead of saying as one does about any other King or Emperor, "He is in his council chamber," here one always said, "The Emperor is in his dressing-room."

Life was very gay in the great town where he lived; hosts of strangers came to visit it every day, and among them one day two swindlers. They gave themselves out as weavers, and said that they knew how to weave the most beautiful stuffs imaginable. Not only were the colours and patterns unusually fine, but the clothes that were made of the stuffs had the peculiar quality of becoming invisible to every person who was not fit for the office he held, or if he was impossibly dull.

"Those must be splendid clothes," thought the Emperor. "By wearing them I should be able to discover which men in my kingdom are unfitted for their posts. I shall distinguish the wise men from the fools. Yes, I certainly must order some of that stuff to be woven for me."

He paid the two swindlers a lot of money in advance so that they might begin their work at once.

They did put up two looms and pretended to weave, but they had nothing whatever upon their shuttles. At the outset they asked for a quantity of the finest silk and the purest gold thread, all of which they put into their own bags while they worked away at the empty looms far into the night.

"THOSE MUST BE SPLENDID CLOTHES," THOUGHT THE EMPEROR.

" I should like to know how those weavers are getting on with the stuff," thought the Emperor; but he felt a little queer when he reflected that anyone who was stupid or unfit for his post would not be able to see it. He certainly thought that he need have no fears for himself, but still he thought he would send somebody else first to see how it was getting on. Everybody in the town knew what wonderful power the stuff possessed, and everyone was anxious to see how stupid his neighbour was.

" I will send my faithful old minister to the weavers," thought the Emperor. " He will be best able to see how the stuff looks, for he is a clever man and no one fulfils his duties better than he does! "

So the good old minister went into the room where the two swindlers sat working at the empty loom.

" Heaven preserve us! " thought the old minister, opening his eyes very wide. " Why I can't see a thing! " But he took care not to say so.

Both the swindlers begged him to be good enough to step a little nearer, and asked if he did not think it a good pattern and beautiful colouring. They pointed to the empty loom, and the poor old minister stared as hard as he could but he could not see anything, for of course there was nothing to see.

" Good heavens! " thought he, " is it possible that I am a fool? I have never thought so and nobody must know it. Am I not fit for my post? It will never do to say that I cannot see the stuffs."

" Well, sir, you don't say anything about the stuff," said the one who was pretending to weave.

" Oh, it is beautiful! quite charming! " said the old minister looking through his spectacles; " this pattern and these colours! I will certainly tell the Emperor that the stuff pleases me very much."

" We are delighted to hear you say so," said the swindlers, and then they named all the colours and described the peculiar pattern. The old minister paid great attention to what they said, so as to be able to repeat it when he got home to the Emperor.

Then the swindlers went on to demand more money, more silk, and more gold, to be able to proceed with the weaving; but they put it all into their own pockets—not a single strand was ever put into the loom, but they went on as before weaving at the empty loom.

The Emperor soon sent another faithful official to see how the stuff was getting on, and if it would soon be ready. The same thing happened to him as to the minister; he looked and looked, but as there was only the empty loom, he could see nothing at all.

"Is not this a beautiful piece of stuff?" said both the swindlers, showing and explaining the beautiful pattern and colours which were not there to be seen.

"I know I am not a fool!" thought the man, "so it must be that I am unfit for my good post! It is very strange though! however one must not let it appear!" So he praised the stuff he did not see, and assured them of his delight in the beautiful colours and the originality of the design. "It is absolutely charming!" he said to the Emperor. Everybody in the town was talking about this splendid stuff.

Now the Emperor thought he would like to see it while it was still on the loom. So, accompanied by a number of selected courtiers, among whom were the two faithful officials who had already seen the imaginary stuff, he went to visit the crafty impostors, who were working away as hard as ever they could at the empty loom.

"It is magnificent!" said both the honest officials. "Only see, your Majesty, what a design! What colours!" And they pointed to the empty loom, for they thought no doubt the others could see the stuff.

"What!" thought the Emperor; "I see nothing at all! This is terrible! Am I a fool? Am I not fit to be Emperor? Why, nothing worse could happen to me!"

"Oh, it is beautiful!" said the Emperor. "It has my highest approval!" and he nodded his satisfaction as he gazed at the empty loom. Nothing would induce him to say that he could not see anything.

The whole suite gazed and gazed, but saw nothing more than all the others. However, they all exclaimed with his Majesty, "It is very beautiful!" and they advised him to wear a suit made of this wonderful cloth on the occasion of a great procession which was just about to take place. "It is magnificent! gorgeous! excellent! went from mouth to mouth; they were all equally delighted with it. The

Emperor gave each of the rogues an order of knighthood to be worn in their buttonholes and the title of "Gentlemen weavers."

The swindlers sat up the whole night, before the day on which the procession was to take place, burning sixteen candles; so that people might see how anxious they were to get the Emperor's new clothes ready. They pretended to take the stuff off the loom. They cut it out in the air with a huge pair of scissors, and they stitched away with needles without any thread in them. At last they said: "Now the Emperor's new clothes are ready!"

The Emperor, with his grandest courtiers, went to them himself, and both the swindlers raised one arm in the air, as if they were holding something, and said: "See, these are the trousers, this is the coat, here is the mantle!" and so on. "It is as light as a spider's web. One might think one had nothing on, but that is the very beauty of it!"

"Yes!" said all the courtiers, but they could not see anything, for there was nothing to see.

"Will your imperial majesty be graciously pleased to take off your clothes," said the impostors, "so that we may put on the new ones, along here before the great mirror."

The Emperor took off all his clothes, and the impostors pretended to give him one article of dress after the other, of the new ones which they had pretended to make. They pretended to fasten something round his waist and to tie on something; this was the train, and the Emperor turned round and round in front of the mirror.

"How well his majesty looks in the new clothes! How becoming they are!" cried all the people round. "What a design, and what colours! They are most gorgeous robes!"

"The canopy is waiting outside which is to be carried over your majesty in the procession," said the master of the ceremonies.

"Well, I am quite ready," said the Emperor. "Don't the clothes fit well?" and then he turned round again in front of the mirror, so that he should seem to be looking at his grand things.

The chamberlains who were to carry the train stooped and pretended to lift it from the ground with both hands, and they walked along with their hands in the air. They dared not let it appear that they could not see anything.

Then the Emperor walked along in the procession under the gorgeous canopy, and everybody in the streets and at the windows exclaimed, " How beautiful the Emperor's new clothes are! What a splendid train! And they fit to perfection! " Nobody would let it appear that he could see nothing, for then he would not be fit for his post, or else he was a fool.

None of the Emperor's clothes had been so successful before.

" But he has got nothing on," said a little child.

" Oh, listen to the innocent," said its father; and one person whispered to the other what the child had said. " He has nothing on; a child says he has nothing on! "

" But he has nothing on! " at last cried all the people.

The Emperor writhed, for he knew it was true, but he thought " the procession must go on now," so held himself stiffer than ever, and the chamberlains held up the invisible train.

THE TINDER BOX

A SOLDIER came marching along the high road. One, two! One, two! He had his knapsack on his back and his sword at his side, for he had been to the wars and he was on his way home now. He met an old witch on the road, she was so ugly, her lower lip hung right down on to her chin.

She said "Good evening, soldier! What a nice sword you've got, and such a big knapsack; you are a real soldier! You shall have as much money as ever you like!"

"Thank you kindly, you old witch!" said the soldier.

"Do you see that big tree!" said the witch, pointing to a tree close by. "It is hollow inside! Climb up to the top and you will see a hole into which you can let yourself down, right down under the tree! I will tie a rope round your waist so that I can haul you up again when you call!"

"What am I to do down under the tree?" asked the soldier.

"Fetch money!" said the witch. "You must know that when you get down to the bottom of the tree you will find yourself in a wide passage; it's quite light there, for there are over a hundred blazing lamps. You will see three doors which you can open, for the keys are there. If you go into the first room you will see a big box in the middle of the floor. A dog is sitting on the top of it, and he has eyes as big as saucers, but you needn't mind that. I will give you my blue checked apron, which you can spread out on the floor; then go quickly forward, take up the dog and put him on my apron, open the box and take out as much money as ever you like. It is all copper, but if you like silver better, go into the next room. There you will find a dog with eyes as big as millstones; but never mind that, put him on my apron and take the money. If you prefer gold you can have it too, and as much as you can carry, if you go into the third room. But the dog sitting on that box has eyes as big as the Round Tower. He *is* a dog, indeed, as you may imagine! But don't let it trouble you; you only have to put him on to my apron and then he won't hurt you, and you can take as much gold out of the box as you like!"

"That's not so bad!" said the soldier. "But what am I to give you, old witch? For you'll want something, I'll be bound."

"No," said the witch, "not a single penny do I want; I only want you to bring me an old tinder box that my grandmother forgot the last time she was down there!"

"Well! tie the rope round my waist!" said the soldier.

"Here it is," said the witch, "and here is my blue-checked apron."

Then the soldier climbed up the tree, let himself slide down the hollow trunk, and found himself, as the witch had said, in the wide passage where the many hundred lamps were burning.

Now he opened the first door. Ugh! There sat the dog with eyes as big as saucers staring at him.

"You are a nice fellow!" said the soldier, as he put him on to the witch's apron, and took out as many pennies as he could cram into his pockets. Then he shut the box, and put the dog on the top of it again, and went into the next room. Hallo! there sat the dog with eyes as big as millstones.

"You shouldn't stare at me so hard; you might get a pain in your eyes!" Then he put the dog on the apron, but when he saw all the silver in the box he threw away all the coppers and stuffed his pockets and his knapsack with silver. Then he went into the third room. Oh! how horrible! that dog really had two eyes as big as the Round Tower, and they rolled round and round like wheels.

"Good evening!" said the soldier, saluting, for he had never seen such a dog in his life; but after looking at him for a bit he thought "that will do," and then he lifted him down on to the apron and opened the chest. Preserve us! What a lot of gold! He could buy the whole of Copenhagen with it, and all the sugar pigs from the cake-women, all the tin soldiers, whips and rocking-horses in the world! That was money indeed! Now the soldier threw away all the silver he had filled his pockets and his knapsack with, and put gold in its place. Yes, he crammed all his pockets, his knapsack, his cap and his boots so full that he could hardly walk! Now, he really had got a lot of money. He put the dog back on to the box, shut the door, and shouted up through the tree, " Haul me up, you old witch! "

" Have you got the tinder box? "

" Oh! to be sure! " said the soldier. " I had quite forgotten it." And he went back to fetch it. The witch hauled him up, and there he was standing on the high road again with his pockets, boots, knapsack and cap full of gold.

" What do you want the tinder box for? " asked the soldier.

" That's no business of yours," said the witch. " You've got the money; give me the tinder box! "

" Rubbish! " said the soldier. " Tell me directly what you want with it, or I will draw my sword and cut off your head."

" I won't! " said the witch.

Then the soldier cut off her head; there she lay! But he tied all the money up in her apron, slung it on his back like a pack, put the tinder box in his pocket, and marched off to the town.

It was a beautiful town, and he went straight to the finest hotel, ordered the grandest rooms and all the food he liked best, because he was a rich man now that he had so much money.

Certainly the servant who had to clean his boots thought they were very funny old things for such a rich gentleman, but he had not had time yet to buy any new ones; the next day he bought new boots and fine clothes. The soldier now became a fine gentleman, and the people told him all about the grand things in the town, and about their king, and what a lovely princess his daughter was.

" Where is she to be seen? " asked the soldier.

" You can't see her at all! " they all said; " she lives in a great copper castle surrounded with walls and towers. Nobody but the king dare go in and out, for it has been prophesied that she will marry a common soldier, and the king doesn't like that! "

" I should like to see her well enough! " thought the soldier. But there was no way of getting leave for that.

He now led a very merry life; went to theatres, drove about in the King's Park, and gave away a lot of money to poor people, which was very nice of him; for he remembered how disagreeable it used to be not to have a penny in his pocket. Now he was rich, wore fine clothes, and had a great many friends, who all said what a nice fellow he was—a thorough gentleman—and he liked to be told that.

But as he went on spending money every day and his store was never renewed, he at last found himself with only two pence left. Then he was obliged to move out of his fine rooms. He had to take a tiny little attic up under the roof, clean his own boots, and mend them himself with a darning needle. None of his friends went to see him, because there were far too many stairs.

One dark evening when he had not even enough money to buy a candle with, he suddenly remembered that there was a little bit in the old tinder box he had brought out of the hollow tree, when the witch helped him down. He got out the tinder box with the candle end in it and struck fire, but as the sparks flew out from the flint the door burst open and the dog with eyes as big as saucers, which he had seen down under the tree, stood before him and said, " What does my lord command? "

" By heaven! " said the soldier, " this is a nice kind of tinder box, if I can get whatever I want like this! Get me some money," he said to the dog, and away it went.

It was back in a twinkling with a big bag full of pennies in its mouth.

Now the soldier saw what a treasure he had in the tinder box. If he struck once, the dog which sat on the box of copper came; if he struck twice, the dog on the silver box came, and if he struck three times, the one from the box of gold.

He now moved down to the grand rooms and got his

fine clothes again, and then all his friends knew him once more and liked him as much as ever.

Then he suddenly began to think: After all it's a curious thing that no man can get a sight of the princess! Everyone says she is so beautiful! But what is the good of that, when she always has to be shut up in that big copper palace with all the towers. Can I not somehow manage tc see her? Where is my tinder box? Then he struck the flint, and, whisk, came the dog with eyes as big as saucers.

"It certainly is the middle of the night," said the soldier, "but I am very anxious to see the princess, if only for a single moment."

The dog was out of the door in an instant, and before the soldier had time to think about it, he was back again with the princess. There she was fast asleep on the dog's back, and she was so lovely that anybody could see that she must be a real princess! The soldier could not help it, but he was obliged to kiss her, for he was a true soldier.

Then the dog ran back again with the princess, but in the morning when the king and queen were having breakfast, the princess said that she had had such a wonderful dream about a dog and a soldier. She had ridden on the dog's back, and the soldier had kissed her.

"That's a pretty tale," said the queen.

After this an old lady-in-waiting had to sit by her bed at night to see if this was really a dream, or what it could be.

The soldier longed so intensely to see the princess again that at night the dog came to fetch her. He took her up and ran off with her as fast as he could, but the old lady-in-waiting put on her galoshes and ran just as fast behind them; when she saw that they disappeared into a large house, she thought now I know where it is, and made a big cross with chalk on the gate. Then she went home and lay down, and presently the dog came back, too, with the princess. When he saw that there was a cross on the gate, he took a bit of chalk, too, and made crosses on all the gates in the town; now this was very clever of him, for the lady-in-waiting could not possibly find the gate when there were crosses on all the gates.

Early next morning the king, the queen, the lady-in-waiting, and all the court officials went to see where the princess had been.

"There it is," said the king, when he saw the first door with the cross on it.

"No, my dear husband, it is there," said the queen, who saw another door with a cross on it.

"But there is one, and there is another!" they all cried out.

They soon saw that it was hopeless to try and find it.

Now the queen was a very clever woman; she knew more than how to drive in a chariot. She took her big gold scissors and cut up a large piece of silk into small pieces, and made a pretty little bag, which she filled with fine grains of buckwheat. She then tied it on to the back of the princess, and when that was done she cut a little hole in the bag, so that the grains could drop out all the way wherever the princess went.

At night the dog came again, took the princess on his back, and ran off with her to the soldier, who was so fond of her that he longed to be a prince, so that he might have her for his wife.

The dog never noticed how the grain dropped out all along the road from the palace to the soldier's window, where he ran up the wall with the princess.

In the morning the king and the queen easily saw where their daughter had been, and they seized the soldier and threw him into the dungeons.

There he lay! Oh, how dark and tiresome it was, and then one day they said to him, "To-morrow you are to be hanged." It was not amusing to be told that, especially as he had left his tinder box behind him at the hotel.

In the morning he could see through the bars in the little window that the people were hurrying out of town to see him hanged. He heard the drums and saw the soldiers marching along. All the world was going; among them was a shoemaker's boy in his leather apron and slippers. He was in such a hurry that he lost one of his slippers, and it fell close under the soldier's window where he was peeping out through the bars.

"I say, you boy! Don't be in such a hurry," said the soldier to him. "Nothing will happen till I get there! But if you will run to the house where I used to live, and fetch me my tinder box, you shall have a penny! You must put your best foot foremost! "

The boy was only too glad to have the penny, and tore off to get the tinder box, gave it to the soldier, and—yes, now we shall hear.

Outside the town a high scaffold had been raised, and the soldiers were drawn up round about it, as well as crowds of townspeople. The king and the queen sat upon a beautiful throne exactly opposite the judge and all the councillors.

The soldier mounted the ladder, but when they were about to put the rope round his neck, he said that before undergoing his punishment a criminal was always allowed the gratification of a harmless wish, and he wanted very much to smoke a pipe, as it would be his last pipe in this world.

The king would not deny him this, so the soldier took out his tinder box and struck fire, once, twice, three times, and there were all the dogs. The one with eyes like saucers, the one with eyes like millstones, and the one whose eyes were as big as the Round Tower.

" Help me! Save me from being hanged! " cried the soldier.

And then the dogs rushed at the soldiers and the councillors; they took one by the legs, and another by the nose, and threw them up many fathoms into the air; and when they fell down, they were broken all to pieces.

" I won't! " cried the king, but the biggest dog took both him and the queen and threw them after all the others. Then the soldiers became alarmed, and the people shouted, " Oh! good soldier, you shall be our king and marry the beautiful princess! "

Then they conducted the soldier to the king's chariot, and all three dogs danced along in front of him and shouted " Hurrah! " The boys all put their fingers in their mouths and whistled, and the soldiers presented arms. The princess came out of the copper palace and became queen, which pleased her very much. The wedding took place in a week, and the dogs all had seats at the table, where they sat staring with all their eyes.

THE SWINEHERD

THERE was once a poor Prince; he had only quite a tiny kingdom, but it was big enough to allow him to marry, and he was bent upon marrying.

Now, it certainly was rather bold of him to say to the Emperor's daughter, " Will you have me? " He did, however, venture to say so, for his name was known far and wide; and there were hundreds of Princesses who would have said " Yes," and " Thank you, kindly," but see if *she* would!

Just let us hear about it.

A rose tree grew on the grave of the Prince's father, it was such a beautiful rose tree; it only bloomed every fifth year, and then only bore one blossom; but what a rose that was! By merely smelling it one forgot all one's cares and sorrows.

Then he had a nightingale which sang as if every lovely melody in the world dwelt in her little throat. This rose and this nightingale were to be given to the Princess, so they were put into great silver caskets and sent to her.

The Emperor had them carried before him into the great Hall where the Princess was playing at " visiting " with her ladies-in-waiting; they had nothing else to do. When she saw the caskets with the gifts she clapped her hands with delight!

" If only it were a little pussy cat! " said she,—but there was the lovely rose.

" Oh, how exquisitely it is made! " said all the ladies-in-waiting.

" It is more than beautiful," said the Emperor; " it is neat."

But the Princess touched it, and then she was ready to cry.

"Fie, papa!" she said; "it is not made, it is a real one!"

"Fie," said all the ladies-in-waiting; "it is a real one!"

"Well, let us see what there is in the other casket, before we get angry," said the Emperor, and out came the nightingale. It sang so beautifully that at first no one could find anything to say against it.

"*Superbe! charmant!*" said the ladies-in-waiting, for they all had a smattering of French, one spoke it worse than the other.

"How that bird reminds me of our lamented Empress's musical box," said an old courtier. "Ah, yes, they are the same tunes, and the same beautiful execution."

"So they are," said the Emperor, and he cried like a little child.

"I should hardly think it could be a real one," said the Princess.

"Yes, it is a real one," said those who had brought it.

"Oh, let that bird fly away then," said the Princess, and she would not hear of allowing the Prince to come. But he was not to be crushed; he stained his face brown and black, and, pressing his cap over his eyes, he knocked at the door.

"Good morning, Emperor," said he; "can I be taken into service in the palace?"

"Well, there are so many wishing to do that," said the Emperor; "but let me see!—yes, I need somebody to look after the pigs, for we have so many of them."

So the prince was made imperial swineherd. A horrid little room was given him near the pig-sties, and here he had to live. He sat busily at work all day, and by the evening he had made a beautiful little cooking pot; it had bells all round it and when the pot boiled they tinkled delightfully and played the old tune:

"Ach du lieber Augustin,
Alles ist weg, weg, weg!" [1]

But the greatest charm of all about it was, that by holding one's finger in the steam one could immediately smell

[1] Alas! dear Augustin,
All is lost, lost, lost!

all the dinners that were being cooked at every stove in the town. Now this was a very different matter from a rose.

The Princess came walking along with all her ladies-in-waiting, and when she heard the tune she stopped and looked pleased for she could play " Ach du lieber Augustin " herself; it was her only tune, and she could only play it with one finger.

" Why, that is my tune," she said; " this must be a cultivated swineherd. Go and ask him what the instrument costs."

So one of the ladies-in-waiting had to go into his room, but she put pattens on first.

" How much do you want for the pot," she asked.

" I must have ten kisses from the Princess," said the swineherd.

" Heaven preserve us! " said the lady.

" I won't take less," said the swineherd.

" Well, what does he say? " asked the Princess.

" I really cannot tell you," said the lady-in-waiting, " it is so shocking."

" Then you must whisper it." And she whispered it.

" He is a wretch! " said the Princess, and went away at once. But she had only gone a little way when she heard the bells tinkling beautifully:

" Ach du lieber Augustin."

" Go and ask him if he will take ten kisses from the ladies-in-waiting."

" No, thank you," said the swineherd; " ten kisses from the Princess, or I keep my pot."

" How tiresome it is," said the Princess. " Then you will have to stand round me, so that no one may see."

So the ladies-in-waiting stood round her and spread out their skirts while the swineherd took his ten kisses, and then the pot was hers.

What a delight it was to them. The pot was kept on the boil day and night. They knew what was cooking on every stove in the town, from the chamberlain's to the shoemaker's. The ladies-in-waiting danced about and clapped their hands.

" We know who has sweet soup and pancakes for dinner, and who has cutlets; how amusing it is."

One of the Ladies-in-waiting had to go into his Room.

" Highly interesting," said the mistress of the robes.

" Yes, but hold your tongues, for I am the Emperor's daughter."

" Heaven preserve us! " they all said.

The swineherd—that is to say, the Prince, only nobody knew that he was not a real swineherd—did not let the day pass in idleness, and he now constructed a rattle. When it was swung round it played all the waltzes, galops and jig tunes which have ever been heard since the creation of the world.

" But this is *superbe*! " said the Princess, as she walked by. " I have never heard finer compositions. Go and ask him what the instrument costs, but let us have no more kissing."

" He wants a hundred kisses from the Princess! " said the lady-in-waiting.

" I think he is mad! " said the Princess, and she went away, but she had not gone far when she stopped.

" One must encourage art," she said; " I am the Emperor's daughter. Tell him he can have ten kisses, the same as yesterday, and he can take the others from the ladies-in-waiting."

" But we don't like that at all," said the ladies.

" Oh, nonsense! If I can kiss him you can do the same. Remember that I pay your wages as well as give you board and lodging." So the lady-in-waiting had to go again.

" A hundred kisses from the Princess, or let each keep his own."

" Stand in front of me," said she, and all the ladies stood round, while he kissed her.

" Whatever is the meaning of that crowd round the pigsties? " said the Emperor as he stepped out on to the verandah; he rubbed his eyes and put on his spectacles. " Why it is the ladies-in-waiting, what games are they up to? I must go and see! " so he pulled up the heels of his slippers for they were shoes which he had trodden down.

Bless us, what a hurry he was in! When he got into the yard, he walked very softly and the ladies were so busy counting the kisses, so that there should be fair play, and neither too few nor too many kisses, that they never heard the Emperor. He stood on tiptoe.

" What is all this? " he said when he saw what was

going on, and he hit them on the head with his slipper just as the swineherd was taking the eighty-sixth kiss.

"Out you go!" said the Emperor, for he was furious, and both the Princess and the Prince were put out of his realm.

There she stood crying, and the swineherd scolded, and the rain poured down in torrents.

"Oh, miserable creature that I am! if only I had accepted the handsome Prince. Oh, how unhappy I am!"

The swineherd went behind a tree, wiped the black and brown stain from his face, and threw away his ugly clothes. Then he stepped out dressed as a Prince, he was so handsome that the Princess could not help curtseying to him.

"I am come to despise thee," he said. "Thou wouldst not have an honourable prince, thou couldst not prize the rose or the nightingale, but thou wouldst kiss the swineherd for a trumpery musical box! As thou hast made thy bed, so must thou lie upon it!"

Then he went back into his own little kingdom and shut and locked the door. So she had to stand outside and sing in earnest—

"Ach du lieber Augustin,
Alles ist weg, weg, weg!"

THE UGLY DUCKLING

THE country was lovely just then; it was summer. The wheat was golden and the oats still green; the hay was stacked in the rich low-lying meadows, where the stork was marching about on his long red legs, chattering Egyptian, the language his mother had taught him.

Round about field and meadow lay great woods, in the midst of which were deep lakes. Yes, the country certainly was delicious. In the sunniest spot stood an old mansion surrounded by a deep moat, and great dock leaves grew from the walls of the house right down to the water's edge; some of them were so tall that a small child could stand upright under them. In amongst the leaves it was as secluded as in the depths of a forest; and there a duck was sitting on her nest. Her little ducklings were just about to be hatched, but she was nearly tired of sitting, for it had lasted such a long time. Moreover, she had very few visitors, as the other ducks liked swimming about in the moat better than waddling up to sit under the dock leaves and gossip with her.

At last one egg after another began to crack. "Cheep, cheep!" they said. All the chicks had come to life, and were poking their heads out.

"Quack! quack!" said the duck; and then they all quacked their hardest, and looked about them on all sides among the green leaves; their mother allowed them to look as much as they liked, for green is good for the eyes.

"How big the world is to be sure!" said all the young ones; for they certainly had ever so much more room to move about, than when they were inside in the eggshell.

"Do you imagine this is the whole world?" said the mother. "It stretches a long way on the other side of the garden, right into the parson's field; but I have never been as far as that! I suppose you are all here now? " and she got up. " No! I declare I have not got you all yet! The biggest egg is still there; how long is it going to last? " and then she settled herself on the nest again.

" Well, how are you getting on? " said an old duck who had come to pay her a visit.

" This one egg is taking such a long time," answered the sitting duck, " the shell will not crack; but now you must look at the others; they are the finest ducklings I have ever seen! they are all exactly like their father, the rascal! he never comes to see me."

" Let me look at the egg which won't crack," said the old duck. " You may be sure that it is a turkey's egg! I have been cheated like that once, and I had no end of trouble and worry with the creatures, for I may tell you that they are afraid of the water. I could not get them into it, I quacked and snapped at them, but it was no good. Let me see the egg! Yes, it is a turkey's egg! You just leave it alone and teach the other children to swim."

" I will sit on it a little longer, I have sat so long already, that I may as well go on till the Midsummer Fair comes round."

" Please yourself," said the old duck, and she went away.

At last the big egg cracked. " Cheep, cheep! " said the young one and tumbled out; how big and ugly he was! The duck looked at him.

" That is a monstrous big duckling," she said; " none of the others looked like that; can he be a turkey chick? well we shall soon find that out; into the water he shall go, if I have to kick him in myself."

Next day was gloriously fine, and the sun shone on all the green dock leaves. The mother duck with her whole family went down to the moat.

Splash, into the water she sprang. " Quack, quack! " she said, and one duckling plumped in after the other. The water dashed over their heads, but they came up again and floated beautifully; their legs went of themselves, and they were all there, even the big ugly grey one swam about with them.

"No, that is no turkey," she said; "see how beautifully he uses his legs and how erect he holds himself: he is my own chick! after all, he is not so bad when you come to look at him properly. Quack, quack! Now come with me and I will take you into the world, and introduce you to the duckyard; but keep close to me all the time, so that no one may tread upon you, and beware of the cat!"

Then they went into the duckyard. There was a fearful uproar going on, for two broods were fighting for the head of an eel, and in the end the cat captured it.

"That's how things go in this world," said the mother duck, and she licked her bill for she wanted the eel's head herself.

"Use your legs," said she; "mind you quack properly, and bend your necks to the old duck over there! She is the grandest of them all; she has Spanish blood in her veins and that accounts for her size, and, do you see? she has a red rag round her leg; that is a wonderfully fine thing, and the most extraordinary mark of distinction any duck can have. It shows clearly that she is not to be parted with, and that she is worthy of recognition both by beasts and men! Quack now! don't turn your toes in, a well brought up duckling keeps his legs wide apart just like father and mother; that's it, now bend your necks, and say quack!"

They did as they were bid, but the other ducks round about looked at them and said, quite loud; "Just look there! now we are to have that tribe! just as if there were not enough of us already, and, oh dear! how ugly that duckling is, we won't stand him!" and a duck flew at him at once and bit him in the neck.

"Let him be," said the mother; "he is doing no harm."

"Very likely not, but he is so ungainly and queer," said the biter; "he must be whacked."

"They are handsome children mother has," said the old duck with the rag round her leg; "all good looking except this one, and he is not a good specimen; it's a pity you can't make him over again."

"That can't be done, your grace," said the mother duck; "he is not handsome, but he is a thorough good creature, and he swims as beautifully as any of the others; nay, I think I might venture even to add that I think he will improve as he goes on, or perhaps in time he may grow smaller! he was too long in the egg, and so he has not come out with a very good figure." And then she patted his neck and stroked him down. "Besides he is a drake," said she; "so it does not matter so much. I believe he will be very strong, and I don't doubt but he will make his way in the world."

"The other ducklings are very pretty," said the old duck. "Now make yourselves quite at home, and if you find the head of an eel you may bring it to me!"

After that they felt quite at home. But the poor duckling which had been the last to come out of the shell, and who was so ugly, was bitten, pushed about, and made fun of both by the ducks and the hens. "He is too big," they all said; and the turkey-cock, who was born with his spurs on, and therefore thought himself quite an emperor, puffed himself up like a vessel in full sail, made for him, and gobbled and gobbled till he became quite red in the face. The poor duckling was at his wit's end, and did not know which way to turn; he was in despair because he was so ugly, and the butt of the whole duckyard.

So the first day passed, and afterwards matters grew worse and worse. The poor duckling was chased and hustled by all of them, even his brothers and sisters ill-used him; and they were always saying, "If only the cat would get hold of you, you hideous object!" Even his mother said, "I wish to goodness you were miles away." The ducks bit him, the hens pecked him, and the girl who fed them kicked him aside.

Then he ran off and flew right over the hedge, where the little birds flew up into the air in a fright.

"That is because I am so ugly," thought the poor duckling, shutting his eyes, but he ran on all the same. Then he came to a great marsh where the wild ducks lived; he was so tired and miserable that he stayed there the whole night.

In the morning the wild ducks flew up to inspect their new comrade.

"What sort of a creature are you?" they inquired, as the duckling turned from side to side and greeted them as well as he could. "You are frightfully ugly," said the wild ducks; "but that does not matter to us, so long as you do not marry into our family!" Poor fellow! he had no thought of marriage, all he wanted was permission to lie among the rushes, and to drink a little of the marsh water.

He stayed there two whole days, then two wild geese came, or rather two wild ganders, they were not long out of the shell, and therefore rather pert.

"I say, comrade," they said, "you are so ugly that we have taken quite a fancy to you; will you join us and be a bird of passage? There is another marsh close by, and there are some charming wild geese there; all sweet young ladies, who can say quack! You are ugly enough to make your fortune among them." Just at that moment, bang! bang! was heard up above, and both the wild geese fell dead among the reeds, and the water turned blood red. Bang! bang! went the guns, and whole flocks of wild geese flew up from the rushes and the shot peppered among them again.

There was a grand shooting party, and the sportsmen lay hidden round the marsh, some even sat on the branches of the trees which overhung the water; the blue smoke rose like clouds among the dark trees and swept over the pool.

The water-dogs wandered about in the swamp, splash! splash! The rushes and reeds bent beneath their tread on all sides. It was terribly alarming to the poor duckling. He twisted his head round to get it under his wing and just at that moment a frightful, big dog appeared close beside him; his tongue hung right out of his mouth and his eyes glared wickedly. He opened his great chasm of a mouth close to the duckling, showed his sharp teeth—and—splash—went on without touching him.

"Oh, thank Heaven!" sighed the duckling, "I am so ugly that even the dog won't bite me!"

Then he lay quite still while the shot whistled among the bushes, and bang after bang rent the air. It only became quiet late in the day, but even then the poor duckling did not dare to get up; he waited several hours more before he looked about and then he hurried away from the marsh as fast as he could. He ran across fields and meadows, and there was such a wind that he had hard work to make his way.

Towards night he reached a poor little cottage; it was

such a miserable hovel that it could not make up its mind which way to fall even, and so it remained standing. The wind whistled so fiercely round the duckling that he had to sit on his tail to resist it, and it blew harder and harder; then he saw that the door had fallen off one hinge and hung so crookedly that he could creep into the house through the crack and by this means he made his way into the room. An old woman lived there with her cat and her hen. The cat, which she called "Sonnie," could arch his back, purr, and give off electric sparks, that is to say if you stroked his fur the wrong way. The hen had quite tiny short legs and so she was called "Chuckie-low-legs." She laid good eggs, and the old woman was as fond of her as if she had been her own child.

In the morning the strange duckling was discovered immediately, and the cat began to purr and the hen to cluck.

"What on earth is that!" said the old woman looking round, but her sight was not good and she thought the duckling was a fat duck which had escaped. "This is a capital find," said she; "now I shall have duck's eggs if only it is not a drake! we must find out about that!"

So she took the duckling on trial for three weeks, but no eggs made their appearance. The cat was the master of the house and the hen the mistress, and they always spoke of "we and the world," for they thought that they represented the half of the world, and that quite the better half.

The duckling thought there might be two opinions on the subject, but the cat would not hear of it.

"Can you lay eggs?" she asked.

"No!"

"Will you have the goodness to hold your tongue then!"

And the cat said, "Can you arch your back, purr, or give off sparks?"

"No."

"Then you had better keep your opinions to yourself when people of sense are speaking!"

The duckling sat in the corner nursing his ill-humour; then he began to think of the fresh air and the sunshine, an uncontrollable longing seized him to float on the water, and at last he could not help telling the hen about it.

"What on earth possesses you?" she asked; "you have nothing to do, that is why you get these freaks into your head. Lay some eggs or take to purring, and you will get over it."

"But it is so delicious to float on the water," said the duckling; "so delicious to feel it rushing over your head when you dive to the bottom."

"That would be a fine amusement," said the hen. "I think you have gone mad. Ask the cat about it, he is the wisest creature I know; ask him if he is fond of floating on the water or diving under it. I say nothing about myself, Ask our mistress yourself, the old woman, there is no one in the world cleverer than she is. Do you suppose she has any desire to float on the water, or to duck underneath it?"

"You do not understand me," said the duckling.

"Well, if we don't understand you, who should? I suppose you don't consider yourself cleverer than the cat or the old woman, not to mention me. Don't make a fool of yourself, child, and thank your stars for all the good we have done you! Have you not lived in this warm room, and in such society that you might have learnt something? But you are an idiot, and there is no pleasure in associating with you. You may believe me I mean you well, I tell you home truths, and there is no surer way than that, of knowing who are one's friends. You just see about laying some eggs, or learn to purr, or to emit sparks."

"I think I will go out into the wide world," said the duckling.

"Oh, do so by all means," said the hen.

So away went the duckling, he floated on the water and ducked underneath it, but he was looked askance at by every living creature for his ugliness. Now the autumn came on, the leaves in the woods turned yellow and brown; the wind took hold of them, and they danced about. The sky looked very cold, and the clouds hung heavy with snow and hail. A raven stood on the fence and croaked Caw! Caw! from sheer cold; it made one shiver only to think of it, the poor duckling certainly was in a bad case.

One evening, the sun was just setting in wintry splendour, when a flock of beautiful large birds appeared out of the bushes; the duckling had never seen anything so beautiful. They were dazzling white with long waving necks; they were swans, and uttering a peculiar cry they spread out their magnificent broad wings and flew away from the cold regions to warmer lands and open seas. They mounted so high, so very high, and the ugly little duckling became strangely uneasy, he circled round and round in the water like a wheel, craning his neck up into the air after them. Then he uttered a shriek so piercing and so strange, that he was quite frightened by it himself. Oh, he could not forget those beautiful birds, those happy birds, and as soon as they were out of sight he ducked right down to the bottom, and when he came up again he was quite beside himself. He did not know what the birds were, or whither they flew, but all the same he was more drawn towards them than he had ever been by any creatures before. He did not envy them in the least, how could it occur to him even to wish to be such a marvel of beauty; he would have been thankful if only the ducks would have tolerated him among them—the poor ugly creature!

The winter was so bitterly cold that the duckling was obliged to swim about in the water to keep it from freezing, but every night the hole in which he swam got smaller and smaller. Then it froze so hard that the surface ice cracked, and the duckling had to use his legs all the time, so that the ice should not close in round him; at last he was so weary that he could move no more, and he was frozen fast into the ice.

Early in the morning a peasant came along and saw him; he went out on to the ice and hammered a hole in it with his heavy wooden shoe, and carried the duckling home to his wife. There it soon revived. The children wanted to play with it, but the duckling thought they were going to ill-use him, and rushed in his fright into the milk pan, and the milk spurted out all over the room. The woman shrieked and threw up her hands, then it flew into the butter cask, and down into the meal tub and out again. Just imagine what it looked like by this time! The woman screamed and tried to hit it with the tongs, and the children tumbled over one another in trying to catch it, and they screamed with laughter—by good luck the door stood open, and the duckling flew out among the bushes and the new fallen snow—and it lay there thoroughly exhausted.

But it would be too sad to mention all the privation and misery it had to go through during that hard winter. When the sun began to shine warmly again, the duckling was in the marsh, lying among the rushes; the larks were singing and the beautiful spring had come.

Then all at once it raised its wings and they flapped with much greater strength than before, and bore him off vigorously. Before he knew where he was, he found himself in a large garden where the apple trees were in full blossom, and the air was scented with lilacs, the long branches of which overhung the indented shores of the lake! Oh! the spring freshness was so delicious!

Just in front of him he saw three beautiful white swans advancing towards him from a thicket; with rustling feathers they swam lightly over the water. The duckling recognized the majestic birds, and he was overcome by a strange melancholy.

" I will fly to them, the royal birds, and they will hack me to pieces, because I, who am so ugly, venture to approach them! But it won't matter; better be killed by them than be snapped at by the ducks, pecked by the hens, or spurned by the henwife, or suffer so much misery in the winter."

So he flew into the water and swam towards the stately swans; they saw him and darted towards him with ruffled feathers.

" Kill me, oh, kill me! " said the poor creature, and bowing his head towards the water he awaited his death. But what did he see reflected in the transparent water?

He saw below him his own image, but he was no longer a clumsy dark grey bird, ugly and ungainly, he was himself a swan! It does not matter in the least having been born in a duckyard, if only you come out of a swan's egg!

He felt quite glad of all the misery and tribulation he had gone through; he was the better able to appreciate his good fortune now, and all the beauty which greeted him. The big swans swam round and round him, and stroked him with their bills.

Some little children came into the garden with corn and pieces of bread, which they threw into the water; and the smallest one cried out: " There is a new one! " The other children shouted with joy, " Yes, a new one has come! " And they clapped their hands and danced about, running after their father and mother. They threw the bread into the water, and one and all said that " the new one was the prettiest; he was so young and handsome." And the old swans bent their heads and did homage before him.

He felt quite shy, and hid his head under his wing; he did not know what to think; he was so very happy, but not at all proud; a good heart never becomes proud. He thought of how he had been pursued and scorned, and now he heard them all say that he was the most beautiful of all beautiful birds. The lilacs bent their boughs right down into the water before him, and the bright sun was warm and cheering, and he rustled his feathers and raised his slender neck aloft, saying with exultation in his heart: " I never dreamt of so much happiness when I was the Ugly Duckling! "

GREAT FAIRY STORIES FROM GRIMM

THE GOLDEN GOOSE

THERE was a man who had three sons. The youngest was called Dummling, which is much the same as Dunderhead, for all thought he was more than half a fool, and he was at all times mocked and ill-treated by the whole household.

It happened that the eldest son took it into his head one day to go into the wood to cut fuel; and his mother gave him a nice pasty and a bottle of wine to take with him, that he might refresh himself at his work. As he went into the wood, a little old man bid him good day, and said, "Give me a little piece of meat from your plate, and a little wine out of your bottle; for I am very hungry and thirsty." But this clever young man said, "Give you my meat and wine? No, thank you; I should not have enough left for myself:" and away he went. He soon began to cut down a tree; but he had not worked long before he missed his stroke, and cut himself, and was forced to go home to have the wound dressed. Now it was the little old man that sent him this mischief.

Next went out the second son to work; and his mother gave him too a pasty and a bottle of wine. And the same little old man met him also, and asked him for something to eat and drink. But he too thought himself very clever, and said, "The more you eat the less there would be for me; so go your way!" The little man took care that he too should have his reward, and the second stroke that he aimed against a tree hit him on the leg; so that he too was forced to go home.

Then Dummling said, "Father, I should like to go and cut wood too." But his father said, "Your brothers have both lamed themselves; you had better stay at home,

THE GOLDEN GOOSE

THERE was a man who had three sons. The youngest was called Dummling—which is much the same as Dunderhead, for all thought he was more than half a fool—and he was at all times mocked and ill-treated by the whole household.

It happened that the eldest son took it into his head one day to go into the wood to cut fuel; and his mother gave him a nice pasty and a bottle of wine to take with him, that he might refresh himself at his work. As he went into the wood, a little old man bid him good day, and said, "Give me a little piece of meat from your plate, and a little wine out of your bottle, for I am very hungry and thirsty." But this clever young man said, "Give you my meat and wine? No, thank you, I should not have enough left for myself:" and away he went. He soon began to cut down a tree; but he had not worked long before he missed his stroke, and cut himself, and was forced to go home to have the wound dressed. Now it was the little old man that sent him this mischief.

Next went out the second son to work: and his mother gave him too a pasty and a bottle of wine. And the same little old man met him also, and asked him for something to eat and drink. But he too thought himself very clever, and said, "The more you eat the less there would be for me: so go your way!" The little man took care that he too should have his reward, and the second stroke that he aimed against a tree hit him on the leg; so that he too was forced to go home.

Then Dummling said, "Father, I should like to go and cut wood too." But his father said, "Your brothers have both lamed themselves; you had better stay at home, for you know nothing about the business of wood-cutting." But Dummling was very pressing; and at last his father said, "Go your way! you will be wiser when you have smarted for your folly." And his mother gave him only some dry bread and a bottle of sour beer. But when he went into the wood, he met the little old man, who said, "Give me some meat and drink, for I am very hungry and thirsty." Dummling said, "I have only dry bread and sour beer; if that will suit you we will sit down and eat it, such as it is, together." So they sat down; and when the lad pulled out his bread, behold it was turned into a rich pasty: and his sour beer, when they tasted it, was delightful wine. They ate and drank heartily; and when they had done, the little man said, "As you have a kind heart, and have been willing to share everything with me, I will send a blessing upon you. There stands an old tree; cut it down, and you will find something at the root." Then he took his leave, and went his way.

Dummling set to work, and cut down the tree; and when it fell, he found, in a hollow under the roots, a goose with feathers of pure gold. He took it up, and went on to a little inn by the roadside, where he thought to sleep for the night on his way home. Now the landlord had three daughters; and when they saw the goose they were very eager to look what this wonderful bird could be, and wished very much to pluck one of the feathers out of its tail. At last the eldest said, "I must and will have a feather." So she waited till Dummling was gone to bed, and then seized the goose by the wing; but to her great wonder there she stuck, for neither hand nor finger could she get away again. Then in came the second sister, and thought to have a feather too; but the moment she touched her sister, there she too hung fast. At last came the third, and she also wanted a feather; but the other two cried out "Keep away! for Heaven's sake, keep away!" However, she did not understand what they meant. "If they are there," thought she, "I may as well be there too." So she went up to them; but the moment she touched her sisters she stuck fast, and hung to the goose, as they did. And so they kept company with the goose all night in the cold.

The next morning Dummling got up and carried off

the goose under his arm. He took no notice at all of the three girls, but went out with them sticking fast behind. So wherever he travelled, they too were forced to follow, whether they would or no, as fast as their legs could carry them.

In the middle of a field the parson met them; and when he saw the train, he said, " Are you not ashamed of yourselves, you bold girls, to run after a young man in that way over the fields? Is that good behaviour? " Then he took the youngest by the hand to lead her away; but as soon as he touched her he too hung fast, and followed in the train; though sorely against his will, for he was not only in rather too good plight for running fast, but just then he had a little touch of the gout in the great toe of his right foot. By and bye up came the clerk; and when he saw his master, the parson, running after the three girls, he wondered greatly and said, " Holla! holla! your reverence! whither so fast? there is a christening to-day." Then he ran up and took him by the gown; when, lo and behold, he stuck fast too. As the five were thus trudging along, one behind another, they met two labourers with their mattocks coming from work; and the parson cried out lustily to them to help him. But scarcely had they laid hands on him, when they too fell into the rank; and so they made seven, all running together after Dummling and his goose.

Now Dummling thought he would see a little of the world before he went home; so he and his train journeyed on, till at last they came to a city where there was a king who had an only daughter. The princess was of so thoughtful and moody a turn of mind that no one could make her laugh; and the king had made known to all the world, that whoever could make her laugh should have her for his wife. When the young man heard this, he went to her, with his goose and all its train; and as soon as she saw the seven all hanging together, and running along, treading on each other's heels, she could not help bursting into a long and loud laugh. Then Dummling claimed her for his wife, and married her; and he was heir to the kingdom, and lived long and happily with his wife.

But what became of the goose and the goose's tail, I never could hear.

THE WISHING TABLE, THE GOLD ASS AND THE CUDGEL

A LONG time ago there lived a tailor who had three sons but only one goat. As the goat supplied the whole family with milk, she had to be well fed and taken daily to pasture. This the sons did in turn. One day the eldest son led her into the churchyard, where he knew there was fine herbage to be found, and there let her browse and skip about till evening. It being then time to return home, he said to her, "Goat, have you had enough to eat?" and the goat answered,—

"I have eaten so much
Not a leaf can I touch, Nan, Nan."

"Come along home then," said the boy, and he led her by the cord round her neck back to the stable and tied her up.

"Well," said the old tailor, "has the goat had her proper amount of food?"

"Why, she has eaten so much, not a leaf can she touch," answered the son.

The father, however, thinking he should like to assure himself of this, went down to the stable, patted the animal and said caressingly, "Goat, have you really had enough to eat?" The goat answered,—

"How can my hunger be allayed?
About the little graves I played
And could not find a single blade, Nan, Nan."

"What is this I hear!" cried the tailor, and running upstairs to his son, "You young liar!" he exclaimed, "to tell me the goat had had enough to eat, and all the while she is starving." And overcome with anger, he took his yard-measure down from the wall, and beat his son out of doors.

The next day it was the second son's turn, and he found a place near a garden hedge, where there were the juiciest plants for the goat to feed upon, and she enjoyed them so much that she ate them all up. Before taking her home in the evening, he said to her, "Goat, have you had enough to eat?" and the goat answered,—

"I have eaten so much
Not a leaf can I touch, Nan, Nan."

"Come along home then," said the boy, and he led her away to the stable and tied her up.

"Well," said the old tailor, "has the goat had her proper amount of food?"

"Why, she has eaten so much, not a leaf can she touch," answered the boy.

But the tailor was not satisfied with this, and went down to the stable. "Goat, have you really had enough to eat?" he asked; and the goat answered,—

"How can my hunger be allayed?
About the little graves I played
And could not find a single blade, Nan, Nan."

"The shameless young rascal!" cried the tailor, "to let an innocent animal like this starve!" and he ran upstairs, and drove the boy from the house with the yard-measure.

It was now the third son's turn, who, hoping to make things better for himself, let the goat feed on the leaves of all the shrubs he could pick out that were covered with the richest foliage. "Goat, have you had enough to eat?" he said, as the evening fell, and the goat answered,——

"I have eaten so much
Not a leaf can I touch, Nan, Nan."

"Come along home then," said the boy, and he took her back and tied her up.

"Well," said the old tailor, "has the goat had her proper amount of food?"

"Why, she has eaten so much, not a leaf can she touch," answered the boy.

But the tailor felt mistrustful, and went down and asked, "Goat, have you really had enough to eat?" and the mischievous animal answered,—

"How can my hunger be allayed?
About the little graves I played
And could not find a single blade, Nan, Nan."

"Oh! what a pack of liars!" cried the tailor. "One as wicked and deceitful as the other, but they shall not make a fool of me any longer." And beside himself with anger, he rushed upstairs, and so belaboured his son with the yard-measure, that the boy fled from the house.

The old tailor was now left alone with his goat. The following morning he went down to the stable and stroked and caressed her. "Come along, my pet," he said, "I will take you out myself to-day," and he led her by the green hedgerows and weed-grown banks, and wherever he knew that goats love to feed. "You shall eat to your heart's content for once," he said to her, and so let her browse till evening. "Goat, have you had enough to eat?" he asked her at the close of the day, and she answered,—

"I have eaten so much
Not a leaf can I touch, Nan, Nan."

"Come along home then," said the tailor, and he led her to the stable and tied her up. He turned round, however, before leaving her, and said once more, "You have really had enough to eat for once?" But the goat gave him no better answer than her usual one, and replied,—

"How can my hunger be allayed?
About the little graves I played
And could not find a single blade, Nan, Nan."

On hearing this, the tailor stood, struck dumb with astonishment. He saw now how unjust he had been in driving away his sons. When he found his voice, he cried: "Wait, you ungrateful creature! it is not enough to drive you away, but I will put such a mark upon you, that you will not dare to shew your face again among honest tailors." And so saying, he sprang upstairs, brought down his razor, lathered the goat's head all over, and shaved it till it was as smooth as the back of his hand. Then he fetched the whip,—his yard-measure he considered was too good for such work,—and dealt the animal such blows, that she leapt into the air and away.

Sitting now quite alone in his house, the tailor fell into great melancholy, and would gladly have had his sons back again, but no one knew what had become of them.

The eldest had apprenticed himself to a joiner, and had set himself cheerfully and diligently to learn his trade. When the time came for him to start as a journeyman, his master made him a present of a table, which was of ordinary wood, and to all outward appearance exactly like any other table. It had, however, one good quality, for if anyone set it down, and said, "Table, serve up a meal," it was immediately covered with a nice fresh cloth, laid with a plate, knife and fork, and dishes of boiled and baked meats, as many as there was room for, and a glass of red wine, which only to look at made the heart rejoice.

"I have enough now to last me as long as I live," thought the young man to himself, and accordingly he went about enjoying himself, not minding whether the inns he stayed at were good or bad, whether there was food to be had there or not. Sometimes it pleased him not to seek shelter within them at all, but to turn into a field or a wood, or wherever else he fancied. When there he put down his table, and said, "Serve up a meal," and he was at once supplied with everything he could desire in the way of food.

After he had been going about like this for some time, he bethought him that he should like to go home again. His father's anger would by this time have passed away, and now that he had the wishing-table with him, he was sure of a ready welcome.

He happened, on his homeward way, to come one evening to an inn full of guests. They bid him welcome, and invited him to sit down with them and share their supper, otherwise, they added, he would have a difficulty in getting anything to eat.

But the joiner replied, "I will not take from you what little you have, I would rather that you should consent to be my guests," whereupon they all laughed, thinking he was only joking with them. He now put down his table in the middle of the room, and said, " Table, serve up a meal," and in a moment it was covered with a variety of food of better quality than any the host could have supplied, and a fragrant steam rose from the dishes and greeted the nostrils of the guests. " Now, friends, fall to," said the young man, and the guests, seeing that the invitation was well intended, did not wait to be asked twice, but drew up their chairs and began vigorously to ply their knives and forks. What astonished them most was the way in which, as soon as a dish was empty, another full one appeared in its place. Meanwhile the landlord was standing in the corner of the room looking on; he did not know what to think of it all, but said to himself, " I could make good use of a cook like that."

The joiner and his friends kept up their merriment late into the night, but at last they retired to rest, the young journeyman placing his table against the wall before going to bed.

The landlord, however, could not sleep for thinking of what he had seen; at last it occurred to him that up in his lumber-room he had an old table, which was just such another one to all appearance as the wishing-table; so he crept away softly to fetch it, and put it against the wall in place of the other.

When the morning came, the joiner paid for his night's lodging, took up his table, and left, never suspecting that the one he was carrying was not his own.

He reached home at mid-day, and was greeted with joy by his father. " And now, dear son," said the old man, " what trade have you learnt? "

" I am a joiner, father."

" A capital business," responded the father, " and what have you brought home with you from your travels? "

" The best thing I have brought with me, father, is that table."

The tailor carefully examined the table on all sides. " Well," he said at last, " you have certainly not brought a master-piece back with you; it is a wretched, badly-made old table."

" But it is a wishing-table," interrupted his son, " if I put it down and order a meal, it is at once covered with the best of food and wine. If you will only invite your relations and friends, they shall, for once in their lives, have a good meal, for no one ever leaves this table unsatisfied."

When the guests were all assembled, he put his table down as usual, and said, "Table, serve up a meal," but the table did not stir, and remained as empty as any ordinary table at such a command. Then the poor young man saw that his table had been changed, and he was covered with shame at having to stand there before them all like a liar. The guests made fun of him, and had to return home without bite or sup. The tailor took out his cloth and sat down once more to his tailoring, and the son started work again under a master-joiner.

The second son had apprenticed himself to a miller. When his term of apprenticeship had expired, the miller said to him, "As you have behaved so well, I will make you a present of an ass; it is a curious animal, it will neither draw a cart nor carry a sack."

"Of what use is he then?" asked the young apprentice.

"He gives gold," answered the miller, "if you stand him on a cloth, and say "Bricklebrit," gold pieces will fall from his mouth."

"That is a handsome present," said the young miller, and he thanked his master and departed.

After this, whenever he was in need of money, he had only to say "Bricklebrit," and a shower of gold pieces fell on the ground, and all he had to do was to pick them up. He ordered the best of everything wherever he went, in short, the dearer the better, for his purse was always full.

He had been going about the world like this for some time, when he began to think he should like to see his father again. When he sees my gold ass, he said to himself, he will forget his anger, and be glad to have me back.

It came to pass that he arrived one evening at the same inn in which his brother had had his table stolen from him. He was leading his ass up to the door, when the landlord came out and offered to take the animal, but the young miller refused his help. "Do not trouble yourself," he said, "I will take my old Greycoat myself to the stable and fasten her up, as I like to know where she is."

The landlord was very much astonished at this; the man cannot be very well off, he thought, to look after his own ass. When the stranger, therefore, pulled two gold pieces out of his pocket, and ordered the best of everything that could be got in the market, the landlord opened his eyes, but he ran off with alacrity to do his bidding.

Having finished his meal, the stranger asked for his bill, and the landlord thinking he might safely overcharge such a rich customer, asked for two more gold pieces. The miller felt in his pocket but found he had spent all his gold. " Wait a minute," he said to the landlord, " I will go and fetch some more money." Whereupon he went out, carrying the table-cloth with him.

This was more than the landlord's curiosity could stand, and he followed his guest to the stable. As the latter bolted the door after him, he went and peeped through a hole in the wall, and there he saw the stranger spread the cloth under his ass, and heard him say, " Bricklebrit," and immediately the floor was covered with gold pieces which fell from the animal's mouth.

" A good thousand, I declare," cried the host, " the gold pieces do not take long to coin! it's not a bad thing to have a money-bag like that."

The guest settled his account and went to bed. During the night the landlord crept down to the stable, led away the gold-coining ass, and fastened up another in its place.

Early the next morning the young miller went off with his ass, thinking all the time that he was leading his own. By noonday he had reached home, where his father gave him a warm welcome.

" What have you been doing with yourself, my son? " asked the old man.

" I am a miller, dear father," he answered.

" And what have you brought home with you from your travels? "

" Nothing but an ass, father."

" There are asses enough here," said the father, " I should have been better pleased if it had been a goat."

" Very likely," replied the son, " but this is no ordinary ass, it is an ass that coins money; if I say " Bricklebrit " to it, a whole sackful of gold pours from its mouth. Call all your relations and friends together, I will turn you all

The Table remained Empty.

into rich people."

"I shall like that well enough," said the tailor, "for then I shall not have to go on plaguing myself with stitching," and he ran out himself to invite his neighbours. As soon as they were all assembled, the young miller asked them to clear a space, and he then spread his cloth and brought the ass into the room. "Now see," said he, and cried "Bricklebrit," but not a single gold piece appeared, and it was evident that the animal knew nothing of the art of gold-coining, for it is not every ass that attains to such a degree of excellence.

The poor young miller pulled a long face, for he saw that he had been tricked; he begged forgiveness of the company, who all returned home as poor as they came. There was nothing to be done now but for the old man to go back to his needle, and the young one to hire himself to a miller.

The third son had apprenticed himself to a turner, which, being a trade requiring a great deal of skill, obliged him to serve a longer time than his brothers. He had, however, heard from them by letter, and knew how badly things had gone with them, and that they had been robbed of their property by an innkeeper on the last evening before reaching home.

When it was time for him to start as a journeyman, his master, being pleased with his conduct, presented him with a bag, saying as he did so, "You will find a cudgel inside."

"The bag I can carry over my shoulder, and it will no doubt be of great service to me, but of what use is a cudgel inside; it will only add to the weight."

"I will explain," said the master; "if any one at any time should behave badly to you, you have only to say, 'Cudgel, out of the bag,' and the stick will jump out, and give him such a cudgelling, that he will not be able to move or stir for a week afterwards, and it will not leave off till you say, 'Cudgel, into the bag.'"

The young man thanked him, hung the bag on his back, and when any one threatened to attack him, or in any way to do him harm, he called out, "Cudgel, out of the bag," and no sooner were the words said, than out jumped the stick, and beat the offenders soundly on the into rich people."

"I shall like that well enough," said the tailor, "for then I shall not have to go on plaguing myself with stitching," and he ran out himself to invite his neighbours. As soon as they were all assembled, the young miller asked them to clear a space, and he then spread his cloth and brought the ass into the room. "Now see," said he, and cried "Bricklebrit," but not a single gold piece appeared, and it was evident that the animal knew nothing of the art of gold-coining, for it is not every ass that attains to such a degree of excellence.

The poor young miller pulled a long face, for he saw that he had been tricked: he begged forgiveness of the company, who all returned home as poor as they came. There was nothing to be done now but for the old man to go back to his needle, and the young one to hire himself to a miller.

The third son had apprenticed himself to a turner, which, being a trade requiring a great deal of skill, obliged him to serve a longer time than his brothers. He had, however, heard from them by letter, and knew how badly things had gone with them, and that they had been robbed of their property by an innkeeper on the last evening before reaching home.

When it was time for him to start as a journeyman, his master, being pleased with his conduct, presented him with a bag, saying as he did so, "You will find a cudgel inside."

"The bag I can carry over my shoulder, and it will no doubt be of great service to me, but of what use is a cudgel inside, it will only add to the weight?"

"I will explain," said the master, "if any one at any time should behave badly to you, you have only to say, 'Cudgel, out of the bag,' and the stick will jump out, and give him such a cudgelling, that he will not be able to move or stir for a week afterwards, and it will not leave off till you say, 'Cudgel, into the bag.'"

The young man thanked him, hung the bag on his back, and when any one threatened to attack him, or in any way to do him harm, he called out, "Cudgel, out of the bag," and no sooner were the words said than out jumped the stick, and beat the offenders soundly on the back, till their clothes were in ribbons, and it did it all so quickly, that the turn had come round to each of them before he was aware.

It was evening when the young turner reached the inn where his brothers had been so badly treated. He laid his bag down on the table, and began giving an account of all the wonderful things he had seen while going about the world.

"One may come across a wishing-table," he said, "or an ass that gives gold, and such like; all very good things in their way, but not all of them put together are worth the treasure of which I have possession, and which I carry with me in that bag."

The landlord pricked up his ears. "What can it be?" he asked himself, "that bag must be filled with precious stones; I must try and get hold of that cheaply too, for there is luck in odd numbers."

Bed-time came, and the guest stretched himself out on one of the benches and placed his bag under his head for a pillow. As soon as the landlord thought he was fast asleep, he went up to him, and began gently and cautiously pulling and pushing at the bag to see if he could get it away and put another in its place.

But the young turner had been waiting for this and just as the landlord was about to give a good last pull, he cried, "Cudgel, out of the bag," and the same moment the stick was out, and beginning its usual dance. It beat him with such a vengeance that the landlord cried out for mercy, but the louder his cries, the more lustily did the stick beat time to them, until he fell to the ground exhausted.

"If you do not give back the wishing-table and the gold ass," said the young turner, "the game shall begin over again."

"No, no," cried the landlord in a feeble voice, "I will gladly give every thing back, if only you will make that dreadful demon of a stick return to the bag."

"This time," said the turner, "I will deal with you according to mercy rather than justice, but beware of offending in like manner again." Then he cried, "Cudgel, into the bag," and let the man remain in peace.

The turner journeyed on next day to his father's house,

taking with him the wishing-table and the gold ass. The tailor was delighted to see his son again, and asked him, as he had the others, what trade he had learnt since he left home.

"I am a turner, dear father," he answered.

"A highly skilled trade," said the tailor, "and what have you brought back with you from your travels?"

"An invaluable thing, dear father," replied the son, "a cudgel."

"What! a cudgel!" exclaimed the old man, "that was certainly well worth while, seeing that you can cut yourself one from the first tree you come across."

"But not such a one as this, dear father; for, if I say to it, 'Cudgel, out of the bag,' out it jumps, and gives any one who has evil intentions towards me such a bad time of it, that he falls down and cries for mercy. And know, that it was with this stick that I got back the wishing-table and the gold ass, which the dishonest inn-keeper stole from my brothers. Now, go and call them both here, and invite all your relations and friends, and I will feast them and fill their pockets with gold."

The old tailor was slow to believe all this but nevertheless he went out and gathered his neighbours together. Then the turner put down a cloth, and led in the gold ass, and said to his brother, "Now, dear brother, speak to him." The miller said "Bricklebrit," and the cloth was immediately covered with gold pieces, which continued to pour from the ass's mouth until everyone had taken as many as he could carry. (I see by your faces that you are all wishing you had been there.)

Then the turner brought in the wishing-table, and said, "Now, dear brother, speak to it." And scarcely had the joiner cried, "Table, serve up a meal," than it was covered with a profusion of daintily dressed meats. Then the tailor and his guests sat down to a meal such as they had never enjoyed before in their lives, and they all sat up late into the night, full of good cheer and jollity.

The tailor put away his needle and thread, his yard-measure and his goose, and he and his three sons lived together henceforth in contentment and luxury.

Meanwhile, what had become of the goat, who had been

the guilty cause of the three sons being driven from their home? I will tell you.

She was so ashamed of her shaven crown, that she ran and crept into a fox's hole. When the fox came home, he was met by two large glittering eyes that gleamed at him out of the darkness, and he was so frightened that he ran away. The bear met him, and perceiving that he was in some distress said, "What is the matter, brother Fox, why are you pulling such a long face?" "Ah!" answered Redskin, "there is a dreadful animal sitting in my hole, which glared at me with fiery eyes."

"We will soon drive him out," said the Bear, and he trotted back with his friend to the hole and looked in, but the sight of the fiery eyes was quite enough for him, and he turned and took to his heels.

The bee met him and noticing that he was somewhat ill at ease, said, "Bear, you look remarkably out of humour, where have you left your good spirits?" "It's easy for you to talk," replied the bear, "a horrible animal with red goggle-eyes is sitting in the fox's hole, and we cannot drive it out."

The bee said, "I really am sorry for you, Bear; I am but a poor weak little creature that you scarcely deign to look at in passing, but, for all that, I think I shall be able to help you."

With this the bee flew to the fox's hole, settled on the smooth shaven head of the goat, and stung her so violently, that she leaped high into the air, crying, "Nan, nan!" and fled away like a mad thing into the open country; but no one, to this hour, has found out what became of her after that.

THE TWELVE BROTHERS

THERE were once a king and queen who had lived happily together for many years. They had twelve children, but it so happened that all these children were boys. One day the king said to the queen, " If our next child should be a girl, all the boys must die, for I should like my daughter to be very rich and to inherit the whole of my kingdom." Hereupon he ordered twelve coffins to be made, and after a little pillow had been placed in each and they had all been filled with shavings, they were locked up in a room in the castle. Then the king gave the key to his wife, and told her on no account to say a word of this matter to anyone.

But the poor mother could do nothing but sit and grieve the whole day long, and seeing her so sorrowful, her youngest boy, whom she had named Benjamin after the little son in the Bible, and who always liked to be near his mother, went to her and said, " Dear mother, why are you so sad? "

" I may not tell you, dearest child," she answered.

The boy, however, gave her no peace with his questionings, until at last she rose and led him to the room in which the coffins were kept.

" Dearest Benjamin," she said, " your father had these coffins prepared for you and your brothers, for, if ever I have a little daughter, you are all to be killed and buried in them." She wept so bitterly as she told him this, that her son tried to comfort her, and said: " Do not weep, dear mother; we will go away from here, and I am sure we shall be able to look after ourselves." Then his mother bade him go with his brothers into the wood, and there find the highest tree; " and let one of you," she continued,

" be always at the top watching, for you must keep your eyes on the castle-tower. If I have a little son, I will put up a white flag, and then you will know that it is safe for you to return home; if I have a little daughter, I will put up a red flag, and then you must flee for your lives, and may God help and protect you. Every night I shall rise and pray for you; in winter, that you may not be without a fire to warm yourselves by; in summer, that you may be sheltered from the heat."

She then blessed them, and the boys went off to the wood, and kept watch in turn on the top of the highest oak-tree. The day came when it was Benjamin's turn to watch, and as he was looking towards the tower, he saw a flag put up. But, alas! it was no white flag, but a blood-red flag, warning them that the hour had come when their father's cruel sentence was to be carried out.

When the others heard this, they flew into a great rage, and exclaimed in their anger: "Are we to be put to death, just for the sake of a girl! but we will have our revenge!" So they swore one and all, that they would take the life of any girl who should cross their path.

They now thought it safer to go farther into the wood, and when they had made their way to where the trees were thickest and the shade deepest, they suddenly came upon a little empty house, that had been raised by the magic of some good or evil fairy.

"Oh!" they cried, "this is just the place for us to live in; you, Benjamin, as you are the youngest and weakest, must stay at home and keep house, while we go and look for provisions."

So the elder brothers went into the wood, and there they found plenty of game to shoot: wild deer, hares, pigeons and other birds, as well as many other things that were good for food. When they had finished their day's sport, they went home, and then it was Benjamin's turn to busy himself with preparing and cooking the food, and glad enough they were of a meal, for by this time they were all very hungry. In this way they lived on in the little house for ten years, and the time passed so quickly that the brothers never found it long.

Meanwhile, the little daughter who had been born at the castle, was growing up. She was good at heart and beautiful in face, and had a gold star on her forehead.

One day about this time, she happened to catch sight of twelve little shirts which were lying among some of her mother's things.

"Mother," she said, "to whom do those shirts belong? for they are too small for my father to wear."

It was with a heavy heart that the poor mother answered. "Those shirts, dear child, belong to your twelve brothers."

"My twelve brothers," cried the girl, "why I never even heard of them. Where are they now?"

"God alone knows," replied her mother, "but they are wandering somewhere about the world."

Then she took her little daughter to the room where the coffins were hidden, and unlocking the door, shewed them to her, and said, "These were meant for your brothers, but they ran away and escaped," and she related to her all that had happened before she was born.

"Dear mother," said the girl, "do not weep; I will go and try to find my brothers."

So she took the twelve shirts and started through the wood in search of them. On and on she went all through the day, and as evening fell she came to the little house. She stepped in, and there she found a young boy, who looked with astonishment at this beautiful girl, who was dressed like a princess and had a gold star on her forehead. "Whence come you?" he asked, "and what are you seeking?"

"I am a king's daughter," she answered, "and I am seeking my twelve brothers; and as far as the blue sky reaches overhead, will I wander till I find them," and she shewed him the twelve shirts. Then Benjamin knew that it was his sister. "I am Benjamin," he cried, "your youngest brother," and at this, they were both so overcome with delight, that they began to cry for joy, and kissed and embraced one another.

At last Benjamin said: "There is one thing that troubles me; my brothers and I were so angry at being driven out of our kingdom on account of a girl, that we made a vow to kill every girl whom we met."

"I would gladly die," said his sister, "if by so doing I could restore my dear brothers to their home."

"No, no, you shall not die," cried Benjamin, "hide yourself under this tub, and when the others return, I will soon come to an understanding with them."

The sister did as she was bid, and as soon as it was dark, in came the brothers from hunting.

They sat down to their supper, and while eating and drinking, asked, "Well, Benjamin, what news have you to tell us?"

"Have you yourselves heard nothing," said Benjamin.

"Nothing," they replied.

"That is strange," continued Benjamin, "for you have been out all day, and I have only been in the house, and yet I know more than you."

"What is it?" they all cried at once, "tell us what it is."

"Only on condition," said Benjamin, "that you promise me not to kill the first girl you see."

"We promise, we promise; she shall find mercy at our hands," they all cried again, "only let us hear your news."

Benjamin went to the tub, and lifting it up, said, "Our sister is here," and the king's daughter stepped forth in her royal attire, with the gold star on her forehead, and stood before them full of tenderness, grace, and beauty. When the brothers saw her, they greatly loved her, and came about her and kissed her, and there was great rejoicing among them.

So now the sister stayed at home with Benjamin and helped him in the house, while the others continued to hunt in the wood for game. Among other things, she gathered the wood for cooking, and the herbs for vegetables, and put the pots and kettles on the fire, so that there might always be food ready for her brothers when they came in. She kept the house in beautiful order, and made the little beds look sweet and clean with pretty white covers, and altogether it was no wonder that the brothers were very happy and comfortable, and that they all lived together in great peace and contentment.

One day, the two who stayed at home had prepared a dainty meal, and as soon as they were all assembled they sat down to the table, happy and in good spirits. Now there was a little garden belonging to the house in which grew twelve tall lily plants. The sister went out to pick the lilies, for she thought it would please her brothers to give them each a flower as they sat at table. But scarcely was the last one gathered, when her brothers were suddenly changed into twelve ravens, that flew right away over the trees, and in the same moment both the house and garden entirely disappeared. There was the poor girl, left alone in the wild wood; turning, however, to look around her, she saw an old woman standing near, who said, "My child, what is this that you have done? Why did you not leave those twelve white lilies untouched? Those were your brothers, who are now from this time forth, turned into ravens." The girl asked weeping, "Is there nothing that I can do to set them free?"

"Nothing," replied the old woman, "there is one way only in all the world by which they might be saved, but that would be far too hard a task for you to perform, for you would have to remain dumb for seven years, never either speaking or laughing, and if, when there were only a few minutes wanting to complete the seven years, you were to utter a single word, all your past endeavour would be in vain, and with that one word you would have killed your brothers."

The girl was silent, but in her heart she said, "I will set my dear brothers free; I know that I shall be able to do it."

Then she went and chose out a high tree, and there among its topmost branches she sat and span, and neither spoke nor laughed.

Now it happened, one day, that a king was out hunting in the wood. He had a large greyhound with him, and the dog ran up to the tree whereon the girl was sitting and began leaping about and looking up at her and barking. Then the king came along, and he too looked up and saw the beautiful princess with the gold star on her forehead, and he was so enchanted with her beauty that he called to her to ask if she would be his wife. She did not speak a word, but gave a little nod with her head. Then the king climbed up into the tree himself and carried her down, and lifting her on to his own horse, bore her away to his home.

The marriage was celebrated with great pomp, and amid

great rejoicings, but the bride neither spoke nor laughed.

They had been living happily together for some years, when the king's mother, who was a hard-hearted woman, began to say wicked things about the young queen. "That woman you brought home with you," she said to the king, "is nothing but a common beggar-maid; who knows what evil tricks she may be up to in secret. Even if she is dumb and cannot speak, at least she must be able to laugh, and you know it is said that those who never laugh have a bad conscience." At first the king would not believe any of the things that were said against his wife; but the old mother gave him no peace, accusing the queen first of one wicked thing and then another, until he allowed himself at last to be persuaded of her guilt, and condemned her to death. But the king still dearly loved his wife, and he stood looking out of his window and weeping, while the fire was being kindled in the courtyard, where the young queen was to be burnt.

The queen had been tied to the stake; and now the last moment of the seven years came just as the angry tongues of the fire were beginning to play about her dress. Then there was heard in the air above a rushing sound as of wings, and twelve ravens came flying down, and no sooner had they alighted on the ground, than behold! there were her twelve brothers whom she had set free. They scattered the fire and trampled on the flames, and showered kisses and loving words upon their sister as they untied her from the stake.

And now that she might speak, she was able to tell the king why she had been dumb and had never laughed. And he was rejoiced when he heard her tale and knew that she was guiltless, and they all lived happily together for ever after.

But the wicked old mother-in-law was taken before the judge and tried, and he condemned her to be put in a vat of boiling oil, in which there were poisonous snakes, and so she died a miserable death.

ASHPUTTEL

THE wife of a rich man fell sick; and when she felt that her end drew nigh, she called her only daughter to her bedside, and said, "Always be a good girl, and I will look down from heaven and watch over you." Soon afterwards she shut her eyes and died, and was buried in the garden; and the little girl went every day to her grave and wept, and was always good and kind to all about her. And the snow fell and spread a beautiful white covering over the grave; but by the time the spring came, and the sun had melted it away again, her father had married another wife. This new wife had two daughters of her own, that she brought home with her; they were fair in face but foul at heart, and it was now a sorry time for the poor little girl. "What does the good-for-nothing thing want in the parlour?" said they; "they who would eat bread should first earn it: away with the kitchen-maid!" Then they took away her fine clothes, and gave her an old grey frock to put on, and laughed at her, and turned her into the kitchen.

There she was forced to do hard work; to rise early before daylight, to bring the water, to make the fire, to cook, and to wash. Besides that, the sisters plagued her in all sorts of ways, and laughed at her. In the evening when she was tired, she had no bed to lie down on, but was made to lie by the hearth among the ashes; and as this, of course, made her always dusty and dirty, they called her Ashputtel.

It happened once that the father was going to the fair, and asked his wife's daughters what he should bring them. "Fine clothes," said the first; "Pearls and diamonds," cried the second. "Now, child," said he to his own daughter, " what will you have? " " The first twig, dear father, that brushes against your hat when you turn your face homewards," said she. Then he bought for the first two the fine clothes and pearls and diamonds they had asked for: and on his way home, as he rode through a green copse, a hazel twig brushed against him, and almost pushed off his hat: so he broke it off and brought it away; and when he got home he gave it to his daughter. Then she took it, and went to her mother's grave and planted it there; and cried so much that it was watered with her tears; and there it grew and became a fine tree. Three times every day she went to it and cried; and soon a little bird came and built its nest upon the tree, and talked with her, and watched over her, and brought her whatever she wished for.

Now it happened that the king of that land held a feast, which was to last three days; and out of those who came to it his son was to choose a bride for himself. Ashputtel's two sisters were asked to come; so they called her up, and said, " Now, comb our hair, brush our shoes, and tie our sashes for us, for we are going to dance at the king's feast." Then she did as she was told; but when all was done she could not help crying, for she thought to herself, she should so have liked to have gone with them to the ball; and at last she begged her mother very hard to let her go. " You, Ashputtel! " said she; " you who have nothing to wear, no clothes at all, and who cannot even dance—you want to go to the ball? " And when she kept on begging, she said at last, to get rid of her, " I will throw this dishful of peas into the ash-heap, and if in two hours' time you have picked them all out, you shall go to the feast too."

Then she threw the peas down among the ashes, but the little maiden ran out at the back door into the garden, and cried out—

" Hither, hither, through the sky,
Turtle-doves and linnets, fly!
Blackbird, thrush, and chaffinch gay,
Hither, hither, haste away!
One and all come help me, quick!
Haste ye, haste ye!—pick, pick, pick! "

Then first came two white doves, flying in at the kitchen

window; next came two turtle-doves; and after them came all the little birds under heaven, chirping and fluttering in; and they flew down into the ashes. And the little doves stooped their heads down and set to work, pick, pick, pick; and then the others began to pick, pick, pick: and among them all they soon picked out all the good grain, and put it into a dish, but left the ashes. Long before the end of the hour the work was quite done, and all flew out again at the windows.

Then Ashputtel brought the dish to her mother, overjoyed at the thought that now she should go to the ball. But the mother said, "No, no! you slut, you have no clothes, and cannot dance; you shall not go." And when Ashputtel begged very hard to go, she said, "If you can in one hour's time pick two of those dishes of peas out of the ashes, you shall go too." And thus she thought she should at last get rid of her. So she shook two dishes of peas into the ashes.

But the little maiden went out into the garden at the back of the house, and cried out as before—

"Hither, hither, through the sky,
Turtle-doves and linnets, fly!
Blackbird, thrush, and chaffinch gay,
Hither, hither, haste away!
One and all come help me, quick!
Haste ye, haste ye!—pick, pick, pick!"

Then first came two white doves in at the kitchen window; next came two turtle-doves; and after them came all the little birds under heaven, chirping and hopping about. And they flew down into the ashes; and the little doves put their heads down and set to work, pick, pick, pick; and then the others began pick, pick, pick; and they all put the good grain into the dishes, and left all the ashes. Before half an hour's time all was done, and out they flew again. And then Ashputtel took the dishes to her mother, rejoicing to think that she should now go to the ball. But her mother said, "It is all of no use, you cannot go; you have no clothes, and cannot dance, and you would only put us to shame": and off she went with her two daughters to the ball.

Now when all were gone, and nobody left at home,

Ashputtel went sorrowfully and sat down under the hazel-tree, and cried out—

"Shake, shake, hazel-tree,
Gold and silver over me!"

Then her friend the bird flew out of the tree, and brought a gold and silver dress for her, and slippers of spangled silk; and she put them on, and followed her sisters to the feast. But they did not know her, and thought it must be some strange princess, she looked so fine and beautiful in her rich clothes; and they never once thought of Ashputtel, taking it for granted that she was safe at home in the dirt.

The king's son soon came up to her, and took her by the hand and danced with her, and no one else: and he never left her hand; but when any one else came to ask her to dance, he said, "This lady is dancing with me."

Thus they danced till a late hour of the night; and then she wanted to go home: and the king's son said, "I shall go and take care of you to your home;" for he wanted to see where the beautiful maiden lived. But she slipped away from him, unawares, and ran off towards home; and as the prince followed her, she jumped up into the pigeon-house and shut the door. Then he waited till her father came home, and told him that the unknown maiden, who had been at the feast, had hid herself in the pigeon-house. But when they had broken open the door they found no one within; and as they came back into the house, Ashputtel was lying, as she always did, in her dirty frock by the ashes, and her dim little lamp was burning in the chimney. For she had run as quickly as she could through the pigeon-house and on to the hazel-tree, and had there taken off her beautiful clothes, and put them beneath the tree, that the bird might carry them away, and had laid down again amid the ashes in her little grey frock.

The next day when the feast was again held, and her father, mother, and sisters were gone, Ashputtel went to the hazel-tree, and said—

"Shake, shake, hazel-tree,
Gold and silver over me!"

And the bird came and brought a still finer dress than

WHEN NIGHT CAME SHE WANTED TO GO HOME.

the one she had worn the day before. And when she came in it to the ball, every one wondered at her beauty. But the king's son, who was waiting for her, took her by the hand, and danced with her; and when any one asked her to dance, he said as before, "This lady is dancing with me."

When night came she wanted to go home; and the king's son followed her as before, that he might see into what house she went; but she sprang away from him all at once into the garden behind her father's house. In this garden stood a fine large pear-tree full of ripe fruit; and Ashputtel, not knowing where to hide herself, jumped up into it without being seen. Then the king's son lost sight of her, and could not find out where she was gone, but waited till her father came home, and said to him, "The unknown lady who danced with me has slipt away, and I think she must have sprung into the pear-tree." The father thought to himself, "Can it be Ashputtel?" So he had an axe brought, and they cut down the tree, but found no one upon it. And when they came back into the kitchen, there lay Ashputtel among the ashes; for she had slipped down on the other side of the tree, and carried her beautiful clothes back to the bird at the hazel-tree, and then put on her little grey frock.

The third day, when her father and mother and sisters were gone, she went again into the garden, and said:

"Shake, shake, hazel-tree,
Gold and silver over me!"

Then her kind friend the bird brought a dress still finer than the former one, and slippers which were all of gold; so that when she came to the feast no one knew what to say, for wonder at her beauty; and the king's son danced with nobody but her; and when any one else asked her to dance, he said, "This lady is my partner, sir."

When night came she wanted to go home; and the king's son would go with her, and said to himself, "I will not lose her this time"; but, however, she again slipt away from him, though in such a hurry that she dropped her left golden slipper upon the stairs.

The prince took the shoe, and went the next day to the king, his father, and said, "I will take for my wife the one she had worn the day before. And when she came in it to the ball, every one wondered at her beauty: but the king's son, who was waiting for her, took her by the hand, and danced with her; and when any one asked her to dance, he said as before, " This lady is dancing with me."

When night came she wanted to go home; and the king's son followed her as before, that he might see into what house she went: but she sprang away from him all at once into the garden behind her father's house. In this garden stood a fine large pear-tree full of ripe fruit; and Ashputtel, not knowing where to hide herself, jumped up into it without being seen. Then the king's son lost sight of her, and could not find out where she was gone, but waited till her father came home, and said to him, " The unknown lady who danced with me has slipt away, and I think she must have sprung into the pear-tree." The father thought to himself, " Can it be Ashputtel? " So he had an axe brought; and they cut down the tree, but found no one upon it. And when they came back into the kitchen, there lay Ashputtel among the ashes; for she had slipped down on the other side of the tree, and carried her beautiful clothes back to the bird at the hazel-tree, and then put on her little grey frock.

The third day, when her father and mother and sisters were gone, she went again into the garden, and said—

" Shake, shake, hazel-tree,
Gold and silver over me! "

Then her kind friend the bird brought a dress still finer than the former one, and slippers which were all of gold: so that when she came to the feast no one knew what to say, for wonder at her beauty: and the king's son danced with nobody but her; and when any one else asked her to dance, he said, " This lady is *my* partner, Sir."

When night came she wanted to go home; and the king's son would go with her, and said to himself, " I will not lose her this time; " but however she again slipt away from him, though in such a hurry that she dropped her left golden slipper upon the stairs.

The prince took the shoe, and went the next day to the king his father, and said, " I will take for my wife the lady that this golden slipper fits." Then both the sisters were overjoyed to hear it; for they had beautiful feet, and had no doubt that they could wear the golden slipper. The eldest went first into the room where the slipper was, and wanted to try it on, and the mother stood by. But her great toe could not go into it, and the shoe was altogether much too small for her. Then the mother gave her a knife, and said, "Never mind, cut it off; when you are queen you will not care about toes; you will not want to walk." So the silly girl cut off her great toe, and thus squeezed on the shoe, and went to the king's son. Then he took her for his bride, and set her beside him on the horse, and rode away with her homewards.

But in their way home they had to pass by the hazel-tree that Ashputtel had planted; and on the branch sat a little dove singing—

"Back again! back again! look to the shoe!
The shoe is too small, and not made for you!
Prince! prince! look again for thy bride,
For she's not the true one that sits by thy side."

Then the prince got down and looked at her foot; and he saw, by the blood that streamed from it, what a trick she had played him. So he turned his horse round, and brought the false bride back to her home, and said, "This is not the right bride; let the other sister try and put on the slipper." Then she went into the room and got her foot into the shoe, all but the heel, which was too large. But her mother squeezed it in till the blood came, and took her to the king's son: and he set her as his bride by his side on his horse, and rode away with her.

But when they came to the hazel-tree the little dove sat there still, and sang—

"Back again! back again! look to the shoe!
The shoe is too small, and not made for you!
Prince! prince! look again for thy bride,
For she's not the true one that sits by thy side."

Then he looked down, and saw that the blood streamed so much from the shoe, that her white stockings were quite red. So he turned his horse and brought her also back again. "This is not the true bride," said he to the father; "have you no other daughters?" "No," said he;

" there is only a little dirty Ashputtel here, the child of my first wife; I am sure she cannot be the bride." The prince told him to send her. But the mother said, " No, no, she is much too dirty; she will not dare to show herself." However, the prince would have her come; and she first washed her face and hands, and then went in and courtesied to him, and he reached her the golden slipper. Then she took her clumsy shoe off her left foot, and put on the golden slipper; and it fitted her as if it had been made for her. And when he drew near and looked at her face he knew her, and said, " This is the right bride." But the mother and both the sisters were frightened, and turned pale with anger as he took Ashputtel on his horse, and rode away with her. And when they came to the hazel-tree, the white dove sang—

" Home! home! look at the shoe!
Princess! the shoe was made for you!
Prince! prince! take home thy bride,
For she is the true one that sits by thy side! "

And when the dove had done its song, it came flying, and perched upon her right shoulder, and so went home with her.

RUMPEL-STILTS-KEN

BY the side of a wood, in a country a long way off, ran a fine stream of water; and upon the stream there stood a mill. The miller's house was close by, and the miller, you must know, had a very beautiful daughter. She was, moreover, very shrewd and clever; and the miller was so proud of her, that he one day told the king of the land, who used to come and hunt in the wood, that his daughter could spin gold out of straw. Now this king was very fond of money; and when he heard the miller's boast his greediness was raised, and he sent for the girl to be brought before him. Then he led her to a chamber in his palace where there was a great heap of straw, and gave her a spinning-wheel, and said, "All this must be spun into gold before morning, as you love your life." It was in vain that the poor maiden said that it was only a silly boast of her father, for that she could do no such thing as spin straw into gold: the chamber door was locked, and she was left alone.

She sat down in one corner of the room, and began to bewail her hard fate; when on a sudden the door opened, and a droll-looking little man hobbled in, and said, "Good morrow to you, my good lass; what are you weeping for?" "Alas!" said she, "I must spin this straw into gold, and I know not how." "What will you give me," said the hobgoblin, "to do it for you?" "My necklace," replied the maiden. He took her at her word, and sat himself down to the wheel, and whistled and sang—

"Round about, round about,
Lo and behold!
Reef away, reef away,
Straw into gold!"

And round about the wheel went merrily; the work was

quickly done, and the straw was all spun into gold.

When the king came and saw this, he was greatly astonished and pleased; but his heart grew still more greedy of gain, and he shut up the poor miller's daughter again with a fresh task. Then she knew not what to do, and sat down once more to weep; but the dwarf soon opened the door, and said, "What will you give me to do your task?" "The ring on my finger," said she. So her little friend took the ring, and began to work at the wheel again, and whistled and sang—

"Round about, round about,
Lo and behold!
Reef away, reef away,
Straw into gold!"

till, long before morning, all was done again.

The king was greatly delighted to see all this glittering treasure; but still he had not enough; so he took the miller's daughter to a yet larger heap, and said, "All this must be spun to-night; and if it is, you shall be my queen." As soon as she was alone the dwarf came in, and said, "What will you give me to spin gold for you this third time?" "I have nothing left," said she. "Then say you will give me," said the little man, "the first little child that you may have when you are queen." "That may never be," thought the miller's daughter: and as she knew no other way to get her task done, she said she would do what he asked. Round went the wheel again to the old song, and the manikin once more spun the heap into gold. The king came in the morning, and, finding all he wanted, was forced to keep his word; so he married the miller's daughter and she really became queen.

At the birth of her first little child she was very glad, and forgot the dwarf, and what she had said. But one day he came into her room, where she was sitting playing with her baby, and put her in mind of it. Then she grieved sorely at her misfortune, and said she would give him all the wealth of the kingdom if he would let her off, but in vain; till at last her tears softened him, and he said, "I will give you three days' grace, and if during that time you tell me my name, you shall keep your child."

Now the queen lay awake all night, thinking of all the odd names that she had ever heard; and she sent messengers all over the land to find out new ones. The next day the little man came, and she began with TIMOTHY, ICHABOD, BENJAMIN, JEREMIAH, and all the names she could remember; but to all and each of them he said, "Madam, that is not my name."

The second day she began with all the comical names she could hear of, BANDY-LEGS, HUNCH-BACK, CROOK-SHANKS, and so on; but the little gentleman still said to every one of them, "Madam, that is not my name."

The third day one of the messengers came back, and said, "I travelled two days without hearing of any other names; but yesterday, as I was climbing a high hill, among the trees of the forest where the fox and the hare bid each other good night, I saw a little hut; and before the hut burnt a fire; and round about the fire a funny little dwarf was dancing upon one leg, and singing,—

"'Merrily the feast I'll make,
To-day I'll brew, to-morrow bake;
Merrily I'll dance and sing,
For next day will a stranger bring.
Little does my lady dream
Rumpel-stilts-ken is my name!'"

When the queen heard this she jumped for joy, and as soon as her little friend came she sat down upon her throne, and called all her court round to enjoy the fun; and the nurse stood by her side with the baby in her arms, as if it was quite ready to be given up. Then the little man began to chuckle at the thoughts of having the poor child, to take home with him to his hut in the woods; and he cried out, "Now, lady, what is my name?" "Is it JOHN?" asked she. "No, madam!" "Is it TOM?" "No, madam!" "Is it JEMMY?" "It is not." "Can your name be RUMPEL-STILTS-KEN?" said the lady slily. "Some witch told you that!—some witch told you that!" cried the little man, and dashed his right foot in a rage so deep into the floor, that he was forced to lay hold of it with both hands to pull it out.

Then he made the best of his way off, while the nurse laughed and the baby crowed; and all the court jeered at him for having had so much trouble for nothing, and said, "We wish you a very good morning, and a merry feast, Mr. RUMPEL-STILTS-KEN!"

THE MAN IN THE BAG

THERE were two brothers, who were both soldiers, the one had grown rich, but the other had had no luck, and was very poor. The poor man thought he would try to better himself; so pulling off his red coat, he became a gardener, and dug his ground well, and sowed turnips.

When the crop came up, there was one plant bigger than all the rest; and it kept getting larger and larger, and seemed as if it would never cease growing; so that it might have been called the prince of turnips, for there never was such a one seen before and never will again. At last it was so big that it filled a cart, and two oxen could hardly draw it; but the gardener did not know what in the world to do with it, nor whether it would be a blessing or a curse to him. One day he said to himself, "What shall I do with it? if I sell it, it will bring me no more than another would; and as for eating, the little turnips I am sure are better than this great one: the best thing perhaps that I can do will be to give it to the king, as a mark of my respect."

Then he yoked his oxen, and drew the turnip to the court, and gave it to the king. "What a wonderful thing!" said the king. "I have seen many strange things in my life, but such a monster as this I never saw before. Where did you get the seed, or is it only your good luck? If so, you are a true child of fortune."

"Ah, no!" answered the gardener, "I am no child of fortune; I am a poor soldier, who never yet could get enough to live upon: so I set to work, tilling the ground. I have a brother who is rich, and your majesty knows him well, and all the world knows him; but as I am poor, everybody forgets me."

Then the king took pity on him, and said, "You shall be poor no longer. I will give you so much, that you shall be even richer than your brother." So he gave him money, and land, and flocks, and herds; and made him so rich, that his brother's wealth could not at all be compared with his.

When the brother heard of all this, and how a turnip had made the gardener so rich, he envied him sorely; and bethought himself how he could please the king and get the same good luck for himself. However, he thought he would manage more cleverly than his brother; so he got together a rich gift of jewels and fine horses for the king, thinking that he must have a much larger gift in return: for if his brother had so much given him for a turnip, what must his gift be worth?

The king took the gift very graciously, and said he knew not what he could give in return more costly and wonderful than the great turnip; so the soldier was forced to put it into a cart, and drag it home with him. When he reached home, he knew not upon whom to vent his rage and envy; and at length wicked thoughts came into his head, and he sought to kill his brother.

So he hired some villains to murder him; and having shown them where to lie in ambush, he went to his brother, and said, "Dear brother, I have found a hidden treasure; let us go and dig it up, and share it between us." The other had no thought or fear of his brother's roguery: so they went out together; and as they were travelling along, the murderers rushed out upon him, bound him, and were going to hang him on a tree.

But whilst they were getting all ready, they heard the trampling of a horse afar off, which so frightened them that they pushed their prisoner neck and shoulders together into a sack, and swung him up by a cord to the tree; where they left him dangling, and ran away, meaning to come back and despatch him in the evening.

Meantime, however, he worked and worked away, till he had made a hole large enough to put out his head. When the horseman came up, he proved to be a student, a merry fellow, who was journeying along on his nag, and singing as he went. As soon as the man in the bag saw him passing under the tree, he cried out, "Good morning! good morning to thee, my friend!" The student looked about, and seeing no one, and not knowing where the voice came from, cried out, "Who calls me?"

Then the man in the bag cried out, "Lift up thine eyes, for behold here I sit in the sack of wisdom! Here have I, in a short time, learned great and wondrous things. Compared to what is taught in this seat, all the learning of the schools is as empty air. A little longer and I shall know all that man can know, and shall come forth wiser than the wisest of mankind. Here I discern the signs and motions of the heavens and the stars; the laws that control the winds; the number of the sands on the sea-shore; the healing of the sick; the virtues of all simples, of birds, and of precious stones. Wert thou but once here, my friend, thou wouldst soon feel the power of knowledge."

The student listened to all this, and wondered much. At last he said, "Blessed be the day and hour when I found you! cannot you let me into the sack for a little while?" Then the other answered, as if very unwillingly, "A little space I may allow thee to sit here, if thou wilt reward me well and treat me kindly: but thou must tarry yet an hour below, till I have learnt some little matters that are yet unknown to me."

So the student sat himself down and waited awhile; but the time hung heavy upon him, and he begged hard that he might ascend forthwith, for his thirst of knowledge was very great. Then the other began to give way, and said, "Thou must let the bag of wisdom descend, by untying yonder cord, and then thou shalt enter." So the student let him down, opened the bag, and set him free. "Now then," cried he, "let me mount quickly!" As he began to put himself into the sack heels first, "Wait a while!" said the gardener, "that is not the way." Then he pushed him in head first, tied up the bag's mouth, and soon swung up the searcher after wisdom, dangling in the air. "How is it with thee, friend?" said he; "dost thou not feel that wisdom cometh unto thee? Rest there in peace, till thou art a wiser man than thou wert."

So saying, he borrowed the student's nag to ride home upon, and trotted off as fast as he could, for fear the villains should return; and he left the poor student to gather wisdom, till somebody should come and let him down, when he had found out in which posture he was wisest,—on his head or his heels.

THE FORBIDDEN ROOM

ONCE upon a time there was a wizard, who changed himself into the form of a poor man, and went about begging from house to house and carrying away all the pretty girls he could find. No one ever knew what became of them, for when they had once disappeared they were never seen again.

One day he went to the door of a man who had three beautiful daughters, looking just like a feeble old beggar, with a basket slung over his shoulder, as if he were collecting the scraps given to him out of charity. He asked for a morsel of food; the eldest girl came out and handed him a piece of bread, and as she did so, he gave her one little touch, and she was at once obliged to jump into his basket.

He then hurried off with long strides and carried her to his house in the middle of a dark wood. Everything in the house was magnificent, and she had but to express a wish for anything and he gave it her at once. " You are happy here with me, dearest one, are you not? " he said; " for you have everything that your heart can wish for." This went on for some days, and then he told her that he must go away and leave her alone for a little while.

" Here are the house-keys," he said. " You can go where you like, and look at what you like; there is only one room into which I forbid you to enter on pain of death; this little key belongs to it."

He also gave her an egg, and begged her to take great care of it. " Always carry it about with you, if possible," he added, " for if it were to be lost, a great misfortune would happen."

She took the keys and the egg, and promised to carry

out his wishes.

As soon as he had left she went over the house, looking at everything from top to bottom. The rooms shone with silver and gold, and she thought she had never before seen anything so splendid. At last she found herself close to the forbidden room, and was going to pass it, when her curiosity became too much for her, and she paused. First she looked at the key—it did not seem to her to be in any way different to the others; then she put it in the lock and gave it a little turn, and—the door flew open. But what a sight met her eyes as she stepped inside! There in the middle of the room stood a block, and on it lay a glittering axe, and all around there was blood upon the floor and the bodies of those who had been seized and cruelly murdered. She was so terrified that she let the egg she held in her hand fall to the ground. She picked it up and saw that there was blood upon it; she tried to wipe it off, but in vain, for rub and scrape as she would, the mark of the blood still remained.

Not long after this, the man returned, and the first things he asked for were the key and the egg. Trembling with fear, she gave them to him, but he knew at once when he saw the mark on the egg, that she had been into the forbidden room. "Since you have been into that room," he cried, "against my will, you shall now go there again against your own. Your life is ended." With these words he threw her to the ground, and dragging her by her hair to where the block stood, he cut off her head and her limbs, so that her blood flowed over the floor, and there he left her with the bodies of his other victims.

"I will now go and fetch the second one," he said; and once again he went to the same house, begging like a poor old man. The second daughter brought him a piece of bread, and he caught her and carried her away as he had the eldest one.

She did not meet with any better fate than her sister; for she was also overcome by her curiosity and looked into the forbidden room, and had to pay for it with her life on the man's return.

He next went and carried away the third sister. Now this sister was wiser and more cunning than the others, and after the wizard had given her the key and the egg, and had left her, the first thing she did was to put the egg safely away. Then she looked over the house, and, finally, went into the forbidden room. Alas! what did she see! her two dear sisters lying murdered and cut to pieces. But she took the head and the body, and the arms and the legs, of each, and put them carefully together, and she had no sooner done this than the limbs began to move, and the different parts became joined to one another, and both sisters opened their eyes and were alive again. Then they kissed and embraced each other in their great joy.

As soon as the wizard returned he asked for the key and the egg, and when he saw that there was no trace of blood upon this, he said, " You have stood the test, you shall be my wife."

He had now lost all power over her, and was obliged in his turn to do whatever she wished.

" Very well," she answered, " but you must first take a basketful of gold to my father and mother, and carry it to them yourself; meanwhile I will prepare for our marriage."

Then she ran to the little room where she had hidden her sisters, and cried, " The moment has come for me to save you; the villain shall carry you home himself; but be sure you send someone to help me as soon as you get there." She put them both in a basket and covered them with gold, so that nothing of them could be seen. Then she called the wizard, and said to him, " Now carry away this basket, and mind you do not stop on the way to rest, for I shall be watching you from my little window." The wizard slung the basket over his shoulder and went off, but he found it such a weight to carry that the perspiration ran down his face, and he felt ready to die of exhaustion. He longed so to rest, that he stopped and sat down, but immediately a voice called out from the basket, " I am watching from my little window; I can see you stopping to rest; will you please to go on! " He thought it was his bride calling after him, so he got up and went on. Presently he sat down again, but the same voice called out, " I am watching you from my little window; I can see you stopping to rest; will you please to go on at once! " And as often as he stopped to rest, he heard the same voice, so that he was obliged to go on till, gasping for breath, he had carried the girls and the gold into the parents' house.

At home, meanwhile, the bride was preparing for the wedding festivities. She took one of his victims' heads, put a smart head-dress and wreath of flowers upon it, and placed it looking out of the garret window. She then invited all the wedding-guests, and when that was done, she got into a barrel of honey, and then cut open a bed and rolled herself in the feathers, so that she looked like some wonderful bird, and no one would have known who she was. Then she left the house, and as she went along she met some of the wedding guests, who said—

"Fitcher's bird, whence come you I pray?
I come from Fitcher's house to-day,
And what is the young bride doing now?
She has swept the house, all round and about,
And sits at her window looking out."

By and by she met the bridegroom returning, and he also said—

"Fitcher's bird, whence come you I pray?
I come from Fitcher's house to-day,
And what is the young bride doing now?
She has swept the house, all round and about,
And sits at her window looking out."

The bridegroom looked up and saw the head at the window, and thinking it was his bride, he nodded and smiled at it. But no sooner were he and his guests assembled in the house, than the friends arrived who had been sent by the sisters. They locked all the doors, so that no one might escape, and then set fire to the house, and the wizard and all his companions were burnt to death.

TOM THUMB

A POOR woodman sat in his cottage one night, smoking his pipe by the fireside, while his wife sat by his side spinning. "How lonely it is, wife," said he, as he puffed out a long curl of smoke, "for you and me to sit here by ourselves, without any children to play about and amuse us, while other people seem so happy and merry with their children!" "What you say is very true," said the wife, sighing, and turning round her wheel; "how happy should I be if I had but one child! If it were ever so small—nay, if it were no bigger than my thumb—I should be very happy, and love it dearly." Now—odd as you may think it—it came to pass that this good woman's wish was fulfilled, just in the very way she had wished it; for, not long afterwards, she had a little boy, who was quite healthy and strong, but was not much bigger than my thumb. So they said, "Well, we cannot say we have not got what we wished for, and, little as he is, we will love him dearly." And they called him Thomas Thumb.

They gave him plenty of food, yet for all they could do he never grew bigger, but kept just the same size as he had been when he was born. Still his eyes were sharp and sparkling, and he soon showed himself to be a clever little fellow, who always knew well what he was about.

One day, as the woodman was getting ready to go into the wood to cut fuel, he said, "I wish I had some one to bring the cart after me, for I want to make haste." "Oh, father," cried Tom, "I will take care of that; the cart shall be in the wood by the time you want it." Then the woodman laughed, and said, "How can that be? you cannot reach up to the horse's bridle." "Never mind that, father," said Tom; "if my mother will only harness the horse, I will get into his ear and tell him which way to go." "Well," said the father, "we will try for once."

When the time came the mother harnessed the horse to the cart, and put Tom into his ear; and as he sat there the little man told the beast how to go, crying out, "Go on!" and "Stop!" as he wanted: and thus the horse went on just as well as if the woodman had driven it himself into the wood. It happened that as the horse was going a little too fast, and Tom was calling out, "Gently! gently!" two strangers came up. "What an odd thing that is!" said one; "there is a cart going along, and I hear a carter talking to the horse, but yet I can see no one." "That is queer, indeed," said the other; "let us follow the cart, and see where it goes." So they went on into the wood, till at last they came to the place where the woodman was. Then Tom Thumb, seeing his father, cried out, "See, father, here I am with the cart, all right and safe! now take me down!" So his father took hold of the horse with one hand, and with the other took his son out of the horse's ear, and put him down upon a straw, where he sat as merry as you please.

The two strangers were all this time looking on, and did not know what to say for wonder. At last one took the other aside, and said, "That little urchin will make our fortune, if we can get him, and carry him about from town to town as a show: we must buy him." So they went up to the woodman, and asked him what he would take for the little man; "He will be better off," said they, "with us than with you." "I won't sell him at all," said the father; "my own flesh and blood is dearer to me than all the silver and gold in the world." But Tom, hearing of the bargain they wanted to make, crept up his father's coat to his shoulder, and whispered in his ear, "Take the money, father, and let them have me; I'll soon come back to you."

So the woodman at last said he would sell Tom to the strangers for a large piece of gold, and they paid the price. "Where would you like to sit?" said one of them. "Oh, put me on the rim of your hat; that will be a nice gallery for me; I can walk about there, and see the country as we go along." So they did as he wished; and when Tom had taken leave of his father they took him away with them.

They journeyed on till it began to be dusky, and then the little man said, "Let me get down, I'm tired." So the man took off his hat, and put him down on a clod of earth, in a ploughed field by the side of the road. But Tom ran about amongst the furrows, and at last slipt into an old mouse-hole. "Good night, my masters!" said he; "I'm off! mind and look sharp after me the next time." Then they ran at once to the place, and poked the ends of their sticks into the mouse-hole, but all in vain; Tom only crawled farther and farther in; and at last it became quite dark, so that they were forced to go their way without their prize, as sulky as could be.

When Tom found they were gone, he came out of his hiding-place. "What dangerous walking it is," said he, "in this ploughed field! If I were to fall from one of these great clods, I should undoubtedly break my neck." At last, by good luck, he found a large empty snail-shell. "This is lucky," said he, "I can sleep here very well"; and in he crept.

Just as he was falling asleep, he heard two men passing by, chatting together; and one said to the other, "How can we rob that rich parson's house of his silver and gold?" "I'll tell you," cried Tom. "What noise was that?" said the thief, frightened; "I'm sure I heard some one speak." They stood still listening, and Tom said, "Take me with you, and I'll soon show you how to get the parson's money." "But where are you?" said they. "Look about on the ground," answered he, "and listen where the sound comes from." At last the thieves found him out, and lifted him up in their hands. "You little urchin!" they said, "what can you do for us?" "Why I can get between the iron window-bars of the parson's house, and throw you out whatever you want." "That's a good thought," said the thieves; "come along, we shall see what you can do."

When they came to the parson's house, Tom slipt through the window-bars into the room, and then called out as loud as he could bawl, "Will you have all that is here?" At this the thieves were frightened, and said,

"Softly, softly! Speak low, that you may not awaken anybody." But Tom seemed as if he did not understand them, and bawled out again, "How much will you have? shall I throw it all out?" Now the cook lay in the next room; and hearing a noise she raised herself up in her bed and listened. Meantime the thieves were frightened, and ran off a little way; but at last they plucked up their hearts, and said, "The little urchin is only trying to make fools of us." So they came back and whispered softly to him, saying, "Now let us have no more of your roguish jokes; but throw us out some of the money." Then Tom called out as loud as he could, "Very well! hold your hands! here it comes."

The cook heard this quite plain, so she sprang out of bed, and ran to open the door. The thieves ran off as if a wolf was at their tails; and the maid, having groped about and found nothing, went away for a light. By the time she came back, Tom had slipt off into the barn; and when she had looked about and searched every hole and corner, and found nobody, she went to bed, thinking she must have been dreaming with her eyes open.

The little man crawled about in the hay-loft, and at last found a snug place to finish his night's rest in; so he laid himself down, meaning to sleep till daylight, and then find his way home to his father and mother. But alas! how woefully was he undone! what crosses and sorrows happen to us all in this world! The cook got up early, before daybreak, to feed the cows; and going straight to the hay-loft, carried away a large bundle of hay, with the little man in the middle of it, fast asleep. He still, however, slept on, and did not awake till he found himself in the mouth of the cow; for the cook had put the hay into the cow's rick, and the cow had taken Tom up in a mouthful of it. "Good lack-a-day!" said he, "how came I to tumble into the mill?" But he soon found out where he really was; and was forced to have all his wits about him, that he might not get between the cow's teeth, and so be crushed to death. At last down he went into her stomach. "It is rather dark here," said he; they forgot to build windows in this room to let the sun in; a candle would be no bad thing."

Though he made the best of his bad luck, he did not like

his quarters at all; and the worst of it was, that more and more hay was always coming down, and the space left for him became smaller and smaller. At last he cried out as loud as he could, " Don't bring me any more hay! Don't bring me any more hay!"

The maid happened to be just then milking the cow; and hearing someone speak, but seeing nobody, and yet being quite sure it was the same voice that she had heard in the night, she was so frightened that she fell off her stool, and overset the milk-pail. As soon as she could pick herself up out of the dirt, she ran off as fast as she could to her master the parson, and said, " Sir, sir, the cow is talking!" But the parson said, " Woman, thou art surely mad!" However, he went with her into the cow-house, to try and see what was the matter.

Scarcely had they set their foot on the threshold, when Tom called out, " Don't bring me any more hay!" Then the parson himself was frightened; and thinking the cow was surely bewitched, told his man to kill her on the spot. So the cow was killed, and cut up; and the stomach, in which Tom lay, was thrown out upon a dunghill.

Tom soon set himself to work to get out, which was not a very easy task; but at last, just as he had made room to get his head out, fresh ill-luck befell him. A hungry wolf sprang out, and swallowed up the whole stomach, with Tom in it, at one gulp, and ran away.

Tom, however, was still not disheartened; and thinking the wolf would not dislike having some chat with him as he was going along, he called out, " My good friend, I can show you a famous treat." " Where's that?" said the wolf. " In such and such a house," said Tom, describing his own father's house: " you can crawl through the drain into the kitchen, and then into the pantry, and there you will find cakes, ham, beef, cold chicken, roast pig, apple-dumplings, and every thing that your heart can wish."

The wolf did not want to be asked twice; so that very night he went to the house and crawled through the drain into the kitchen, and then into the pantry, and ate and drank there to his heart's content. As soon as he had had enough he wanted to get away; but he had eaten so much that he could not go out by the same way that he came in.

This was just what Tom had reckoned upon; and now

he began to set up a great shout, making all the noise he could. "Will you be easy?" said the wolf: "you'll awaken everybody in the house if you make such a clatter." "What's that to me?" said the little man: "you have had your frolic, now I've a mind to be merry myself"; and he began again, singing and shouting as loud as he could.

The woodman and his wife being awakened by the noise, peeped through a crack in the door; but when they saw that a wolf was there, you may well suppose that they were sadly frightened; and the woodman ran for his axe, and gave his wife a scythe. "Do you stay behind," said the woodman, "and when I have knocked him on the head you must rip him up with the scythe." Tom heard all this said, and cried out, "Father, father! I am here, the wolf has swallowed me." And his father said, "Heaven be praised! we have found our dear child again"; and he told his wife not to use the scythe for fear she should hurt him. Then he aimed a great blow, and struck the wolf on the head, and killed him on the spot; and when he was dead they cut open his body, and set Tommy free. "Ah!" said the father, "what fears we have had for you!" "Yes, father," answered he: "I have travelled all over the world, I think, in one way or other, since we parted; and now I am very glad to come home and get fresh air again." "Why, where have you been?" said his father. "I have been in a mouse-hole,—and in a snail-shell,—and down a cow's throat,—and in the wolf's belly; and yet here I am again, safe and sound."

"Well," said they, "you are come back, and we will not sell you again for all the riches in the world."

Then they hugged and kissed their dear little son, and gave him plenty to eat and drink, for he was very hungry; and then they fetched new clothes for him for his old ones had been quite spoiled on his journey. So Master Thumb stayed at home with his father and mother, in peace; for though he had been so great a traveller, and had done and seen so many fine things, and was fond enough of telling the whole story, he always agreed that, after all,—There's no place like HOME!

THE DANCING SHOES

OVER the seas and far away there is a fine country that neither you nor I, nor anybody else that we know, ever saw; but a very great king once reigned there who had no son at all, but twelve most beautiful daughters. Now this king had no queen to help him to take care of all these twelve young ladies; and so you may well think that they gave him no little trouble. They slept in twelve beds, all in a row, in one room: and when they went to bed the king always went up, and shut and locked the door. But, for all this care that was taken of them, their shoes were every morning found to be quite worn through, as if they had been danced in all night; and yet nobody could find out how it happened, or where they could have been.

Then the king, you may be sure, was very angry at having to buy so many new shoes; and he made it known to all the land, that if anybody could find out where it was that the princesses danced in the night, he should have the one he liked best of the whole twelve for his wife, and should be king after his death; but that whoever tried, and could not, after three days and night, make out the truth, should be put to death.

A king's son soon came. He was well lodged and fed, and in the evening was taken to the chamber next to the one where the princesses lay in their twelve beds. There he was to sit and watch where they went to dance; and in order that nothing might pass without his hearing it, the door of his chamber was left open. But the prince soon fell asleep; and when he awoke in the morning, he found that the princesses had all been dancing, for the soles of their shoes were full of holes. The same thing happened the second and third nights: so the king soon had this young gentleman's head cut off.

After him came many others; but they had all the same luck, and lost their lives in the same way.

Now it chanced that an old soldier, who had been wounded in battle, and could fight no longer, passed through this country; and as he was travelling through a wood, he met a little old woman, who asked him where he was going. "I hardly know where I am going, or what I had better do," said the soldier; "but I think I should like very well to find out where it is that these princesses dance, about whom people talk so much; and then I might have a wife, and in time I might be a king, which would be a mighty pleasant sort of thing for me in my old days." "Well, well," said the old dame, nodding her head, "that is no very hard task: only take care not to drink the wine that one of the princesses will bring to you in the evening; and as soon as she leaves you, you must seem to fall fast asleep."

Then she gave him a cloak, and said, "As soon as you put that on you will become invisible; and you will then be able to follow the princesses wherever they go, without their being at all aware of it." When the soldier heard this he thought he would try his luck: so he went to the king, and said he was willing to undertake the task.

He was as well lodged as the others had been, and the king ordered fine royal robes to be given him; and when the evening came, he was led to the other chamber. Just as he was going to lie down, the eldest of the princesses brought him a cup of wine; but the soldier slily threw it all away, taking care not to drink a drop. Then he laid himself down on his bed, and in a little while began to snore very loud, as if he was fast asleep. When the twelve princesses heard this they all laughed heartily; and the eldest said, "This fellow, too, might have done a wiser thing than lose his life in this way!" Then they rose up and opened their drawers and boxes, and took out all their fine clothes, and dressed themselves at the glass; and put on the twelve pairs of new shoes that the king had just bought them, and skipped about as if they were eager to begin dancing. But the youngest said, "I don't know how it is, but though you are so happy, I feel very uneasy;

I am sure some mischance will befall us." "You simpleton!" said the eldest, "you are always afraid; have you forgotten how many kings' sons have already watched us in vain? As for this soldier, he had one eye shut already, when we came into the room; and even if I had not given him his sleeping draught he would have slept soundly enough."

When they were all ready, they went and looked at the soldier; but he snored on, and did not stir hand or foot: so they thought they were quite safe; and the eldest went up to her own bed, and clapped her hands, and the bed sank into the floor, and a trap door flew open. The soldier saw them going down through the trap-door, one after another, the eldest leading the way; and thinking he had no time to lose, he jumped up, put on the cloak which the old fairy had given him, and followed them. In the middle of the stairs he trod on the gown of the youngest, and she cried out, "All is not right; some one took hold of my gown." "You silly thing!" said the eldest; "it was nothing but a nail in the wall."

Then down they all went, and then ran along a dark walk, till they came to a door; and there they found themselves in a most delightful grove of trees; and the leaves were all of silver, and glittered and sparkled beautifully. The soldier wished to take away some token of the place; so he broke off a little branch, and there came a loud noise from the tree. Then the youngest daughter said again, "I am sure all is not right: did not you hear that noise? That never happened before." But the eldest said, "It is only the princes, who are shouting for joy at our approach."

They soon came to another grove of trees, where all the leaves were of gold; and afterwards to a third, where the leaves were all glittering diamonds. And the soldier broke a branch from each; and every time there came a loud noise, that made the youngest sister shiver with fear: but the eldest still said, it was only the princes, who were shouting for joy. So they went on till they came to a great lake; and at the side of the lake there lay twelve little boats, with twelve handsome princes in them, waiting for the princesses.

One of the princesses went into each boat, and as the

boats were very small the soldier hardly knew what to do. "My company will not be very agreeable to any of them," said he; "but, however, I must not be left behind": so he stepped into the same boat with the youngest. As they were rowing over the lake, the prince who was in the boat with the youngest princess and the soldier said, "I do not know how it is, but, though I am rowing with all my might, we get on very slowly, and I am quite tired: the boat seems very heavy to-day, especially at one end." "It is only the heat of the weather," said the princess; "I feel it very warm, too."

On the other side of the lake stood a fine illuminated castle, from which came the merry music of horns and trumpets. There they all landed, and went into the castle, and each prince danced with his princess; and the soldier, who was all the time invisible, danced with them too; and when any of the princesses had a cup of wine set by her, he drank it all up, so that when she put the cup to her mouth it was empty. At this, too, the youngest sister was sadly frightened; but the eldest always stopped her mouth. They danced on till three o'clock in the morning, and then all their shoes were worn out, so that they were forced to leave off. The princes rowed them back again over the lake; but this time the soldier sat himself in the boat by the eldest princess, and her friend too found it very hard work to row that night. On the other shore they all took leave, saying they would come again the next night.

When they came to the stairs, the soldier ran on before the princesses, and laid himself down; and as they came up slowly, panting for breath and very much tired, they heard him snoring in his bed, and said, "Now all is quite safe." Then they undressed themselves, put away their fine clothes, pulled off their shoes, and went to bed, and to sleep.

In the morning the soldier said nothing about what had happened, for he wished to see more of this sport. So he went again the second and third night, and every thing happened just as before, the princesses dancing each time till their shoes were worn to pieces, and then going home tired; but the third night the soldier carried away one of the golden cups, as a token of where he had been.

On the morning of the fourth day he was ordered to appear before the king; so he took with him the three branches and the golden cup. The twelve princesses stood listening behind the door, to hear what he would say, laughing within themselves to think how cleverly they had taken him in, as well as all the rest who had watched them. Then the king asked him, " Where do my twelve daughters dance at night? " and the soldier said, " With twelve princes in a castle under ground." So he told the king all that had happened, and showed him the three branches and the golden cup, that he had brought with him. On this the king called for the princesses, and asked them whether what the soldier said was true or not; and when they saw they were found out, and that it was of no use to deny what had happened, they said it was all true.

Then the king asked the soldier which of them he would choose for his wife: and he said, " I am not very young, so I think I had better take the eldest." And they were married that very day, and the soldier in due time was heir to the kingdom, after the king his father-in-law died; but what became of the other eleven princesses, or of the twelve princes, I never heard.

HANSEL AND GRETHEL

THERE was once a poor man, who was a woodman, and went every day to cut wood in the forest. One day as he went along, he heard a cry like a little child's: so he followed the sound, till at last he looked up a high tree, and on one of the branches sat a very little child. Now its mother had fallen asleep, and a vulture had taken it out of her lap and flown away with it, and left it on the tree. Then the woodcutter climbed up, took the little child down, and found it was a pretty little girl; and he said to himself, "I will take this poor child home, and bring her up with my own son Hansel." So he brought her to his cottage, and both grew up together: he called the little girl Grethel, and the two children were so very fond of each other that they were never happy but when they were together.

But the wodcutter became very poor, and had nothing in the world he could call his own; and indeed he had scarcely bread enough for his wife and the two children to eat. At last the time came when even that was all gone, and he knew not where to seek for help in his need. Then at night, as he lay on his bed, and turned himself here and there, restless and full of care, his wife said to him, "Husband, listen to me, and take the two children out early to-morrow morning; give each of them a piece of bread, and then lead them into the midst of the wood, where it is thickest, make a fire for them, and go away and leave them alone to shift for themselves, for we can no longer keep them here." "No, wife," said the husband, "I cannot find it in my heart to leave the children to the wild beasts of the forest; they would soon tear them to pieces." "Well, if you will not do as

I say," answered the wife, "we must all starve together." And she would not let him have any peace until he came into her hard-hearted plan.

Meantime the poor children too were lying awake restless, and weak from hunger, so that they heard all that Hansel's mother said to her husband. "Now," thought Grethel to herself, "it is all up with us": and she began to weep. But Hansel crept to her bedside, and said, "Do not be afraid, Grethel, I will find out some help for us." Then he got up, put on his jacket, and opened the door and went out.

The moon shone bright upon the little court before the cottage, and the white pebbles glittered like daisies on the green meadows. So he stooped down, and put as many as he could into his pocket, and then went back to the house. "Now, Grethel," said he, "rest in peace!" and he went to bed and fell fast asleep.

Early in the morning, before the sun had risen, the woodman's wife came and awoke them. "Get up, children," said she, "we are going into the wood; there is a piece of bread for each of you, but take care if it, and keep some for the afternoon." Grethel took the bread, and carried it in her apron, because Hansel had his pocket full of stones; and they made their way into the wood.

After they had walked on for a time, Hansel stood still and looked towards home; and after a while he turned again, and so on several times. Then his father said, "Hansel, why do you keep turning and lagging about so? move on a little faster." "Ah, father," answered Hansel, "I am stopping to look at my white cat, that sits on the roof, and wants to say good-bye to me." "You little fool!" said his mother, "that is not your cat; it is the morning sun shining on the chimney-top." Now Hansel had not been looking at the cat, but had all the while been lingering behind, to drop from his pocket one white pebble after another along the road.

When they came into the midst of the wood the woodman said, "Run about, children, and pick up some wood, and I will make a fire to keep us all warm." So they piled up a little heap of brushwood, and set it on fire; and as the flames burnt bright, the mother said, "Now set yourselves by the fire, and go to sleep, while we go and cut wood in the forest; be sure you wait till we come again and fetch you." Hansel and Grethel sat by the fireside till the afternoon, and then each of them ate their piece of bread. They fancied the woodman was still in the wood, because they thought they heard the blows of his axe; but it was a bough, which he had cunningly hung upon a tree, in such a way that the wind blew it backwards and forwards against the other boughs; and so it sounded as the axe does in cutting. Thus they waited till evening: but the woodman and his wife kept away, and no one came to fetch them.

When it was quite dark Grethel began to cry; but then Hansel said, "Wait awhile till the moon rises." And when the moon rose he took her by the hand, and there lay the pebbles along the ground, glittering like new pieces of money, and marking out the way. Towards morning they came again to the woodman's house, and he was glad in his heart when he saw the children again, for he had grieved at leaving them alone. His wife also seemed to be glad; but in her heart she was angry at it.

Not long afterwards there was again no bread in the house, and Hansel and Grethel heard the wife say to her husband, "The children found their way back once, and I took it in good part; but now there is only half a loaf of bread left for them in the house; to-morrow you must take them deeper into the wood, that they may not find their way out, or we shall all be starved." It grieved the husband in his heart to do as his selfish wife wished, and he thought it would be better to share their last morsel with the children; but as he had done as she said once, he did not dare now to say no. When the children heard all their plan, Hansel got up, and wanted to pick up pebbles as before; but when he came to the door, he found his mother had locked it. Still he comforted Grethel, and said, "Sleep in peace, dear Grethel! God is very kind, and will help us."

Early in the morning, a piece of bread was given to each of them, but still smaller than the one they had before. Upon the road Hansel crumbled his in his pocket and often stood still, and threw a crumb upon the ground. "Why do you lag so behind, Hansel?" said the woodman; "go your ways on before." "I am looking at my little dove that is sitting upon the roof, and wants to say good-bye to me." "You silly boy!" said the wife, "that is not your little dove; it is the morning sun, that shines on the chimney-top." But Hansel still went on crumbling his bread, and throwing it on the ground. And thus they went on still further into the wood, where they had never been before in all their life.

There they were again told to sit down by a large fire, and go to sleep; and the woodman and his wife said they would come in the evening and fetch them away. In the afternoon Hansel shared Grethel's bread, because he had strewed all his upon the road; but the day passed away, and evening passed away too, and no one came to the poor children. Still Hansel comforted Grethel, and said, "Wait till the moon rises; and then I shall be able to see the crumbs of bread which I have strewed, and they will show us the way home."

The moon rose; but when Hansel looked for the crumbs they were gone, for hundreds of little birds in the wood had found them and picked them up. Hansel, however, set out to try and find his way home; but they soon lost themselves in the wilderness, and went on through the night and all the next day, till at last they laid down and fell asleep for weariness. Another day they went on as before, but still did not come to the end of the wood; and they were as hungry as could be, for they had had nothing to eat.

In the afternoon of the third day they came to a strange little hut, made of bread, with a roof of cake, and windows of barley-suger. "Now we will sit down and eat till we have had enough," said Hansel; "I will eat off the roof for my share; do you eat the windows, Grethel, they will be nice and sweet for you." Whilst Grethel, however, was picking at the barley-sugar, a pretty voice called softly from within,

> "Tip, tap! who goes there?"

But the children answered,

> "The wind, the wind,
> That blows through the air!"

and went on eating. Now Grethel had broken out a round pane of the window for herself, and Hansel had torn off a large piece of cake from the roof, when the door opened, and a little old fairy came gliding out. At this Hansel and Grethel were so frightened, that they let fall what they had in their hands. But the old lady nodded to them, and said, "Dear children, where have you been wandering about? Come in with me; you shall have something good."

So she took them both by the hand, and led them into her little hut, and brought out plenty to eat,—milk and pancakes, with sugar, apples, and nuts; and then two beautiful little beds were got ready, and Grethel and Hansel laid themselves down, and thought they were in heaven. But the fairy was a spiteful one, and made her pretty sweetmeat house to entrap little children. Early in the morning, before they were awake, she went to their little beds; and though she saw the two sleeping and looking so sweetly, she had no pity on them, but was glad they were in her power. Then she took up Hansel, and fastened him up in a coop by himself, and when he awoke he found himself behind a grating, shut up safely, as chickens are; but she shook Grethel, and called out, "Get up, you lazy little thing, and fetch some water; and go into the kitchen, and cook something good to eat: your brother is shut up yonder; I shall first fatten him, and when he is fat, I think I shall eat him."

When the fairy was gone poor Grethel watched her time, and got up, and ran to Hansel, and told him what she had heard, and said, "We must run away quickly, for the old woman is a bad fairy, and will kill us." But Hansel said, "You must first steal away her fairy wand, that we may save ourselves if she should follow; and bring the pipe too that hangs up in her room." Then the little maiden ran back, and fetched the magic wand and the pipe, and away they went together; so when the old fairy came back and could see no one at home, she sprang in a great rage to the window, and looked out into the wide world (which she could do far and near), and a long way off she spied Grethel, running away with her dear Hansel. "You are already a great way off," said she; "but you will still fall into my hands."

Then she put on her boots, which walked several miles at a step, and scarcely made two steps with them before she overtook the children; but Grethel saw that the fairy was coming after them, and, by the help of the wand, turned her friend Hansel into a lake of water, and herself into a swan, which swam about in the middle of it. So the fairy sat herself down on the shore, and took a great deal of trouble to decoy the swan, and threw crumbs of bread to it; but it would not come near her, and she was forced to go home in the evening without taking her revenge. Then Grethel changed herself and Hansel back into their own forms once more, and they went journeying on the whole night, until the dawn of day: and then the maiden turned herself into a beautiful rose, that grew in the midst of a quickset hedge; and Hansel sat by the side.

The fairy soon came striding along. "Good piper," said she, "may I pluck yon beautiful rose for myself?" "O yes," answered he. "And then," thought he to himself, "I will play you a tune meantime." So when she had crept into the hedge in a great hurry, to gather the flower—for she well knew what it was,—he pulled out the pipe slily, and began to play. Now the pipe was a fairy pipe, and, whether they liked it or not, whoever heard it was obliged to dance. So the old fairy was forced to dance a merry jig, on and on without any rest, and without being able to reach the rose. And as he did not cease playing a moment, the thorns at length tore the clothes from off her body, and pricked her sorely, and there she stuck quite fast.

Then Grethel set herself free once more, and on they went; but she grew very tired, and Hansel said, "Now I will hasten home for help." And Grethel said, "I will stay here in the meantime, and wait for you." Then Hansel went away, and Grethel was to wait for him.

But when Grethel had staid in the field a long time, and found he did not come back, she became quite sorrowful, and turned herself into a little daisy, and thought to herself, "Some one will come and tread me under foot, and so my sorrows will end." But it so happened that, as a shepherd was keeping watch in the field, he saw the daisy; and thinking it very pretty, he took it home, placed it in a box in his room, and said, "I have never found so pretty a daisy before." From that time everything throve wonderfully at the shepherd's house. When he got up in the morning, all the household work was ready done; the room was swept and cleaned, the fire made, and the water fetched; and in the afternoon, when he came home, the table-cloth was laid, and a good dinner ready set for him. He could not make out how all this happened, for he saw no one in his house; and although it pleased him well enough, he was at length troubled to think how it could be, and went to a cunning woman who lived hard by, and asked her what he should do. She said, "There must be witchcraft in it; look out to-morrow morning early, and see if anything stirs about in the room: if it does, throw a white cloth at once over it, and then the witchcraft will be stopped." The shepherd did as she said, and the next morning saw the box open, and the daisy come out: then he sprang up quickly, and threw a white cloth over it: in an instant the spell was broken, and Grethel stood before him, for it was she who had taken care of his house for him; and she was so beautiful, that he asked her if she would marry him. She said, "No," because she wished to be faithful to her dear Hansel; but she agreed to stay, and keep house for him till Hansel came back.

Time passed on, and Hansel came back at last; for the spiteful fairy had led him astray, and he had not been able for a long time to find his way, either home or back to Grethel. Then he and Grethel set out to go home; but after travelling a long way, Grethel became tired, and she and Hansel laid themselves down to sleep in a fine old hollow tree that grew in a meadow by the side of the wood. But as they slept the fairy—who had got out of the bush at last—came by; and finding her wand was glad to lay hold of it, and at once turned poor Hansel into a fawn while he was asleep.

Soon after Grethel awoke, and found what had happened; and she wept bitterly over the poor creature; and the tears too rolled down her eyes, as he laid himself down beside her. Then she said, "Rest in peace, dear fawn; I will never, never leave thee." So she took off her golden necklace, and put it round his neck, and plucked some rushes, and plaited them into a soft string to fasten to it, and led the poor little thing by her side when she went to walk in the wood; and when they were tired they came back, and laid down to sleep by the side of the hollow tree, where they lodged at night: but nobody came near them except the little dwarfs that lived in the wood, and these watched over them while they were asleep.

At last one day they came to a little cottage; and Grethel having looked in, and seen that it was quite empty, thought to herself, " We can stay and live here." Then she went and gathered leaves and moss to make a soft bed for the fawn; and every morning she went out and plucked nuts, roots, and berries for herself, and sweet shrubs and tender grass for her friend; and it ate out of her hand, and was pleased, and played and frisked about her. In the evening, when Grethel was tired, and had said her prayers, she laid her head upon the fawn for her pillow, and slept; and if poor Hansel could but have his right form again, she thought they should lead a very happy life.

They lived thus a long while in the wood by themselves, till it chanced that the king of that country came to hold a great hunt there. And when the fawn heard all around the echoing of the horns, and the baying of the dogs, and the merry shouts of the huntsmen, he wished very much to go and see what was going on. " Ah, sister! sister!" said he, " let me go out into the wood, I can stay no longer." And he begged so long, that she at last agreed to let him go. " But," said she, " be sure to come to me in the evening; I shall shut up the door, to keep out those wild huntsmen; and if you tap at it and say, ' Sister, let me in!' I shall know you: but if you don't speak, I shall keep the door fast." Then away sprang the fawn, and frisked and bounded along in the open air. The king and his huntsmen saw the beautiful creature, and followed, but could not overtake him; for when they thought they were sure of their prize, he sprang over the bushes, and was out of sight at once.

As it grew dark he came running home to the hut and tapped, and said, " Sister, sister, let me in!" Then she opened the little door, and in he jumped, and slept soundly all night on his soft bed.

Next morning the hunt began again; and when he heard

the huntsmen's horns, he said, "Sister, open the door for me, I must go again." Then she let him out, and said, "Come back in the evening, and remember what you are to say." When the king and the huntsmen saw the fawn with the golden collar again, they gave him chase; but he was too quick for them. The chase lasted the whole day; but at last the huntsmen nearly surrounded him, and one of them wounded him in the foot, so that he became sadly lame, and could hardly crawl home. The man who had wounded him followed close behind, and hid himself, and heard the little fawn say, "Sister, sister, let me in!" upon which the door opened, and soon shut again. The huntsman marked all well, and went to the king and told him what he had seen and heard; then the king said, "To-morrow we will have another chase."

Grethel was very much frightened when she saw that her dear little fawn was wounded; but she washed the blood away, and put some healing herbs on it, and said, "Now go to bed, dear fawn, and you will soon be well again." The wound was so slight, that in the morning there was nothing to be seen of it; and when the horn blew, the little thing said, "I can't stay here, I must go and look on; I will take care that none of them shall catch me." But Grethel said, "I am sure they will kill you this time: I will not let you go." "I shall die of grief," said he, "if you keep me here; when I hear the horns, I feel as if I could fly." Then Grethel was forced to let him go: so she opened the door with a heavy heart, and he bounded out gaily into the wood.

When the king saw him, he said to his huntsmen, "Now chase him all day long, till you catch him; but let none of you do him any harm." The sun set, however, without their being able to overtake him, and the king called away the huntsmen, and said to the one who had watched, "Now come and show me the little hut." So they went to the door and tapped, and said, "Sister, sister, let me in!" Then the door opened, and the king went in, and there stood a maiden more lovely than any he had ever seen. Grethel was frightened to see that it was not her fawn, but a king with a golden crown that was come into her hut: however, he spoke kindly to her, and took her hand, and said, "Will you come with me to my castle, and be my wife?" "Yes," said the maiden, "I will go to your castle, but I cannot be your wife; and my fawn must go with me, I cannot part with that." "Well," said the king, "he shall come and live with you all your life, and want for nothing." Just then in sprang the little fawn; and his sister tied the string to his neck, and they left the hut in the wood together.

Then the king took Grethel to his palace, and on the way she told him all her story: and then he sent for the fairy, and made her change the fawn into Hansel again; and he and Grethel loved one another, and were married, and lived happily together all their days in the good king's palace.

GREAT FAIRY STORIES FROM THE ARABIAN NIGHTS

THE LOSS OF THE TALISMAN

SOON after his marriage Prince Camaralzaman dreamt one night that he saw his father Schahzaman on his death-bed, and heard him speak thus to his attendants: "My son, my son, whom I so tenderly loved, has abandoned me." He awoke with a great sigh, which aroused the princess, who asked him the cause of it. Next morning the princess went to her own father, and finding him alone kissed his hand and thus addressed herself to him: "Sir, I have a favour to beg of your majesty; it is that you will give me leave to go with the prince my husband to see King Schahzaman, my father-in-law."

"Daughter," replied the king, "though I shall be very sorry to part with you for so long a time, your resolution is worthy of you: go, child, I give you leave, but on condition that you stay no longer than a year in King Schahzaman's court."

The princess communicated the King of China's consent to Prince Camaralzaman, who was transported with joy to hear it.

The King of China gave orders for preparations to be made for the journey; and when all things were ready, he accompanied the prince and princess several days' journey on their way. They parted at length with great weeping on all sides: the king embraced them, and having desired the prince to be kind to his daughter, and to love her always, he left them to proceed on their journey, and, to divert his thoughts, hunted all the way home.

Prince Camaralzaman and the Princess Badoura travelled for about a month, and at last came to a meadow of great extent, planted with tall trees, forming an agreeable shade. The day being unusually hot, Camaralzaman thought it best to encamp there. They alighted in one of the finest spots, and the prince ordered his servants to pitch their tents, and went himself to give directions. The princess, weary with the fatigue of the journey, bade her women untie her girdle, which they laid down by her, and when she fell asleep, her attendants left her by herself.

Prince Camaralzaman having seen all things in order came to the tent where the princess was sleeping; he entered, and sat down without making any noise, intending to take a nap himself; but observing the princess's girdle lying by her, he took it up, and looked at the diamonds and rubies one by one. In doing this, he saw a little purse hanging to it, sewed neatly on to the stuff, and tied fast with a ribbon; he felt it, and found there was something solid inside it. Desirous to know what it was, he opened the purse, and took out a cornelian, engraven with unknown figures and characters. "This cornelian," said the prince to himself, "must be something very valuable, or my princess would not carry it with so much care." It was Badoura's talisman, which the Queen of China had given her daughter as a charm, to keep her, as she said, from any harm as long as she had it about her.

The prince, the better to look at the talisman, took it out to the light, the tent being dark; and while he was holding it up in his hand, a bird darted down from the air and snatched it away from him.

Imagine the concern and grief of Prince Camaralzaman when he saw the bird fly away with the talisman. He was more troubled at it than words can express, and cursed his unseasonable curiosity, by which his dear princess had lost a treasure that was so precious and so much valued by her.

The bird having got her prize settled on the ground not far off, with the talisman in her mouth. The prince drew near, in hopes she would drop it; but, as he approached, the bird took wing, and settled again on the ground further off. Camaralzaman followed, and the bird, having swallowed the talisman, took a further flight: the prince still followed; the further she flew, the more eager he grew in pursuing her. Thus the bird drew him along from hill to valley, and valley to hill all day, every step leading him further away from the field where he had left his camp and the Princess Badoura; and instead of perching at night on a bush where he might probably have taken her, she roosted on a high tree, safe from pursuit. The prince, vexed to the heart for taking so much pains to no purpose, thought of returning to the camp; "but," said he to himself, "which way shall I return? Shall I go down the hills and valleys which I passed over? Shall I wander in darkness? and will my strength bear me out? How dare I appear before my princess without her talisman?" Overwhelmed with such thoughts, and tired with the pursuit, he lay down under a tree, where he passed the night.

He awoke the next morning before the bird had left the tree, and, as soon as he saw her on the wing, followed her again that whole day, with no better success, eating nothing but herbs and fruits all the way. He did the same for ten days together, pursuing the bird, and keeping his eye upon her from morning to night, always lying under the tree where she roosted. On the eleventh day the bird continued flying, and came near a great city. When the bird came to the walls, she flew over them, and the prince saw no more of her; so he despaired of ever recovering the Princess Badoura's talisman.

Camaralzaman, whose grief was beyond expression, went into the city, which was built by the seaside, and had a fine port; he walked up and down the streets without knowing where he was, or where to stop. At last he came to the port, in as great uncertainty as ever what he should do. Walking along the river-side, he perceived the gate of a garden open, and an old gardener at work. The good man looked up and saw that he was a stranger and a Mussulman, so he asked him to come in, and to shut the door after him.

Camaralzaman entered, and, as the gardener bade him shut the door, demanded of the gardener why he was so cautious.

"Because," replied the old man, "I see you are a stranger newly arrived, and a Mussulman, and this city is inhabited for the most part by idolaters, who have a mortal aversion to us Mussulmans, and treat those few of us that are here with great barbarity. I suppose you did not know this, and it is a miracle that you have escaped as you have thus far, these idolaters being very apt to fall upon the Mussulmans that are strangers, or to draw them into a snare, unless those strangers know how to beware of them."

Camaralzaman thanked the honest gardener for his advice, and the safety he offered him in his house: he would have said more, but the good man interrupted him, saying, "You are weary, and must want to refresh yourself. Come in and rest." He conducted him into his little hut, and after the prince had eaten heartily of what he set before him, he requested him to relate how he came there.

Camaralzaman complied with his request, and when he had ended his story, he asked him which was the nearest way to the king his father's territories; "for it is in vain," said he, "for me to think of finding my princess where I left her, after wandering eleven days from the spot. Ah!" continued he, "how do I know she is alive?" and so saying, he burst into tears.

The gardener replied that there was no possibility of his going thither by land, the roads were so difficult and the journey so long; besides, he must necessarily pass through the countries of so many barbarous nations that he would never reach his father's. It was a year's journey from the city where he was to any country inhabited only by Mussulmans; the quickest passage for him would be to go to the Isle of Ebony, whence he might easily transport himself to the Isles of the Children of Khaledan: a ship sailed from the port every year to Ebony, and he might take that opportunity of returning to those islands. "The ship departed," said the gardener, "but a few days ago: if you had come a little sooner you might have taken your passage in it. If you will wait the year round until it makes the voyage again, and will stay with me in my house, such as it is, you will be as welcome to it as to your own."

Prince Camaralzaman was glad he had met with such a place of refuge, in a place where he had no acquaintances. He accepted the offer, and lived with the gardener till the time came that the ship was to sail to the Isle of Ebony. He spent his time in working all day in the garden, and all night in sighs, tears and complaints, thinking of his dear Princess Badoura.

We must leave him in this place, to return to the princess, whom we left asleep in her tent.

The princess slept a long time, and, when she awoke, wondered that Prince Camaralzaman was not with her; she called her women, and asked them if they knew where he was. They told her they saw him enter the tent, but did not see him go out again. While they were talking to her, she took up her girdle, found the little purse open, and the talisman gone. She did not doubt but that Camaralzaman had taken it to see what it was, and that he would bring it back with him. She waited for him impatiently till night, and could not imagine what made him stay away from her so long.

When it was quite dark, and she could hear no news of him, she fell into violent grief; she cursed the talisman, and the man that made it. She could not imagine how her talisman should have caused the prince's separation from her: she did not however lose her judgment, and came to a courageous decision as to what she should do.

She only and her women knew of the prince's being gone; for his men were asleep in their tents. The princess, fearing they would betray her if they had any knowledge of it, moderated her grief, and forbade her women to say or do anything that might create the least suspicion. She then laid aside her robe, and put on one of Prince Camaralzaman's, being so like him that next day, when she came out, his men took her for him.

She commanded them to pack up their baggage and begin their march; and when all things were ready, she ordered one of her women to go into her litter, she herself mounting on horseback, and riding by her side.

They travelled for several months by land and sea; the princess continuing the journey under the name of Camaralzaman. They took the Isle of Ebony on their way to the Isles of the Children of Khaledan. They went to the capital of the Isle of Ebony, where a king reigned whose name was Armanos. The persons who first landed gave out that the ship carried Prince Camaralzaman, who was returning from a long voyage and was driven in there by a storm, and the news of his arrival was presently carried to the court.

King Armanos, accompanied by most of his courtiers, went immediately to meet the prince, and met the princess just as she was landing, and going to the lodging that had been taken for her. He received her as the son of a king who was his friend, and conducted her to the palace, where an apartment was prepared for her and all her attendants, though she would fain have excused herself, and have lodged in a private house. He showed her all possible honour, and entertained her for three days with extraordinary magnificence. At the end of this time, King Armanos, understanding that the princess, whom he still took for Prince Camaralzaman, talked of going on board again to proceed on her voyage, charmed with the air and qualities of such an accomplished prince as he took her to be, seized an opportunity when she was alone, and spoke to her in this manner: "You see, prince, that I am old, and cannot hope to live long; and, to my great mortification, I have not a son to whom I may leave my crown. Heaven has only blest me with one daughter, the Princess Haïatalnefous whose beauty cannot be better matched than with a prince of your rank and accomplishments. Instead of going home, stay and marry her from my hand, with my crown, which I resign in your favour. It is time for me to rest, and nothing could be a greater pleasure to me in my retirement than to see my people ruled by so worthy a successor to my throne."

The King of the Isle of Ebony's generous offer to bestow his only daughter in marriage, and with her his kingdom, on the Princess Badoura, put her into unexpected perplexity. She thought it would not become a princess of her rank to undeceive the king, and to own that she was not Prince Camaralzaman, but his wife, when she had assured him that she was he himself, whose part she had hitherto acted so well. She was also afraid to refuse the honour he offered her, lest, as he was much bent upon the marriage, his kindness might turn to aversion and hatred, and he might attempt something even against her life. Besides, she was not sure whether she might not find Prince Camaralzaman in the court of King Schahzaman his father.

These considerations, added to the prospect of obtaining a kingdom for the prince her husband, in case she found him again, determined her to accept the proposal of King Armanos, and marry his daughter; so after having stood silent for some minutes, she with blushes, which the king took for a sign of modesty, answered, "Sir, I am infinitely obliged to your majesty for your good opinion of me, for the honour you do me, and the great favour you offer me, which I cannot pretend to merit, and dare not refuse.

"But, sir," continued she, "I cannot accept this great alliance on any other condition than that your majesty will assist me with your counsel, and that I do nothing without first having your approbation."

The marriage treaty being thus concluded and agreed on, the ceremony was put off till next day. In the mean time Princess Badoura gave notice to her officers, who still took her for Prince Camaralzaman, of what she was going to do so that they might not be surprised at it, assuring them that the Princess Badoura consented. She talked also to her women, and charged them to continue to keep the secret.

The King of the Isle of Ebony, rejoicing that he had got a son-in-law so much to his satisfaction, next morning summoned his council, and acquainted them with his design of marrying his daughter to Prince Camaralzaman, whom he introduced to them; and having made him sit down by his side, told them he resigned the crown to the prince, and required them to acknowledge him for king, and swear fealty to him. Having said this, he descended from his throne, and the Princess Badoura, by his order, ascended it. As soon as the council broke up, the new king was proclaimed through the city, rejoicings were appointed for several days, and couriers despatched all over the kingdom to see the same ceremonies observed with the same demonstrations of joy.

As soon as they were alone, the Princess Badoura told the Princess Haïatalnefous the secret, and begged her to keep it, which she promised faithfully to do.

"Princess," said Haïatalnefous, "your fortune is indeed strange, that a marriage, so happy as yours was, should be shortened by so unaccountable an accident. Pray heaven you may meet with your husband again soon, and be sure that I will religiously keep the secret committed to me. It will be to me the greatest pleasure in the world to be the only person in the great kingdom of the Isle of Ebony who knows what and who you are, while you go on governing the people as happily as you have begun. I only ask of you at present to be your friend." Then the two princesses tenderly embraced each other, and after a thousand expressions of mutual friendship lay down to rest.

While these things were taking place in the court of the Isle of Ebony, Prince Camaralzaman stayed in the city of idolaters with the gardener, who had offered him his house till the ship sailed.

One morning when the prince was up early, and, as he used to do, was preparing to work in the garden, the gardener prevented him, saying, "This day is a great festival among the idolaters, and because they abstain from all work themselves, so as to spend the time in their assemblies and public rejoicings, they will not let the Mussulmans work. Their shows are worth seeing. You will have nothing to do to-day: I leave you here. As the time approaches in which the ship is accustomed to sail for the Isle of Ebony, I will go and see some of my friends, and secure you a passage in it." The gardener put on his best clothes, and went out.

When Prince Camaralzaman was alone, instead of going out to take part in the public joy of the city, the solitude he was in brought to his mind, with more than usual violence, the loss of his dear princess. He walked up and down the garden sighing and groaning, till the noise which two birds made on a neighbouring tree tempted him to lift up his head, and stop to see what was the matter.

Camaralzaman was surprised to behold a furious battle between these two birds, fighting one another with their beaks. In a very little while one of them fell down dead at the foot of a tree; the bird that was victorious took wing again, and flew away.

In an instant, two other large birds, that had seen the fight at a distance, came from the other side of the garden, and pitched on the ground, one at the feet and the other at the head of the dead bird: they looked at it some time, shaking their heads in token of grief; after which they dug a grave with their talons, and buried it. When they had filled up the grave with the earth they flew away, and returned in a few minutes, bringing with them the bird that had committed the murder, the one holding one of its wings in its beak, and the other one of its legs; the criminal all the while crying out in a doleful manner, and struggling to escape. They carried it to the grave of the bird which it had lately sacrificed to its rage, and there sacrificed it in just revenge for the murder it had committed. They killed the murderer with their beaks. They then opened it, tore out the entrails, left the body on the spot unburied, and flew away.

Camaralzaman remained in great astonishment all the time that he stood beholding this sight. He drew near the tree, and casting his eyes on the scattered entrails of the bird that was last killed, he spied something red hanging out of its body. He took it up, and found it was his beloved Princess Badoura's talisman, which had cost him so much pain and sorrow and so many sighs since the bird snatched it out of his hand. "Ah, cruel monster!" said he to himself, still looking at the bird, "thou tookest delight in doing mischief, so I have the less reason to complain of that which thou didst to me: but the greater it was, the more do I wish well to those that revenged my quarrel on thee, in punishing thee for the murder of one of their own kind."

It is impossible to express Prince Camaralzaman's joy: "Dear princess," continued he to himself, "this happy minute, which restores to me a treasure so precious to thee, is without doubt a presage of our meeting again, perhaps even sooner than I think."

So saying, he kissed the talisman, wrapped it up in a ribbon, and tied it carefully about his arm. Till now he had been almost every night a stranger to rest, his trouble always keeping him awake, but the next night he slept soundly: he rose somewhat later the next morning than he was accustomed to, put on his working clothes, and went to the gardener for orders. The good man made him root up an old tree which bore no fruit.

Camaralzaman took an axe and began his work. In cutting off a branch of the root, he found that his axe struck against something that resisted the blow and made a great noise. He removed the earth, and discovered a broad plate of brass, under which was a staircase of ten steps. He went down, and at the bottom saw a cavity about six yards square, with fifty brass urns placed in order around it, each with a cover over it. He opened them all, one after another, and there was not one of them which was not full of gold-dust. He came out of the cave, rejoicing that he had found such a vast treasure: he put the brass plate over the staircase, and rooted up the tree against the gardener's return.

The gardener had learned the day before that the ship which was bound for the Isle of Ebony would sail in a few days, but the exact time was not yet fixed. His friend promised to let him know the day, if he called upon him on the morrow; and while Camaralzaman was rooting up the tree, he went to get his answer. He returned with a joyful countenance, by which the prince guessed that he brought him good news. "Son," said the old man (so he always called him, on account of the difference of age between him and the prince), "be joyful, and prepare to embark in three days, for the ship will then certainly set sail: I have arranged with the captain for your passage."

"In my present situation," replied Camaralzaman, "you could not bring me more agreeable news; and in return, I have also tidings that will be as welcome to you; come along with me, and you shall see what good fortune heaven has in store for you."

The prince led the gardener to the place where he had rooted up the tree, made him go down into the cave, and when he was there showed him what a treasure he had discovered, and thanked Providence for rewarding his virtue, and the labour he had done for so many years.

"What do you mean?" replied the gardener: "do you imagine I will take these riches as mine? They are yours: I have no right to them. For fourscore years, since my father's death, I have done nothing but dig in this garden, and could not discover this treasure, which is a sign that it was destined for you, since you have been permitted to find it. It suits a prince like you, rather than me: I have one foot in the grave, and am in no want of anything. Providence has bestowed it upon you, just when you are returning to that country which will

PRINCE CAMARALZAMAN DISCOVERS THE CAVE.

one day be your own, where you will make a good use of it."

Prince Camaralzaman would not be outdone in generosity by the gardener. They had a long dispute about it. At last the prince solemnly protested that he would have none of it unless the gardener would divide it with him and take half. The good man, to please the prince, consented, so they parted it between them, and each had twenty-five urns.

Having thus divided it, "Son," said the gardener to the prince, "it is not enough that you have got this treasure; we must now contrive how to carry it so privately on board the ship that nobody may know anything of the matter, otherwise you will run the risk of losing it. There are no olives in the Isle of Ebony, and those that are exported thence are wanted there; you know I have plenty of them; take what you will; fill fifty pots, half with the gold dust, and half with olives, and I will get them carried to the ship when you embark."

Camaralzaman followed this good advice, and spent the rest of the day in packing up the gold and the olives in the fifty pots, and fearing lest the talisman, which he wore on his arm, might be lost again, he carefully put it into one of the pots, marking it with a particular mark, to distinguish it from the rest. When they were all ready to be shipped, the prince retired with the gardener, and talking together, he related to him the battle of the birds, and how he had found the Princess Badoura's talisman again. The gardener was equally surprised and joyful to hear it for his sake.

Whether the old man was quite worn out with age, or had exhausted himself too much that day, he had a very bad night; he grew worse the next day, and on the third day, when the prince was to embark, was so ill that it was plain he was near his end. As soon as day broke, the Captain of the ship came in person with several seamen to the gardener's; they knocked at the garden-door, and Camaralzaman opened it to them. They asked him where the passenger was that was to go with him. The prince answered, "I am he; the gardener who arranged with you for my passage is ill, and cannot be spoken with; come in, and let your men carry those one day be your own, where you will make a good use of it."

Prince Camaralzaman would not be outdone in generosity by the gardener. They had a long dispute about it. At last the prince solemnly protested that he would have none of it, unless the gardener would divide it with him and take half. The good man, to please the prince, consented; so they parted it between them, and each had twenty-five urns.

Having thus divided it, "Son," said the gardener to the prince, "it is not enough that you have got this treasure; we must now contrive how to carry it so privately on board the ship that nobody may know anything of the matter, otherwise you will run the risk of losing it. There are no olives in the Isle of Ebony, and those that are exported hence are wanted there; you know I have plenty of them; take what you will; fill fifty pots, half with the gold dust, and half with olives, and I will get them carried to the ship when you embark."

Camaralzaman followed this good advice, and spent the rest of the day in packing up the gold and the olives in the fifty pots, and fearing lest the talisman, which he wore on his arm, might be lost again, he carefully put it into one of the pots, marking it with a particular mark, to distinguish it from the rest. When they were all ready to be shipped, the prince retired with the gardener, and talking together, he related to him the battle of the birds, and how he had found the Princess Badoura's talisman again. The gardener was equally surprised and joyful to hear it for his sake.

Whether the old man was quite worn out with age, or had exhausted himself too much that day, he had a very bad night; he grew worse the next day, and on the third day, when the prince was to embark, was so ill that it was plain he was near his end. As soon as day broke, the captain of the ship came in person with several seamen to the gardener's; they knocked at the garden-door, and Camaralzaman opened it to them. They asked him where the passenger was that was to go with him. The prince answered, "I am he; the gardener who arranged with you for my passage is ill, and cannot be spoken with: come in, and let your men carry those pots of olives and my baggage aboard. I will only take leave of the gardener, and follow you."

The seamen took up the pots and the baggage, and the captain bade the prince make haste, for the wind being fair they were waiting for nothing but him.

When the captain and his men were gone, Camaralzaman went to the gardener, to take leave of him, and thank him for all his good offices: but he found him in the agonies of death, and had scarcely time to bid him rehearse the articles of his faith, which all good Mussulmans do before they die, when the gardener expired in his presence.

The prince being under the necessity of embarking immediately hastened to pay the last duty to the deceased. He washed his body, buried him in his own garden (for the Mahometans had no cemetery in the city of the idolaters, where they were only tolerated), and as he had nobody to assist him it was almost evening before he had put him in the ground. As soon as he had done it he ran to the waterside, carrying with him the key of the garden, intending, if he had time, to give it to the landlord; otherwise to deposit it in some trusty person's hand before a witness, that he might leave it when he was gone. When he came to the port, he was told the ship had sailed several hours before he came and was already out of sight. It had waited three hours for him, and the wind standing fair, the captain dared not stay any longer.

It is easy to imagine that Prince Camaralzaman was exceedingly grieved to be forced to stay longer in a country where he neither had nor wished to have any acquaintance: to think that he must wait another twelvemonth for the opportunity he had lost. But the greatest affliction of all was his having let go the Princess Badoura's talisman, which he now gave over for lost. The only course that was left for him to take was to return to the garden to rent it of the landlord, and to continue to cultivate it by himself, deploring his misery and misfortunes. He hired a boy to help him to do some part of the drudgery; and that he might not lose the other half of the treasure, which came to him by the death of the gardener, who died without heirs, he put the gold-dust into fifty other pots, which he filled up with olives, to be ready against the time of the ship's return.

While Prince Camaralzaman began another year of labour, sorrow and impatience, the ship, having a fair wind, continued her voyage to the Isle of Ebony, and happily arrived at the capital.

The palace being by the sea-side, the new king, or rather the Princess Badoura, espying the ship as she was entering the port, with all her flags flying, asked what vessel it was; she was told that it came anually from the city of the idolaters, and was generally richly laden.

The princess, who always had Prince Camaralzaman in her mind amidst the glories which surrounded her, imagined that the prince might be on board, and resolved to go down to the ship and meet him. Under pretence of inquiring what merchandise was on board, and having the first sight of the goods, and choosing the most valuable, she commanded a horse to be brought, which she mounted, and rode to the port, accompanied by several officers in waiting, and arrived at the port just as the captain came ashore. She ordered him to be brought before her, and asked whence he came, how long he had been on his voyage, and what good or bad fortune he had met with: if he had any stranger of quality on board, and particularly with what his ship was laden.

The captain gave a satisfactory answer to all her demands; and as to passengers, assured her that there were none but merchants in his ship, who were used to come every year and bring rich stuffs from several parts of the world to trade with, the finest linens painted and plain, diamonds, musk, ambergris, camphor, civet, spices, drugs, olives, and many other articles.

The Princess Badoura loved olives extremely: when she heard the captain speak of them, she said, " Land them, I will take them off your hands: as to the other goods, tell the merchants to bring them to me, and let me see them before they dispose of them, or show them to any one else."

The captain, taking her for the King of the Isle of Ebony, replied, " Sire, there are fifty great pots of olives, but they belong to a merchant whom I was forced to leave behind. I gave him notice myself that I was waiting for him, and waited a long time; but as he did not come, and the wind was good, I was afraid of losing it, and so set sail."

The princess answered, "No matter; bring them ashore; we will make a bargain for them."

The captain sent his boat aboard, and in a little time it returned with the pots of olives. The princess demanded how much the fifty pots might be worth in the Isle of Ebony. "Sir," said the captain, "the merchant is very poor, and your majesty will do him a singular favour if you give him a thousand pieces of silver."

"To satisfy him," replied the princess, "and because you tell me he is poor, I will order you a thousand pieces of gold for him, which do you take care to give him." The money was accordingly paid, and the pots carried to the palace in her presence.

Night was drawing on when the princess withdrew into the inner palace, and went to the Princess Haïatalnefous' apartment, ordering the fifty pots of olives to be brought thither. She opened one, to let the Princess Haïatalnefous taste them, and poured them into a dish. Great was her astonishment when she found the olives mingled with gold-dust. "What can this mean?" said she, "it is wonderful beyond comprehension." Her curiosity increasing, she ordered Haïatalnefous' women to open and empty all the pots in her presence; and her wonder was still greater, when she saw that the olives in all of them were mixed with gold-dust; but when she saw her talisman drop out of that into which the prince had put it, she was so surprised that she fainted away. The Princess Haïatalnefous and her women restored the Princess Badoura by throwing cold water on her face. When she recovered her senses, she took the talisman and kissed it again and again; but not being willing that the Princess Haïatalnefous' women, who were ignorant of her disguise, should hear what she said, she dismissed them.

"Princess," said she to Haïatalnefous, as soon as they were gone, "you, who have heard my story, surely guessed that it was at the sight of the talisman that I fainted. This is the talisman, the fatal cause of my losing my dear husband Prince Camaralzaman; but as it was that which caused our separation, so I foresee it will be the means of our meeting again soon."

The next day, as soon as it was light, she sent for the captain of the ship; and when he came she spoke to him thus: "I want to know something more of the merchant to whom the olives belong, that I bought of you yesterday. I think you told me you had left him behind you in the city of the idolaters: can you tell me what he is doing there?"

"Yes, sire," replied the captain, "I can speak on my own knowledge. I arranged for his passage with a very old gardener, who told me I should find him in his garden, where he worked under him. He showed me the place, and for that reason I told your majesty he was poor. I went there to call him. I told him what haste I was in, spoke to him myself in the garden, and cannot be mistaken in the man."

"If what you say is true," replied the Princess Badoura, "you must set sail this very day for the city of idolaters, and fetch me that gardener's man, who is my debtor; else I will not only confiscate all your goods and those of your merchants, but your and their lives shall answer for his. I have ordered my seal to be put on the warehouses where they are, which shall not be taken off till you bring me that man. This is all I have to say to you; go, and do as I command you."

The captain could make no reply to this order, the disobeying of which would be a very great loss to him and his merchants. He told them about it, and they hastened him away as fast as they could after he had laid in a stock of provisions and fresh water for his voyage. They were so diligent, that he set sail the same day. He had a prosperous voyage to the city of the idolaters, where he arrived in the night. When he was as near to the city as he thought convenient, he would not cast anchor, but let the ship ride off the shore; and going into his boat, with six of his stoutest seamen, he landed a little way off the port, whence he went directly to Camaralzaman's garden.

Though it was about midnight when he arrived there, the prince was not asleep. His separation from the fair Princess of China his wife afflicted him as usual. He cursed the minute in which his curiosity tempted him to touch the fatal girdle.

Thus did he pass those hours which are devoted to rest, when he heard somebody knock at the garden door. He ran hastily to it, half-dressed as he was; but he had no sooner opened it, than the captain and his seamen took hold of him, and carried him by force on board the boat, and so to the ship, and as soon as he was safely lodged, they set sail immediately, and made the best of their way to the Isle of Ebony.

Hitherto Camaralzaman, the captain, and his men had not said a word to one another; at last the prince broke silence, and asked the captain, whom he recognised, why they had taken him away by force? The captain in his turn demanded of the prince whether he was not a debtor of the King of Ebony?

" I the King of Ebony's debtor! " replied Camaralzaman in amazement; " I do not know him, I never had anything to do with him in my life, and never set foot in his kingdom."

The captain answered, " You should know that better than I; you will talk to him yourself in a little while: till then, stay here and have patience."

Though it was night when he cast anchor in the port, the captain landed immediately, and taking Prince Camaralzaman with him hastened to the palace, where he demanded to be introduced to the king.

The Princess Badoura had withdrawn into the inner palace; however, as soon as she had heard of the captain's return and Camaralzaman's arrival, she came out to speak to him. As soon as she set her eyes on the prince, for whom she had shed so many tears, she knew him in his gardener's clothes. As for the prince, who trembled in the presence of a king, as he thought her, to whom he was to answer for an imaginary debt, it did not enter into his head that the person whom he so earnestly desired to see stood before him. If the princess had followed the dictates of her inclination, she would have run to him and embraced him, but she put a constraint on herself, believing that it was for the interest of both that she should act the part of a king a little longer before she made herself known. She contented herself for the present with putting him into the hands of an officer, who was then in waiting, with a charge to take care of him till the next day.

When the Princess Badoura had provided for Prince Camaralzaman, she turned to the captain, whom she was now to reward for the important service he had done her. She commanded another officer to go immediately and take the seal off the warehouse where his and his merchants' goods were, and gave him a rich diamond, worth much more than the expense of both his voyages. She bade him besides keep the thousand pieces of gold she had given him for the pots of olives, telling him she would make up the account with the merchant herself.

This done, she retired to the Princess of the Isle of Ebony's apartment, to whom she communicated her joy, praying her to keep the secret still. She told her how she intended to manage to reveal herself to Prince Camaralzaman, and to give him the kingdom.

The Princess of the Isle of Ebony was so far from betraying her, that she rejoiced and entered fully into the plan.

The next morning the Princess of China ordered Prince Camaralzaman to be apparelled in the robes of an emir or governor of a province. She commanded him to be introduced into the council, where his fine person and majestic air drew all the eyes of the lords there present upon him.

The Princess Badoura herself was charmed to see him again, as handsome as she had often seen him, and her pleasure inspired her to speak the more warmly in his praise. When she addressed herself to the council, having ordered the prince to take his seat among the emirs, she spoke to them thus: "My lords, this emir whom I have advanced to the same dignity with you is not unworthy the place assigned him. I have known enough of him in my travels to answer for him, and I can assure you he will make his merit known to all of you."

Camaralzaman was extremely amazed to hear the King of the Isle of Ebony, whom he was far from taking for a woman, much less for his dear princess, name him, and declare that he knew him, while he thought himself certain that he had never seen him before in his life. He was much more surprised when he heard him praise him so excessively. Those praises, however, did not disconcert him, though he received them with such modesty as showed that he did not grow vain. He prostrated himself before the throne of the king, and rising again, " Sire," said he, " I want words to express my gratitude to your majesty for the honour you have done me: I shall do all in my power to render myself worthy of your royal favour."

From the council-board the prince was conducted to a palace, which the Princess Badoura had ordered to be fitted up for him; where he found offices and domestics ready to obey his commands, a stable full of fine horses, and everything suitable to the rank of an emir. Then the steward of his household brought him a strong box full of gold for his expenses.

The less he understood whence came his great good fortune, the more he admired it, but never once imagined that he owed it to the Princess of China.

Two or three days after, the Princess Badoura, that he might be nearer to her, and in a more distinguished post, made him high treasurer, which office had lately become vacant. He behaved himself in his new charge with so much integrity, yet obliging everybody, that he not only gained the friendship of the great but also the affections of the people, by his uprightness and bounty.

Camaralzaman would have been the happiest man in the world, if he had had his princess with him. In the midst of his good fortune he never ceased lamenting her, and grieved that he could hear no tidings of her, especially in a country where she must necessarily have come on her way to his father's court after their separation. He would have suspected something had the Princess Badoura still gone by the name of Camaralzaman, but on her accession to the throne she changed it, and took that of Armanos, in honour of the old king her father-in-law. She was now known only by the name of the young King Armanos. There were very few courtiers who knew that she had ever been called Camaralzaman, which name she assumed when she arrived at the court of the Isle of Ebony, nor had Camaralzaman so much acquaintance with any of them yet as to learn more of her history.

The princess fearing he might do so in time, and desiring that he should owe the discovery to herself only, resolved to put an end to her own torment and his; for she had observed that as often as she discoursed with him about the affairs of his office, he fetched such deep sighs as could be addressed to nobody but her. She herself also lived under such constraint that she could endure it no longer.

The Princess Badoura had no sooner made this decision with the Princess Haïatalnefous, than she took Prince Camaralzaman aside, saying, "I must talk with you about an affair, Camaralzaman, which requires much consideration, and on which I want your advice. Come hither in the evening, and leave word at home that you will not return; I will take care to provide you a bed."

Camaralzaman came punctually to the palace at the hour appointed by the princess; she took him with her into the inner apartment, and having told the chief chamberlain, who was preparing to follow her, that she had no occasion for his service, and that he should only keep the door shut, she took him into a different apartment.

When the prince and princess entered the chamber she shut the door, and, taking the talisman out of a little box, gave it to Camaralzaman, saying, "It is not long since an astrologer presented me with this talisman; you being skilful in all things, may perhaps tell me its use."

Camaralzaman took the talisman, and drew near a lamp to look at it. As soon as he recollected it, with an astonishment which gave the princess great pleasure, "Sire," said he to the princess, "your majesty asked me what this talisman is good for. Alas! it is only good to kill me with grief and despair, if I do not quickly find the most charming and lovely princess in the world to whom it belonged, whose loss it occasioned by a strange adventure, the very recital of which will move your majesty to pity such an unfortunate husband and lover, if you would have patience to hear it."

"You shall tell me that another time," replied the princess; "I am very glad to tell you I know something of it already; stay here a little, and I will return to you in a moment."

At these words she went into her dressing-room, put off her royal turban, and in a few minutes dressed herself like a woman; and having the girdle round her which she wore on the day of their separation, she entered the chamber.

Prince Camaralzaman immediately knew his dear

princess, ran to her, and tenderly embraced her, crying out, " How much I am obliged to the king, who has so agreeably surprised me! "

" Do not expect to see the king any more," replied the princess, embracing him in her turn, with tears in her eyes; " you see him in me: sit down, and I will explain this enigma to you."

They sat down, and the princess told the prince the resolution she came to, in the field where they encamped the last time they were together, as soon as she perceived that she waited for him to no purpose; how she went through with it till she arrived at the Isle of Ebony, where she had been obliged to marry the Princess Haïatalnefous, and accept the crown which King Armanos offered her as a condition of the marriage: how the princess, whose merit she highly extolled, had kept the secret, and how she found the talisman in the pots of olives mingled with the gold-dust, and how the finding it was the cause of her sending for him to the city of the idolaters.

The Princess Badoura and Prince Camaralzaman rose next morning as soon as it was light, but the princess would no more put on her royal robes as king; she dressed herself in the dress of a woman, and then sent the chief chamberlain to King Armanos, her father-in-law, to desire he would be so good as to come to her apartment.

When the king entered the chamber, he was amazed to see there a lady who was unknown to him, and the high treasurer with her, who was not permitted to come within the inner palace. He sat down and asked where the king was.

The princess answered, " Yesterday I was king, sir, and to-day I am the Princess of China, wife of the true Prince Camaralzaman, the true son of King Schahzaman. If your majesty will have the patience to hear both our stories, I hope you will not condemn me for putting an innocent deceit upon you." The king bade her go on, and heard her discourse from the beginning to the end with astonishment. The princess on finishing it said to him, " Sir, in our religion men may have several wives; if your majesty will consent to give your daughter the Princess Haïatalnefous in marriage to Prince Camaralzaman, I will with all my heart yield up to her the rank and quality of queen, which of right belongs to her, and content myself with the second place. If this precedence was not her due, I would, however, give it her, after she has kept my secret so generously."

King Armanos listened to the princess with astonishment, and when she had done, turned to Prince Camaralzaman, saying, " Son, since the Princess Badoura your wife, whom I have all along thought to be my son-in-law, through a deceit of which I cannot complain, assures me that she is willing, I have nothing more to do but to ask you if you are willing to marry my daughter and accept the crown, which the Princess Badoura would deservedly wear as long as she lived, if she did not quit it out love to you."

" Sir," replied Prince Camaralzaman, " though I desire nothing so earnestly as to see the king my father, yet the obligation I am under to your majesty and the Princess Haïatalnefous is so weighty, I can refuse her nothing." Camaralzaman was proclaimed king, and married the same day with all possible demonstrations of joy.

Not long afterwards they all resumed the long interrupted journey to the Isles of the Children of Khaledan, where they were fortunate enough to find the old King Schahzaman still alive and overjoyed to see his son once more; and after several months' rejoicing, King Camaralzaman and the two queens returned to the Island of Ebony, where they lived in great happiness for the remainder of their lives.

THE STORY OF ALI BABA AND THE FORTY THIEVES

PART I

IN a town in Persia, there lived two brothers, one named Cassim, the other Ali Baba. Their father left them no great property; though as he had divided it equally between them, their fortune should have been equal; but it was otherwise.

Cassim married a widow, who, soon after their marriage, became heiress to a large estate, and a good shop and warehouse full of rich merchandize; so that all at once he became one of the richest merchants, and lived at his ease.

Ali Baba, on the other hand, who married a woman as poor as himself, lived in a very mean dwelling, and had no other means of maintaining his wife and children than his daily labour in cutting wood in a forest near the town, and bringing it upon three asses to town to sell.

One day, when Ali Baba was in the forest, and had just cut wood enough to load his asses, he saw at a distance a great cloud of dust, which seemed to approach towards him: he observed it very attentively, and distinguished a large body of horse coming briskly on; and though they did not fear robbers in that country, Ali Baba began to think that they might prove such, and, without considering what might become of his asses, he resolved to save himself. He climbed up a large tree, whose branches, at a little distance from the ground, divided in a circular form so close to one another that there was but little space between them. He placed himself in the middle, from whence he could see all that passed without being seen. This tree stood at the bottom of a single rock, which was very high, and so steep and craggy that nobody could climb it.

The troop, who were all well mounted and well armed,

came to the foot of this rock, and there dismounted. Ali Baba counted forty of them, and by their looks never doubted that they were thieves; nor was he mistaken; for they were a troop of banditti, who, without doing any harm in the neighbourhood, robbed at a distance, and made that place their rendezvous. Every man unbridled his horse, and tied him to a shrub, and hung about his neck a bag of corn. Then each of them took his saddle-bags, which seemed to Ali Baba to be full of gold and silver by the weight. One, whom he took to be their captain, came with his saddle-bags on his back under the tree in which Ali Baba was hidden, and, making his way through some shrubs, pronounced these words, "Open, Sesame," so distinctly, that Ali Babi heard him. As soon as the captain of the robbers uttered these words, a door opened; and after he had made all his troop go in before him, he followed them, and the door shut again of itself.

The robbers stayed some time within the rock, and Ali Baba, who feared that some or all of them together might come out and catch him if he endeavoured to make his escape, was obliged to sit patiently in the tree. He was nevertheless tempted once or twice to get down and mount one of their horses, and, leading another, to drive his asses before him to the town with all the haste he could; but uncertainty made him choose the safest way.

At last the door opened again, and the forty robbers came out. As the captain went in last, so he came out first, and stood to see them all pass by; and then Ali Baba heard him make the door fast by pronouncing the words, "Shut, Sesame." Every man went and bridled his horse, fastened his saddle-bags, and mounted again; and when the captain saw them all ready, he put himself at their head, and they returned the way they came.

Ali Baba did not immediately quit his tree; "for," said he to himself, "they may have forgotten something and come back again, and then I shall be caught." He followed them with his eyes as far as he could see them; and after that waited some time before he came down. Remembering the words the captain of the robbers had made use of to cause the door to open and shut, he had the curiosity to try whether his pronouncing them would have the same effect. Accordingly, he went among the shrubs, and perceiving the door concealed behind them, he stood before it, and said, "Open, Sesame." The door instantly flew open.

Ali Baba, who expected a dark dismal place, was very much surprised to see it well lighted and spacious, cut out by men's hands in the form of a vault, which received the light from an opening at the top of the rock. He saw all sorts of provisions, and rich bales of merchandize, of silk, stuff, brocade, and valuable carpeting, piled one upon another; and, above all, gold and silver in great heaps, and money in great leather purses. The sight of all these riches made him believe that the cave had been occupied for ages by robbers, who succeeded one another.

Ali Baba did not stand long to consider what to do, but went immediately into the cave, and as soon as he was in, the door shut. But this did not disturb him, because he knew the secret of opening it again. He disregarded the silver, but made the best use of his time in carrying out as much of the gold coin, which was in bags, as he thought his three asses could carry. When he had done, he fetched his asses which had strayed, and, when he had loaded them with the bags, laid the wood on them in such a manner that the bags could not be seen. When he had done, he stood before the door, and pronouncing the words, "Shut, Sesame," the door closed after him; for it had shut of itself while he was within, and remained open while he was out. He then made the best of his way to the town.

When Ali Baba got home, he drove his asses into a little yard, and shut the gates very carefully, threw off the wood that covered the bags, carried them into his house, and ranged them in order before his wife, who sat on a sofa.

His wife handled the bags, and finding them full of money, suspected that her husband had been stealing, insomuch that when he had brought them all in, she could not help saying, "Ali Baba, have you been so unhappy as to——"

"Be quiet, wife," interrupted Ali Baba; "do not frighten yourself: I am no robber, unless he can be one who steals from robbers. You will no longer have a bad opinion of me, when I tell you my good fortune." Then he emptied the bags, which raised such a great heap of gold as dazzled his wife's eyes; and when he had done, he told

Ali Baba counted forty of them.

her the whole adventure from beginning to end, and, above all, recommended her to keep it secret.

The wife recovered, and cured of her fears, rejoiced with her husband at their good luck, and wanted to count all the gold, piece by piece. "Wife," replied Ali Baba, "you do not know what you are undertaking, when you try to count the money; you will never have done. I will go and dig a hole, and bury it; there is no time to be lost."

"You are in the right, husband," replied the wife; "but let us know, as nearly as possible, how much we have. I will go and borrow a small measure in the neighborhood, and measure it, while you dig the hole."

"What you are going to do is to no purpose, wife," said Ali Baba; "if you take my advice, you had better let it alone; but be sure to keep the secret, and do what you please."

Away the wife ran to her brother-in-law Cassim, who lived close by, but was not then at home; and addressing herself to his wife, asked her to lend her a measure for a little while. Her sister-in-law asked her whether she would have a large or a small one. "A small one," said she. Cassim's wife bade her wait a little, and she would readily fetch one.

The sister-in-law did so, but as she knew very well Ali Baba's poverty, she was curious to know what sort of grain his wife wanted to measure, and bethought herself of artfully putting some suet at the bottom of the measure; then she brought it to her with the excuse that she was sorry that she had made her wait so long, but that she could not find it sooner.

Ali Baba's wife went home, set the measure upon the heap of gold, and filled it and emptied it, at a small distance upon the sofa, till she had done; and she was very well satisfied to find that the number of measures amounted to so many as they did, and went to tell her husband, who had almost finished digging the hole. While Ali Baba was burying the gold, his wife, to show her punctuality to her sister-in-law, carried the measure back again, without noticing that a piece of gold stuck at the bottom. "Sister," said she, giving it back to her again, "you see that I have not kept your measure long; I am much obliged to you, and return it with thanks."

her the whole adventure from beginning to end; and, above all, recommended her to keep it secret.

The wife recovered, and, cured of her fears, rejoiced with her husband at their good luck, and wanted to count all the gold, piece by piece. " Wife," replied Ali Baba, " you do not know what you are undertaking when you try to count the money; you will never have done. I will go and dig a hole, and bury it; there is no time to be lost."

" You are in the right, husband," replied the wife; " but let us know, as nearly as possible, how much we have. I will go and borrow a small measure in the neighbourhood, and measure it, while you dig the hole."

" What you are going to do is to no purpose, wife," said Ali Baba; " if you take my advice, you had better let it alone; but be sure to keep the secret, and do what you please."

Away the wife ran to her brother-in-law Cassim, who lived close by, but was not then at home; and addressing herself to his wife, asked her to lend her a measure for a little while. Her sister-in-law asked her whether she would have a large or a small one. " A small one," said she. Cassim's wife bade her wait a little, and she would readily fetch one.

The sister-in-law did so, but as she knew very well Ali Baba's poverty, she was curious to know what sort of grain his wife wanted to measure, and bethought herself of artfully putting some suet at the bottom of the measure; then she brought it to her with the excuse that she was sorry that she had made her wait so long, but that she could not find it sooner.

Ali Baba's wife went home, set the measure upon the heap of gold, and filled it and emptied it, at a small distance upon the sofa, till she had done: and she was very well satisfied to find that the number of measures amounted to so many as they did, and went to tell her husband, who had almost finished digging the hole. While Ali Baba was burying the gold, his wife, to show her punctuality to her sister-in-law, carried the measure back again, without noticing that a piece of gold stuck at the bottom. " Sister," said she, giving it back to her again, " you see that I have not kept your measure long: I am much obliged to you, and return it with thanks."

As soon as Ali Baba's wife's back was turned, Cassim's wife looked at the bottom of the measure, and was inexpressibly surprised to find a piece of gold sticking to it. Envy immediately possessed her heart. "What!" said she, "has Ali Baba gold so plentifully as to measure it? Where has that poor wretch got all this gold?" Cassim, her husband, was at his shop, which he left always in the evening. His wife waited for him, and thought the time an age; so great was her impatience to tell him the news, at which he would be so much surprised.

When Cassim came home, his wife said to him, "Cassim, you think yourself rich, but you are much mistaken; Ali Baba is infinitely richer than you; he does not count his money, but measures it." Cassim desired her to explain the riddle, which she did, telling him the stratagem by which she had made the discovery, and showing him the piece of money, which was so old a coin that they could not tell in what prince's reign it was coined.

Cassim, instead of being pleased at his brother's prosperity, could not sleep all that night for jealousy, but went to him in the morning before sunrise. Now Cassim, after he had married the rich widow, never treated Ali Baba as a brother, but forgot him. "Ali Baba," said he, "you are very reserved in your affairs; you pretend to be miserably poor, and yet you measure gold!"

"What, brother?" replied Ali Baba; "I do not know what you mean: explain yourself."

"Do not pretend ignorance," replied Cassim, showing him the piece of gold his wife had given him. "How many of these pieces have you? My wife found this at the bottom of the measure you borrowed yesterday."

By this Ali Baba perceived that Cassim and his wife, through his own wife's folly, knew what they had such good reason to keep secret; but what was done could not be recalled; therefore without showing the least surprise or vexation, he confessed all, and told his brother by what chance he had discovered this retreat of the thieves, and where it was; and offered him part of his treasure to keep the secret. "I expected as much," replied Cassim haughtily; "but I will know exactly where this treasure is and the signs and tokens by which I may go to it myself when I have a mind; otherwise I will go and inform against you, and then you will not only get no more, but will lose all you have got, and I shall have my share for my information.''

Ali Baba, more out of his natural good temper than frightened by the insulting threats of a barbarous brother, told him all he desired, and even the very words he was to make use of to go into the cave and to come out again.

Cassim, who wanted no more of Ali Baba, left him, resolving to be beforehand with him, and hoping to get all the treasure to himself. He rose early the next morning, a long time before sunrise, and set out with ten mules laden with great chests, which he designed to fill: intending to carry many more the next time, according to the riches he found; and followed the road which Ali Baba had told him. It was not long before he came to the rock, and found out the place by the tree. When he came to the door, he pronounced the words, "Open, Sesame," and it opened; and when he was in, shut again. In examining the cave, he was astonished to find much more riches than he had supposed from Ali Baba's story. He was so covetous and fond of riches that he could have spent the whole day in feasting his eyes with so much treasure, if the thought that he came to carry some away with him had not hindered him. He laid as many bags of gold as he could carry away by the entrance, and, coming at last to open the door, his thoughts were so full of the great riches he should possess that he could not think of the necessary word; but instead of "Open, Sesame," said, "Open, Barley," and was very much amazed to find that the door did not open, but remained fast shut. He named several sorts of grain,—all but the right one,—and the door would not open.

Cassim had never expected such an accident, and was so frightened at the danger he was in that the more he endeavoured to remember the word "Sesame," the more his memory failed, and he had as much forgotten it as if he had never heard it in his life. He threw down the bags with which he had laden himself, and walked hastily up and down the cave, without the least attention to all the riches that were around him. In this miserable condition we will leave him, bewailing his fate, and undeserving of pity.

About noon the robbers returned to their cave, and from

some distance saw Cassim's mules straggling about the rock with great chests on their backs. Alarmed at this unexpected sight, they galloped full speed to the cave. They drove away the mules, which Cassim had neglected to fasten, and which strayed away through the forest so far that they were soon out of sight. The robbers never gave themselves the trouble of pursuing the mules: they were more concerned to know to whom they belonged. And while some of them searched about the rock, the captain and the rest went straight to the door, with naked sabres in their hands, and on their pronouncing the words, it opened.

Cassim, who heard the noise of the horses' feet from the middle of the cave, never doubted the coming of the robbers, and his approaching death; but he was resolved to make one effort to escape. To this end he stood ready at the door, and no sooner heard the word "Sesame," which he had forgotten, and saw the door open, than he jumped briskly out, and threw the captain down, but could not escape the other robbers, who with their sabres soon deprived him of life.

The first care of the robbers after this was to go into the cave. They found all the bags which Cassim had brought to the door, and carried them all back again to their places, without perceiving what Ali Baba had taken away before. Then holding a council, and deliberating upon the matter, they guessed that Cassim, when he was in, could not get out again; but they could not imagine how he had got in. It came into their heads that he might have got down by the top of the cave; but the opening by which it received light was so high, and the top of the rock so inaccessible without—besides that, nothing showed that he had done so—that they believed it hopeless for them to find out. That he came in at the door they could not feel sure, unless he had the secret of making it open. In short, none of them could imagine which way he entered; for they were all persuaded that nobody knew their secret, little imagining that Ali Baba had watched them. But, however it had happened, it was a matter of the greatest importance to them to secure their riches. They agreed, therefore, to cut Cassim's body into four quarters, and to hang two on one side, and two on the other, inside the door of the cave, to terrify any person who might attempt the same thing.

They had no sooner taken this resolution than they executed it; and when they had nothing more to detain them, they left the place of their retreat well closed. They mounted their horses, and went to range the roads again, and to attack the caravans they might meet.

In the meantime Cassim's wife was very uneasy when night came, and her husband had not returned. She ran to Ali Baba in a terrible fright, and said, "I believe, brother-in-law, you know that Cassim, your brother, has gone to the forest, and why; it is now night, and he has not returned; I am afraid some misfortune has befallen him." Ali Baba, who never doubted that his brother, after what he had said, would go to the forest, told her, without any reflection upon her husband's unhandsome behaviour, that she need not alarm herself, for that certainly Cassim would not think it proper to come into the town till the night was pretty far advanced.

Cassim's wife, considering how much it behoved her husband to keep this thing secret, was the more easily persuaded to believe him. She went home again, and waited patiently till midnight. Then her fear redoubled, and she repented of her foolish curiosity, and cursed her desire to penetrate into the affairs of her brother and sister-in-law. She spent all that night in weeping; and as soon as it was light, went to them, showing by her tears the reason of her coming.

Ali Baba did not wait for his sister-in-law to ask him to go and see what had become of Cassim, but went immediately with his three asses, begging her first to moderate her grief. He went to the forest, and when he came near the rock, having seen neither his brother nor his mules on the way, he was very much surprised to see some blood spilt by the door. This he took for an ill omen, but when he had pronounced the words, and the door opened, he was much more startled at the dismal sight of his brother in quarters. He was not long in determining how he should pay the last dues to his brother, and without remembering how little brotherly friendship he had shown to him, went into the cave to find something to wrap the remains in, put them on one of his asses, and covered them over with wood. The other two asses he loaded with bags of gold, covering them with wood also as before.

Then bidding the door shut, he came away; but was cautious enough to stop some time at the end of the forest, that he might not go into the town before nightfall. When he came home, he drove the two asses laden with gold into his little yard, and left the care of unloading them to his wife, while he led the other to his sister-in-law's.

Ali Baba knocked at the door, which was opened by Morgiana, an intelligent slave, clever in inventing plans for the most difficult undertakings: and Ali Baba knew she was. When he came into the court, he unloaded the ass, and taking Morgiana aside, said to her, " The first thing I ask of you is inviolable secrecy, which you will find is necessary both for your mistress' sake and mine. Your master's body is contained in these two bundles, and our business is to bury him as if he had died a natural death. Go and tell your mistress I want to speak to her, and mind what I say."

Morgiana went to her mistress, and Ali Baba followed. " Well, brother," said she, with great impatience, " what news do you bring me of my husband? I perceive no comfort in your face."

" Sister," answered Ali Baba, " I cannot tell you anything before you hear my story from the beginning to the end, without speaking a word; for it is of as great importance to you as to me to keep what has happened secret."

" Alas! " said she, " this tells me that my husband is dead; but as I know the necessity of the secrecy you require of me, I must constrain myself: say on, I will hear you."

Then Ali Baba told his sister all about his journey, till he came to the finding of Cassim's body. " Now," said he, " sister, I have something to tell you which will distress you much more, because it is what you so little expect; but it cannot now be remedied. We must now think of acting so that my brother may appear to have died a natural death. I think you may leave the management of it to Morgiana, and I will contribute all that lies in my power."

What could Cassim's widow do better than accept this proposal? Ali Baba left the widow, and, recommending Morgiana to act her part well, then returned home with his ass.

Morgiana went out to an apothecary, and asked him for some lozenges which he prepared, and which were very efficacious in the most dangerous illnesses. The apothecary asked her who was ill at her master's. She replied, with a sigh, her good master Cassim himself: they knew not what his illness was, but he could neither eat nor speak. After these words, Morgiana carried the lozenges home with her, and the next morning went to the same apothecary's again, and, with tears in her eyes, asked for an essence which they used to give sick people only when at the last extremity. " Alas! " said she, taking it from the apothecary, " I am afraid that this remedy will have no better effect than the lozenges, and that I shall lose my good master."

On the other hand, as Ali Baba and his wife were often seen to go between Cassim's and their own house all that day, and to seem melancholy, nobody was surprised in the evening to hear the lamentable shrieks and cries of Cassim's wife and Morgiana, who told everyone that her master was dead.

Next morning, soon after daylight appeared, Morgiana, who knew a certain old cobbler who opened his stall early, before other people, went to him, and bidding him good-morning, put a piece of gold into his hand. " Well," said Baba Mustapha, which was his name, and who was a merry old fellow, looking at the gold, though it was hardly daylight, and seeing what it was, " this is good handling; what must I do for it? I am ready."

" Baba Mustapha," said Morgiana, " you must take with you your sewing tackle, and go with me; but I shall blindfold you when you come to a certain place."

Baba Mustapha seemed to hesitate a little at these words. " Oh, ho! " replied he, " you would have me do something against my conscience, or against my honour."

" Nay," said Morgiana, putting another piece of gold into his hand, " only come along with me and fear nothing."

Baba Mustapha went with Morgiana, who, after she had bound his eyes with a handkerchief, at the place she told him of, took him to her deceased master's house, and never unbandaged his eyes till he came in. " Baba Mustapha," said she, " you must make haste and sew these pieces of my master together; and when you have done, I will give you another piece of gold."

After Baba Mustapha had done, she blindfolded him again, gave him the third piece of gold as she had promised, imposed secrecy on him, and led him back to the place where she first bound his eyes. Then she pulled off the bandage, and let him go home, but watched till he was quite out of sight, for fear he should have the curiosity to return and dodge her; and then went home.

Morgiana had scarcely got home before the iman and the other ministers of the mosque came. Four neighbours carried the coffin on their shoulders to the burying-ground, following the iman, who recited some prayers. Morgiana, as a slave of the deceased, followed, weeping, beating her breast, and tearing her hair; and Ali Baba came after with some neighbours.

Cassim's wife stayed at home mourning, uttering lamentable cries with the women of the neighbourhood, who came according to custom during the funeral, and, joining their lamentations with hers, filled the quarter far and near with sorrow.

In this manner Cassim's melancholy death was concealed and hushed up between Ali Baba, his wife, Cassim's widow, and Morgiana, so that nobody in the city had the least knowledge or suspicion of the reason of it.

Three or four days after the funeral, Ali Babi removed his few goods to his brother's widow's house; the money he had taken from the robbers he conveyed thither by night; and soon afterwards the marriage with his sister-in-law was published, and as these marriages are common in the Mussulman religion, nobody was surprised.

As for Cassim's shop, Ali Baba gave it to his own eldest son, who had been some time out of his apprenticeship to a great merchant, promising him withal that, if he managed well, he would soon give him a fortune to marry upon.

PART II

LET us now return to the forty robbers.

They came again at the appointed time to visit their retreat in the forest; but how great was their surprise to find Cassim's body taken away, and some of their bags of gold! "We are certainly discovered," said the captain, "and shall be undone, if we do not take care; otherwise we shall gradually lose all the riches which our ancestors have been so many years amassing together with so much pains and danger. All that we can think of is that the thief whom we surprised had the secret of opening the door, and we came luckily as he was coming out; but his body being removed, and with it some of our money, plainly shows that he had an accomplice. As it is likely that there were but two who had got the secret, and one has been caught, we must look narrowly after the other. What say you to it, my lads? ''

All the robbers thought the captain's proposal so reasonable that they unanimously approved of it, and agreed that they must lay all other enterprises aside, to follow this closely, and not give it up till they had succeeded.

'' I expected no less,'' said the captain, '' from your courage and bravery: but, first of all, one of you who is bold, artful, and enterprising, must go into the town dressed like a traveller, and stranger, and do all he can to see if he can hear any talk of the strange death of the man whom we killed, as he deserved, and to find out who he was, and where he lived. This is a matter of the first importance for us to know, that we may do nothing which we may have reason to repent of, by revealing ourselves in a country where we have lived so long unknown, and where we have so much reason to remain: but to warn the man who shall take upon himself this commission, and to prevent our being deceived by his giving us a false report, which might be the cause of our ruin, I ask you all, whether you do not think it fit that if he does he shall suffer death? ''

Without waiting for his companions, one of the robbers started up, and said, '' I submit to this law, and think it an honour to expose my life by taking such a commission upon me; but remember, at least, if I do not succeed, that I wanted neither courage nor good-will to serve the troop.''

After this robber had received great commendation from the captain and his comrades, he disguised himself so that nobody would take him for what he was; and taking leave of the troop that night, went into the town just at day-break; and walked up and down till he came to Baba Mustapha's stall, which was always open before any of the shops of the town.

Baba Mustapha was sitting on his seat with an awl in his hand, just going to work. The robber saluted him, and perceiving that he was very old, he said, "Honest man, you begin to work very early: is it possible that any one of your age can see so well? I question whether you can see to stitch."

"Certainly," replied Baba Mustapha, "you must be a stranger, and not know me; for old as I am, I have extraordinarily good eyes; and you will not doubt it when I tell you that I sewed the pieces of a dead man together in a place where I had not so much light as I have now."

The robber was overjoyed to think that he had addressed himself, at his first coming into the town, to a man who gave him the information he wanted, without being asked. "A dead man!" replied he with amazement. "What could you sew up a dead man for? You mean you sewed up his winding sheet."

"No, no," answered Baba Mustapha, "I know what I say; you want to have me speak out, but you shall know no more."

The robber needed no great insight to be persuaded that he had discovered what he came about. He pulled out a piece of gold, and putting it into Baba Mustapha's hand, said "I do not want to know your secret, though I can assure you I would not divulge it, if you trusted me. The only thing which I request of you is to do me the favour to point out the house where you stitched up the dead man."

"If I wanted to do you that favour," replied Baba Mustapha, holding the money in his hand, ready to return it, "I assure you I cannot; on my word, I was taken to a certain place, where they first blindfolded me, and then led me to the house, and brought me back again after the same manner; therefore you see the impossibility of doing what you desire."

"Well," replied the robber, "you may remember a little of the way that you were led blindfold. Come, let me bind your eyes at the same place. We will walk together by the same way and turnings; perhaps you may remember some part; and as everybody ought to be paid for their trouble, there is another piece of gold for you: gratify me in what I ask you." So saying, he put another piece of gold into his hand.

The two pieces of gold were a great temptation to Baba Mustapha. He looked at them a long time in his hand, without saying a word, thinking what he should do; but at last he pulled out his purse, and put them in. "I cannot assure you," said he to the robber, "that I remember the way exactly; but, since you desire it, I will try what I can do." At these words Baba Mustapha rose up, to the great satisfaction of the robber, and without shutting up his shop, where he had nothing valuable to lose, he led the robber to the place where Morgiana had bound his eyes. "It was here," said Baba Mustapha, "that I was blindfolded; and I turned as you see me." The robber, who had his handkerchief ready, tied it over his eyes, and walked by him till he stopped, partly leading him, and partly guided by him. "I think," said Baba Mustapha, "I went no further," and he had now stopped directly opposite Cassim's house, where Ali Baba lived then; upon which the thief, before he pulled off the handkerchief, marked the door with a piece of chalk, which he had ready in his hand; and when he had pulled it off, he asked him if he knew whose house that was: to which Baba Mustapha replied, that as he did not live in the neighbourhood, he could not tell.

The robber, finding he could discover no more from Baba Mustapha, thanked him for the trouble he had taken, and left him to go back to his stall, while he returned to the forest, persuaded that he would be very well received.

A little while after the robber and Baba Mustapha parted, Morgiana went out of Ali Baba's house for something, and coming home again, she saw the mark the robber had made, and stopped to observe it. "What is the meaning of this?" said she to herself: "either somebody intends my master no good, or else some boy has been playing the rogue: with whatever intention it was done, it is good to guard against the worst." Accordingly she went and fetched a piece of chalk, and marked two or three doors on each side in the same manner, without saying a word to her master or mistress.

In the meantime the thief rejoined his troop again in the forest, and told them the success he had had, dwelling upon his good fortune in meeting so soon with the only person who could tell him what he wanted to know. All the robbers listened to him with the utmost satisfaction. Then the captain, after commending his diligence, addressed himself to them all and said, "Comrades, we have no time to lose: let us all set off well armed, without its appearing who we are; and that we may not give any suspicion, let one or two go privately into the town together, and appoint the rendezvous in the great square; and in the meantime our comrade, who brought us the good news, and myself will go and find out the house."

This speech and plan was approved by all, and they were soon ready. They filed off in small groups of two or three, at the proper distance from each other; and all got into the town without being in the least suspected. The captain and he that came in the morning as spy came in last of all. He led the captain into the street where he had marked Ali Baba's house, and when they came to one of the houses which Morgiana had marked, he pointed it out. But going a little further, to avoid being noticed, the captain observed that the next door was chalked after the same manner, and in the same place; and showing it to his guide, asked him which house it was, that, or the first. The guide was so bewildered, that he knew not what answer to make; much less, when he and the captain saw five or six houses marked in the same manner. He assured the captain that he had marked but one, and could not tell who had chalked the rest; and owned, in his confusion, that he could not distinguish it.

The captain, finding that their design proved abortive, went at once to the place of rendezvous, and told the first of his troop that he met that they had lost their labour, and must return to their cave. He himself set them the example, and they all returned as they came.

When the troop was all together, the captain told them the reason of their returning; and presently the conductor was declared by all to be worthy of death. He condemned himself, acknowledging that he ought to have taken better precautions, and knelt down to receive the stroke from him that was appointed to cut off his head.

But as it was for the safety of the troop that an injury should not go unpunished, another of the gang, who promised that he would succeed better, presented himself; and his offer being accepted, he went and corrupted Baba Mustapha, as the other had done, and being shown the house, marked it, in a place more remote from sight, with red chalk.

Not long after, Morgiana, whose eyes nothing could escape, went out. She saw the red chalk, and, arguing after the same manner with herself, marked the neighbours' houses in the same place and manner.

The robber, on his return to his company, prided himself very much upon the precaution he had taken, which he looked upon as an infallible way of distinguishing Ali Baba's house from those of his neighbours, and the captain and all of them thought it must succeed. They conveyed themselves into the town in the same manner as before, and when the robber and his captain came to the street, they found the same difficulty, at which the captain was enraged, and the robber in as great confusion as his predecessor.

Thus the captain and his troop were forced to retire a second time, still more dissatisfied; and the robber, as the author of the mistake, underwent the same punishment, to which he willingly submitted.

The captain, having lost two brave fellows of his troop, was afraid of diminishing it too much by pursuing this plan to get information about Ali Baba's house. He found, by their example, that their heads were not so good as their hands on such occasions, and therefore resolved to take upon himself this important commission.

Accordingly, he went and addressed himself to Baba Mustapha who did him the same service as he had done to the former men. He did not amuse himself with setting any particular mark on the house, but examined and observed it so carefully, by passing and repassing, that it was impossible for him to mistake it.

The captain, very well satisfied with his journey, and informed of what he wanted to know, returned to the forest; and when he came into the cave, where the troops awaited him, he said: "Now, comrades, nothing can prevent our full revenge. I am certain of the house, and on my way hither I have thought how to act, and if any one knows a better plan, let him communicate it." Then he ordered them to go into the towns and villages round about, and buy nineteen mules, and thirty-eight large leather jars, one full, and the others all empty.

In two or three days' time the robbers purchased the mules and jars, and as the mouths of the jars were rather too narrow for his purpose, the captain caused them to be widened; and after having put one of his men into each, with the weapons which he thought suitable, and leaving open the seam which had been undone so as to leave them room to breathe, he rubbed the jars on the outside with oil from the full vessel.

Things being thus prepared, when the nineteen mules were loaded with thirty-seven robbers in jars and the jar of oil, the captain as their driver set out with them, and reached the town by the dusk of the evening, as he intended. He led them through the streets till he came to Ali Baba's, at whose door he had intended to knock. Ali Baba was sitting there, after supper, to take a little fresh air. The robber captain stopped his mules, and said, "I have brought some oil here a great way to sell at to-morrow's market, and it is now so late that I do not know where to lodge. If I should not be troublesome to you, do me the favour to let me pass the night here, and I shall be very much obliged to you."

Though Ali Baba had seen the captain of the robbers in the forest, and had heard him speak, it was impossible for him to know him in the disguise of an oil-merchant. He told him he would be welcome, and immediately opened his gates for the mules to go into the yard. At the same time he called to a slave, and ordered him, when the mules were unloaded, not only to put them into the stable, but to give them corn and hay, and then went to Morgiana, to bid her get a good hot supper for his guest, and make him a good bed.

To make his guest as welcome as possible, when he saw the captain had unloaded his mules, that they were put into the stables as he had ordered, and that he was looking for a place to pass the night out of doors, he brought him into the hall, telling him he could not suffer him to remain in the court. The captain excused himself, on pretence of not being troublesome, but really to have room to execute his design; and it was not until after the most pressing importunity that he yielded. Ali Baba, not content with showing hospitality to the man who had a design on his life, continued talking with him till supper was ended, and repeated his offer of service.

The captain rose up at the same time, and went with

him to the door, and, while Ali Baba went into the kitchen to speak to Morgiana, he went into the yard, under pretence of looking at his mules. Ali Baba, after charging Morgiana afresh to take great care of his guest, said to her, " To-morrow morning I intend to go to the baths before dawn. Take care that my bathing linen is ready, and give it to Abdalla," (which was the slave's name), " and make me some good broth by the time I come back." After this he went to bed.

In the meantime, the captain of the robbers went from the stable to give his people orders what to do, and beginning at the first jar, and so on to the last, said to each man, " As soon as I throw some stones out of my window, do not fail to cut open the jar with the knife you have about you, pointed and sharpened for the purpose, and come out, and I will be with you at once." After this he returned into the kitchen, and Morgiana, taking a light, conducted him to his chamber, where, after she had asked him if he wanted anything, she left him; and he, to avoid any suspicion put the light out soon after, and laid himself down in his clothes, that he might be the more ready to get up again.

Morgiana, remembering Ali Baba's orders, got his bathing linen ready, and ordered Abdalla, who was not then gone to bed, to set on the pot for the broth; but while she scummed the pot the lamp went out, and there was no more oil in the house, nor any candles. What to do she did not know, for the broth must be made.

Abdalla, seeing her very uneasy, said, " Do not fret and tease yourself, but go into the yard and take some oil out of one of the jars."

Morgiana thanked Abdalla for his advice, and he went to bed, when she took the oil-pot and went into the yard, and as she came near the first jar, the robber within said softly, " Is it time? "

Though the robber spoke low, Morgiana was struck with the voice, the more because the captain, when he unloaded the mules opened this and all the other jars, to give air to his men, who were cramped and ill at ease.

Any other slave but Morgiana, surprised to find a man in a jar, instead of the oil she wanted, would have made such a noise as to have given an alarm, which would have been attended with evil consequences; whereas Morgiana, apprehending immediately the importance of keeping the secret and the danger Ali Baba, his family, and she herself were in, and the necessity of taking quiet action at once, collected herself without showing the least alarm, and answered, "Not yet, but presently." She went in this manner to all the jars, giving the same answer, till she came to the jar of oil.

By this means Morgiana found out that her master, Ali Baba, who thought that he had entertained an oil-merchant, had admitted thirty-eight robbers into his house, with this pretended merchant as their captain. She made what haste she could to fill her oil-pot, and returned into her kitchen; where as soon as she had lighted the lamp, she took a great kettle, and went again to the oil jar, filled the kettle, and set it on a great wood fire to boil. As soon as it boiled, she went and poured enough into every jar to stifle and destroy the robber within.

When this action, worthy of the courage of Morgiana, was executed, without any noise, as she had intended, she returned to the kitchen with an empty kettle, and shut the door; and having put out the great fire she had made to boil the oil, and leaving just enough to make the broth, put out also the lamp, and remained silent; resolving not to go to bed till she had observed what was to follow through a window of the kitchen, which opened into the yard, so far as the darkness of the night permitted.

She had not waited a quarter of an hour before the captain of the robbers got up, and opened the window; and finding no light, and hearing no noise, or any one stirring in the house, he gave the signal by throwing little stones, several of which hit the jars, as he doubted not by the sound they made. Then he listened, and not hearing or perceiving any thing whereby he could judge that his companions stirred, he began to grow very uneasy, and threw stones again a second and a third time, and could not comprehend the reason why none of them answered his signal. Much alarmed, he went softly down into the yard, and going to the first jar, asked the robber, whom he thought alive, if he was asleep. Then he smelt the hot boiled oil, which sent forth a steam out of the jar, and knew thereby that his plot to murder Ali Baba and plunder his house was discovered. Examining all the jars one after another, he found that all his gang were dead; and by the oil he missed out of the last jar, he guessed at the means and manner of their death. Enraged to despair at having failed in his design, he forced the lock of a door that led from the yard into the garden, and, climbing over the walls of several gardens, at last made his escape.

When Morgiana heard no noise, and found, after waiting some time, that the captain did not return, she guessed that he chose to make his escape by the garden rather than by the street-door, which was double-locked. Satisfied and pleased to have succeeded so well, and to have saved the house, she went to bed and fell asleep.

Ali Baba rose before dawn, and, followed by his slave, went to the baths, entirely ignorant of the amazing event that had happened at home: for Morgiana did not think it right to wake him before for fear of losing her opportunity; and afterwards she thought it needless to disturb him.

When he returned from the baths, and the sun had risen, he was very much surprised to see the oil-jars, and that the merchant had not gone with the mules. He asked Morgiana, who opened the door, and had let all things stand as they were, that he might see them, the reason of it. "My good master," answered she, "you will be better informed of what you wish to know, when you have seen what I have to show you, if you will take the trouble to follow me."

As soon as Morgiana had shut the door, Ali Baba followed her; and when she brought him into the yard, she bade him look into the first jar, and see if there was any oil. Ali Baba did so, and seeing a man, started back frightened, and cried out. "Do not be afraid," said Morgiana; "the man you see there can do neither you nor anybody else any harm. He is dead."

"Ah, Morgiana!" said Ali Baba, "what is this you show me? Explain the meaning."

"I will," replied Morgiana; "do not excite the curiosity of your neighbours; for it is of great importance to keep this affair secret. Look in all the other jars."

Ali Baba examined all the other jars, one after another; and when he came to that which had the oil in it, he found it much sunk, and stood for some time motionless, sometimes looking at the jars, and sometimes at Morgiana, without saying a word, so great was his surprise. At last, when he had recovered himself, he said, " And what has become of the merchant? "

" Merchant! " answered she: " he is as much one as I am. I will tell you who he is, and what has become of him; but you had better hear the story in your own room; for it is time for your health that you had your broth after your bathing."

While Ali Baba went to his room, Morgiana went into the kitchen to fetch the broth, and carry it to him; but before he would drink it, he bade her satisfy his curiosity, and tell him the whole story, and she obeyed him.

" This," said Morgiana, when she had finished, " is the account you asked for; and I am convinced it is the sequel of an observation which I had made two or three days before, but did not think it necessary to acquaint you with; for when I came in one morning, early, I found our street-door marked with white chalk, and the next morning with red; and both times, without knowing what was the meaning of those chalks, I marked two or three neighbours' doors on each side in the same manner. If you reflect on this, and on what has since happened, you will find it to be a plot of the robbers of the forest, of whose gang there are two missing, and now they are reduced to three. All this shows that they had sworn your destruction, and it is right that you should stand upon your guard, while there is one of them alive: for my part, I shall not neglect anything necessary to your preservation, as I am in duty bound."

When Morgiana left off speaking, Ali Baba was so impressed with a sense of the great service she had done him, that he said to her, " I will not die without rewarding you as you deserve. I owe my life to you, and I give you your liberty from this moment, till I can complete your recompense as I intend. I am persuaded, with you, that the forty robbers have laid all manner of snares for me. All that we have to do is to bury the bodies of these pests of mankind immediately, and with all the secrecy imaginable, that nobody may suspect what is become of them. But that Abdalla and I will undertake."

Ali Baba's garden was very long, and shaded at the further end by a great number of large trees. Under these trees he and the slave went and dug a trench, long and wide enough to hold all the robbers, and as the earth was light, they were not long doing it. Afterwards they lifted the robbers out of the jars, took away their weapons, carried them to the end of the garden, laid them in the trench, and levelled the ground again. When this was done, Ali Baba hid the jars and weapons; and as for the mules, as he had not occasion for them, he sent them at different times to be sold in the market by his slave.

While Ali Baba took these measures to prevent the public from knowing how he came by his riches in so short a time, the captain of the forty robbers returned to the forest, in the most inconceivable mortification. He entered the cave, not having been able, all the way from the town, to come to any resolution as to what to do to Ali Baba.

The loneliness of the dark place seemed frightful to him. "Where are you, my brave lads?" cried he, "old companions of my watchings, inroads, and labour! What can I do without you? Did I collect you to lose you by so base a fate, one so unworthy of your courage? Had you died with your sabres in your hands, like brave men, my regret had been less! When shall I get such a gallant troop again? And if I could, can I undertake it without exposing so much gold and treasure to him who has already enriched himself out of it? I cannot, I ought not to think of it, before I have taken away his life. I will undertake that myself which I could not accomplish with powerful assistance; and when I have taken care to secure this treasure from being pillaged, I will provide for it new masters and successors after me, who shall preserve and augment it to all posterity." This resolution being taken, he became easy in his mind, and, full of hope, he slept all that night very quietly.

When he woke early the next morning as he had proposed he dressed himself in accordance with the project he had in his head, went down to the town, and took a lodging in a khan. And as he expected that what had happened at Ali Baba's might make a great noise in the town, he asked his host, casually, what news there was in the city. Upon which the innkeeper told him a great many things which did not concern him in the least. He judged by this that the reason why Ali Baba kept the affair so secret was lest people should find out where the treasure lay, and the means of getting at it. And this urged him the more to neglect nothing which might rid himself of so dangerous a person.

The next thing that the captain had to do was to provide himself with a horse, and to convey a great many sorts of rich stuffs and fine linen to his lodging, which he did by a great many journeys to the forest, with all the precautions imaginable to conceal the place whence he brought them. In order to dispose of the merchandize when he had amassed it together, he took a furnished shop, which happened to be opposite to Cassim's, which Ali Baba's son had not long occupied.

He took upon him the name of Cogia Houssain, and, as a new comer, was, according to custom, extremely civil and complaisant to all the merchants his neighbours. And as Ali Baba's son was young and handsome, and a man of good sense, and was often obliged to converse with Cogia Houssain, he soon introduced them to him. He strove to cultivate his friendship, more particularly when, two or three days after he was settled, he recognised Ali Baba, who came to see his son, and stopped to talk with him as he was accustomed to do; and when he was gone the robber captain learnt from his son who he was. He increased his attentions, made him some small presents, often asked him to dine and sup with him, and treated him very handsomely.

Ali Baba's son did not care to lie under such obligations to Cogia Houssain without making a like return; but he was so much straitened for want of room in his house that he could not entertain him so well as he wished. He therefore told his father Ali Baba that it did not look well for him to receive such favours from Cogia Houssain without inviting him again.

Ali Baba, with great pleasure, took the matter upon himself. "Son," said he, "to-morrow (Friday), which is a day that the shops of such great merchants as Cogia Houssain and yourself are shut, get him to take a walk with you after dinner, and as you come back, pass by my door, and call in. It will look better to have it happen accidentally than if you gave him a formal invitation. I will go and order Morgiana to provide a supper."

The next day, after dinner, Ali Baba's son and Cogia Houssain met by appointment, and took their walk, and, as they returned, Ali Baba's son led Cogia Houssain through the street where his father lived; and when they came to the house, he stopped and knocked at the door.

"This sir," said he, "is my father's house; when I told him of your friendship, he charged me to gain him the honour of your acquaintance."

Though it was the sole aim of Cogia Houssain to introduce himself into Ali Baba's house, that he might kill him without hazarding his own life or making any noise, he excused himself, and offered to take leave. But a slave having opened the door, Ali Baba's son took him kindly by the hand, and in a manner forced him in.

Ali Baba received Cogia Houssain with a smiling countenance, and in the most obliging manner he could wish. He thanked him for all the favours he had done his son; adding that the obligation was the greater, as his son was a young man not very well acquainted with the world, and that he might learn much from him.

Cogia Houssain returned the compliment by assuring Ali Baba that, though his son might not have acquired the experience of older men, he had good sense equal to the experience of many others. After a little more conversation on different subjects, he offered again to take his leave; when Ali Baba, stopping him, said, "Where are you going, sir, in such haste? I beg you will do me the honour to sup with me, though what I have to give you is not worth your acceptance; but such as it is, I hope you will accept it as heartily as I give it."

"Sir," replied Cogia Houssain, "I am thoroughly persuaded of your good-will; and if I ask you not to take it ill that I do not accept your kind invitation, I beg you to believe that it does not proceed from any slight or intention to affront, but from a certain reason which you would approve of if you knew it."

"And what may that reason be, sir," replied Ali Baba, "if I may be so bold as to ask you?"

"It is," answered Cogia Houssain, "that I can eat no food that has any salt in it."

"If that is the only reason," said Ali Baba, "it ought not to deprive me of the honour of your company at supper; for, in the first place, there is no salt ever put into my bread, and, as for the meat we shall have to-night, I promise you there shall be none. I will go and take care of that. Therefore you must do me the favour to stay; I will come back immediately."

Ali Baba went into the kitchen, and ordered Morgiana to put no salt to the meat that was to be cooked that night; and to make quickly two or three ragoûts besides what he had ordered, but to be sure to put no salt in them.

Morgiana, who was always ready to obey her master, could not help, this time, seeming somewhat dissatisfied at his new order. "Who is this difficult man," said she, "who eats no salt with his meat? Your supper will be spoiled, if I keep it back so long."

"Do not be angry, Morgiana," replied Ali Baba, "he is an honest man; therefore do as I bid you."

Morgiana obeyed, though with no little reluctance; and was curious to see this man who ate no salt. So when she had done what she had to do in the kitchen, and Abdalla had laid the cloth, she helped to carry up the dishes; and looking at Cogia Houssain she knew him at first sight to be the captain of the robbers, notwithstanding his disguise; and examining him very carefully, she perceived that he had a dagger hidden under his garment. "I am not in the least amazed," said she to herself, "that this wicked wretch, who is my master's greatest enemy, would eat no salt with him, since he intends to assassinate him; but I will prevent him."

When Morgiana had sent up the supper by Abdalla, while they were eating, she made the necessary preparations for executing one of the boldest acts which could be thought of, and had just done, when Abdalla came again for the dessert. This she carried up, and as soon as Abdalla had taken the meat away, she set it upon the table; after that, she set a little table and three glasses by Ali Baba, and going out, took Abdalla along with her to supper, and to give Ali Baba the more freedom for conversation with his guest.

Then the pretended Cogia Houssain, or rather captain of the robbers, thought he had a favourable opportunity to kill Ali Baba. "I will," said he to himself, "make the father and son both drunk; and then the son, whose life I intend to spare, will not be able to prevent my stabbing his father to the heart; and while the slaves are at supper, or asleep in the kitchen, I can make my escape over the gardens as before."

Instead of going to supper, Morgiana, who penetrated into the intention of the sham Cogia Houssain, dressed herself neatly with a suitable head-dress like a dancer, girded her waist with a silver-gilt girdle, to which there hung a poniard with a hilt and guard of the same metal, and put a handsome mask on her face. When she had thus disguised herself, she said to Abdalla, "Take your tabor, and let us go and amuse our master and his son's guest, as we do sometimes when he is alone."

Abdalla took his tabor and played before Morgiana all the way into the hall. When she came to the door, she made a low curtsy, with a deliberate air, by way of asking leave to show what she could do. Abdalla, seeing that his master wanted to say something, left off playing. "Come in, Morgiana," said Ali Baba, "and let Cogia Houssain see what you can do, that he may tell us what he thinks of you. But, sir," said he, turning towards Cogia Houssain, "do not think that I put myself to any expense to give you this entertainment, since these are my slave and my cook and housekeeper; and I hope you will not find it disagreeable."

Cogia Houssain, who did not expect this diversion after supper, began to fear that he should not have the opportunity that he thought he had found; but he hoped, if he missed it now, to have one another time, by keeping up a friendly correspondence with the father and son; therefore, though he could have wished Ali Baba to let it alone, he pretended to be much obliged to him for it, and had the good manners to express pleasure at what he saw pleased his host.

As soon as Abdalla saw that Ali Baba and Cogia Houssain had done talking, he began to play an air on the tabor, to which Morgiana, who was an excellent dancer, danced in such a manner as would have created admiration in any company.

After she had danced several dances with the same grace and strength, she drew the poniard, and holding it in her hand, danced a dance in which she outdid herself by the many different figures and light movements, and the surprising leaps and wonderful exertions with which she accompanied it. Sometimes she presented the poniard to one person's breast, sometimes to another's, and oftentimes seemed to strike her own. At last, as if she were out of breath, she snatched the tabor from Abdalla with her left hand, and, holding the dagger in her right presented the other side of the tabor, after the manner of those who get a livelihood by dancing, for the liberality of the spectators.

Ali Baba put a piece of gold into the tabor, as did also his son; and Cogia Houssain, seeing that she was coming to him, pulled out his purse to make her a present; but while he was putting his hand into it, Morgiana, with a courage and resolution worthy of herself, plunged the poniard into his heart.

Ali Baba and his son, frightened at this action, cried out aloud.

"Unhappy wretch!" exclaimed Ali Baba, "what have you done to ruin me and my family?"

"It was to preserve you, not to ruin you," answered Morgiana; "for see here," said she (opening Cogia Houssain's garment, and showing the dagger), "what an enemy you had entertained! Look well at him, and you will find him to be both the pretended oil-merchant, and the captain of the gang of forty robbers. Remember, too, that he would eat no salt with you; and what more would you have to persuade you of his wicked design. I suspected him as soon as you told me you had such a guest. You now find that my suspicion was not groundless."

Ali Baba, who immediately felt the new obligation he was under to Morgiana for saving his life a second time, embraced her.

"Morgiana," said he, "I gave you your liberty, and then promised you that my gratitude should not stop there, but that I would soon complete it. The time is come for me to give you a proof of this, by making you my daughter-in-law." Then addressing himself to his son, he said to him: "I believe you, son, to be so dutiful, that you will not refuse Morgiana for your wife. You see that Cogia Houssain sought your friendship with a treacherous design to take away my life; and, if he had succeeded, there is no doubt but that he would also have sacrificed you to his revenge. Consider that by marrying Morgiana you marry the support of my family and your own."

The son, far from showing any dislike, readily consented to the marriage; not only because he would not disobey his father, but because he loved Morgiana for herself.

After this, they thought of burying the captain of the robbers with his comrades, and did it so privately that nobody knew anything of it till a great many years afterwards.

After a few days, Ali Baba celebrated the marriage of his son and Morgiana with great solemnity and a sumptuous feast, and the usual dancing and shows; and he had the satisfaction of seeing that his friends and neighbours, who were not unacquainted with Morgiana's good qualities, commended his generosity and goodness of heart.

Ali Baba forbore, for a long time after this marriage, to go again to the robbers' cave, for fear of finding them there and being surprised by them. He kept away after the death of the thirty-seven robbers and their captain, supposing that the other two robbers, of whom he could get no account, might be alive.

But at the year's end, when he found that they had not made any attempt to disturb him, he had the curiosity to make another journey, taking the necessary precautions for his safety. He mounted his horse and when he came to the cave, and saw no footsteps of men or horses, he looked upon it as a good sign. He alighted off his horse, and tied him to a tree; and on his presenting himself before the door, and pronouncing the words, "Open, Sesame," the door opened. He went in, and, by the condition that he found things in, he judged that nobody had been there since the false Cogia Houssain, when he fetched the goods for his shop, and that the gang of forty robbers was completely destroyed; and he never doubted that he was the only person in the world who had the secret of opening the cave, and that all the treasure was solely at his disposal. With as much gold as his horse would carry, he returned to town.

Afterwards Ali Baba took his son to the cave and told him the secret, which they handed down to their posterity; and using their good fortune with moderation, lived in great honour and splendour, and filled the highest offices of the city.

THE STORY OF ALADDIN; OR, THE WONDERFUL LAMP

PART I

IN the capital of one of the large and rich provinces of the kingdom of China there lived a tailor, whose name was Mustapha, so poor, that he could hardly, by his daily labour, maintain himself and his family, which consisted of a wife and son.

His son, who was called Aladdin, had been brought up after a very careless and idle manner, and by that means had contracted many vicious habits. He was wicked, obstinate, and disobedient to his father and mother, who, when he grew up, could not keep him within doors, but he would go out early in the morning, and stay out all day, playing in the streets and public places with little vagabonds of his own age.

When he was old enough to learn a trade, his father, not being able to put him out to any other, took him into his own shop, and showed him how to use his needle; but neither good words nor the fear of chastisement were capable of fixing his attention. All that his father could do to keep him at home to mind his work was in vain; for no sooner was his back turned than Aladdin had gone for that day. Mustapha chastised him, but Aladdin was incorrigible; and his father, to his great grief, was forced to abandon him to his own devices; and was so much troubled at not being able to reclaim him, that he fell into an illness, of which he died in a few months.

The mother of Aladdin, finding that her son would not follow his father's business, shut up the shop, sold off the implements of the trade, and with the money she got for them, and what she could get by spinning cotton, hoped to maintain herself and her son.

Aladdin, who was now no longer restrained by the fear of a father, and who cared so little for his mother that, whenever she chid him, he would fly in her face, gave himself entirely over to dissipation, and was never out of the streets from his companions. This course he followed till he was fifteen years old, without giving his mind to any thing whatever, or the least reflection on what would become of him. Things being thus, as he was one day playing, according to custom, in the street, with his vagabond troop, a stranger passing by stood still to observe him.

This stranger was a famous magician, called the African Magician, as he was a native of Africa, and had been but two days come from thence.

The African magician had observed in Aladdin's countenance something which was absolutely necessary for the execution of the plan he came about; he enquired artfully about his family, who he was, and what was his disposition; and when he had learned all he desired to know, he went up to him, and taking him aside from his comrades, said to him, "Child, was not your father called Mustapha the tailor?"

"Yes, sir," answered Aladdin, "but he has been dead a long time."

At these words the African magician threw his arms about Aladdin's neck, and kissed him several times with tears in his eyes. "Alas! my son," cried the African magician with a sigh, "how can I forbear? I am your uncle; your good father was my own brother. I have been a great many years abroad travelling, and now that I am come home in the hope of seeing him, you tell me he is dead. It is a great grief to me to be deprived of the comfort I expected. But it is some relief, that, so far as I can remember him, you are so like him." Then he asked Aladdin, putting his hand into his purse, where his mother lived; and as soon as Aladdin had informed him, he gave him a handful of small money, saying "Go, my son, to your mother, give my love to her, and tell her that I will come and see her to-morrow, if I have time, that I may have the satisfaction of seeing where my good brother lived so long, and ended his days."

As soon as the African magician left his newly-adopted nephew, Aladdin ran to his mother, overjoyed at the money his uncle had given him. "Mother," said he, "have I an uncle?"

"No, child," replied his mother, "you have no uncle on your father's side, or mine."

"I have just now come," answered Aladdin, "from a man who says he is my uncle on my father's side, assuring me that he is his brother. He cried and kissed me when I told him my father was dead; and to show you that what I tell you is the truth," added he, pulling out the money, "see what he has given me; he charged me to give his love to you, and to tell you, if he has any time to-morrow, he will come and pay you a visit, that he may see the house my father lived and died in."

"Indeed, child," replied his mother, "your father had a brother, but he has been dead a long time, and I never heard of another."

The mother and son talked no more then of the African magician; but the next day Aladdin's uncle found him playing in another part of the town with other children, and embracing him as before, put two pieces of gold into his hand, and said to him, "Carry this, child, to your mother, and tell her that I will come and see her to-night, and bid her get us something for supper; but first show me the house where you live."

After Aladdin had showed the African magician the house, he carried the two pieces of gold to his mother, and when he had told her of his uncle's intentions, she went out and bought provisions. She spent the whole day in preparing the supper; and at night, when it was ready, she said to Aladdin, "Perhaps your uncle knows not how to find our house; go and see, and bring him if you meet with him."

Though Aladdin had showed the magician the house, he was very ready to go, when somebody knocked at the door, which Aladdin immediately opened; and the magician came in loaded with wine, and all sorts of fruit, which he had brought for dessert.

After the African magician had given what he brought into Aladdin's hands, he saluted his mother, and desired her to show him the place where his brother Mustapha used to sit on the sofa; and when she had so done, he presently fell down and kissed it several times, crying out, with tears in his eyes, "My poor brother! how unhappy am I, not to have come soon enough to give you one last embrace!" Aladdin's mother desired him to sit down in the same place, but he would not. "No," said he, "I shall take care how I do that; but give me leave to sit here over against it, that if I am deprived of seeing the master of a family so dear to me, I may at least have the pleasure of seeing the place where he used to sit." Aladdin's mother pressed him no farther, but left him at liberty to sit where he pleased.

When the magician had sat down, he began to enter into conversation with Aladdin's mother: "My good sister," said he, "do not be surprised at your never having seen me all the time you were married to my brother Mustapha, of happy memory. I have been forty years absent from this country, which is my native place, as well as my late brother's; and during that time have travelled into the Indies, Persia, Arabia, Syria, and Egypt, and have resided in the finest towns of those countries; and afterwards crossed over into Africa, where I made a longer stay. At last, as it is natural for a man, how distant soever it may be, to remember his native country, relations, and acquaintances, I was very desirous to see mine again, and to embrace my dear brother; and finding I had strength and courage enough to undertake so long a journey, I immediately made the necessary preparations, and set out. I will not tell you the time it took me, all the obstacles I met with, what fatigues I have endured, to come hither; but nothing ever mortified and afflicted me so much as hearing of my brother's death, for whom I always had a brotherly love and friendship. I observed his features in the face of my nephew, your son, and distinguished him from among a number of children with whom he was at play; he can tell you how I received the most melancholy news that ever reached my ears. But it is a comfort to me to find him again in a son who has his most remarkable features."

The African magician, perceiving that Aladdin's mother began to weep at the remembrance of her husband, changed the conversation, and turning towards Aladdin, asked him his name.

"I am called Aladdin," said he.

"Well, Aladdin," replied the magician, "what business do you follow? Are you of any trade?"

At this question Aladdin hung down his head, and was not a little abashed when his mother made answer, "Aladdin is an idle fellow; his father, when alive, strove all he could to teach him his trade, but could not succeed; and since his death, notwithstanding all I can say to him, he does nothing but idle away his time in the streets, as you saw him, without considering that he is no longer a child; and if you do not make him ashamed of it, and make him leave it off, I despair of his ever coming to any good. He knows that his father left him no fortune, and sees me endeavour to get bread by spinning cotton every day; for my part, I am resolved one of these days to turn him out of doors, and let him provide for himself."

After these words, Aladdin's mother burst into tears; and the magician said, "This is not well, nephew; you must think of helping yourself, and getting your livelihood. There are a great many sorts of trades; consider if you have not a liking for some of them; perhaps you did not like your father's trade, and would prefer another: come, do not disguise your feelings from me; I will endeavour to help you." But finding that Aladdin returned no answer, "If you have no mind," continued he, "to learn any trade and prove an honest man, I will take a shop for you, and furnish it with all sorts of fine stuffs and linens, and set you to trade with them; and the money you make of them lay out in fresh goods, and then you will live in an honourable way. Tell me freely what you think of it: you shall always find me ready to keep my word."

This proposal greatly flattered Aladdin, who mortally hated work, and had sense enough to know that such shops were very much esteemed and frequented, and the owners honoured and respected. He told the magician he had a greater liking for that business than for any other, and that he should be very much obliged to him all his life for his kindness. "Since this profession is agreeable to you," said the African magician, "I will take you with me to-morrow, and clothe you as richly and handsomely as the best merchants in the city, and after that we will think of opening such a shop as I mean."

Aladdin's mother, who never till then could believe that

the magician was her husband's brother, no longer doubted it after his promises of kindness to her son. She thanked him for his good intentions; and after having exhorted Aladdin to render himself worthy of his uncle's favour by his good behaviour, served up supper, at which they talked of several different matters; and then the magician, who saw that the night was pretty far advanced, took his leave of the mother and son, and retired.

He came again the next day, as he promised, and took Aladdin with him to a great merchant, who sold all sorts of clothes for different ages and ranks, ready made, and a variety of fine stuffs. He asked to see some that suited Aladdin in size; and after choosing a suit which he liked best, and rejecting others which he did not think handsome enough, he bid Aladdin choose those he preferred. Aladdin, charmed with the liberality of his new uncle, made choice of one, and the magician immediately bought it, and all things necessary, and paid for it without haggling,

When Aladdin found himself so handsomely equipped from top to toe, he returned his uncle all imaginable thanks: who, on the other hand, promised never to forsake him, but always to take him with him; which he did to the most frequented places in the city, and particularly to where the chief merchants kept their shops. When he brought him into the street where they sold the richest stuffs and finest linens, he said to Aladdin, "As you are soon to be a merchant as well as these, it is proper you should frequent these shops, and be acquainted with them." Then he showed him the largest and finest mosques, and took him to the khans or inns where the merchants and travellers lodged, and afterwards to the sultan's palace, where he had free access; and at last he took him to his own khan, where, meeting with some merchants he had got acquainted with since his arrival, he treated them, to make them and his pretended nephew acquainted.

This treat lasted till night, when Aladdin would have taken his leave of his uncle to go home; but the magician would not let him go by himself, but conducted him safe to his mother, who, as soon as she saw him so finely dressed, was transported with joy, and bestowed a thousand blessings upon the magician, for being at so great an expense for her child. "Generous relation!" said she, "I know not how to thank you for your liberality! I know that my son is not deserving of your favours; and was he never so grateful, he would be unworthy of them. For my part," added she, "I thank you with all my soul, and hope you may live long enough to be a witness of my son's gratitude, which he cannot better show than by regulating his conduct by your good advice."

"Aladdin," replied the magician, "is a good boy, and minds well enough, and I believe we shall do very well; but I am sorry for one thing, which is, that I cannot perform to-morrow what I promised, because it is Friday, and the shops will be shut up, and therefore we cannot hire or furnish one, but must leave it till Saturday. But I will call on him to-morrow, and take him to walk in the gardens, where the most fashionable people generally walk. Perhaps he has never seen these amusements, he has only been hitherto among children; but now he must see men." Then the African magician took his leave of the mother and son, and retired. Aladdin, who was overjoyed to be so well clothed, looked forward to the pleasure of walking in the gardens which lay about the town. He had never been out of the town, nor seen the environs, which were very beautiful and pleasant.

Aladdin rose early the next morning, and dressed himself, to be ready when his uncle called on him; and after he had waited some time, he began to be impatient, and stood watching for him at the door; but as soon as he perceived him coming, he told his mother, took leave of her, and ran to meet him.

The magician caressed Aladdin when he came to him. "Come along, my dear child," said he, "and I will show you fine things." Then he led him out at one of the gates of the city, to some large fine houses, or rather palaces, with beautiful gardens, into which anybody might go. At every house he came to, he asked Aladdin if he did not think it fine; and Aladdin was ready to answer, "Here is a finer house, uncle, than any we have seen yet." By this artifice, the cunning magician got Aladdin a good long way into the country; and, pretending to be tired, the better to rest Aladdin, he took the opportunity to sit down in one of the gardens by a fountain of clear water, which fell from a lion's mouth of bronze into a great basin, "Come, nephew," said he, "you must be weary as well as I; let us rest ourselves, and we shall be better able to walk."

After they had sat down, the magician pulled from his girdle a handkerchief with cakes and fruit, which he had provided on purpose, and laid them on the edge of the basin. He broke a cake in two, gave one half to Aladdin, and ate the other himself. During this short repast, he exhorted his nephew to leave off keeping company with children, and to seek that of wise and prudent men, to improve by their conversation; "for," said he, "you will soon be at man's estate, and you cannot too early begin to imitate them." When they had eaten as much as they liked, they got up, and pursued their walk through the gardens, which were separated from one another only by small ditches, which marked out the limits without interrupting the commuication; so great was the confidence the inhabitants reposed in each other. By this means, the African magician drew Aladdin insensibly beyond the gardens, and crossed the country, till they almost came to the mountains.

Aladdin, who had never been so far in his life before, began to feel much tired with so long a walk, and said to the magician, "Where are we going, uncle? We have left the gardens a great way behind us, and I see nothing but mountains; if we go much further, I do not know whether I shall be able to reach the town again."

"Never fear, nephew," said the false uncle; "I will show you another garden which surpasses all we have yet seen; it is not far off, it is but a little step; and when we come there, you will say that you would have been sorry to be so near it, and not to have seen it." Aladdin was soon persuaded; and the magician, to make the way seem shorter and less fatiguing, told him a great many stories.

At last they came between two mountains of moderate height and equal size, divided by a narrow valley, which was the place where the magician intended to bring Aladdin, to put into execution a design that had brought him from Africa to China. "We will go no further now," said he to Aladdin; "I will show you here some very extraordinary things, such as nobody ever saw before; when you have seen them, you will thank me; but while I strike fire, do you gather up all the loose dry sticks you can see, to kindle a fire with."

Aladdin found there so many dried sticks that, before the magician had lighted a match, he had gathered up a great heap. The magician presently set them on fire, and when they were all in a blaze, the magician threw in some incense he had about him, which raised a great cloud of smoke. This he dispersed on each side, by pronouncing several magical words which Aladdin did not understand.

At the same time the earth trembled a little, and opened just before the magician and Aladdin, and showed a stone about half a yard square, laid horizontally, with a brass ring fixed into the middle of it, to raise it up by. Aladdin was so frightened at what he saw, that he would have run away; but he was to be useful to the magician, who caught hold of him, scolded him, and gave him such a box on the ear that he knocked him down, and nearly beat his teeth down his throat. Poor Aladdin got up again trembling, and, with tears in his eyes, said to the magician, "What have I done, uncle, to be treated in this severe manner?"

"I have my reasons for it," replied the magician: "I am your uncle, and supply the place of your father, and you ought to make no reply. But, child," added he, softening, "do not be afraid of anything; for I shall not ask anything of you, except that you should obey me punctually, if you would reap the advantages which I intended you should." These fair promises calmed Aladdin's fears and resentment; and when the magician saw that he was come to himself, he said to him: "You see what I have done by virtue of my incense, and the words I pronounced. Know, then, that under this stone there is hidden a treasure, which is destined to be yours, and which will make you richer than the greatest monarch in the world: this is so true, that no other person but yourself is permitted to touch this stone, and to pull it up and go in; for I am forbidden ever to touch it, or to set foot in this treasure when it is opened; so you must without fail execute what I tell you, for it is a matter of great consequence both to you and to me."

Aladdin, amazed at all he saw and heard the magician say of the treasure, which was to make him happy for ever, forgot what was past, and rising up, said to the magician: "Well, uncle, what is to be done? Command me; I am ready to obey you."

"I am overjoyed, child," said the African magician, embracing him, "to see you make the resolution: come, take hold of the ring, and lift up that stone."

"Indeed, uncle," replied Aladdin, "I am not strong enough to lift it; you must help me."

"You have no occasion for my assistance," answered the magician; "if I help you, we shall not be able to do anything; you must lift it up yourself; take hold of the ring, only pronounce the names of your father and grandfather, then lift it up, and you will find it will come easily." Aladdin did as the magician bade him, and raised the stone with a great deal of ease, and laid it on one side.

When the stone was pulled up, there appeared a cavity of about three or four feet deep, with a little door, and steps to go down lower.

"Observe, my son," said the African magician, "what I am going to say to you: go down into that cave, and when you are at the bottom of those steps you will find a door open, which will lead you into a large vaulted place, divided into three great halls, in each of which you will see four large brass vessels placed on each side, full of gold and silver; but take care you do not meddle with them. Before you go into the first hall, be sure to tuck up your gown, and wrap it well about you, and then go through the second into the third without stopping. Above all take care that you do not touch the walls, so much as with your clothes; for if you do, you will die instantly. At the end of the third hall, you will find a door which leads into a garden planted with fine trees loaded with fruit; walk direct across the garden by a path which will lead you to five steps that will bring you upon a terrace, where you will see a niche before you, and in that niche a lighted lamp. Take the lamp down, and put it out; when you have thrown away the wick, and poured out the liquor, put it in your breast and bring it to me. Do not be afraid that the liquor will spoil your clothes, for it is not oil; and the lamp will be dry as soon as it is thrown out. If you have a mind for any of the fruit in the garden, you may gather as much as you please."

After these words, the magician drew a ring off his finger, and put it upon one of Aladdin's, telling him that it was a charm against all evil, so long as he observed what he had prescribed to him. After these instructions he said, "Go down boldly, child, and we shall both be rich all our lives."

Aladdin jumped into the cave, went down the steps, and found the three halls just as the African magician had described them. He went through them with all the precaution the fear of death could inspire; crossed the garden without stopping, took down the lamp from the niche, threw out the wick and the liquor, and, as the magician told him, put it in his bosom. But as he came down from the terrace, he stopped in the garden to observe the fruit, which he had only had a glimpse of in crossing it. All the trees were loaded with extraordinary fruit, of different colours on each tree. Some bore fruit entirely white, and some clear and transparent as crystal; some pale red, and others deeper, some green, blue, and purple, and others yellow: in short there were fruits of all colours. The white were pearls, the clear and transparent, diamonds; the deep red, rubies; the paler, ballas rubies; the green, emeralds; the blue, turquoises; the purple, amethysts; and those that were of yellow cast, sapphires; and so on with the rest. All these fruits were so large and beautiful that nothing was ever seen like them. Aladdin was altogether ignorant of their value, and would have preferred figs and grapes, or any other fruits instead. And though he took them only for coloured glass of little value, yet he was so pleased with the colours and the beauty and extraordinary size of the fruit, that he gathered some of every sort, and accordingly filled his two pockets, and the two new purses his uncle had bought for him with the clothes; and as he could not put them in his pockets, he fastened them to his girdle. Some he wrapped up in the skirts of his gown, which was of silk, large and wrapping, and crammed his breast as full as it could hold.

Having thus loaded himself with riches he knew not the value of, Aladdin returned through the three halls with the same precaution, and made all the haste he could, that he might not make his uncle wait, and soon arrived at the mouth of the cave, where the African magician awaited him with the utmost impatience. As soon as Aladdin saw him, he cried out, "Pray, uncle, lend me your hand, to help me out."

"Give me the lamp first," replied the magician, "it will be troublesome to you."

"Indeed, uncle," answered Aladdin, "I cannot now; it is not troublesome to me: but I will as soon as I am up."

The African magician was so obstinate, that he would have the lamp before he would help him up; and Aladdin, who had encumbered himself so much with his fruit that he could not well get at it, refused to give it to him till he was out of the cave. The African magician, provoked at this obstinate refusal of the lad, flew into a terrible passion, and threw a little of his incense into the fire, which he had taken care to keep in, and no sooner had he pronounced two magical words than the stone which had closed the mouth of the cave moved into its place, with the earth over it, in the same manner as it had been at the arrival of the magician and Aladdin.

This action of the African magician plainly showed him to be neither Aladdin's uncle, nor Mustapha the tailor's brother; but a true African. For as Africa is a country whose inhabitants delight more in magic than those of any other part of the whole world, he had applied himself to it from his youth; and after about forty years' experience in enchantments, fumigations, and reading of magic books, he had found out that there was in the world a wonderful lamp, the possession of which, if he could obtain it, would render him more powerful than any monarch in the world; and by a recent operation he found out that his lamp lay concealed in a subterranean place in the midst of China. Fully persuaded of the truth of this discovery, he set out from the furthest part of Africa; and after a long and fatiguing journey, he came to the town nearest to this treasure. But though he had a certain knowledge of the place where the lamp was, he was not permitted to take it himself, nor to enter the subterranean place where it was, but must receive it from the hands of another person. For this reason he addressed himself to Aladdin, whom he looked upon as a young lad of no consequence, and fit to serve his purpose, resolving, as soon as he got the lamp into his hands, to sacrifice poor Aladdin to his avarice and wickedness by making the fumigation mentioned before, and saying those two magical words, the effect of which was to remove the stone into its place again, that he might have no witness of what he had done.

The blow he gave Aladdin, and the authority he assumed over him, were only to accustom him to fear him, and to make him obey the more readily, and give him the lamp as soon as he asked for it. But his too great hurry in executing his wicked intention on poor Aladdin, and his fear lest somebody should come that way during their dispute and discover what he wished to keep secret, produced an effect quite contrary to what he proposed.

When the African magician saw that all his great hopes were frustrated for ever, he started that same day for Africa; but went quite round the town, and at some distance from it, for fear lest any persons who had seen him walk out with the boy should see him come back without him, entertain suspicions, and stop him.

According to all appearances there was no prospect of Aladdin being heard of any more. But when the magician plotted his death, he had forgotten the ring he put on his finger, which preserved him, though he knew not its virtue; and it is amazing that the loss of that, together with the lamp, did not drive the magician to despair; but magicians are so much used to misfortunes that they do not lay them to heart, but still feed themselves, all their lives, with unsubstantial notions.

As for Aladdin, who never suspected this bad usage from his pretended uncle, after all his caresses and what he had done for him, his surprise is more easily imagined than described. When he found himself buried alive, he cried, and called out to his uncle, to tell him he was ready to give him the lamp; but all in vain, since his cries could not be heard, and he remained in this dark abode. At last, when he had quite tired himself out with crying, he went to the bottom of the steps, to get into the garden, where it was light; but the door, which was opened before by enchantment, was now shut by the same means. Then he redoubled his cries and tears, and sat down on the steps, without any hope of ever seeing the light again, and in a melancholy certainty of passing from the present darkness into a speedy death.

Aladdin remained in this state for two days, without eating or drinking, and on the third day looked upon death as inevitable. Clasping his hands with entire resignation, he said, " There is no strength or power but in the great and high God." In joining his hands he rubbed the ring which the magician had put on his finger, and of which he knew not yet the virtue, and immediately a genie of enormous size and frightful look rose out of the earth, his head reaching the vault, and said to him, " What wouldst thou? I am ready to obey thee as thy slave, and the slave of all who have the ring on thy finger; I and the other slaves of that ring."

At another time, Aladdin, who had not been used to such visions, would have been so frightened, that he would not have been able to speak; but the danger he was in made him answer without hesitation, " Whoever thou art, deliver me from this place, if thou art able." He had no sooner made an end of these words, than the earth opened, and he found himself on the very spot where the magician had first brought him.

It was some time before Aladdin's eyes could bear the light, after having been so long in total darkness: but after he had endeavoured by degrees to look about him, he was very much surprised not to find the earth open, and could not comprehend how he had got so soon out of it. There was nothing to be seen but the place where the fire had been, by which he could nearly judge whereabouts the cave was. Then turning towards the town, he perceived it in the midst of the gardens that surrounded it, and knew the way back by which the magician had brought him; then, returning God thanks to see himself once more in the world, where he had never expected to be, he made the best of his way home. When he got to his mother's door, his joy at seeing her, and his faintness for want of food for three days, made him swoon, and he remained for a long time as dead. His mother, who had given him over for lost or dead, seeing him in this condition, omitted nothing to bring him to himself again. As soon as he recovered, the first words he spake, were, " Pray, mother, give me something to eat, for I have not put a morsel of anything into my mouth these three days." His mother brought what she had, and set it before him. " My son," said she, " be not too eager, for it is dangerous; eat but a little at a time, and take care of yourself. Besides, I would not have you talk; you will have time enough to tell me what has happened to you, when you have recovered. It is a great comfort to me to see you again, after the grief I have been in since Friday, and the pains I have taken to learn what had become of you, ever since night came, and you had not returned."

Aladdin took his mother's advice, and ate and drank moderately. When he had done, "Mother," said he, "you believed he was my uncle, as well as I; and what other thoughts could we entertain of a man who was so kind to me? But I must tell you, mother, he is a rogue and a cheat, and only did what he did, and made me all those promises, to accomplish my death; but for what reason neither you nor I can guess. For my part, I can assure you I never gave him any cause to deserve the least ill treatment from him. You shall judge of it yourself, when you have heard all that passed from the time I left you, till he came to the execution of his wicked plan."

Then Aladdin began to tell his mother all that had happened to him from the Friday, when the magician took him to see the palaces and gardens about the town, and what happened on the way, till they came to the place between the two mountains, where the strange deeds were performed; how, with incense which the magician threw into the fire, and some magical words which he pronounced, the earth opened, and discovered a cave, which led to an inestimable treasure. He did not forget the blow the magician gave him, and in what manner he softened again. and got him by great promises, putting a ring on his finger, to go down into the cave. He did not omit the least item of what he saw in crossing the three halls and the garden, and in taking the wonderful lamp, which he showed to his mother, as well as the transparent fruit of different colours, which he had gathered in the garden as he returned. But, though these fruits were precious stones, brilliant as the sun, she was as ignorant of their worth as her son, and cared nothing for them. She had been brought up in a middling rank of life, and her husband's poverty prevented his being possessed of such things, nor had she, or her relations or neighbours, ever seen them; so that we must not wonder that she looked on them as things of no value, and only pleasing to the eye by the variety of their colours.

Aladdin put them behind one of the cushions of the sofa he sat upon, and continued his story. When he came to the end, he said to his mother, "I need say no more; you know the rest. This is my adventure, and the danger I have been exposed to since you saw me."

Aladdin's mother heard, with patience, this surprising and wonderful story, though it caused no small affliction to a mother who loved her son tenderly; but yet in the part which disclosed the perfidy of the African magician, she could not help showing, by the greatest indignation, how much she detested him; and when Aladdin had finished his story, she broke out into a thousand reproaches against that vile impostor. She called him perfidious traitor, barbarian, assassin, deceiver, magician, and an enemy and destroyer of mankind. "Without doubt, child," added she, "he is a magician, and they are plagues to the world, and by their enchantments and sorçeries have commerce with the Evil One. Bless God for preserving you from his wicked designs; for your death would have been inevitable, if you had not called upon Him, and implored His assistance." She said a great deal more against the magician's treachery; but finding that whilst she talked her son Aladdin began to nod, she put him to bed.

Aladdin, who had not had one wink of sleep while he was in the subterranean abode, slept very heartily all that night, and never waked till late the next morning; when the first thing he said to his mother was, he wanted something to eat. "Alas! child," said she, "I have not a bit of bread to give you; you ate up all the provisions I had in the house yesterday; but have a little patience, and it shall not be long before I will bring you some: I have a little cotton, which I have spun; I will go and sell it, and buy bread, and something for our dinner."

"Mother," replied Aladdin, "keep your cotton for another time, and give me the lamp I brought home with me yesterday; I will go and sell that, and the money I shall get for it will serve both for breakfast and dinner, and perhaps supper too."

Aladdin's mother took the lamp, and said to her son, "Here it is, but it is very dirty; if it was a little cleaner I believe it would fetch something more." She took a little fine sand and water to clean it; but no sooner had she begun to rub it than a hideous genie of gigantic size appeared before her, and said in a voice like thunder, "What wouldst thou have? I am ready to obey thee as thy slave, and the slave of all those who have that lamp in their hands; I, and the other slaves of the lamp."

Aladdin's mother was not able to speak at the sight of this frightful genie, but fainted away; when Aladdin, who had seen such a genie in the cavern, without losing time on reflection, snatched the lamp out of his mother's hands, and said to the genie boldly, "I am hungry; bring me something to eat." The genie disappeared immediately, and in an instant returned with a large silver basin on his head, and twelve covered plates of the same metal, which contained excellent meats; six large white loaves on two other plates, two bottles of wine, and two silver cups in his hands. All these things he placed upon a table, and disappeared; and all this was done before Aladdin's mother came out of her swoon.

Aladdin went and fetched some water, and threw it on her face, to recover her. Whether that or the smell of the meats the genie procured brought her to life again, it was not long before she came to herself. "Mother," said Aladdin, "do not mind this; it is nothing at all; get up, and come and eat; do not let such fine meat get cold, but fall to."

His mother was very much surprised to see the great basin, twelve plates, six loaves, and the two bottles and cups, and to smell the delicious odour which exhaled from the plates. "Child," said she to Aladdin, "to whom are we indebted for this great plenty? Has the sultan been made acquainted with our poverty, and had compassion on us?"

"It is no matter, mother," said Aladdin; "let us sit down and eat; for you are in almost as much need of a good breakfast as myself; when we have done, I will tell you." Accordingly both mother and son sat down, and ate with first-rate appetites. But all the time Aladdin's mother could not forbear looking at and admiring the basin and plates, though she could not well tell whether they were silver or any other metal, so little accustomed were she and her son to see such things.

In short, the mother and son sat at breakfast till it was dinner-time, and then they thought it would be best to put the two meals together; yet after this they found they should have enough left for supper, and two meals for the next day.

When Aladdin's mother had taken away and set by what was left, she went and sat down by her son on the sofa. "Aladdin," said she, "I expect now that you should tell me exactly what passed between the genie and you while I was in a swoon;" which he at once complied with.

She was in as great amazement at what her son told her as at the appearance of the genie; and said to him, "But, son, what have we to do with genies? I never in my life heard that any of my acquaintance had ever seen one. How came that vile genie to address himself to me, and not to you, to whom he had appeared before in the cave?"

"Mother," answered Aladdin, "the genie you saw is not the same who appeared to me, though he resembles him in size; no, they had quite a different appearance and habits; they belong to different masters. If you remember, he that I first saw called himself the slave of the ring on my finger; and this one you saw called himself the slave of the lamp you had in your hand; but you did not hear him, for I think you fainted away as soon as he began to speak."

"What!" cried his mother, "was your lamp the occasion of that cursed genie's addressing himself to me rather than to you. Ah! my son, take it out of my sight, and put it where you please. I will never touch it. I had rather you would sell it than run the risk of being frightened to death again by touching it: and if you would take my advice, you would part also with the ring, and not have anything to do with genies, who, as our prophet has told us, are only devils."

"With your leave, mother," replied Aladdin, "I shall take care how I sell a lamp which may be so serviceable both to you and me. Have you not seen what it has procured us? It shall still continue to furnish us with subsistence. My false and wicked uncle would not have taken so much pains, and undertaken so long and tedious a journey, if it had not been to get into his possession this wonderful lamp, which he preferred before all the gold and silver which he knew was in the halls, and which I have seen with my own eyes. He knew too well the merit and worth of this lamp; and since chance has shown the virtue of it to us, let us make a profitable use of it, without making any great stir, and drawing the envy and jealousy of our neighbours upon us. However, since the genies frighten you so much, I will take it out of your sight, and put it where I may find it when I want it. As for the ring, I cannot resolve to part with that either, for without that you would never have seen me again; and though I am alive now, perhaps, if it was gone, I might not be so some moments hence; therefore I hope you will give me leave to keep that, and to wear it always on my finger. Who knows what dangers you and I may be exposed to, which neither of us can foresee, and from which it may deliver us?"

As Aladdin's arguments were just, and had great weight, his mother had nothing to say against them; but only replied, that he might do what he pleased, but for her part she would have nothing to do with genies, but would wash her hands of them, and never say anything more about them.

By the next day they had eaten all the provisions the genie had brought; and the next day Aladdin, who could not bear the thought of hunger, took one of the silver plates under his coat and went out early to sell it, and addressing himself to a Jew whom he met in the streets, took him aside, and pulling out the plate, asked him if he would buy it. The cunning Jew took the plate and examined it, and no sooner found that it was good silver than he asked Aladdin at how much he valued it. Aladdin, who knew not the value of it, and never had been used to such traffic, told him he would trust to his judgment and honour. The Jew was somewhat taken aback at this plain dealing; and, doubting whether Aladdin understood the material or the full value of what he offered him, he took a piece of gold out of his purse and gave it him, though it was but the sixtieth part of the worth of the plate. Aladdin took the money very eagerly, and as soon as he got it in his pocket, retired with so much haste, that the Jew, not content with his exorbitant profit, was vexed he had not penetrated into Aladdin's ignorance, and was going to run after him to get some change out of the piece of gold; but Aladdin ran so fast, and had got so far, that it would have been impossible to overtake him.

Before Aladdin went home to his mother, he called at a baker's, bought a loaf, changed his money, and went home, and gave the rest to his mother, who went and bought provisions enough to last them some time. After this manner they lived, till Aladdin had sold the twelve plates, one at a time, to the Jew, for the same money; who, after the first time, durst not offer him less, for fear of losing so good a customer. When he had sold the last plate, he had recourse to the basin, which weighed ten times as much as the plate, and would have carried it to his old purchaser, except that it was too large and cumbersome; therefore he was obliged to bring him home with him to his mother's, where, after the Jew had examined the weight of the basin, he laid down ten pieces of gold, with which Aladdin was very well satisfied.

They lived on these ten pieces in a frugal manner a good while; and Aladdin, though formerly used to an idle life, had left off playing with young lads of his own age ever since his adventure with the African magician. He spent his time in walking about, and talking with people with whom he had got acquainted. Sometimes he would stop at the best merchants' shop, where people of distinction met, and listen to their talk, by which he gained some little knowledge of the world.

When all the money was spent, Aladdin had recourse again to the lamp. He took it in his hand, looked for the place where his mother had rubbed it with the sand, and rubbed it also, and the genie immediately appeared, and said, "What wouldst thou have? I am ready to obey thee as thy slave, and the slave of those who have that lamp in their hands; I, and the other slaves of the lamp."

"I am hungry," said Aladdin; "bring me something to eat."

The genie disappeared, and presently returned with a basin, and the same number of covered plates, etc., and set them down on a table, and vanished again.

Aladdin's mother, knowing what her son was going to do, went out at that time about some business, on purpose to avoid being in the way when the genie came; and when she returned, which was not long afterwards, and found the table and sideboard so furnished a second time, she was almost as much surprised as before at the prodigious effect of the lamp. However she sat down with her son, and when they had eaten as much as they wanted, she set enough by to last them two or three days.

As soon as Aladdin found that their provisions and money were spent, he took one of these plates, and went to look for the Jew again; but as he passed by the shop of a goldsmith, who had the character of a very fair and honest man, the goldsmith called to him, and said, "My lad, I have often observed you go by, loaded as you are at present, and talk with a certain Jew, and then come back again empty handed. I imagine that you carry something to sell to him; but perhaps you do not know what a rogue he is; he is the greatest rogue among all the Jews, and is so well known that nobody will have anything to do with him. What I tell you is for your own good. If you will show me what you now carry, and if it is to be sold, I will give you the full value of it; or I will direct you to other merchants who will not cheat you."

The hope of getting more money for his plate induced Aladdin to pull it from under his coat and show it to the goldsmith. The old man, who at first sight saw it was made of the finest silver, asked him if he had sold any such as that to the Jew, and Aladdin told him plainly that he had sold him twelve such for a piece of gold each.

"What a villain!" cried the goldsmith; "but," added he, "my son, what is past cannot be recalled. By showing you the value of this plate, which is of the finest silver we use in our shops, I will let you see how much the Jew has cheated you."

The goldsmith took a pair of scales, weighed the plate, and after he had told Aladdin how much an ounce of fine silver was worth, he showed him that his plate was worth by weight sixty pieces of gold, which he paid him down immediately. "If you dispute my honesty," said he, "you may go to any other of our trade, and if he gives you any more, I will forfeit twice as much."

Aladdin thanked him for his good advice, so greatly to his advantage, and never after went to any other person, but sold him all his plates and the basin, and had as much for them as the weight came to.

Though Aladdin and his mother had an inexhaustible treasure of money in their lamp, and might have had whatever they had a mind to, yet they lived with the same frugality as before, except that Aladdin went wore neat; as for his mother, she wore no clothes but what she earned by spinning cotton. Hence the money for which Aladdin had sold the plates and basin was sufficient to maintain them some time. They went on for many years by the help of the produce that Aladdin, from time to time, made of his lamp.

During this time Aladdin frequented the shops of the principal merchants, where they sold cloth of gold and silver, and linens, silk stuffs and jewellery, and oftentimes joining in their conversation, acquired a complete knowledge of the world, and assumed its manners. From his acquaintance with the jewellers, he came to know that the fine fruit which he had gathered, when he took the lamp, was not coloured glass, but stones of extraordinary value. For as he had seen all sorts of jewels bought and sold in the shops, but none so beautiful or so large as his, he found that instead of coloured glass he possessed an inestimable treasure; but he had the prudence not to say anything of it to any one.

One day, as Aladdin was walking about the town, he chanced to see the Princess Badroulboudour, the sultan's daughter, attended by a great crowd of ladies, slaves, and attendants, just at a moment when she unveiled her face. Aladdin had never seen any woman unveiled except his mother, and the princess was so beautiful that he was filled with amazement, and could think of nothing else for several days and nights. At last his mother inquired why he was so silent and absent-minded. "Mother," said Aladdin, "I cannot live without the beautiful and amiable Princess Badroulboudour, and I am firmly resolved to ask her in marriage from her father."

Aladdin's mother listened with attention to what her son told her; but when he talked of asking the Princess Badroulboudour in marriage of the sultan, she could not help bursting out into a loud laugh. Aladdin would have gone on, but she interrupted him: "Alas! child," said she, "what are you thinking of? you must be mad to talk so."

"I assure you, mother," replied Aladdin, "that I am not mad, but in my right senses: I foresaw that you would reproach me for folly and extravagance; but I must tell you once more, that I am resolved to demand the Princess Badroulboudour of the sultan in marriage, and your remonstrances shall not prevent me."

"Indeed, son," replied his mother, seriously, "I cannot help telling you that you have quite forgotten yourself; and I do not see who you can get to venture to propose it for you."

"You, yourself," replied he immediately.

"I go to the sultan!" answered his mother, amazed and surprised. "I shall take good care how I engage in such an affair. Why, who are you, son," continued she, "that you can have the assurance to think of your sultan's daughter? Have you forgotten that your father was one of the poorest tailors in the capital, and that I am of no better extraction; and do not you know that sultans never marry their daughters but to princes, sons of sultans like themselves?"

"Mother," answered Aladdin, "I have already told you that I foresaw all that you have said, or can say: and tell you again that neither your discourse nor your remonstrances shall make me change my mind. I have told you that you must ask the Princess Badroulboudour in marriage for me: it is a favour I request with all the respect I owe you, and I beg of you not to refuse me, unless you would rather see me in my grave, than by so doing give me new life."

The good old woman was very much embarrassed, when she found Aladdin so obstinately persisting in so foolish a design. "My son," said she again, "I am your mother, and there is nothing reasonable that I would not readily do for you. If I were to go and treat about your marriage with some neighbour's daughter, whose circumstances were equal to yours, I would do it with all my heart; and even then they would expect you to have some little estate or fortune, or be of some trade. When such poor folks as we marry, the first thing they ought to think of is how to live. But without reflecting on your lowly birth, and the little merit and fortune you have to recommend you, you aim at the highest; you demand in marriage the daughter of your sovereign, who with one single word can crush you to pieces. How could so extraordinary a thought come into your head, as that I should go to the sultan, and make a proposal to him to give his daughter in marriage to you? Suppose I had, not to say the boldness, but the impudence to present myself before the sultan and make so extravagant a request, to whom should I address myself to be introduced to his majesty? Do you not think the first person I should speak to would take me for a mad woman, and chastise me as I should deserve? Of course, I know there is no difficulty to those who go to ask justice, which he distributes equally among his subjects; I know too that to those who ask some favour he grants it with pleasure when he sees that it is deserved, and the persons are worthy of it. But is that your case? And do you think you have deserved the favour you would have me ask for you? Are you worthy of it? What have you done, either for your prince or country? How have you distinguished yourself? If you have done nothing to merit so great a favour, nor are worthy of it, with what face shall I ask it? How can I open my mouth to make such a proposal to the sultan? His majestic presence and the splendour of his court would immediately silence me. There is another reason, my son, which you do not think of; nobody ever goes to ask a favour of the sultan without a present. But what presents have you to make? And if you had any that was worthy of the least attention of so great a monarch, what proportion could it bear to the favour you would ask? Therefore, reflect well on what you are about, and consider that you aspire to a thing which it is impossible for you to obtain."

Aladdin heard very calmly all that his mother could say to dissuade him from his design, and made answer: "I own, mother, it is great rashness in me to presume so far; and a great want of consideration to ask you with so much suddenness to go and make the proposal of my marriage to the sultan, without first taking proper measures to procure a favourable reception; I therefore beg your pardon. But be not surprised that I did not at first sight see everything that it was necessary to do to procure me the happiness I seek after. I love the Princess Badroulboudour beyond everything you can imagine; and shall always persevere in my design of marrying her, which is a thing I have determined and resolved on. I am much obliged to you for the hint you have given me, and look upon it as the first step I ought to take.

"You say it is not customary to go to the sultan without a present, and that I have nothing worthy of his acceptance. As to what you say about the present, do you not think, mother, that what I brought home with me the day on which I was delivered from certain death, may be an agreeable present? I mean those things you and I both took for coloured glass; they are jewels of inestimable value, and fit for the greatest monarch. I know the worth of them through frequenting the jewellers' shops; and you may take my word for it, all the jewels that I have seen in the best jewellers' shops were not to be compared to those we have, either for size or beauty. Neither you nor I know the value of ours; but I am persuaded that they will be received very favourably by the sultan; you have a large porcelain dish fit to hold them; fetch it, and let us see how they will look, when we have arranged them according to their different colours."

Aladdin's mother fetched the china dish, and he took the jewels out of the two purses in which he had kept them, and placed them in the dish. But the brightness and lustre they had in the daytime, and the variety of the colours, so dazzled the eyes of both mother and son that they were astonished beyond measure; for they had only seen them by the light of a lamp; and though Aladdin had seen them hang on the trees like fruit, beautiful to the eye, yet as he was then but a boy, he did not take much notice of them.

After they had admired the beauty of this present some time, Aladdin said to his mother, "Now you cannot excuse yourself from going to the sultan, under the pretext of not having a present to make him, since here is one which will gain you a favourable reception."

Though Aladdin's mother did not believe it to be so valuable as her son esteemed it, she thought it might nevertheless be agreeable to the sultan, and found that she had not anything to say against it, but kept thinking of the request Aladdin wanted her to make to the sultan. "My son," said she, "I cannot conceive that your present will have its desired effect, and that the sultan will look upon me with a favourable eye; and I am sure, if I attempt this message of yours, I shall have no power to open my mouth; and, therefore, I shall not only lose my labour, but the present, which you say is so extraordinarily valuable, and shall return home again in confusion. I have told you the consequences, and you ought to believe me; but," added she, "I will do my best to please you; though certainly he will either laugh at me, or send me back like a fool, or be in so great a rage as to make us both the victims of his fury."

She used a great many more arguments to make him change his mind; but Aladdin persisted, and his mother, as much out of tenderness as for fear he should be guilty of some worse piece of extravagance, consented.

As it was now late, and the time for going to the sultan's palace was past, it was put off till the next day. The mother and son talked of different matters the remaining part of the day; and Aladdin took a great deal of pains to encourage his mother in the task she had undertaken; while she, notwithstanding all his arguments, could not persuade herself that she could ever succeed; and it must be confessed she had reason enough to doubt. "Child," said she to Aladdin, "if the sultan should receive me as favourably as I wish for your sake, and hear my proposal with calmness, and after this kind reception should think of asking me where lie your riches and your estate (for he will sooner enquire after these than your person), if, I say, he should ask me the question, what answer would you have me give him?"

"Let us not be so uneasy, mother," replied Aladdin, "about what may never happen. First, let us see how the sultan receives you, and what answer he gives. If it should so happen that he desires to be informed of all that you mention, I have thought of an answer, and am confident that the lamp, which has assisted us so long, will not fail me in time of need."

Aladdin's mother could not say anything against what her son then proposed; but reflected that the lamp might be capable of doing greater wonders than merely providing food for them. This satisfied her, and at the same time removed all the difficulties which might have prevented her from undertaking the service she had promised her son; when Aladdin who penetrated into his mother's thoughts, said to her, "Above all things, mother, be sure to keep the secret, for thereon depends the success;" and after this caution, Aladdin and his mother parted to go to bed. Aladdin rose at daybreak, and went and awakened his mother, begging her to get dressed to go to the sultan's palace, and to get in first, as the grand vizier, the other viziers, and all the great officers of state went in to take their seats in the divan, where the sultan always presided in person.

Aladdin's mother did all that her son desired. She took the china dish, in which they had put the jewels the day before, tied up in two napkins, one finer than the other, and set out for the sultan's palace, to the great satisfaction of Aladdin. When she came to the gates, the grand vizier, and other viziers and most distinguished lords of the court, were just gone in; and, notwithstanding the crowd of people who had business there, which was extraordinarily great, she got into the divan, which was a large spacious hall. She placed herself just before the sultan, the grand vizier, and the great lords, who sat in that council, on his right and left hand. Several cases were called, according to their order, and pleaded and adjudged, until the time the divan generally broke up, when the sultan rising, dismissed the council, and returned to his apartment, attended by the grand vizier; the other viziers and ministers of state returned, as also did all those whose business called them thither; some pleased with gaining their cases, others dissatisfied at the sentences pronounced against them, and some in expectation of theirs being heard at the next sitting.

Aladdin's mother, seeing the sultan rise and retire, and all the people go away, rightly judged that he would not come again that day, and resolved to go home. When Aladdin saw her return with the present, he knew not at first what to think, and from the fear he was in lest she should bring him some bad news, he had not courage enough to ask her any questions, till his mother, who had never set foot in the sultan's palace before, and knew not what was done there every day, freed him from his embarrassment, and said, "Son, I have seen the sultan, and am very well persuaded he has seen me too; for I placed myself just before him, and nothing could hinder him from seeing me; but he was so much taken up with all those who talked on all sides of him, that I pitied him, and wondered at his patience to hear them. At last I believe he was heartily tired, for he rose up suddenly, and would not hear a great many who were prepared to speak to him, but went away, at which I was very well pleased, for indeed I began to lose all patience, and was extremely tired with staying so long. But there is no harm done; I will go again to-morrow; perhaps the sultan may not be so busy."

Though Aladdin was very violent, he was forced to be satisfied with this, and to fortify himself with patience. He had at least the satisfaction of finding that his mother had got over the greatest difficulty, which was to procure access to the sultan, and hoped that the example of those whom she saw speak to him would embolden her to acquit herself better when a favourable opportunity offered.

The next morning she went to the sultan's palace with the present, as early as the day before, but when she came there, she found the gates of the divan shut, and understood that the council only sat every other day, and that therefore she must come again the next. This news she carried her son, whose only relief was patience. She went six times afterwards on the days appointed, placed herself always directly before the sultan, but with as little success as on the first time, and might have perhaps come a thousand times to as little purpose, if the sultan himself had not taken particular notice of her.

At last, after the council had broken up, and when the sultan returned to his own apartment, he said to his grand vizier, "I have for some time observed a certain woman, who comes constantly every day that I go into council, and has something wrapped up in a napkin: she always stands up from the beginning to the breaking up of the council, and places herself just before me. Do you know what she wants?"

"Sir," replied the grand vizier, who knew no more than the sultan, but did not like to seem uninformed, "perhaps this woman has come to complain to your majesty that somebody has sold her some bad flour, or some such trifling matter." The sultan was not satisfied with this answer, but replied, "If this woman comes again next council-day, do not fail to call her, that I may hear what she has to say." The grand vizier made answer by kissing his hand, and lifting it up above his head, signifying his willingness to lose it if he failed.

By this time, Aladdin's mother was so much accustomed to go to the council, and stand before the sultan, that she did not think it any trouble, if she could but satisfy her son that she neglected nothing that lay in her power: so the next council-day she went to the divan, and placed herself before the sultan as usual; and before the grand vizier had made his report of business, the sultan perceived her, and compassionating her for having waited so long, he said to the vizier, " Before you enter upon any business, remember the woman I spoke to you about: bid her come near, and let us hear and despatch her business first." The grand vizier immediately called the chief of the officers; and pointing to her, bid him go to the woman, and tell her to come before the sultan.

The chief of the officers went to Aladdin's mother, and at a sign she followed him to the foot of the sultan's throne, where he left her, and retired to his place by the grand vizier. Aladdin's mother, following the example of a great many others whom she saw salute the sultan, bowed her head down to the carpet, which covered the steps of the throne, and remained in that posture till the sultan bade her rise, which she had no sooner done than the sultan said to her, " Good woman, I have observed you a long time; what business brings you here? "

At these words, Aladdin's mother prostrated herself a second time; and when she got up again, said, " Monarch of monarchs, before I tell your majesty the extraordinary and almost incredible business which brings me before your high throne, I beg of you to pardon the boldness or rather impudence of the demand I am going to make, which is so uncommon that I tremble, and am ashamed to propose it to my sultan." In order to give her the more freedom to explain herself, the sultan ordered everybody to go out of the divan but the grand vizier, and then told her she might speak without restraint.

Aladdin's mother, notwithstanding this favour of the sultan's to save her the trouble and confusion of speaking before so many people, was not a little apprehensive; therefore, she said, " I beg your majesty, if you should think my demand the least injurious or offensive, to assure me first of your pardon and forgiveness."

"Well," replied the sultan, "I will forgive you, be it what it will, and no hurt shall come to you: speak boldly."

When Aladdin's mother had taken all these precautions, for fear of the sultan's anger, she told him faithfully how Aladdin had seen the Princess Badroulboudour, and had fallen in love with her, the declaration he had made to her when he came home, and what she had said to dissuade him, "But," continued she, "my son, instead of taking my advice and reflecting on his boldness, was so obstinate as to threaten me with some desperate act if I refused to come and ask the princess in marriage of your majesty; and it was not till after doing violence to my feelings that I was forced to come, for which I beg your majesty once more to pardon not only me but Aladdin my son for entertaining such a rash thought."

The sultan hearkened mildly, without showing the least anger; but before he gave her any answer, he asked her what she had brought tied up in that napkin. She took the china dish, which she had set down at the foot of the throne, before she prostrated herself before him; she untied it, and presented it to the sultan.

The sultan's amazement and surprise were inexpressible, when he saw so many large, beautiful, and valuable jewels collected in one dish. He remained for some time motionless with admiration. At last, when he had recovered himself, he received the present from Aladdin's mother's hand, crying out in a transport of joy, "How rich and how beautiful!" After he had admired and handled all the jewels, one after another, he turned about to his grand vizier, and showing him the dish, said, "Look here, and confess that your eyes never beheld anything so rich and beautiful before." The vizier was charmed. "Well," continued the sultan, "what sayest thou to such a present? Is it not worthy of the princess my daughter? And ought I not to bestow her on one who values her at so great a price?"

These words put the grand vizier into a great fright. The sultan had some time before signified to him his intention of bestowing the princess his daughter on a son of his; therefore he was afraid, and not without grounds, that the sultan might change his mind. Thereupon, going up to him, and whispering he said, "Sir, I cannot but own that the present is worthy of the princess; but I beg of your majesty to grant me three months before you come to a decision. I hope before that time that my son, on whom you have had the goodness to look with a favourable eye, will be able to make a nobler present than Aladdin, who is an entire stranger to your majesty."

Though the sultan was very sure that it was not possible for the vizier to provide so considerable a present for his son to make, he hearkened to him, and granted the favour. So turning to Aladdin's mother, he said to her, "Good woman, go home, and tell your son that I agree to the proposal you have made me; but I cannot marry the princess my daughter till some furniture I intend for her be got ready, which cannot be finished for three months; but at the end of that time come again."

Aladdin's mother returned home much more overjoyed than she could have imagined, and told Aladdin all that had happened.

Aladdin thought himself the most happy of all men at hearing this news, and thanked his mother for all the pains she had taken. When two of the three months were past, his mother one evening went to light the lamp, and finding no oil in the house, went out to buy some, and when she came into the city, found a general rejoicing. The shops, instead of being shut up, were open. The streets were crowded with officers in robes of ceremony, mounted on horses richly caparisoned, each attended by a great many footmen. Aladdin's mother asked the oil-merchant what was the meaning of all these doings. "Whence come you, good woman," said he, "that you don't know that the grand vizier's son is to marry the Princess Badroulboudour, the sultan's daughter, to-night? These officers that you see are to assist at the procession to the palace, where the ceremony is to be solemnised."

This was news enough for Aladdin's mother. She ran till she was quite out of breath home to her son, who little suspected any such thing. "Child," cried she, "you are undone! you depend upon the sultan's fine promises, but they will come to nothing." Aladdin was terribly alarmed at these words. "Mother," replied he, "how do you know the sultan has been guilty of breaking his promise?"

"This night," answered his mother, "the grand vizier's

son is to marry the Princess Badroulboudour." She then related how she had heard it; so that he had no reason to doubt the truth of what she said.

At this Aladdin was thunderstruck. Any other man would have sunk under the shock; but soon he bethought himself of the lamp, which had till then been so useful to him; and without venting his rage in empty words against the sultan, the vizier or his son, he only said, "Perhaps, mother, the vizier's son may not be so happy to-night as he thinks: while I go into my room, do you go and get supper ready." She accordingly went about it, and guessed that her son was going to make use of the lamp, to prevent the marriage if possible.

When Aladdin had got into his room, he took the lamp, and rubbed it in the same place as before, and immediately the genie appeared, and said to him, "What wouldst thou have? I am ready to obey thee as thy slave, and the slave of all those who have that lamp in their hands; I and the other slaves of the lamp."

"Hear me," said Aladdin; "thou hast hitherto brought me whatever I wanted as to provisions; but now I have business of the greatest importance for thee to execute. I have demanded the Princess Badroulboudour in marriage of the sultan her father; he promised her to me, but only asked three months' time; and instead of keeping that promise, he has planned to marry her to the grand vizier's son. I have just heard this, and have no doubt of it. What I ask of you is, that you bring them both hither to me."

"Master," replied the genie, "I will obey you. Have you any other commands?"

"None at present," answered Aladdin; and then the genie disappeared.

Aladdin went downstairs to his mother, with the same tranquillity of mind as usual; and after supper talked of the princess's marriage as of an affair wherein he had not the least concern; and afterwards sat up till the genie had executed his orders.

In the mean time, everything was prepared with the greatest magnificence in the sultan's palace to celebrate the princess's wedding; and the evening was spent with all the usual ceremonies and great rejoicings.

Suddenly the genie, as the faithful slave of the lamp, to

the great amazement of bride and bridegroom, took them up, and transported them in an instant to Aladdin's house, where he set them down.

Aladdin had waited impatiently for this moment. "Take this man," said he to the genie, "and shut him up, and come again to-morrow." The genie took the vizier's son and carried him away; and after he had breathed upon him, which prevented his stirring, he left him.

Great as was Aladdin's love for the Princess Badroulboudour, he did not talk much to her, but only said, "Fear nothing, adorable princess; you are in safety. If I have been forced to come to this extremity, it is not with any intention of affronting you, but to prevent an unjust rival's marrying you contrary to the sultan your father's promise to me."

The princess, who knew nothing of these particulars, gave very little attention to what Aladdin said. The fright and amazement of so surprising and unexpected an adventure had put her into such a condition that he could not get one word from her.

Next morning the genie came at the hour appointed, and said to him, "I am here, master; what are your commands?"

"Go," said Aladdin, "fetch the vizier's son out of the place where you left him, and then take them back to the sultan's palace." Then genie presently returned with the vizier's son, and in an instant they were transported into the palace. But we must observe, that all this time the genie never appeared to either the princess or the grand vizier's son. His hideous form would have made them die with fear. Neither did they hear anything of the discourse between Aladdin and him; they only perceived the motion, and their transportation from one place to another; which we may well imagine was enough to frighten them.

Next day the princess was very melancholy and alarmed, and the sultan and his wife thought she must either be mad, or else have had a bad dream.

The rejoicings lasted all that day in the palace, and the sultaness, who never left the princess, did all she could to divert her.

But the princess continued so gloomy and ill-tempered that the sultan, provoked with his daughter, said to her in a rage, with his sabre in his hand, " Daughter, tell me what is the matter, or I will cut off your head immediately."

The princess, more frightened at the menaces and tone of the enraged sultan than at the sight of the drawn sabre, at last broke silence, and said, with tears in her eyes, " My dear father and sultan, I ask your majesty's pardon if I have offended you, and hope you will have compassion on me when I have told you what a dreadful thing has happened." Then she told him all.

The sultan felt extreme uneasiness at so surprising an adventure. " Daughter," said he, " efface all these troublesome ideas out of your memory; I will take care and give orders that you shall have no more such disagreeable and insupportable adventures."

As soon as the sultan got back to his own apartment, he sent for the grand vizier. " Vizier," said he, " have you seen your son, and has he told you anything? "

The vizier replied, " No."

Then the sultan related all that the Princess Badroulboudour had told him, and said, " I do not doubt that my daughter has told me the truth; but nevertheless I should be glad to have it confirmed by your son; therefore go and ask him."

The grand vizier went immediately to his son, and communicated what the sultan had told him, and enjoined him to conceal nothing, but to tell him the whole truth.

" I will disguise nothing from you, father," replied the son, " for indeed all that the princess says is true. All this ill-usage does not the least lessen the respect and gratitude I entertain for the princess, and of which she is so deserving; but I must confess that, notwithstanding all the honour and splendour that attends my marrying my sovereign's daughter, I would much rather die than marry her if I must undergo again what I have already endured. I do not doubt but that the princess entertains the same sentiments, and that she will readily agree to part, which is so necessary both for her repose and mine. Therefore, father, I beg you to get the sultan's consent that our marriage may be broken off."

Notwithstanding the grand vizier's ambition to have his son allied to the sultan, the firm resolution which he saw he had formed to be separated from the princess made him go and give the sultan an account of what he had told him, assuring him that all was but too true, and begging him to give his son leave to retire from the palace, alleging, for an excuse, that it was not just that the princess should be a moment longer exposed to so terrible a persecution upon his son's account.

The grand vizier found no great difficulty in obtaining what he asked. From that instant the sultan, who had determined upon it already, gave orders to put a stop to all rejoicings in the palace and town, and sent post-haste to all parts of his dominions to countermand his first orders; and in a short time all rejoicings ceased.

This sudden and unexpected change gave rise, in both the city and kingdom, to various speculations and inquiries; but no other account could be given of it except that both the vizier and his son went out of the palace very much dejected. Nobody but Aladdin knew the secret. He rejoiced over the happy success procured for him by his lamp. But neither the sultan nor the grand vizier, who had forgotten Aladdin and his request, had the least thought that he had any hand in the enchantment which caused the marriage to be broken off.

Nevertheless, Aladdin waited till the three months were completed, which the sultan had appointed for the marriage between the Princess Badroulboudour and himself; but the next day sent his mother to the palace, to remind the sultan of his promise.

Aladdin's mother went to the palace, as her son had bidden her, and stood before the divan in the same place as before. The sultan no sooner cast his eyes upon her than he knew her again, and remembered her business, and how long he had put her off: therefore when the grand vizier was beginning to make his report, the sultan interrupted him, and said, "Vizier, I see the good woman who made me the present some months ago; forbear your report till I have heard what she has to say." The vizier presently perceived Aladdin's mother, and sent the chief of the officers for her.

Aladdin's mother came to the foot of the throne, and prostrated herself as usual, and when she rose up again, the sultan asked her what she wanted. "Sir," said she,

"I come to represent to your majesty, in the name of my son Aladdin, that the three months, at the end of which you ordered me to come again, are expired; and to beg you to remember your promise."

The sultan had little thought of hearing any more of a marriage which he imagined would be very disagreeable to the princess, when he considered only the meanness and poverty of Aladdin's mother, and this summons for him to be as good as his word was somewhat embarrassing to him; he declined giving an answer till he had consulted his vizier.

The grand vizier freely told the sultan his thoughts on the matter, and said to him, "In my opinion, sir, there is one certain way for your majesty to avoid so unequal a match without giving Aladdin any cause of complaint; which is, to set so high a value upon the princess, that were he never so rich, he could not come up to it. This is the only way to make him desist from so bold, not to say rash, an undertaking."

The sultan, approving of the grand vizier's advice, turned about to Aladdin's mother, and after some reflection, said to her, "Good woman, it is true sultans ought to be as good as their word, and I am ready to keep mine, by making your son happy by his marriage with the princess my daughter. But as I cannot marry her without some valuable present from your son, you may tell him, I will fulfil my promise as soon as he shall send me forty basins of massy gold, brim-full of the same things you have already made me a present of, and carried by the like number of black slaves, who shall be led by as many young and handsome white slaves, all dressed magnificently. On these conditions I am ready to bestow the princess my daughter on him; therefore, good woman, go and tell him so, and I will wait till you bring me his answer."

Aladdin's mother prostrated herself a second time before the sultan's throne, and retired. On her way home she laughed to herself at her son's foolish imagination. "Where," said she, "can he get so many large gold basins, and enough of the coloured glass to fill them? Must he go again to that subterranean abode, the entrance into which is stopped up, and gather them off the trees? But where will he get so many slaves such as the sultan requires? It is altogether out of his power, and I believe he will not be so well satisfied with my embassy this time." When she came home, full of these thoughts, she said to her son, "Indeed, child, I would not have you think any further of your marriage with the Princess Badroulboudour. The sultan received me very kindly, and I believe he was well disposed to you; but if I am not very much deceived, the grand vizier has made him change his mind." Then she gave her son an exact account of what the sultan said to her, and the conditions on which he consented to the match. Afterwards she said to him, "The sultan expects your answer immediately; but," continued she, laughing, "I believe he may wait long enough."

"Not so long, mother, as you imagine," replied Aladdin; "the sultan is mistaken if he thinks by this exorbitant demand to prevent my entertaining thoughts of the princess; his demand is but a trifle to what I could have done for her. But go and get us something for dinner, and leave the rest to me."

As soon as Aladdin's mother was gone out to the market, Aladdin took the lamp, and rubbed it; the genie appeared, and offered his services as usual. "The sultan," said Aladdin to him, "demands forty large basins of massy gold, brim-full of the fruits of the garden from whence I took this lamp you are slave to; and these he expects to have carried by as many black slaves, each preceded by a young, handsome, well-made white slave, richly clothed. Go and fetch me this present as soon as possible, that I may send it to him before the divan breaks up." The genie told him his command should be immediately obeyed, and disappeared.

A little while afterwards the genie returned with forty black slaves, each bearing on his head a basin of massy gold of twenty marks' weight, full of pearls, diamonds, rubies, and emeralds, all larger and more beautiful than those presented to the sultan before. Each basin was covered with a silver stuff, embroidered with flowers of gold: all these, and the white slaves, quite filled the house, which was but a small one, and the little court before it, and a little garden behind. The genie asked Aladdin if he had any other commands. Aladdin told him that he wanted nothing further then, and the genie disappeared.

When Aladdin's mother came from market, she was greatly surprised to see so many people and such vast riches. As soon as she had laid down her provisions, Aladdin said, "Mother, let us lose no time; before the sultan and the divan rise, I would have you return to the palace, and go with this present as the dowry he asked for the Princess Badroulboudour, that he may judge by my diligence and exactness how anxious I am to procure the honour of this alliance." Without waiting for his mother's reply, Aladdin opened the street-door, and made the slaves walk out; a white slave followed always by a black one with a basin on his head. When they were all out, the mother followed the last black slave, and he shut the door, full of hope that the sultan, after this present, which was such as he required, would at length receive him as his son-in-law.

The first white slave that went out of the house made all the people, who were going by and saw him, stop; and before they were all out of the house, the streets were crowded with spectators, who ran to see so extraordinary and noble a sight. The dress of each slave was so rich, both from the stuff and the jewels, that those who were dealers in them valued each at no less than a million of money. Besides the neatness and propriety of the dress, the good grace, noble air, and beauty of each slave was unparalleled; their grave walk at an equal distance from each other, the lustre of the jewels, which were large, and curiously set in their girdles of massy gold, and the precious stones in their hats, put the crowds of spectators into such great admiration that they could not weary of gazing at them, and followed them with their eyes as far as possible; but the streets were so crowded with people, that none could move out of the spot they stood on. As the procession had to pass through a great many streets to get to the palace, a great part of the city had an opportunity of seeing them. As soon as the first of the slaves arrived at the palace-gate, the porters formed themselves into order, and took him for a king, and were going to kiss the hem of his garment; but the slave, who was instructed by the genie, prevented them, and said, "We are only slaves; our master will appear at the proper time."

Then this slave, followed by the rest, advanced into the second court, which was very spacious, and in which the sultan's household was ranged during the sitting of the divan. The magnificence of the officers, who stood at the head of the troops, was very much eclipsed by the slaves who bare Aladdin's present, of which they themselves made a part. Nothing was ever seen so beautiful and brilliant in the sultan's palace before; and all the lustre of the lords of his court was not to be compared to them.

As the sultan, who had been informed of their coming to the palace, had given orders for them to be admitted when they came, they met with no obstacle, but went into the divan in good order, one part filing to the right, and the other to the left. After they had all entered, and had formed a great semicircle before the sultan's throne, the black slaves laid the basins on the carpet, and all prostrated themselves, touching the carpet with their foreheads, and the white slaves did the same. When they all rose again, the black slaves uncovered the basins, and then all stood with their arms crossed over their breasts.

In the meantime Aladdin's mother advanced to the foot of the throne, and having paid her respects, said to the sultan, "Sir, my son Aladdin is aware that this present, which he has sent your majesty, is much below the Princess Badroulboudour's worth; but hopes, nevertheless, that your majesty will accept it."

The sultan was not able to give the least attention to this compliment of Aladdin's mother. The moment he cast his eyes on the forty basins, brim-full of the most precious, brilliant, and beautiful jewels he had ever seen, and the fourscore slaves, who looked, from the comeliness of their persons and the richness and magnificence of their dress, like so many kings, he was so struck that he could not recover from his admiration; but instead of answering the compliment of Aladdin's mother, addressed himself to the grand vizier, who could no more than the sultan comprehend from whence such a profusion of riches could come. "Well, vizier," said he aloud, "who do you think it can be that has sent me so extraordinary a present? Do you think him worthy of the Princess Badroulboudour, my daughter?"

The vizier, notwithstanding his envy and grief to see a stranger preferred to his son, dared not say so. Aladdin's present was more than sufficient, therefore he returned this answer: "I am so far, sir, from thinking that the person who has made your majesty so noble a present is unworthy of the honour you would do him, that I should be bold to say he deserved much more, if I was not persuaded that the greatest treasure in the world ought not to be put on a level with the princess your majesty's daughter." This advice was applauded by all the lords who were then in council.

The sultan no longer hesitated, nor thought whether Aladdin was endowed with the qualifications requisite in one who aspired to be his son-in-law. The sight alone of such immense riches, and Aladdin's diligence in satisfying his demand without the least difficulty, easily persuaded him that he lacked nothing to render him accomplished, and such as he desired. Therefore, to send Aladdin's mother back with all the satisfaction she could desire, he said to her, "Good woman, go and tell your son that I wait to receive him with open arms, and the more haste he makes to come and receive the princess my daughter from my hands, the greater pleasure he will do me."

As soon as Aladdin's mother retired, overjoyed to see her son raised beyond all expectation to such great honour, the sultan put an end to the audience for that day; and rising from his throne, ordered that the princess's servants should come and carry the basins into their mistress's apartment, whither he went himself to examine them with her at his leisure. The fourscore slaves were not forgotten, but were conducted into the palace; and some time after, the sultan, telling the Princess Badroulboudour of their magnificent appearance, ordered them to be brought before her apartment, that she might see them through the lattice.

In the meantime Aladdin's mother got home, and showed in her face the good news she brought her son. "My son," said she to him, "you have now all the reason in the world to be pleased. Not to keep you too long in suspense, the sultan, with the approbation of the whole court, has declared that you are worthy to marry the Princess Badroulboudour, and waits to embrace you, and arrange your marriage; therefore lose no time in going to him."

Aladdin, charmed with this news, made very little reply, but retired to his room. There, after he had rubbed his lamp, the obedient genie appeared. "Genie," said Aladdin, "I want to bathe immediately, and you must afterwards provide me the richest and most magnificent robe ever worn by a monarch." No sooner were the words out of his mouth, than the genie rendered him, as well as himself, invisible, and transported him into a bath of the finest marble of all sorts of colours; where he was undressed, without seeing by whom, in a neat and spacious hall. From the hall he was led to the bath, and there rubbed and washed with all sorts of scented water. After he had passed through several degrees of heat, he came out, quite a different man from what he was before. When he returned into the hall, he found, instead of his own clothes, a suit the magnificence of which very much surprised him. The genie helped him to dress, and when he had done, transported him back to his own room, where he asked him if he had any other commands. "Yes," answered Aladdin, "I expect you to bring me, as soon as possible, a horse that surpasses in beauty and goodness the best in the sultan's stables, with a saddle, bridle, and harness worth a million of money. I want also twenty slaves, as richly clothed as those who carried the present to the sultan, to walk by my side and follow me, and twenty more to go before me in two ranks. Besides these, bring my mother six women-slaves to wait on her, as richly dressed at least as any of the Princess Badroulboudour's, each loaded with a complete suit fit for any sultaness. I want also ten thousand pieces of gold in ten purses. Go, and make haste."

As soon as Aladdin had given these orders, the genie disappeared and presently returned with the horse, the forty slaves, ten of whom carried each a purse with one thousand pieces of gold, and six women-slaves, each carrying on her head a different dress for Aladdin's mother, wrapped up in a piece of silver stuff, and presented them all to Aladdin.

Of the ten purses Aladdin took but four, which he gave to his mother, telling her that those were to supply her with necessaries; the other six he left in the hands of the slaves who brought them, with an order to throw them by handfuls among the people as they went to the sultan's palace. The six slaves who carried the purses, he ordered likewise to march before him, three on the right hand and three on the left. Afterwards he presented the six women-slaves to his mother, telling her they were her slaves, and that the dresses they had brought were for her use.

When Aladdin had thus settled matters, he told the genie he would call for him when he wanted him, and thereupon the genie disappeared. Aladdin's thoughts now were only of answering, as soon as possible, the desire the sultan had shown to see him. He despatched one of the forty slaves to the palace, with an order to address himself to the chief of the officers, to know when he might have the honour to come and throw himself at the sultan's feet. The slave soon acquitted himself of his message, and brought for answer that the sultan waited for him with impatience.

Aladdin immediately mounted his horse, and began his march in the order we have already described; and though he never was on a horse's back before, he rode with such extraordinary grace that the most experienced horseman would not have taken him for a novice. The streets through which he was to pass were almost instantly filled with an enormous crowd of people, who made the air echo with their shouts, especially every time the six slaves who carried the purses threw handfuls of gold into the air on both sides. Those who knew him once when he played in the streets like a vagabond, did not know him again; those who had seen him but a little while before hardly knew him, so greatly were his features altered: such were the effects of the lamp.

Much more attention was paid to Aladdin than to the pomp and magnificence of his attendants, which had been taken notice of the day before, when the slaves walked in procession with the present to the sultan. Nevertheless the horse was very much admired by good judges, who knew how to discern his beauties without being dazzled with the jewels and richness of the harness: and when the report was everywhere spread about that the sultan was going to give the Princess Badroulboudour in marriage to him, nobody thought of his birth, nor envied his good fortune, so worthy he seemed of it.

When he arrived at the palace everything was prepared for his reception; and when he came to the second gate, he would have alighted off his horse, agreeable to the custom observed by the grand vizier, the generals of the armies, and governors of provinces of the first rank; but the chief of the officers who waited on him by the sultan's order prevented him, and attended him to the council-hall, where he helped him to dismount. The officers formed themselves into two ranks at the entrance of the hall. The chief put Aladdin on his right hand, and through the midst of them led him to the sultan's throne.

As soon as the sultan perceived Aladdin, he was surprised to see him more richly and magnificently clothed than ever he had been himself. Besides, he had a certain air of unexpected grandeur, very different from the poverty his mother had appeared in.

But notwithstanding, his surprise did not hinder him from rising off his throne, and descending two or three steps, quick enough to prevent Aladdin's throwing himself at his feet. He embraced him with all the demonstrations of friendship. After this, Aladdin would have cast himself at his feet again; but the sultan held him fast by the hand, and obliged him to sit between him and the grand vizier.

Then Aladdin said, "I receive, sir, the honour which your majesty out of your great goodness is pleased to confer on me; but permit me to tell you that I have not forgotten that I am your slave; that I know the greatness of your power, and that I am not unaware how much my birth is below the splendour and lustre of the high rank to which I am raised. I ask your majesty's pardon for my rashness, but I cannot dissemble that I should die with grief if I should lose my hope of marrying the princess."

"My son," answered the sultan, embracing him a second time, "you would wrong me to doubt my sincerity for a moment."

After these words the sultan gave a signal, and immediately the air echoed with the sound of trumpets and hautboys, and other musical instruments: and at the same time the sultan led Aladdin into a magnificent hall, where there was prepared a noble feast. The sultan and Aladdin ate by themselves; the grand vizier and the great lords of the court, according to their dignity and rank, waited all the time. The conversation turned on different subjects; but all the while the sultan hardly ever took his eyes off him; and throughout all their conversation Aladdin showed so much good sense, that it confirmed the sultan in the good opinion he had of him.

After the feast, the sultan sent for the chief judge of his capital, and ordered him to draw up immediately a contract of marriage between the Princess Badroulboudour, his daughter, and Aladdin.

When the judge had drawn up the contract in all the requisite forms, the sultan asked Aladdin if he would stay in the palace, and solemnise the ceremonies of marriage that day. To which he answered, " Sir, though great is my impatience, yet I beg of you to give me leave to defer it till I have built a palace fit to receive the princess in; I therefore desire you to grant me a convenient spot of ground near your palace, that I may come the more frequently to pay my respects to you, and I will take care to have it finished with all diligence."

" Son," said the sultan, " take what ground you think proper; there is land enough before my palace." After these words he embraced Aladdin again, who took his leave with as much politeness as if he had always lived at court.

Aladdin mounted his horse again, and returned home in the order he came, with the acclamations of the people, who wished him all happiness and prosperity. As soon as he dismounted he retired to his own room, took the lamp and called the genie as before. " Genie," said Aladdin, " I have had all the reason in the world to commend you hitherto, but now if you have any regard for the lamp your mistress, you must show, if possible, more zeal and diligence than ever. I want you to build me, as soon as you can, a palace at a proper distance from the sultan's, fit to receive my wife the Princess Badroulboudour. I leave the choice of the materials to you, that is to say, porphyry, jasper, agate, lapis lazuli, and the finest marble of the most varied colours; and the style of the building. But in the highest story of this palace you shall build me a large hall with a dome and four equal fronts; and instead of layers of bricks, the walls shall be made of massy gold and silver, laid alternately; each front shall contain six windows, the lattices of all of which shall be so enriched with diamonds, rubies and emeralds that they shall exceed everything of the kind that has ever been seen in the world. I would have an inner and outer court before this palace, and a garden, but above all things take care that there be laid in a place, which you shall point out to me, a treasure of gold and silver coin. This palace must be well provided with kitchens and offices, store-houses, and rooms in which to keep choice furniture for every season of the year. I must have stables full of the finest horses, with their equerries and grooms, and hunting equipage. There must be officers to attend the kitchens and offices, and women-slaves to wait on the princess. You understand what I mean, therefore go about it, and come and tell me when all is finished."

By the time Aladdin had instructed the genie with his intentions respecting the building of his palace, the sun was set. The next morning by break of day, Aladdin was no sooner up than the genie presented himself, and said, "Sir, your palace is finished; come and see how you like it." The genie transported him thither in an instant, and he found it so much beyond his expectation that he could not enough admire it. The genie led him through all the apartments, where he met with nothing but what was rich and magnificent, with officers and slaves, all dressed according to their rank and the services to which they were appointed. Then the genie showed him the treasury, which was opened by a treasurer, where Aladdin saw heaps of purses of different sizes, piled up to the top of the ceiling. The genie assured him of the treasurer's fidelity, and thence led him to the stables, where he showed him some of the finest horses in the world, and the grooms busy dressing them. From thence they went to the store-houses, which were filled with all necessary provisions, for both the food and ornament of the horses.

When Aladdin had examined the palace from top to bottom, and particularly the hall with the four-and-twenty windows, and found it much beyond whatever he could have imagined, he said to the genie, "Genie, no one can be better satisfied than I am, and indeed I should be very much to blame if I found any fault. There is only one thing wanting, which I forgot to mention. That is, to lay from the sultan's palace to the door of the apartment designed for the princess, a carpet of fine velvet for her to walk upon." The genie immediately disappeared, and Aladdin saw what he desired executed that minute. Then the genie returned, and carried Aladdin home before the gates of the sultan's palace were opened.

When the porters, who had always been used to an open view, came to open the gates, they were amazed to find it obstructed, and to see a carpet of velvet spread. They did not immediately see what it meant, but when they saw Aladdin's palace distinctly, their surprise was increased. The news of so extraordinary a wonder spread through the palace. The grand vizier, who came soon after the gates were open, was no less amazed than the others, but ran and told the sultan, and endeavoured to make him believe it to be all enchantment. "Vizier," replied the sultan, "why do you say it is enchantment? You know as well as I that it is Aladdin's palace, which I gave him leave to build to receive my daughter in. After the proof we have had of his riches, can we think it strange that he should build a palace in so short a time? He intends to surprise us, and let us see what wonders are to be done with ready money every day. Confess sincerely to me that that enchantment you talk of proceeds from a little envy."

When Aladdin had been conveyed home, and had dismissed the genie, he found his mother up, and dressing herself in one of the suits that were brought her. By the time the sultan came from the council, Aladdin had prepared his mother to go to the palace with her slaves, and desired her, if she saw the sultan, to tell him she came to do herself the honour of attending the princess towards evening to her palace. Accordingly she went, but though she and the women-slaves who followed her were all dressed like sultanesses, yet the crowd was nothing like so great, because they were all veiled. As for Aladdin, he mounted his horse, and took leave of his paternal house for ever, taking care not to forget his wonderful lamp, and went to the palace with the same pomp as the day before.

As soon as the porters of the sultan's palace saw Aladdin's mother, they went and informed the sultan, who presently ordered the bands of trumpets, cymbals, drums, fifes and hautboys, placed in different parts of the palace, to play and beat, so that the air resounded with sounds which inspired the whole city with joy; the merchants began to adorn their shops and houses with fine carpets and cushions, and bedeck them with boughs, and prepare illuminations for the night. The artists of all sorts left their work, and the people all repaired to the great space between the sultan's and Aladdin's palaces; which last drew all their attention, not only because it was new to them, but because there was no comparison between the two buildings. But they could not imagine by what unheard-of miracle so magnificent a palace could be so soon built, it being apparent to all that there were no prepared materials, or any foundations laid the day before.

Aladdin's mother was received in the palace with honour, and introduced into the Princess Badroulboudour's apartment. As soon as the princess saw her, she went and saluted her, and desired her to sit down on her sofa: and while her women finished dressing her, and adorning her with the jewels with which Aladdin had presented her, a collation was served up. At the same time the sultan, who wanted to be as much with his daughter as possible before he parted with her, came and paid her great respect. The sultan, who had always seen Aladdin's mother dressed very meanly, not to say poorly, was surprised to find her as richly and magnificently clothed as the princess his daughter. This made him think Aladdin equally prudent and wise in whatever he undertook.

When it was night, the princess took leave of the sultan her father, and set out for Aladdin's palace, with his mother on her left hand, followed by a hundred women-slaves, dressed with surprising magnificence. All the bands of music, which played from the time Aladdin's mother arrived, joined together and led the procession. Four hundred of the sultan's young pages carried torches on each side, which, together with the illuminations of the sultan's and Aladdin's palaces, made it as light as day.

At length the princess arrived at the new palace. Aladdin ran with all imaginable joy to receive her at the entrance. His mother had taken care to point him out to the princess, in the midst of the officers that surrounded him, and she was charmed as soon as she saw him. "Adorable princess," said Aladdin to her, saluting her respectfully, "if I have displeased you by my boldness in aspiring to so lovely a princess, and my sultan's daughter, I must tell you that you ought to blame yourself, not me."

"Prince (as I may now call you)," answered the princess, "I am obedient to the will of my father; and it is enough for me to have seen you, to tell you that I obey without reluctance."

Aladdin, charmed with so agreeable and satisfactory an answer, would not keep the princess standing after she had walked so far, but took her by the hand, which he kissed with joy, and led her into a large hall, illuminated with an infinite number of wax candles, where, by the care of the genie, a noble feast was served up. The plates were of massy gold. The vases, basins, and goblets, with which the sideboard was furnished, were gold also, and of exquisite workmanship. The princess, dazzled to see so much riches collected in one place, said to Aladdin, "I thought, Prince, that nothing in the world was so beautiful as the sultan my father's palace; but the sight of this hall alone is enough to show that I was deceived."

Then Aladdin led the princess to the place appointed for her, and as soon as she and his mother were sat down, a band of the most harmonious instruments, accompanied with the voices of beautiful ladies, began a concert, which lasted without intermission to the end of the repast. The princess was so charmed that she declared she never heard anything like it in the sultan her father's court; but she knew not that these musicians were fairies chosen by the genie, slaves of the lamp.

When the supper was ended, and the table taken away, there entered a company of dancers. At length, Aladdin, according to the custom of that time in China, rose up and presented his hand to the Princess Badroulboudour to dance with her, and to finish the ceremonies. They danced with so good a grace that they were the admiration of all the company. Thus ended the ceremonies and rejoicings at the marriage of Aladdin with the Princess Badroulboudour.

PART II

ALADDIN and his wife had lived happily after this manner for several years, when the African magician, who undesignedly had been the means of raising him to such good fortune, bethought himself of him in Africa, whither, after his expedition, he had returned. And though he was almost persuaded that Aladdin had died miserably in the subterranean abode where he left him, he had the curiosity to learn about his end with certainty. As he was a great magician, he took out of a cupboard a square covered box, which he made use of in his observations; then sat himself down on his sofa, set it before him, and uncovered it. After he had prepared and levelled the sand which was in it, to discover whether or no Aladdin died in the subterranean abode, he cast the points, drew the figures, and formed a horoscope, by which, when he came to examine it, he found that Aladdin, instead of dying in the cave, had escaped out of it, lived splendidly, was very rich, had married a princess, and was very much honoured and respected.

The magician no sooner understood by the rules of his diabolical art that Aladdin had arrived at that height of good fortune, than a colour came into his face, and he cried out in a rage, "This poor sorry tailor's son has discovered the secret and virtue of the lamp! I believed his death to be certain, but find too plainly he enjoys the fruit of my labour and study! But I will prevent his enjoying it long, or perish in the attempt." The next morning the magician mounted a horse which was in his stable, set out, and stopped only to refresh himself and horse till he arrived at the capital of China. He alighted, took up his lodgings in a khan, and stayed there the remainder of the day and the night, to rest after so long a journey.

The next day his first object was to inquire what people said of Aladdin; and, taking a walk through the town, he went to the most public and frequented places, where people of the highest distinction met to drink a certain warm liquor, which he had drunk often when he was there before. As soon as he sat down he was given a glass of it, which he took; but listening at the same time to the discourse of the company on each side of him, he heard them talking of Aladdin's palace. When he had drunk off his glass, he joined them, and taking the opportunity, asked them what palace it was they spoke so well of. "From whence come you?" said the person to whom he addressed himself; "you must certainly be a stranger not to have seen or heard talk of Prince Aladdin's palace (for he was called so after his marriage with the Princess Badroulboudour). I do not say," continued the man, "that it is one of the wonders of the world, but that it is the only wonder of the world; since nothing so grand, rich, and magnificent was ever seen. Certainly you must have come from a great distance, not to have heard of it; it must have been talked of all over the world. Go and see it, and then judge whether I have told you more than the truth."

"Forgive my ignorance," replied the African magician; "I arrived here but yesterday, and came from the furthest part of Africa, where the fame of this palace had not reached when I came away. For the affair which brought me hither was so urgent, that my sole object was to get here as soon as I could, without stopping anywhere, or making any acquaintance. But I will not fail to go and see it; I will go immediately and satisfy my curiosity, if you will do me the favour to show me the way."

The person to whom the African magician addressed himself was pleased to show him the way to Aladdin's palace. When he came to the palace, and had examined it on all sides, he doubted not that Aladdin had made use of the lamp to build it; for he knew that none but the genies, the slaves of the lamp, could have performed such wonders; and piqued to the quick at Aladdin's happiness and greatness, he returned to the khan where he lodged.

The next thing was to learn where the lamp was; if Aladdin carried it about with him, or where he kept it; and this he was able to discover by an operation of magic. As soon as he entered his lodging, he took his square box of sand, which he always carried with him when he travelled, and after he had performed some operations, he knew that the lamp was in Aladdin's palace, and so great was his joy at the discovery that he could hardly contain himself. " Well," said he, " I shall have the lamp, and I defy Aladdin to prevent my carrying it off and making him sink to his original meanness, from which he has taken so high a flight."

It was Aladdin's misfortune at that time to have gone hunting for eight days, of which only three were past. After the magician had performed the operation which gave him so much joy, he went to the master of the khan, entered into talk with him on indifferent matters, and among the rest, told him he had been to see Aladdin's palace; and added, " and I shall not be easy till I have seen the person to whom this wonderful edifice belongs."

" That will be no difficult matter," replied the master of the khan; " there is not a day passes but he gives an opportunity when he is in town, but at present he is not at home, and has been gone these three days on a hunting-match, which will last eight."

The magician wanted to know no more: he took leave of the master of the khan, and returning to his own chamber, said to himself, " This is an opportunity I ought by no means to let slip." For this purpose he went to a maker and seller of lamps, and asked for a dozen copper lamps: the master of the shop told him he had not so many by him, but if he would have patience till the next day, he would get them for him. The magician appointed his time, and bid him take care that they should be handsome and well polished. After promising to pay him well, he returned to his inn.

The next day the magician called for the twelve lamps, paid the man his full price for them, put them into a basket which he bought on purpose, and with the basket hanging on his arm, went straight to Aladdin's palace; and when he came near it, he began crying, " Who will change old lamps for new ones? " As he went along, he gathered a crowd of children about him, who hooted at him, and thought him, as did all who chanced to be passing by, mad or a fool, to offer to change new lamps for old ones.

The African magician never minded all their scoffs and hootings, but still continued crying, " Who will change old lamps for new ones? " He repeated this so often, walking backwards and forwards about the Princess Badroulboudour's palace, that the princess, who was then in the hall with the four-and-twenty windows, hearing a man cry something, and not being able to distinguish his words, by reason of the hooting of the children and increasing mob about him, sent one of her women-slaves down to know what he cried.

It was not long before the slave returned, and ran into the hall, laughing heartily. "Well, giggler," said the princess, "will you tell me what are you laughing at?"

"Madam," answered the slave, laughing still, "who can help laughing to see a fool with a basket on his arm, full of fine new lamps, ask to change them for old ones; the children and mob, crowding about him so that he can hardly stir, make all the noise they can by deriding him."

Another woman-slave, hearing this, said, "Now you speak of lamps, I know not whether the princess has observed it, but there is an old one on the shelf, and whoever owns it will not be sorry to find a new one in its stead. If the princess has a mind she may have the pleasure of trying if this fool is so silly as to give a new lamp for an old one without taking anything for the exchange."

The lamp this slave spoke of was Aladdin's wonderful lamp, which he, for fear of losing, had laid on the shelf before he went hunting, which precaution he had taken several times before, but neither the princess, the slaves, nor the attendants had ever taken any notice of it. At all other times he carried it about with him, and then indeed he might have locked it up, but other people have been guilty of oversight as great, and will be so to the end of time.

The Princess Badroulboudour, who knew not the value of this lamp, and the importance for Aladdin, not to mention herself, of keeping it safe from everybody else, entered into the joke, and bade an attendant take it, and go and make the exchange. The attendant obeyed, went out of the hall, and no sooner got to the palace gates than he saw the African magician, called to him, and showing him the old lamp, said to him, "Give me a new lamp for this."

The magician never doubted but this was the lamp he wanted. There could be no other like it in this palace, where all was gold or silver. He snatched it eagerly out of the man's hand, and thrusting it as far as he could into his breast, offered him his basket, and bid him choose which he liked best. The man picked out one, and carried it to the Princess Badroulboudour, but the exchange was no sooner made than the place rang with the shouts of the children, deriding the magician's folly.

The African magician gave everybody leave to laugh as much as they pleased. He stayed not long about Aladdin's palace, but made the best of his way back without crying any longer "New lamps for old ones." His end was answered, and by his silence he got rid of the children and the mob.

As soon as he got out of the square between the two palaces he skulked down the streets which were the least frequented, and having no more need for his lamps or basket, set them all down in the midst of a street where nobody saw him; then scouring another street or two, he walked till he came to one of the city gates, and pursuing his way through the suburbs, which were very long, he bought some provisions before he left the city, got into the fields, and turned into a road which led to a lonely remote place, where he stopped for a time to execute the design he came about, never thinking about his horse, which he had left at the khan, but considering himself perfectly compensated by the treasure he had acquired.

In this place the African magician passed the remainder of the day, till the darkest time of night, when he pulled the lamp out of his breast and rubbed it. At that summons the genie appeared, and said, "What wouldst thou have? I am ready to obey thee as thy slave, and the slave of all those who have that lamp in their hands, both I and the other slaves of the lamp."

"I command thee," replied the magician, "to transport me immediately and the palace which thou and the other slaves of the lamp have built in this town, just as it is, with all the people in it, to a place in Africa." The genie made no reply, but with the assistance of the other genies, the slaves of the lamp, transported him and the palace entire immediately to Africa, where we will leave the magician, palace, and the Princess Badroulboudour, to speak of the surprise of the sultan.

As soon as the sultan rose the next morning, according to custom, he looked out of the window to have the pleasure of contemplating and admiring Aladdin's palace.

But when he first looked that way, and instead of a palace saw an empty space such as it had been before the palace was built, he thought he was mistaken, and rubbed his eyes. He looked again, and saw nothing more the second time than the first, though the weather was fine, the sky clear, and the daybreak had made all objects very distinct. He looked through the two openings on the right and left, and saw nothing more than he had formerly been used to see out of them. His amazement was so great that he stood for some time turning his eyes to the spot where the palace had stood, but where it was no longer to be seen. He could not comprehend how so large a palace as Aladdin's, which he saw plainly every day, and but the day before, should vanish so soon and not leave the least trace behind. " Certainly," said he, to himself, " I am not mistaken. It stood there. If it had tumbled down, the materials would have lain in heaps, and if it had been swallowed up by an earthquake there would be some mark left." Though he was convinced that no palace stood there, he could not help staying there some time, to see whether he might not be mistaken. At last he retired to his apartment, not without looking behind him before he quitted the spot, and ordered the grand vizier to be fetched in all haste, and in the meantime sat down, his mind agitated by many different thoughts.

The grand vizier did not make the sultan wait long for him, but came with so much haste that neither he nor his attendants as they passed by missed Aladdin's palace; neither did the porters, when they opened the palace gates; observe any alteration.

When he came into the sultan's presence, he said to him, " Sir, the haste with which your majesty has sent for me makes me believe something very extraordinary has happened, since you know this is a council-day, and I should not fail to attend you there very soon."

" Indeed," said the sultan, " it *is* something very extraordinary, as you say, and you will allow it to be so. Tell me what has become of Aladdin's palace."

" Aladdin's palace! " replied the grand vizier, in great amazement, " I thought, as I passed by, that it stood in its usual place; such substantial buildings are not so easily removed."

"Go to my window," said the sultan, "and tell me if you can see it."

The grand vizier went to the window, where he was struck with no less amazement than the sultan had been. When he was well assured that there was not the least appearance of this palace, he returned to the sultan. "Well," said the sultan, "have you seen Aladdin's palace?"

"Sir," answered the vizier, "your majesty may remember that I had the honour to tell you that that palace, which was the subject of your admiration, with all its immense riches, was only the work of magic and a magician, but your majesty would not pay the least attention to what I said."

The sultan, who could not deny what the grand vizier had represented to him, flew into a great passion. "Where is that impostor, that wicked wretch," said he, "that I may have his head cut off immediately?"

"Sir," replied the grand vizier, "it is some days since he came to take his leave of your majesty; he ought to be sent to to know what is become of his palace, since he cannot be ignorant of what has been done."

"That is too great a favour," replied the sultan: "go and order a detachment of thirty horse, to bring him to me loaded with chains." The grand vizier went and gave orders for a detachment of thirty horse, and instructed the officer who commanded them how they were to act, that Aladdin might not escape them. The detachment pursued their orders; and about five or six leagues from the town they met him returning from hunting. The officer went up to him, and told him that the sultan was so impatient to see him, that he had sent them to accompany him home.

Aladdin had not the least suspicion of the true reason of their meeting him, but pursued his way hunting; but when he came within half a league of the city, the detachment surrounded him, and the officer addressed himself to him, and said, "Prince Aladdin, it is with great regret that I declare to you the sultan's order to arrest you, and to carry you before him as a criminal; I beg of you not to take it ill that we acquit ourselves of our duty, and to forgive us."

Aladdin, who felt himself innocent, was very much surprised at this declaration, and asked the officer if he knew what crime he was accused of; who replied he did not. Then Aladdin, finding that his retinue was much smaller than this detachment, alighted off his horse, and said to the officer, "Execute your orders; I am not conscious that I have committed any crime against the sultan's person or government." A large long chain was immediately put about his neck, and fastened round his body, so that both his arms were pinioned down; then the officer put himself at the head of the detachment, and one of the troopers took hold of the end of the chain, and proceeding the officer, led Aladdin, who was obliged to follow him on foot, into the town.

When this detachment entered the suburbs, the people who saw Aladdin thus led as a state criminal, never doubted but that his head was to be cut off; and as he was generally beloved, some took sabres and other arms; and those who had none, gathered stones, and followed the detachment. The last five of the detachment faced about to disperse them; but their number presently increased so much that the detachment began to think that it would be well if they could get into the sultan's palace before Aladdin was rescued; to prevent which, according to the different extent of the streets, they took care to cover the ground by extending or closing. In this manner they arrived at the palace square, and there drew up in a line, and faced about till their officer and the troopers that led Aladdin had got within the gates, which were immediately shut.

Aladdin was carried before the sultan, who waited for him attended by the grand vizier in a balcony; and as soon as he saw him, he ordered the executioner, who waited there on purpose, to cut off his head, without hearing him, or giving him leave to clear himself.

As soon as the executioner had taken off the chain that was fastened about Aladdin's neck and body, and laid laid down a skin stained with the blood of the many criminals he had executed, he made Aladdin kneel down, and tied a bandage over his eyes. Then drawing his sabre, he prepared to strike the blow by flourishing it three times in the air, waiting for the sultan's signal to separate his head from his body.

At that instant the grand vizier, perceiving that the populace had forced the guard of horse, and crowded the great square before the palace, and were scaling the walls in several places and beginning to pull them down to force their way in, said to the sultan, before he gave the signal, "I beg of your majesty to consider what you are going to do, since you will risk your palace being forced; and who knows what fatal consequences may attend it?"

"My palace forced!" replied the sultan; "who can have such boldness?"

"Sir," answered the grand vizier, "if your majesty will but cast your eyes towards the great square, and on the palace walls, you will know the truth of what I say."

The sultan was so frightened when he saw so great a crowd and perceived how enraged they were, that he ordered the executioner to put his sabre in the scabbard immediately, and to unbind Aladdin; and at same time bade the officers declare to the people that the sultan had pardoned him and that they might retire.

Then all those who had already got upon the walls and were witnesses of what had passed, got quickly down, overjoyed that they had saved the life of a man they dearly loved, and published the news among the rest, which was presently confirmed by the officers from the top of the terraces. The justice which the sultan had done to Aladdin soon disarmed the populace of their rage; the tumult abated, and the mob dispersed.

When Aladdin found himself at liberty, he turned towards the balcony, and perceiving the sultan, raised his voice, and said to him in a moving manner, "I beg of your majesty to add one favour more to that which I have already received, which is to let me know my crime."

"Your crime!" answered the sultan; "perfidious wretch! do you not know it? Come up, hither, and I will show you."

Aladdin went up and presented himself to the sultan, who walked in front, without looking at him, saying, "Follow me;" and then led him into his room. When he came to the door, he said, "Go in; you ought to know whereabouts your palace stood; look round, and tell me what has become of it."

Aladdin looked round but saw nothing. He perceived very well the spot of ground his palace had stood on; but not being able to divine how it had disappeared, this extraordinary and surprising event threw him into such great confusion and amazement that he could not answer one word.

The sultan growing impatient, said to him again, "Where is your palace, and what has become of my daughter?"

Then Aladdin, breaking silence, said to him, "Sir, I see very well, and own that the palace which I have built is not in the place where it was, but is vanished; neither can I tell your majesty where it may be, but I can assure you I have had no hand in it."

"I am not so much concerned about your palace," replied the sultan; "I value my daughter ten thousand times before it, and would have you find her out, otherwise I will cause your head to be struck off, and no consideration shall prevent it."

"I beg your majesty," answered Aladdin, "to grant me forty days to make my inquiries; and if in that time I have not the success I wish for, I will come again and offer my head at the foot of your throne, to be disposed of at your pleasure."

"I give you the forty days you ask for," said the sultan; "but think not to abuse the favour I show you by imagining you shall escape my resentment; for I will find you out in whatsoever part of the world you are."

Aladdin went out of the sultan's presence with great humiliation, and in a condition worthy of pity. He crossed the courts of the palace, hanging down his head, and in such great confusion that he dared not lift up his eyes. The principal officers of the court, who had all professed themselves his friends, and whom he had never disobliged, instead of going up to comfort him, and offer him a refuge in their houses, turned their backs on him to avoid seeing him, lest he should know them. But had they accosted him with a word of comfort or offer of service, they would not have known Aladdin. He did not know himself, and was no longer in his senses, as plainly appeared by his asking everybody he met, at every house, if they had seen his palace, or could tell him any news of it.

These questions made everybody believe that Aladdin was mad. Some laughed at him, but people of sense and humanity, particularly those who had had any connection of business or friendship with him, really pitied him. For three days he rambled about the city after this manner, without coming to any decision, or eating anything, but what some good people forced him to take out of charity.

At last, as he could no longer, in his unhappy condition, stay in a city where he had formerly made so fine a figure, he quitted it, and took the road to the country; and after he had traversed several fields in frightful uncertainty, at the approach of night he came to a river-side. There, possessed by his despair, he said to himself, "Where shall I seek my palace? In what province, country, or part of the world, shall I find that and my dear princess? I shall never succeed; I had better free myself at once from so much fruitless fatigue and such bitter grief." He was just going to throw himself into the river, but, as a good Mussulman, true to his religion, he thought he could not do it without first saying his prayers. Going to prepare himself, he went first to the river-side to wash his hands and face, according to custom. But that place being steep and slippery, owing to the water's beating against it, he slid down, and would certainly have fallen into the river, but for a little rock which projected about two feet out of the earth. Happily also for him, he still had on the ring which the African magician put on his finger before he went down into the subterranean abode to fetch the precious lamp. In slipping down the bank he rubbed the ring so hard, by holding on the rock, that immediately the genie appeared whom he saw in the cave where the magician left him. "What wouldst thou have?" said the genie. "I am ready to obey thee as thy slave, and the slave of all those that have that ring on their finger; both I and the other slaves of the ring."

Aladdin, agreeably surprised at an apparition he so little expected, replied, "Save my life, genie, a second time, either by showing me to the place where the palace I have caused to be built now stands, or by immediately transporting it back to where it first stood."

"What you command me," answered the genie, "is not in my power; I am only the slave of the ring; you must address yourself to the slave of the lamp."

"If it be so," replied Aladdin, "I command thee, by the power of the ring, to transport me to the place where my palace stands, in what part of the world soever it is, and to set me down under the Princess Badroulboudour's window." These words were no sooner out of his mouth than the genie transported him into Africa, to the midst of a large meadow, where his palace stood, a small distance from a great city, and set him exactly under the windows of the princess's apartment, and then left him. All this was done almost in an instant.

Aladdin, notwithstanding the darkness of the night, knew his palace and the Princess Badroulboudour's apartment again very well; but as the night was far advanced, and all was quiet in the palace, he retired to some distance, and sat down at the foot of a large tree. As he had not slept for five or six days, he was not able to resist the drowsiness which came upon him, but fell fast asleep where he was.

The next morning, as soon as the dawn appeared, Aladdin was agreeably awakened not only by the singing of the birds which had roosted in the tree under which he had passed the night, but of all those which perched in the thick trees of the palace garden. When he cast his eyes on that wonderful building, he felt an inexpressible joy to think he should soon be master of it again, and once more see his dear Princess Badroulboudour. Pleased with these hopes, he immediately got up, went toward the princess's apartment, and walked under her window, in expectation of her rising, that he might see her. Meanwhile, he began to consider with himself from whence his misfortune proceeded; and after mature reflection, he no longer doubted that it was owing to his having put his lamp out of his sight. He accused himself of negligence, and the little care he took of it, to let it be a moment away from him. But what puzzled him most was that he could not imagine who had been so jealous of his happiness. He would soon have guessed this, if he had known that both he and his palace were in Africa, the very name of which would soon have made him remember the magician, his declared enemy; but the genie, the slave of the ring, had not made the least mention of the name of the place, nor had Aladdin asked him.

The Princess Badroulboudour rose earlier that morning than she had done since her transportation into Africa by the magician, whose presence she was forced to endure once a day, because he was master of the palace; but she had always treated him so harshly that he dared not reside in it. As she was dressing, one of the women looking through the window perceived Aladdin, and ran and told her mistress. The princess, who could not believe the news, went herself to the window, and seeing Aladdin, immediately opened it. The noise the princess made in opening the window made Aladdin turn his head that way, and, knowing the princess, he saluted her with an air that expressed his joy. "To lose no time," said she to him, "I have sent to have the private door opened for you; enter, and come up." She then shut the window.

The private door, which was just under the princess's apartment, was soon opened, and Aladdin was conducted up into the princess's room. It is impossible to express their joy at seeing each other after a separation which they both thought was for ever. They embraced several times, and these embracings over, they sat down, shedding tears of joy, and Aladdin said, "I beg you, Princess, before we talk of anything else, to tell me, both for your own sake, the sultan your father's, and mine, what is become of an old lamp which I left upon the shelf in the hall of the four-and-twenty windows, before I went hunting?"

"Alas! dear husband," answered the princess, "I am afraid our misfortune is owing to that lamp: and what grieves me most is that I have been the cause of it."

"Princess," replied Aladdin, "do not blame yourself, since it was entirely my fault, and I ought to have taken more care of it. But let us now think only of repairing the loss; tell me what has happened, and into whose hands it has fallen."

Then the Princess Badroulboudour gave Aladdin an account of how she changed the old lamp for a new one, which she ordered to be fetched, that he might see it, and how the next morning she found herself in the unknown country they were then in, which she was told was Africa by the traitor who had transported her thither by his magic art.

"Princess," said Aladdin, interrupting her, "you have informed me who the traitor is, by telling me we are in Africa. He is the most perfidious of all men; but this is neither the time nor the place to give you a full account of his villainies. I desire you only to tell me what he has done with the lamp, and where he has put it."

"He carries it carefully wrapt up in his bosom," said the princess: "and this I can assure you, because he pulled it out before me, and showed it to me in triumph."

"Princess," said Aladdin, "do not be displeased that I trouble you with so many questions, since they are equally important both to you and me. But tell me, I implore you, how so wicked and perfidious a man treats you."

"Since I have been here," replied the princess, "he comes once a day to see me; and I am persuaded that the little satisfaction he receives from his visits makes him come no oftener. All his discourse tends to persuade me to break that faith I have pledged to you, and to take him for a husband; giving me to understand that I ought not to entertain any hope of ever seeing you again, for that you were dead, and had had your head struck off by the sultan my father's order. He added, to justify himself, that you were an ungrateful wretch; that your good fortune was owing to him, and a great many other things which I forbear to repeat: but, as he received no other answer from me but grievous complaints and tears, he was always forced to retire with as little satisfaction as he came. I doubt not his intention is to allow me time to vanquish my grief, in the hope that I may change my mind; and if I persevere in an obstinate refusal, to use violence. But my dear husband's presence removes all my disquiet."

"I think," replied Aladdin, "I have found means to deliver you from your enemy and mine: to execute this design, it is necessary for me to go to the town. I shall return by noon, and will then communicate my plan to you, and tell you what you must do to ensure success. But that you may not be surprised, I think it proper to tell you that I shall change my apparel, and beg you to give orders that I may not wait long at the private door, but that it may be opened at the first knock," all of which the princess promised to observe.

When Aladdin had got out of the palace by that door, he looked round about him on all sides, and perceiving a peasant going into the country, he hastened after him; and when he had overtaken him, made a proposal to him to change clothes, which the man agreed to. They made the exchange; the countryman went about his business, and Aladdin to the city. After traversing several streets, he came to that part of the town where all sorts of merchants and artisans had their particular streets, according to their trades. He went into that of the druggists; and going into one of the largest and best shops, asked the druggist if he had a certain powder which he named.

The druggist regarding Aladdin from his clothes as very poor, told him he had it, but that it was very dear; upon which Aladdin, penetrating into his thoughts, pulled out his purse, and showing him some gold, asked for half a drachm of the powder, which the druggest weighed, and wrapped up in a piece of paper, and gave him, telling him the price was a piece of gold. Aladdin put the money into his hand, and staying no longer in the town, except just to get a little refreshment, returned to the palace, where he waited not long at the private door. When he came into the princess's apartment, he said to her, "Princess, perhaps the aversion you tell me you have for the magician may hinder your doing what I am going to propose; but give me leave to tell you, it is proper that you should dissemble a little, and do violence to your feelings, if you would deliver yourself from him, and give the sultan your father the satisfaction of seeing you again.

"If you will take my advice," continued he, "dress yourself this moment in one of your richest robes, and when the African magician comes, give him the best reception; receive him with an open countenance, without constraint. From your conversation, let him suppose that you strive to forget me. Invite him to sup with you, and give him to understand you should be glad to taste some of the best wines of his country. He will go and fetch you some. During his absence, put this powder into one of the cups, and setting it by, charge the slave who attends you to bring you that cup at a signal you shall agree on with her. When the magician and you have eaten and drunk as much as you choose, let her bring you the cup, and change cups with him. He will take it as so great a favour that he will not refuse you, and will drain the cup; but no sooner will he have drunk it off than you will see him fall backwards."

When Aladdin had finished, "I own," answered the

princess, "I shall do myself great violence in consenting to make the magician such advances as I see are absolutely necessary for me to make; but what cannot one resolve to do against a cruel enemy? I will therefore follow your advice." After the princess had agreed to the measures proposed by Aladdin, he took his leave of her, and went and spent the rest of the day in the neighbourhood of the palace till it was night, when he might safely return to the private door.

The Princess Badroulboudour, who was inconsolable at being separated not only from her dear husband, but also from the sultan her father, had, ever since that cruel separation, lived in great neglect of her person. She had almost forgotten to keep herself neat, particularly after the first time the magician paid her a visit; for she learned from some of the women, who knew him again, that it was he who took the old lamp in exchange for a new one, which notorious cheat rendered the sight of him more abhorrent. However, the opportunity of punishing him as he deserved made her resolve to gratify Aladdin. As soon, therefore, as he was gone, she sat down at her toilet, and was dressed by her women to the best advantage, in the richest robes. Her girdle was of the finest and largest diamonds set in gold, which she matched with a necklace of pearls, six on a side, so well setting off the one in the middle, which was the largest and most valuable, that the greatest sultanesses and queens would have been proud to be adorned with only two of the smallest. Her bracelets were of diamonds and rubies intermixed.

When the Princess Badroulboudour was completely dressed, she consulted her glass and her women as to how she looked, and when she found she would easily be able to flatter the foolish magician, she sat down on a sofa, awaiting his arrival.

The magician came at the usual hour, and as soon as he entered the great hall, where the princess waited to receive him, she rose up and pointed with her hand to the most honourable place, waiting till he sat down, that she might sit at the same time, which was a piece of civility she had never shown him before.

The African magician was very much surprised. The majestic and graceful air with which she received him, so opposed to her former behaviour, quite bewildered him.

When he had sat down, the princess, to free him from his embarrassment, broke silence first, and said, " You are doubtless amazed to find me so much altered to-day from what I used to be; but your surprise will not be so great when I tell you that I am naturally of a disposition so opposed to melancholy and grief, sorrow and uneasiness, that I always strive to put them as far away as possible when I find the reason of them is past. I have reflected on what you told me of Aladdin's fate, and know the sultan my father's temper so well that I am persuaded that Aladdin could not escape the terrible effects of his rage; therefore, should I continue to lament him all my life, my tears cannot recall him. To begin to cast off all melancholy, I am resolved to banish it entirely; and, persuaded you will bear me company to-night, I have ordered a supper to be prepared; but as I have no wines except those of China, I have a great desire to taste the African wine, and doubt not you will get some of the best."

The African magician, who had looked upon the happiness of coming so soon and so easily into the Princess Badroulboudour's good graces as impossible, could not think of words enough to express his gratitude: but to put an end the sooner to a conversation which would have embarrassed him, he turned it upon the wines of Africa, and said, " Of all the advantages Africa can boast, that of producing the most excellent wines is one of the principal. I have a vessel of seven years old, which has never been broached; and it is indeed not praising it too much to say that it is the finest wine in the world. If my princess," added he, " will give me leave, I will go and fetch two bottles, and return again immediately."

" I should be sorry to give you that trouble," replied the princess; " you had better send for them."

" It is necessary I should go myself," answered the African magician; " for nobody but myself knows where the key of the cellar is laid, or has the secret to unlock the door."

" If it be so," said the princess, " make haste back again; for the longer you stay, the greater will be my impatience, and we shall sit down to supper as soon as you come back."

The African magician, full of hope, flew rather than ran, and returned quickly with the wine. The princess, not doubting in the least but that he would make haste, put with her own hand the powder Aladdin gave her into the cup that was set apart for that purpose. They sat down at the table opposite to each other, the magician's back towards the sideboard. The princess presented him with the best on the table, and said to him, "If it pleases you, I will entertain you with a concert of vocal and instrumental music; but, as we are only two, I think conversation may be more agreeable." This the magician took as a new favour.

After they had eaten some time, the princess called for some wine, and drank the magician's health; and afterwards said to him, "Indeed you were right to commend your wine, since I never tasted any so delicious in my life."

"Charming princess," said he, holding in his hand the cup which had been presented to him, "my wine becomes more exquisite by your approbation of it."

"Then drink my health," replied the princess; "you will find I understand wines." He drank the princess's health, and returning the cup, said, "I think myself happy, princess, that I reserved this wine for so good an occasion; and I own I never before drank any so excellent in every respect."

Presently, the princess, who had completely charmed the African magician by her civility and obliging behaviour, gave the signal to the slave who served them with wine, bidding her bring the cup which had been filled for herself, and at the same time bring the magician a full cup. When they both had their cups in their hands, she presented to him the cup which was in her hand, and held out her hand to receive his. He for his part hastened to make the exchange with the greater pleasure because he looked upon this favour as the most certain token of an entire conquest over the princess, which raised his happiness to its height. Before he drank, he said to her, with the cup in his hand, "Indeed, I shall never, lovely princess, forget my recovering, by drinking out of your cup, that life which your cruelty, had it continued, would have made me despair of."

The Princess Badroulboudour, who began to be tired of this barefaced foolishness of the African magician, interrupted him, and said, " Let us drink first, and then say what you will afterwards; " and at the same time set the cup to her lips, while the African magician, who was eager to get his wine off first, drank up the very last drop. Then he fell backwards lifeless.

The princess had no occasion to order the back-door to be opened to Aladdin; for her women were so arranged from the great hall to the foot of the staircase, that the word was no sooner given that the African magician was fallen backwards than the door was opened that instant.

As soon as Aladdin entered the hall, he saw the magician stretched backwards on the sofa. The Princess Badroulboudour rose from her seat, and ran overjoyed to embrace him; but he stopped her, and said, " Princess, it is not yet time; oblige me by retiring to your apartment, and let me be left alone a moment, while I endeavour to transport you back to China as quickly as you were brought from thence."

When the princess, her women and attendants, had gone out of the hall, Aladdin shut the door, and going to the dead body of the magician, opened his vest, and took out the lamp carefully wrapt up; and on his unfolding and rubbing it, the genie immediately appeared. " Genie," said Aladdin, " I command thee, on the part of thy good mistress this lamp, to transport this palace directly into China." The genie bowed his head in token of obedience, and disappeared. Immediately the palace was transported into China, and its removal was only felt by two little shocks, the one when it was lifted up, the other when it was set down, and both in a very short interval of time.

Aladdin went down to the princess's apartment, and embracing her, said, " I can assure you, princess, that your joy and mine will be complete to-morrow morning." The princess, who had not quite finished supper, guessed that Aladdin might be hungry, and ordered the meats that were served up in the great hall, and were scarcely touched, to be brought down. The princess and Aladdin ate as much as they thought fit, and drank in like manner of the African magician's old wine; then they retired to rest.

From the time of the transportation of Aladdin's palace, and of the Princess Badroulboudour in it, the sultan, that princess's father, was inconsolable. He hardly slept night or day, and instead of taking measures to avoid everything that could keep up his affliction, he indulged it; he went now many times in the day to renew his tears, and plunged himself into the deepest melancholy.

The very morning of the return of Aladdin's palace, the sultan went, at break of day, into his room to indulge his sorrows. Centred in himself, and in a pensive mood, he cast his eyes in a melancholy manner towards the place where he remembered the palace once stood, expecting only to see an open space. Perceiving that vacancy filled up, he at first imagined it to be the effect of a fog; but looking more attentively, he was convinced beyond the power of doubt that it was his son-in-law's palace. Then joy and gladness succeeded to sorrow and grief. He immediately ordered a horse to be saddled, which he mounted that instant, thinking he could not make haste enough to get to Aladdin's palace.

Aladdin, who foresaw what would happen, rose that morning by daybreak, put on one of the most magnificent robes his wardrobe afforded, and went up into the hall of twenty-four windows, from whence he perceived the sultan coming, and got down soon enough to receive him at the foot of the great staircase, and to help him to dismount. "Aladdin," said the sultan, "I cannot speak to you till I have seen and embraced my daughter."

He led the sultan into the Princess Badroulboudour's apartment. She had been told by him when he rose that she was no longer in Africa, but in China, and in the capital of the sultan her father. The sultan embraced her with his face bathed in tears of joy.

At last the sultan broke silence, and said, "You have undergone a great deal; for a large palace cannot be so suddenly transported, as yours has been, without great fright and terrible anguish. Tell me all that has happened, and conceal nothing from me."

The princess, who took great pleasure in complying, gave the sultan a full account of how the African magician disguised himself like a seller of lamps, and offered to change new lamps for old ones; and how she amused herself in making that exchange, being entirely ignorant of the secret and importance of the lamp; how the palace and herself were carried away and transported into Africa, with the African magician, who was recollected by two of her women when he had the boldness to pay her the first visit after the success of his audacious enterprise, to propose that she should marry him; how he persecuted her till Aladdin's arrival; how he and she concerted measures together to get the lamp again, which he carried about him, and the success they had; and how she had invited him to supper, and had given him the cup with the powder, prepared for him. "For the rest," added she, "I leave it to Aladdin to give you an account."

Aladdin had not much to tell the sultan, but only said, "When the private door was opened, I went into the great hall, where I found the magician lying dead on the sofa. As soon as I was alone, and had taken the lamp out of the magician's breast, I made use of the same secret as he had done to remove the palace, and carry off the princess; and by that means the palace was brought into the same place where it stood before; and I have the happiness to bring back the princess to your majesty, as you commanded me. But that your majesty may not think that I impose upon you, if you will go up into the hall, you shall see the magician punished as he deserved."

The sultan, to be assured of the truth, rose up instantly, and went up into the hall, and when he saw the African magician dead, he embraced Aladdin with great tenderness, and said, "My son, be not displeased at my proceedings against you; they arose from my love for my daughter, and therefore you ought to forgive the excesses to which it hurried me."

"Sir," replied Aladdin, "I have not the least reason to complain of your majesty's conduct, since you did nothing but what your duty required of you. This infamous magician, the basest of men, was the sole cause of my misfortune. When your majesty has leisure, I will give you an account of another villainous action he was guilty of to me, which was no less black and base than this, from which I was preserved in a very strange manner."

"I will take an opportunity, and that very shortly," replied the sultan, "to hear it; but in the meantime let us think only of rejoicing, and the removal of this odious object."

Aladdin ordered the magician's dead carcass to be removed. In the meantime the sultan commanded the drums, trumpets, cymbals, and other instruments of music to sound, and a feast of ten days to be proclaimed for joy at the return of the Princess Badroulboudour, and Aladdin with his palace.

Thus Aladdin escaped a second time the danger of losing his life.

But the African magician had a younger brother, who was as great a necromancer, and even surpassed him in villainy and pernicious designs. As they did not live together, or in the same city, but oftentimes when one was in the east the other was in the west, they each failed not every year to discover by their art where the other was, and whether he stood in need of any assistance

Some time after the African magician had failed in his enterprise against Aladdin's happiness, his younger brother, who had not heard any tidings of him for a year, and was not in Africa, but in a distant country, was anxious to know in what part of the world he was, how he did, and what he was doing; and as he, as well as his brother, always carried a geomantic square instrument about with him, he prepared the sand, cast the points, and drew the figures. On examining the "houses" he found that his brother was no longer living, that he had been poisoned, and died suddenly; that it had happened in the capital of the kingdom of China, and that the person who had poisoned him was of low birth, and married to a princess, a sultan's daughter.

When the magician had after this manner learned his brother's fate, he lost no time in useless regret, which could not restore him to life again, but resolving immediately to avenge his death, he took horse, and set out for China, where, after crossing plains, rivers, mountains, deserts, and a long tract of country, without stopping, he arrived after incredible fatigue.

When he came to the capital of China, which his knowledge of geomancy pointed out to him, he took a lodging. The next day he went out and walked through the town, not so much to observe its beauties, to which he was indifferent, as to take proper measures to execute his pernicious design. He went into the most frequented places, where he listened to everybody's conversation. In a place where people went to play at all sorts of games, he heard some persons talking of the virtue and piety of a woman called Fatima, who had retired from the world, and of the miracles she performed. As he fancied that this woman might be serviceable to him for the project he had in his head, he took one of the company aside, and desired him to tell him more particularly who this holy woman was, and what sort of miracles she performed.

"What!" said the person whom he addressed, "have you never seen or heard of her? She is the admiration of the whole town, for her fasting, her austerities, and her exemplary life. Except on Mondays and Fridays, she never stirs out of her little cell; and the days on which she comes into the town she does an infinite deal of good; for there is not a person who has the headache who is not cured by her laying her hand upon him."

The magician wanted no further information. He only asked in what part of the town this holy woman's cell was. After he had been told, he determined on a detestable design; and, that he might know the way again, and be fully informed, he watched her steps the first day she went out after he had made this enquiry, and never lost sight of her till evening, when he saw her re-enter her cell. Then he went to one of those houses where they sell a certain hot liquor, and where any person may pass the night, particularly during the great heats, when the people of that country prefer lying on a mat to going to bed. About midnight, after the magician had paid the master of the house for what little he had called for, he went direct to the cell of Fatima, the holy woman. He had no difficulty in opening the door, which was only fastened with a latch, and he shut it again after he had got in, without any noise. When he entered the cell he perceived Fatima in the moonlight lying on a sofa covered only by an old mat, with her head leaning against the wall. He awakened her, and clapped a dagger to her breast.

Poor Fatima, opening her eyes, was very much surprised to see a man with a dagger at her breast ready to stab her. "If you cry out," he said, "or make the least noise, I will kill you; but get up and do as I bid you."

Fatima, who had lain down in her clothes, got up,

trembling with fear. "Do not be so frightened," said the magician; "I only want your gown: give it me at once, and take mine." Accordingly Fatima and he changed clothes. Then he said, "Colour my face as yours is, that I may look like you;" but perceiving that the poor creature could not help trembling, he said, "I tell you again, you need not fear anything; I will not take away your life." Fatima lighted her lamp, and made him come into the cell; and taking a pencil, and dipping it in a certain liquor, she rubbed it over his face and assured him that the dye would not change, and that his face was of the same colour as her own; after which, she put her own head-dress on his head, with a veil, with which she showed him how to hide his face as he passed through the town. After this, about his neck she put a long string of beads, which hung down to his waist, and, giving him the stick she was accustomed to walk with, she brought him a looking-glass, and bade him see if he were not as like her as possible. The magician found himself as much disguised as he wished to be; but he did not keep the promise he so solemnly gave to the good Fatima, for he killed her at once.

The magician, thus disguised like the holy woman, spent the remainder of the night in the cell. The next morning, two hours after sunrise, though it was not the day the holy woman used to go out, he crept out of the cell, being well persuaded that nobody would ask him any questions about it; or, if they should, he had an answer ready for them. As one of the first things he had done after his arrival was to find out Aladdin's palace, he went straight thither.

As soon as the people saw the holy woman, as they imagined him to be, they gathered about him in a great crowd. Some begged his blessing, others kissed his hand, and some, more reserved, only the hem of his garment; while others, if their heads ached, or they desired to be preserved against their headache, stooped for him to lay his hands upon them; which he did, muttering some words in form of a prayer. In short, he counterfeited so well that everybody took him for the holy woman.

After stopping frequently to satisfy these people, who received neither good nor harm from his imposition of hands, he came at last to the square before Aladdin's palace. The crowd was so great that the eagerness to get at him increased in proportion. Those who were the most zealous and strong forced their way through the crowd to get near. There were such quarrels and so great a noise that the princess, who was in the hall of the four-and-twenty windows, heard it, and asked what was the matter; but nobody being able to give an account, she ordered them to go and see. One of her women looked out of a window, and told her that a great crowd of people was gathered about the holy woman, to be cured of the headache by the imposition of her hands.

The princess, who had for a long time heard a great deal of this holy woman, but had never seen her, felt great curiosity to have some conversation with her, and immediately sent four chamberlains for the pretended holy woman.

As soon as the crowd saw the chamberlains coming, they made way, and the magician advanced to meet them, overjoyed to find his plot work so well. "Holy woman," said one of the officers, "the princess wants to see you, and has sent us for you."

"The princess does me too great an honour," replied the false Fatima, "but I am ready to obey her command," and he followed the chamberlains into the palace.

When the magician, who under a holy garment disguised such a wicked heart, was introduced into the great hall, and perceived the princess, he began a prayer, which contained a long enumeration of vows and good wishes for the princess's health and prosperity, and that she might have everything she desired. Then he displayed all his deceitful, hypocritical rhetoric, to insinuate himself into the princess's favour under the cloak of piety, which it was no hard matter for him to do; for as the princess herself was naturally good, she was easily persuaded that all the world was like her, especially those who made profession of serving God in solitary retreat.

When the pretended Fatima had made an end of his long harangue, the princess said to him, "I thank you, good mother, for your prayers. Come and sit by me." The false Fatima sat down with affected modesty; then the princess said, "My good mother, I have one thing to ask you, which you must not refuse me; which is, to stay with me, that you may teach me your way of living, and that I may learn from your good example."

"Princess," said the counterfeit Fatima, "I beg of you not to ask what I cannot consent to, without neglecting my prayers and devotions."

"That shall be no hindrance to you," answered the princess. "I have a great many apartments unoccupied; you shall choose which you like best, and shall have as much liberty to perform your devotions as if you were in your own cell."

The magician, who wanted nothing better than to introduce himself into Aladdin's palace, where it would be a much easier matter for him to execute his pernicious design, under the favour and protection of the princess, than if he had been forced to come and go from the cell to the palace, did not urge much to excuse himself from accepting the obliging offer the princess made him. "Princess," said he, "whatever resolutions a poor wretched woman, such as I am, may have made to renounce the pomp and grandeur of this world, I dare not presume to oppose the will and command of so pious and charitable a princess."

Upon this the princess rose up and said, "Come along with me, I will show you what empty apartments I have, that you may make choice of those which you like best." The magician followed the Princess Badroulboudour, and made choice of that which was the most poorly furnished, saying, "It is too good for me; I only accept it to please you."

Then the Princess wished to take him back again into the great hall to dine with her; but considering that then he would be obliged to show his face, which he had all the time taken care to hide, and fearing that the princess might find out that he was not Fatima, he begged her earnestly to dispense with him, telling her that he never ate anything but bread and dried fruits, and that he desired to eat a slight repast in his own room. This the princess granted him, saying, "You may be as free here, good mother, as if you were in your own cell. I will order you a dinner, but, remember, I shall expect you as soon as you have finished."

After the princess had dined, the false Fatima failed not to wait upon her. "My good mother," said the princess,

"I am overjoyed to have the company of so holy a woman as yourself, who will confer a blessing upon this palace. But now that I am speaking of this palace, pray how do you like it? And before I show you the rest, tell me first what you think of this hall."

At this question the counterfeit Fatima, who, to act his part the better, pretended to hang down his head without so much as ever once lifting it, at last looked up; and, surveying the hall from one end to the other, he said to the princess, "As far as such a solitary being as I can judge, this hall is truly admirable and most beautiful; it lacks but one thing."

"What is that, good mother?" answered the Princess Badroulboudour, "tell me, I implore you. For my part, I have always believed and have heard that it lacked nothing; but if it does, that want shall be supplied."

"Princess," said the false Fatima, with great dissimulation, "forgive me for the liberty I have taken; but if my opinion can be of any importance, it is that if a roc's egg were hung up in the middle of the dome, this hall would have no parallel in the four quarters of the world, and your palace would be the wonder of the universe."

"My good mother," said the princess, "what is a roc, and where could I get an egg?"

"Princess," replied the pretended Fatima, "it is a bird of prodigious size, which inhabits the top of Mount Caucasus; the architect who built your palace can get you one."

After the Princess Badroulboudour had thanked the false Fatima for what she believed her good advice, she conversed with her upon other matters, but she could not forget the roc's egg, of which she determined to tell Aladdin when he returned from hunting. He had been gone six days, which the magician knew, and therefore took advantage of his absence. But he returned that evening after the false Fatima had taken leave of the princess, and retired to his room. As soon as he arrived, Aladdin went straight up to the princess's apartment, and saluted and embraced her. She seemed to receive him coldly. "My princess," said he, "I think you are not so cheerful as usual. Has anything happened during my absence to give you any trouble or dissatisfaction? If so, do not conceal it from me. I will leave nothing undone that is in my power to please you."

"It is a trifling matter," replied the princess, "which gives me so little concern that I should not have thought you would perceive it in my countenance. But since you have unexpectedly discovered it, I will no longer disguise a matter of so little consequence from you.

"I always believed, as you did," continued the Princess Badroulboudour, "that our palace was the most superb, magnificent, and complete one in the world, but I will tell you now what I find fault with upon examining the hall of four-and-twenty windows. Do you not think, with me, that it would be better if a roc's egg were hung up in the midst of the dome?"

"Princess," replied Aladdin, "it is enough that you think it needs such a thing. You shall see by my diligence that there is nothing which I would not do for your sake."

Aladdin left the Princess Badroulboudour that very moment, and went up into the hall of four-and-twenty windows. Pulling out of his bosom the lamp, which, after the danger he had been exposed to, he always carried about with him, he rubbed it, upon which the genie immediately appeared. "Genie," said Aladdin, "there ought to be a roc's egg hung up in the midst of the dome. I command thee, in the name of this lamp, to repair the deficiency."

Aladdin had no sooner pronounced these words than the genie gave so loud and terrible a cry that the hall shook, and Aladdin could scarcely stand upright. "What? wretch," said the genie, in a voice that would have made the most undaunted man tremble, "is it not enough that I and my companions have done everything for you, that you, with unheard-of ingratitude, must command me to bring my master, and hang him up in the midst of this dome? This attempt deserves that you, your wife, and your palace should be immediately reduced to ashes. You are fortunate, however, in not being the real author of this request. It does not come from yourself. Know, then, that the true author is the brother of the African magician, your enemy, whom you have destroyed as he deserved. He is now in your palace, disguised in the clothes of the holy woman Fatima, whom he has murdered, and it is he who has suggested to your wife to make this pernicious demand.

His design is to kill you, therefore take care of yourself." After these words the genie disappeared.

Aladdin lost not a word of what the genie had said. He had heard of the holy woman Fatima, and how she could cure the headache. He returned to the princess's apartment, and without mentioning a word of what had happened, he sat down, and complained of a great pain which had suddenly seized his head. Upon this the princess immediately ordered the holy woman to be fetched, and then told Aladdin how she had come to the palace.

When the pretended Fatima came, Aladdin said, "Come hither, good mother; I am glad to see you here at so fortunate a time. I am tormented with a violent pain in my head, and request your assistance. I hope you will not refuse me that kindness which you have done to so many persons afflicted with the headache." So saying, he rose up, but held down his head.

The counterfeit Fatima advanced towards him, with his hand all the time on a dagger, concealed in his girdle under his gown. Aladdin saw this, and, seizing his hand, pierced him to the heart with his own dagger, and then threw him down on the floor dead.

"My dear husband, what have you done?" cried the princess in surprise. "You have killed the holy woman!"

"No, my princess," answered Aladdin, without emotion, "I have not killed Fatima, but a wicked wretch that would have assassinated me, if I had not prevented him. This wicked man," added he, uncovering his face, "has strangled Fatima, whom you accuse me of killing, and disguised himself in her clothes, to come and murder me. He is the brother of the African magician." Then Aladdin told her how he came to know these particulars, and afterwards ordered the dead body to be taken away.

Thus was Aladdin delivered from the persecution of the two magicians. Within a few years afterwards, the sultan died in a good old age, and the Princess Badroulboudour, as lawful heir of the crown, succeeded him. She shared her power with Aladdin, and they reigned together many years, and left a numerous and illustrious posterity behind them.